A
Study in Death

BERKLEY
PRIME
CRIME

An imprint of Penguin Random House LLC
375 Hudson Street, New York, New York 10014

This book is an original publication of the Berkley Publishing Group.

Library of Congress Cataloging-in-Publication Data

Huber, Anna Lee.
A study in death / Anna Lee Huber.—First edition.
pages ; cm
ISBN 978-0-425-27752-2
I. Title.
PS3608.U238S78 2015
813'.6—dc23
2015003057

FIRST EDITION: July 2015

PRINTED IN THE UNITED STATES OF AMERICA

10   9   8   7   6   5   4   3   2   1

Cover illustration by Larry Rostant.
Cover design by Lesley Worrell.

Penguin
Random
House

A
STUDY IN DEATH

ANNA LEE HUBER

BERKLEY PRIME CRIME, NEW YORK

For my daughter, my little songbird.
May you always know how beautiful, courageous, and extraordinary you are,
and how very, very much you are loved.
Never let anyone convince you otherwise.

ACKNOWLEDGMENTS

I am so incredibly grateful to all of the many people who help make my books a reality, whether in the production and marketing, the plotting and execution, or in a support capacity. None of this would be possible without all of you, as well as my amazing readers, who get so excited to read Lady Darby's next adventures. I am humbled and blessed.

Special thanks go to the entire team at Berkley Prime Crime for all of their excellent work on the Lady Darby series, particularly the Art Department for their spectacular covers; my wonderful publicist, Danielle Dill; and my uber-talented editor, Michelle Vega, and her sharp assistant, Bethany Blair.

I'm also grateful to my agent, Kevan Lyon, for all of her support, enthusiasm, and brilliant insight.

Tons of thanks go to the impressive women in my writing group— my cousin Jackie Musser, and my friends Stacie Roth Miller and Jackie Adams. Your advice and encouragement are indispensable.

I also want to thank the many author friends who have helped me in innumerable ways, especially my cheerleaders and confidantes— Marci Jefferson and Rebecca Henderson Palmer; my plotting partners—Erin Knightley, Hanna Martine, and Heather Snow; and the ladies of Sleuths in Time Authors.

Thanks and appreciation go to all of my friends and family, particularly my mother, who helped me in so many ways during those last few crazy weeks before my deadline.

And lastly, immense gratitude goes to my husband and our beautiful daughter. You are my greatest blessings, and I am so fortunate to share my life and love with you. Thank you for loving and supporting me through thick and thin. None of this would mean anything without you.

There's the scarlet thread of murder running through the colourless skein of life, and our duty is to unravel it, and isolate it, and expose every inch of it.

—*A Study in Scarlet* by Sir Arthur Conan Doyle

A
STUDY IN DEATH

CHAPTER I

EDINBURGH, SCOTLAND
MARCH 1831

"Can you turn your head a little to the right?"

"Oh, yes. Of course," Lady Drummond gasped, swiftly complying.

At that angle the light fell just so on her honey blond curls, and hid the streak of gray beginning to show at her right temple. It would also allow me to accent the height of her cheekbones and the pert tilt of her chin. I narrowed my eyes to study just how the swirls of butter and goldenrod formed a pattern in her elaborately styled hair, and then I dipped my brush in the paint on my palette.

"Lady Darby, you must grow weary of reminding your subjects not to fidget and turn," she chattered in her light, melodic voice, careful not to move even her mouth too much. "And children! How on earth do you coax them to sit still? My Freddy and Victoria would never last a minute."

A smile curled my lips as I applied the paint carefully to the canvas before me. "Oh, I don't need a subject to remain perfectly still, just when I'm focusing on a particular part of their anatomy. Like your face and hair." I brushed a small dab of the yellow ochre into the goldenrod hue I'd mixed for Lady Drummond's hair. It needed a hint more gold. "When children move about, it actually helps me to better capture them. After all, they're far from static. If I can observe how restless they are when trying to sit still, then I know to paint their vitality. If they giggle frequently, then I know to light their eyes with delight."

"And I suppose you do the same with adults?" she guessed.

"To a certain extent," I replied distractedly, trying to imitate the definition in the ringlets surrounding her face.

She laughed a bit breathlessly. "I think I'm afraid to ask what my twitching says about me."

The sharpness in her tone belied the humor implied by her statement, and I couldn't help but peer around the canvas at her. She sat very still, but the hands that had lain so elegantly in her lap were now clasped together, and her thumbs rubbed against each other, turning the skin pink. Normally I didn't encourage the subjects of my portrait commissions to talk, but from the very beginning there had been something about Lady Drummond that had been different. It was that difference that compelled me to reassure her now.

"Oh, I don't think you have anything to worry about," I replied casually, dabbing my brush in the paint on my palette. However, when I snuck another glance at her, I could see in her troubled blue eyes that she knew I was lying.

Perhaps I should have said something, but how could I admit I recognized her sadness, her loneliness? That I sensed her uneasiness, that her perfect life was not all that it seemed, and that her husband was quite possibly a brute. Although we'd spent several hours together every morning over the past two weeks, we were not friends. And I knew from experience that people did not like to have their carefully cultivated façades ripped away, whether you could see beyond them or not. They preferred the disingenuousness of the lie to the nakedness of the truth.

If any society lady might react differently to such an unveiling, I suspected it would be Lady Drummond, but still I was hesitant to take a chance. I genuinely liked her, and I quailed at the thought of hurting her, even if there was a possibility it might help. She was warmhearted and kind, quick-witted and even quicker to smile, and the sorrow I saw in her eyes called to the same melancholy I buried inside me. All the secret hurts we wished to keep hidden, sometimes even from ourselves. Though I now had my fiancé—and sometimes investigative partner— Sebastian Gage, to share mine. I wasn't certain Lady Drummond had anyone to lighten her burden.

The ornate gold clock on the mantel in the drawing room chimed the hour, recalling me to my task. Lady Drummond had informed me she had an appointment this afternoon, so I would only have an hour more of her time before she would need to ready herself. I rested my brush on my palette and flexed my right hand, trying to work out the stiffness the continued cold weather caused in my joints.

Lady Drummond observed my movements. "Shall I call Jeffers to come stoke up the fire?"

"No. The fire is already burning quite brightly, and I suspect the room is as warm as it's going to get."

"Yes, this winter has been dreadful, hasn't it? But are you certain? I know this room can be quite drafty."

"I'm sure."

"I bet Lady Cromarty doesn't mind the chill." Her lips quirked in amused remembrance. "I recall how dreadfully hot I was when I was enceinte with my children."

My sister, Alana, was eight months heavy with her fourth child, and the growing discomfort had not improved her temperament.

"Yes. Lord Cromarty and I, and even the servants, have taken to wearing extra layers of clothing."

Lady Drummond smiled.

I dipped my brush in the goldenrod hue and focused once more on Lady Drummond's curls. She obliged me by returning to her posed position without my even having to ask. The sun outside the window shone brighter than it had a few minutes ago, indicating there had been a break in the perpetual ceiling of gray clouds—a rare treat for Edinburgh in March. When such a thing happened, nearly the entire city was tempted outside to enjoy the rays of warmth while they could. But Lady Drummond and I stayed where we were.

I had to admit the peacock blue silk wallpaper made a stunning backdrop to the baroness's portrait, and it brought a depth of hue to her somewhat watery blue eyes that would have been lacking otherwise. The forest green pleated fabric of her dress and gold braid were striking, but truly did nothing for her features. If not for the brilliant blue backdrop, I might have broken yet another of my rules and urged her to choose a different gown.

"And how is Lady Cromarty feeling?" Lady Drummond asked kindly.

"Quite well," I admitted. "I was cheered to see her moving about the house yesterday, and some color has returned to her cheeks."

After arriving several minutes late and rather flustered one morning the week before because Alana had been ill, I had hesitantly admitted my concerns over my sister's impending delivery. The birth of Alana's third child had been met with complications, so we were all anxious for her and the new baby's health.

She beamed. "That's wonderful. And I'm sure a relief to you and Lord Cromarty."

"Yes," I replied simply, though I couldn't help thinking of my brother-in-law Philip's increasingly strange behavior over the past month since my return to Edinburgh. There wasn't anything distinct I could point to, but it niggled at the back of my mind nonetheless. I knew he'd been busy with political matters, so perhaps it was just his distraction. I pushed the worrying thought away.

"Well, I have some creams and unctions I would like to send her, if I may. A friend of mine introduced them to me as I was entering the last stage of my confinement when my skin was so taut it was almost unbearable." She swiveled on her gold and ecru Chippendale chair to reach for a piece of foolscap on the desk nearby, forgetting to remain still in her enthusiasm, and nearly upsetting the bowl of sugared plums she had been nibbling on. "I'll send a note around now asking Hinkley's to deliver it."

I thanked her, having grown accustomed to ladies offering me helpful advice for my sister since she'd officially entered her confinement a few weeks ago. Some of their suggestions were beyond bizarre, like avoiding looking in the mirror to prevent giving her baby bad dreams, or inducing sneezing with pepper should her labor prove difficult. At least Lady Drummond's seemed to be truly useful. Alana had been complaining about how dry and itchy her skin felt, particularly over her ever-expanding abdomen. I'd made a note to search out something for her since she'd been discouraged by her physician from making any more outings.

Dropping my brush in the cup of linseed oil I had at the ready, I chose a rigger brush and began to highlight Lady Drummond's curls with the shade of butter. When I glanced up, I could see she was worrying her hands again, as she'd been doing quite frequently this morning. I could tell that something was troubling her, but it didn't seem my place to ask her about it. Perhaps if we'd been acquainted longer, on surer ground, I might have dared, but as things currently stood, it merely seemed prying.

I had just begun to lose myself in the rhythm of my movements when she spoke. "Your fiancé, Mr. Gage . . ." She cleared her throat. "Are you still assisting him with his inquiries?"

I slowly lifted my head, surprised by the question, and the

too-casual way she'd attempted to phrase it. She sat tensely, waiting for my answer.

"Yes, I am," I managed to reply. "Though we've nothing notable to investigate at the moment. Just a few small matters." I tilted my head to the side, trying to decide whether to risk a question of my own. "Why do . . ."

But I was cut off by the sound of the drawing room door bursting open. It thudded against the wall behind it.

"What is the meanin' o' this?" Lord Drummond shouted, crossing the room toward his wife in a few angry strides.

I unconsciously shrank away from him, reminded too intimately of some of the encounters I'd had in the past with my late husband, Sir Anthony. Lady Drummond did the same and then forced herself to sit upright, facing her husband's glare.

He shook the paper he was holding in her face, causing her to flinch. "I asked ye a question. What is this?"

She stared past her husband at me, and I could read the horror and humiliation reflected in her eyes. Lord Drummond followed her gaze, his head rearing backward in shock when he saw me, clearly having neglected to notice my presence.

The muscles in his jaw tensed and then released before he bit out, "Lady Darby, I require a word alone wi' my wife. Please leave us." He turned away from me in dismissal.

I stood there stunned. I wanted to do nothing but comply, but my muscles wouldn't seem to budge. It was as if they remembered all too well the times when Sir Anthony had cornered me, furious about something I'd done or simply frustrated and eager to take it out on me. It was not unlike facing a predator. *Stand still. Don't make any sudden movements. Don't look him in the eye or he'll see it as a challenge.*

Lady Drummond seemed to employ the same tactic, sitting rigidly in her chair, not daring to lift her gaze. The sight of her struggling not to cower from her husband as he towered over her shifted something inside me. It had been nearly two years since my husband's death, and yet I still struggled to escape from his domineering shadow. To watch another woman face such an existence angered me. And suddenly I was tired of remaining quiet.

From our first meeting, I'd suspected Lord Drummond of being a controlling brute. It was written in the hard glares, the proprietorial grip of his hand on his wife's arm, the clipped way he spoke to her. I'd seen no bruises on Lady Drummond, but there were ways to hurt someone without leaving a mark. I knew.

Even if he didn't physically harm her, I'd witnessed enough of his displays of temper to know that he did not treat his wife as he should. A wife who was loved and cherished did not wince when she heard her husband walking through the house.

"No," I stated firmly, swirling my brush through the paint on the palette. Out of the corner of my eye I saw Lord Drummond's shoulders tense, but I told myself to ignore him. I flicked another glance at the clock on the mantel. "I still have thirty-four minutes with Lady Drummond, and I don't intend to waste them."

Lord Drummond turned his hard glare on me. "Ye will do as I ask," he replied, speaking in sharp tones. "I hired ye to paint my wife's portrait . . ."

"No," I replied as coolly as I could manage.

Lord Drummond's posture stiffened further, proving he was unaccustomed to being interrupted. Lady Drummond's eyes were wide and almost wild, as if she couldn't believe what I was doing. I'm not sure I could either.

"You *requested* I paint your wife's portrait. *I* choose which commissions to take. I'm not obliged to accept any of them." I leaned in to pretend to apply my brush to the canvas, though in actuality my hand was shaking. "I have other commissions already lined up, and I do not wish to fall behind schedule. Nor do I intend to waste the costly pigments I mixed this morning specifically for your wife's portrait."

Lord Drummond opened his mouth to argue, and I finally looked up to scowl at him and cut him off. "So I'm afraid you'll just have to throw your tantrum later."

The room fell silent, and I realized with a sick feeling of dread that I might have overstepped myself. My refusal to leave was one thing, but that last remark had been dangerously insulting, no matter how true it was. My heart beat loudly in my ears as I stared Lord Drummond down, knowing if I looked aside now, the argument would be lost, and Lady Drummond would suffer the consequences.

When Lord Drummond's nostrils flared and he turned to stalk from the room, I could hardly believe I'd won, though I dared not move until he'd slammed the door shut behind him. Then I exhaled and turned to stare into the hearth, my heart still galloping in my chest. A feeling of elation began to fill me and I couldn't stop a smile from curling my lips. It felt good to stand up to a bully for once after years of shrinking from my late husband.

However, my pride was short-lived.

"You shouldn't have done that," Lady Drummond murmured so softly I almost didn't hear her. Her eyes were clouded with fear, her hands pressed to her abdomen.

And I suddenly realized what I'd done.

Lord Drummond was little danger to me. For him to strike a woman outside of his protection would have been beyond the pale of gentlemanly conduct. My fiancé or brother or even brother-in-law would have been quite within their rights to demand satisfaction for such a slight to their female relative. However, Lady Drummond had no such defense. Being Lord Drummond's wife, he could do as he wished to her, as Sir Anthony had done to me. Yes, society generally frowned upon physically harming one's wife, but they also expected that husbands should give their wives moderate correction, so spouses who went too far in their discipline were rarely prosecuted. Perhaps my standing up to Lord Drummond had been a personal triumph, but it had also potentially exposed Lady Drummond to harsher treatment.

"I'm sorry. But I couldn't do nothing," I pleaded. "I know what he would have done had I left the room."

Lady Drummond's gaze dropped to the Aubusson rug. I hated saying the words, hurting her by destroying the fiction, but it was the truth.

"Perhaps this will give him some time to calm down." I inhaled shakily before adding, "Sometimes it works."

Her eyes slowly lifted to meet mine, and I could tell she understood I was speaking from experience. Something passed between us then, though neither of us said a word. It was an acceptance similar to what I imagined soldiers felt for each other, having been through the hellish nightmares of war together. Lady Drummond and I had been through a different sort of battle, but a battle it was all the same.

I lifted my brush and turned back toward the canvas, unwilling to push Lady Drummond for more than I was prepared to give.

It was only later that I realized what a mistake that had been. I should have urged her to confide all—what was making her nervous, what cruel acts her husband was capable of, what the contents of the letter that had so angered him had been. Instead, I allowed her to keep her secrets, and by doing so, they almost remained hidden forever.

If only I'd made her talk, the events that followed would have unfolded quite differently.

CHAPTER 2

Edinburgh's brief glimpse of the sun had passed by the time I emerged from Drummond House, and the sky was once more weighted down by dark gray clouds. I hurried down the steps and into Philip's carriage just as the first drops of rain began to splatter against the roof.

Though only half past noon, the Cromarty town house was ablaze with light as we pulled around Charlotte Square and up to the door. I dashed inside as Figgins held the door open for me. I could hear the murmur of happy voices through the open drawing room doors above.

The butler smiled as he took my cloak and gloves. "Mr. Gage is here."

My heart gave a leap, as it always did upon hearing that Sebastian Gage was in the vicinity. I wondered if it always would.

I nodded in thanks and passed my satchel of art supplies, including my set of specially weighted brushes, to the maid standing nearby. She would take it to my bedchamber, and I would transfer it to my locked art studio on the top floor later.

"Please tell Bree I'll be up in a moment," I told her, though I knew the request was pointless. My lady's maid would understand what the arrival of my satchel meant, and she would already have my afternoon dress laid out for me.

Brushing a hand down over my plain slate gray serge dress, I climbed the stairs to the drawing room, knowing I would never be allowed to sneak past to change before greeting them.

Gage sat to the right of my sister where she reclined on a spring green fainting couch near the Georgian windows, her hands resting instinctively and protectively over her full belly. She was smiling at something he said, and I was grateful for the welcome flush it brought to Alana's cheeks. Gage, for his part, also seemed to be enjoying himself. His pale blue eyes crinkled with humor as he leaned back in his chair and rested one booted ankle over his other knee. Though his golden curls had recently been trimmed shorter than usual, they were still artfully arranged in their normal style.

Philip was the first to notice me as he entered through the connecting door from the parlor with a stack of correspondence in his hands. More parliamentary business, I assumed. "Ah, there you are, Kiera." He nodded to Gage with a twinkle in his eyes. "Now you can distract your fiancé from filling my wife's ears full of nonsense."

My fiancé. Those words still astonished me every time I heard them.

After my disastrous marriage to the late great anatomist Sir Anthony Darby, and the scandal that followed the revelation of my forced involvement with his dissections, I had thought never to marry again. I had also thought never again to have anything to do with corpses, and yet a year and half later I'd found myself assisting with the investigation of a gentlewoman's murder. It was during that investigation that I had met Sebastian Gage, gentleman inquiry agent, and now after seven months of tumultuous courtship, and three treacherous inquiries, we were engaged to marry.

"What has he been telling her this time?" I remarked, good-naturedly playing along as Gage rose from his chair.

"Just that the sun made an appearance this morning, even though we all know it's much too early in the year for such a thing in Edinburgh."

"Ah, but it did. I saw it through Lady Drummond's window."

A smile playing across his lips, Gage took hold of my hands and leaned in to kiss my cheek. I inhaled the familiar scent of his cologne as well as the faint odor of sawdust, telling me he'd likely been building something that morning in the workshop in the basement of the building where he rented his bachelor quarters.

"Well, dash it," Philip muttered. "That means I owe Strathblane five quid."

Momentarily distracted, I turned to watch Philip drop into the chair Gage had just vacated. "You wagered on the weather?"

Philip shrugged his broad shoulders. "What else is there to wager on?"

I smiled. My brother-in-law was too chivalrous to gamble on the ridiculous and sometimes scandalous things that most gentlemen bet on—the length of *affairs de coeur*, the measurement of an opera singer's bosom, or whether one man would have a legitimate child before another man. From the fond look in my sister's eyes, I could tell she was thinking the same thing.

I leaned over to kiss her cheek, noticing her maid had added a cherry red ribbon trim to her jonquil floral morning dress, one of the only gowns that still fit her comfortably at this stage of her confinement. It was a welcome addition as the other colors had begun to fade.

"You have paint on your cheek, dear," Alana murmured.

I nodded, promising to return shortly.

After scrubbing my neck, face, and hands clean, and allowing Bree to help me into a Pomona green gown much more suitable to entertaining, I rejoined the others. It had taken longer than expected to fix my hair, which, per usual, was already falling out of its pins. So by the time I settled onto the settee next to Gage, Alana had introduced her new favorite subject—preparations for our wedding.

It was not that I minded my sister's enthusiasm, and in fact, being hopeless myself at social events and planning, I welcomed her assistance. But bit by bit it had all begun to snowball out of control, growing from a small ceremony and wedding breakfast with family and close friends to something more akin now to the event of the season. Oh, Alana wasn't imprudent enough to call it that, knowing how the words would terrify me, but I wasn't fooled. I could see what an enormous, elaborate affair it was becoming.

Several times I had wanted to speak up, to halt the monstrosity my wedding was growing into, to chop the guest list to a tenth its size. But Alana seemed so happy, and it had given her something to occupy her time. I knew how trying she found it to be largely restricted to the house. She was a social creature, eager to interact with others.

As was Gage—the other reason I hadn't opposed their plans. He seemed quite happy inviting half the members of the ton, who all admired and adored him. I was the outsider, the eccentric, the person most likely to trip over her hem as she walked down the aisle.

Philip could sense my tension, and had even tried several times to speak up on my behalf, but Alana had ignored him, insisting this was what I'd wanted. Gage had at least pulled me aside to ask if that was true, and I'd been unable to tell him no. Not when it seemed such a little thing in the grand scheme of it all. Our wedding was just one day. Our marriage would be the rest of our lives, and that was the part I was most looking forward to. Especially when Gage took me in his arms.

Still, Philip shot me a sympathetic look as Alana launched into her recommendation for the floral arrangements. I tried to be attentive, but my thoughts continued to return to Lady Drummond. I couldn't help but wonder if her husband's temper had cooled, or if the delay I forced had only made matters worse for the baroness. After all, there were just as many people who stewed in their anger—building themselves up into a fury—as there were those who reacted without thinking. What if, that very moment, she was suffering her husband's wrath?

Apparently my worries did not go unnoticed, for Gage reached over to still my hand where I had begun to fuss with a piece of my gown's lace trim. I looked up to find him watching me in quiet concern and tried to offer him a reassuring smile. But he was not fooled.

"Lady Cromarty," he interrupted my sister. "Would you mind if I spoke with Kiera alone for a moment before luncheon?"

My sister glanced between us. "Of course." She smiled. "And please, I've told you before. Call me Alana. After all, you're to be my brother."

"You can use my study," Philip offered, never lifting his eyes from his stack of dispatches.

Gage escorted me down the stairs, but did not speak what was on his mind until he'd closed the study door behind us very properly, leaving it slightly ajar. I strolled toward the hearth, where the fire was banked, giving off only a minimum of heat. Lifting my eyes, I stared up at the portrait I'd painted of Alana and the children and tried to gather my thoughts, to decide how much I wanted to reveal. How much Lady Drummond would be comfortable with me divulging.

Gage joined me in my contemplation of the painting. "Kiera," he began. "You know you don't have to defer to your sister's opinion."

I turned to look at him in surprise.

"If you'd rather have forget-me-nots instead of roses, or daffodils instead of tulips, you should say so."

I offered him a gentle smile. "Gage, I don't really care about all of that. You know that."

"Then what's troubling you?" His gaze searched mine. "I can tell when something is wrong."

I lowered my head, staring at the speckled stone slab before the hearth. "Something . . . upsetting happened at Lady Drummond's this morning."

He pivoted to face me more fully. "What do you mean?"

I lifted my eyes, still trying to decide exactly what to say. "Lord

Drummond interrupted us. He was furious with his wife. He shook a letter in her face."

"Well, I suppose there was something about it that displeased him."

"Yes, but it was more than that." I swallowed, wishing Gage would come to the same conclusion I had without my having to disclose so much. "I don't think he treats his wife very well," I told him slowly.

His pupils widened in comprehension.

"Do you know Lord Drummond?"

His mouth flattened into a frown. "Not really. Not nearly enough to be familiar with his temperament."

I nodded, biting my lip as I looked away.

"He's a former navy man. Received his title for services to the Crown during the war with Napoleon. Perhaps, like my father, he still acts like he's commanding his crew from the quarterdeck of his ship," he suggested. The corners of his eyes crinkled, letting me know he was as much concerned for me as he was for the Drummonds.

"It's more than that," I insisted. I smiled tightly. "Remember, I would know."

Though I had never shared all, he knew enough about Sir Anthony's ill treatment of me to understand what I meant.

Gage nodded and pulled me close, tucking my head under his chin. I inhaled deeply and wrapped my arms around him, soaking up the warmth and comfort of his embrace. I hadn't even known how much I needed it.

"Is there something I can do?" His chest rumbled against my ear.

"I don't know," I admitted. "Can . . . can I think about it?"

"Of course."

I closed my eyes as he pressed a kiss into my hair, wishing there were an easy solution to Lady Drummond's predicament.

CHAPTER 3

I glanced up and down Hanover Street, my arms wrapped around me as I shivered in the cold wind. What was taking so long? I reached up to pound the knocker on the door of Number 99 once more, bouncing on my heels, trying to warm myself. Normally, the Drummonds' ever-efficient butler, Jeffers, was prepared to let me in before I'd even climbed the steps, but this morning I'd been waiting at least a full minute, possibly longer, for someone to answer the door.

I looked back at Philip's carriage still parked on the street. The coachman and footman stared up at me, awaiting further instructions. I offered them a weak smile and then turned to wrap on the door for a fourth time.

A sinking feeling settled in my stomach as the royal blue door remained closed. Something must be very wrong for the staff to ignore my knocking for so long. Or perhaps Lady Drummond had ordered them not to answer. If so, how badly had Lord Drummond hurt her?

No. That couldn't have been it. If she hadn't wanted to see me, for whatever reason, she simply would have sent a note to cancel today's portrait session. It must have been something else.

Unless Lady Drummond was too incapacitated even to write.

I lifted my hand to pound yet again, determined to stand there all day if necessary to gain entry, when I heard hurried footsteps approaching. I inhaled in relief and turned to nod at the coachman in dismissal as the door finally opened.

However, it was not Jeffers who greeted me, but a wild-eyed footman gulping breaths.

"Heavens," I exclaimed. "Whatever is wrong?"

"Lady Drummond is no' receiving," he gasped as if prompted.

"What do you mean?" I demanded, pushing past him into the entrance hall. His strange demeanor frightened me.

"M-m'lady. Ye canna come in," he called after me.

"Of course I can."

I marched deeper into the house, ignoring his agitated gestures as he followed me. The sound of voices farther along the corridor drew me toward the back parlor. As I approached the doorway, I could see several servants clustered around something. A maid wringing her apron and a shock-faced footman hung back while another maid and Jeffers kneeled over someone. My heart rate accelerated as I recognized the hem of the woman's dress.

"What happened?" I demanded as I rushed forward. I dropped my satchel and shrugged off my cloak, kneeling beside Lady Drummond's prone form.

Jeffers slid to the side so that I could better see the baroness. She stared wide-eyed up at the ceiling, her facial muscles almost slack, but the rest of her body constricted in pain. Her hands formed into claws wrapped around her abdomen. I reached out to run a hand gently over her hair, letting her know I was there. Her eyes sought mine out, pain and panic shimmering in their depths. The sour stench of fear filled my nostrils. I used my other hand to search for a pulse in her wrist. It raced.

A third maid I hadn't noticed from the doorway sat on Lady Drummond's other side. I had seen her during several previous visits, fussing around her employer, adjusting her hair and clothing. She looked terrified. Her hands hovered over the baroness's body as if wanting to comfort her, but afraid to touch her.

"What happened?" I asked again, this time directly to the maid.

Her head jerked up to look at me, as if she hadn't noticed my presence before. "I . . . I dinna ken. She . . . she was comin' doon the stairs when I heard her stumble. Then she began to retch, all o'er the rug." She glanced up at Jeffers as if he would confirm her story. "We tried to take her upstairs, but we were closer to the parlor and she insisted on bein' brought here. But once inside, she clutched at her chest and collapsed."

"Did you send for the physician?"

"Straightaway."

I leaned over the baroness, looking into her eyes. "Lady Drummond, can you speak? Can you tell us what's wrong? Where does it hurt?" I searched for any sign she could understand me, but she merely stared up at me in pleading.

Reaching out, I ran an exploratory hand over her abdomen, looking for any indication that one spot troubled her more than another. However, contrary to expectation, her rigid muscles suddenly began to relax. My gaze flew back to her face and I reached again for her wrist. Her pulse, which just a moment ago had been so rapid, had slowed, beating weakly against my fingertips.

"Lady Drummond, stay with us. Help is on the way."

But even as I spoke, her pulse continued to drop.

"Lady Drummond," I gasped.

A raspy, anguished breath rattled from her throat as her body exhaled. I watched her chest rise once, twice more, and then it stopped. Her eyes, which had remained locked on mine, grew vacant. Lady Drummond was no longer with us.

I exhaled shakily, an unconscious imitation of the baroness, and sank back on my calves. Shocked silence filled the room, ringing in my ears, broken only by the sound of one of the maids weeping. Her lady's maid clasped her hands over her mouth to stifle a cry. I didn't turn to look at the others, but I assumed they were as appalled and disbelieving as I was that Lady Drummond was dead.

Yesterday she had been so full of life. Distressed and uncertain, but also warm and vital. Now she lay before me growing cold, whatever troubles she'd struggled with still unburdened.

The heavy hand of guilt pressed down on my heart. What if I'd asked? What if I'd tried to make her talk to me? Perhaps this wouldn't have happened. Perhaps she would be settling into her chair as I set out my art supplies, laughing as she shared a humorous anecdote about her young children.

I shook the distressing thoughts aside, and forced myself to focus on what was before me. I could no longer ask her what had worried her, but I could find out what had happened to her.

I reached out to run a hand over her eyelids to close them, and then glanced around at the servants gathered in the room. What had they seen?

"You said Lady Drummond vomited," I said as calmly as I could, turning to her lady's maid. Tears trailed down the girl's cheeks. "Did you notice anything strange in it? Any blood?"

She sniffed and shook her head.

"What did she have to eat?"

The maid had opened her mouth to answer when a gruff male voice in the hall cut her off. "Where is her ladyship?" the man demanded, his footsteps loud on the wooden floor.

The servants standing in the doorway all turned as one to allow a tall, bespectacled man with an expanding waistline past.

He took in the scene with one glance and then waved his hands. "Move."

Jeffers and the two maids hastened to comply, though I moved more slowly. He set aside his bag and knelt on one knee beside Lady

Drummond, reaching out to feel her pulse much as I had. I watched as he studied her pale complexion and the position of her body.

"Did she clutch her chest in pain?" he asked no one in particular, not even bothering to lift his gaze.

The servants all looked to Jeffers, who cleared his throat. "Ah, yes."

The physician nodded and pushed to his feet. "Apoplexy."

I frowned at his hasty diagnosis. "She also vomited."

He reached into his pocket to extract a handkerchief and removed his spectacles to clean the lenses. "That's not uncommon."

"But she wasn't even thirty," I pointed out, my voice growing more agitated. "And her facial features were numb, as if she couldn't move them."

The physician glanced up at me for the first time, his mouth turning downward like his mustache. "And just who are you?" he retorted, replacing his spectacles.

I squared my shoulders. "Lady Darby. I'm a friend of Lady Drummond's."

His eyes narrowed, as I'd known they would. "Oh, I know who you are."

I tried not to react to such a barbed response, though I was quivering with anger and frustration. "Some of her symptoms are strange," I argued. "Are you certain it wasn't poison?"

"Now, see here. You may have assisted your late husband with his dissections and experiments." He nearly spat the words. "But you do not have a medical degree. Furthermore, you're just a woman. One with a rather tarnished reputation." He scoffed. "As if you have any right to question my findings."

I clenched my hands, wanting more than anything to plant the man a facer, but it was far more important that we find the truth for Lady Drummond.

"But don't you want to be certain? We should send for Sergeant Maclean with the Edinburgh City Police . . ."

"We are *not* sending for the police," Lord Drummond declared in his booming voice as he strode into the room. His eyes seemed to skim over the sight of his wife's body, barely giving her notice. "What happened?" he asked the physician.

The medical man shot me another glare before addressing his lordship. "Most likely an apoplexy. Though I suppose it could have been gastric fever."

Lord Drummond nodded. "Then what need would we have for those scurrilous busybodies crawlin' aroond my house, pocketin' my silver?"

"I didn't suggest it," the physician declared, nodding to me.

Lord Drummond scowled, and I decided it would be best to speak before he sent me away.

"My lord, I believe your wife may have been poisoned. Surely you want to be certain."

He studied me with his dark eyes, as if weighing my worth. "Davis, is it possible?"

"Highly unlikely, my lord," the physician sneered.

"My lord, I am not unacquainted with such matters," I argued, infuriated that they would not listen to me. "In fact, I suspect I have more experience than Dr. Davis when it comes to poisons."

"Oh, I'm sure ye do." Lord Drummond's voice had turned nasty. "But I willna have ye attachin' scandal to this household where there is none. *You* may be used to it. Ye may even enjoy it. But I assure ye the rest of us do not."

I stood there stunned. I had meant that I was familiar with poisons through my artistic pursuits. Cautious artists knew that many of our pigments contained poisons—arsenic and aconite and antimony, among others. But, of course, the baron had jumped to a different conclusion.

I swallowed, trying to gather my thoughts, but Lord Drummond had already turned away from me.

"Jeffers, see Lady Darby out."

Then, much as the day before, he showed me his back, dismissing me entirely. However, this time, I could not find the words to protest. In any case, what could I possibly say? It was clear that Lord Drummond and Dr. Davis would not listen to me, whether because of their own prejudice or, more disturbingly, because there was something they wished to hide.

I had not forgotten Lord Drummond's treatment of his wife or his outburst the morning before. Nor had I failed to notice his eagerness to accept his physician's diagnosis and his determination not to involve the city police. He'd scarcely given his dead wife's body a second look, nor did he appear in any way to be grieving. I was deeply suspicious, but sharing my thoughts with him would do no good.

I glanced down at Lady Drummond's slack features. I was reluctant to leave her behind, but I realized I had no choice. I only hoped something could be done before all potential evidence of wrongdoing was discarded or destroyed.

The other servants were careful to keep their eyes averted as I followed Jeffers through the doorway and down the corridor to the front door. He offered me my cloak, which he'd gathered from the parlor. I draped it around my shoulders, staring up at him in determination. His eyes gave very little away, but I could sense his sadness in the heaviness of his eyelids, the slight slouch of his shoulders. I only hoped Lady Drummond's affection for the man would not prove unfounded should a test of his loyalty arise.

"I'll be back," I told him, unwilling to leave without saying something of my intentions.

Jeffers did not reply, but I thought I saw a flicker of consideration in his eyes as he handed me my satchel. Then, with my head held high, I turned to march through the door.

CHAPTER 4

I stood on the pavement outside the Drummonds' town house, uncertain what to do. It felt completely wrong to walk away, but what choice did I have? Lord Drummond had essentially ejected me from his home. I couldn't very well sneak back in through the servants' entrance, though I did contemplate it.

I considered heading straight to the police house off Old Stamp Office Close up in Old Town to look for Sergeant Maclean, but there was no guarantee he would be there, and I didn't know any other officers I could trust. Besides, Gage had warned me about going there alone. No one reputable visited the police house, least of all a genteel woman, and I would only be inviting trouble for myself and Maclean.

I shivered as a gust of wind blew down Hanover Street, pressing my skirts against my legs. I needed to speak to Gage. He would know what to do. Wrapping my forest green cloak tighter around me, I hefted my satchel and hurried south toward George Street. The weight of my art supplies wrenched my shoulder, but there was nothing to be done. Philip kept only one carriage while in Edinburgh, so the coachmen delivered me to my portrait sessions and then picked me up later at the appointed time. It would have been silly for them to wait for me, and inconvenient for Philip or Alana should they need to use the coach.

I glanced down bustling George Street and decided to cross over to Rose Street instead. At half past ten in the morning, with much of society still rising from their beds or seated at breakfast, New Town was not as busy as it would be later in the day, but there were still enough earlier risers and prosperous merchants about to concern me. Considering my ultimate destination, the last thing I wanted to do was draw attention to myself, and I was sure to do that lugging my satchel several blocks. If I were observing the proprieties, I should have returned home to Charlotte Square and sent a note around to Gage asking him to call. But I knew I would never be able to hide from Alana how upset I was. She was already under enough strain. I didn't want to risk sending her into early labor.

Still, I couldn't march up to the door of the building on Princes Street where Gage rented his bachelor quarters and demand to see him. Such a thing simply wasn't done. At least, not by respectable women.

I paused at the intersection of Frederick Street to set my bag down. Rolling my arm in its socket to ease the pain, I glanced around for one of the young lads who hung about, waiting to earn a few pence by running errands or holding the reins of a gentleman's horse. I should have known one of them would find me.

"I'll carry that for ye, m'lady. For a threepence."

The boy stared up at me with restrained eagerness, letting me know he was keen to earn the money, but experienced enough to understand that if he appeared too willing, he might earn less. His clothes were scuffed and dirty, but in good repair, and his face had been scrubbed clean, even if he had missed his neck. Unlike many of the lads, he clearly had someone to go home to. Though whether that was a good thing or not depended on the person he lived with.

I decided he would do.

"No, but I do need you to deliver a message," I replied, kneeling to extract my sketchbook and a lead pencil. I hastily scribbled a note and folded the paper before handing it to the boy along with a half-crown. He nodded once to indicate he understood my directions to Gage's lodging house. "Take this note to Mr. Gage there and he'll give you an additional crown for your trouble."

The lad's eyes lit with an avid gleam and he tipped his hat and took off at a run.

I lifted my satchel and continued down Rose Street. At the last block, I turned left into the mews that led behind the buildings on Princes Street. I could hear the stable lads jesting with one another in one of the carriage houses near the corner, but the rest of the lane was quiet. The servants tucked themselves up inside where it was warm, away from the leaden skies and blustery wind.

I paused to consider two black doors toward the middle of the block of buildings, trying to remember which one was correct. I'd only been here once, in the dark of night two months ago, and I hadn't gotten a good look. The buildings looked the same, though the roofs were slightly different. One was darker than the other. I thought the building on the right was correct, but ultimately decided to stand between the two doors in case I was wrong.

The boy had clearly moved quickly, because I didn't have long to wait. The door on the right opened, but still I hung back until I saw Gage's golden head peer around it.

"Why, Lady Darby, had I only known how eager you were to see my rooms, I would have invited you up long ago and saved myself a crown." His eyes twinkled devilishly. But the teasing light died when he saw my face more fully. "Kiera, what is it? Has something happened?"

"It's Lady Drummond." I had a difficult time choking out the words. "She's dead."

His eyes widened and he reached out to usher me inside. "Come with me."

After taking my satchel from me, he glanced up the stairs with a frown before guiding me downward instead. At the base of the stairs he opened a door I knew to be his woodshop. The air inside was cold and sharp with the scents of sawdust, lacquer, and wood stain. The sunlight filtering in through the dusty windows high on the wall was faint, but bright enough to see the tables and the shelves of equipment.

He shut the door softly behind us before speaking in a low voice. "I would have taken you up to my rooms, but I'm afraid Crawford has visitors in the den." He set my bag on the floor and reached out to clasp my shoulders. "Now, tell me what happened. What do you mean she's dead?"

I swallowed, biting back a wave of unexpected tears I hadn't even known I was suppressing until I'd seen Gage. "I arrived at Lady Drummond's town house this morning at the usual time for her portrait session," I began, speaking slowly. "It took the servants longer than normal to answer the door, and when I was finally allowed in, it was to find Lady Drummond collapsed on the floor." I gripped his arms. "She was in horrible pain. I tried to help, but . . . there was nothing I could do."

He pulled me close, cradling my head against his chest. I burrowed into him for a moment, absorbing his warmth, but then I pushed away, recalling my urgency.

"Gage, I'm almost certain she was poisoned, but the physician who came to examine her declared it an apoplexy. He barely looked at her. And he didn't even bother to ask the servants what had happened." My voice rose in outrage. "Lord Drummond was more than happy to accept his diagnosis, and when I tried to voice my doubts, he implied I was ghoulish and scandal-mongering, and had me escorted out of his house."

His brow furrowed. "Well, given your past, I suppose you can't be surprised by his reaction."

I reared back in shock.

"Not that I agree with him," he protested heatedly. "You know I'm tired of people's ignorance. But it happens all the same. Why do you believe she was poisoned?"

His response appeased me somewhat, but I couldn't help searching his face for even the tiniest bit of disbelief as I relayed the details to him. "Her maid said she vomited forcefully, and she was clutching at her abdomen where she lay on the floor. Her face was also oddly slack, while the rest of her was rigid with pain. Gage, her eyes were pleading with me to help her." I squeezed my own eyes shut, trying to erase the sight. "It was awful."

Gage considered the matter. "It is odd for the physician to diagnose such a thing so quickly in a woman so young."

"She was a healthy woman. There was no reason she should have had an apoplexy." I was beginning to feel agitated that he didn't seem to grasp the seriousness of the situation. "Don't you see? They could be destroying and discarding evidence as we speak. We need to do something."

"Now, calm yourself a moment," he said, gripping my arms again. "We can't simply charge into the Drummonds' house and accuse the man of concealing his wife's murder."

"Oh, I don't think he's just concealing it."

He looked at me more closely. "You think he murdered his wife. Because you suspect he mistreated her?"

I could tell he doubted me already. "Not just that. You should have seen him today. When he arrived, he hardly spared her a glance. There was his wife's dead body splayed out on the floor before him, and he didn't display even a flicker of grief or shock."

He opened his mouth as if to protest, but I spoke over him, knowing what he was going to say.

"It's not that I thought he should have broken down in tears or anything like that. I know all about you gentlemen and your pride in your stiff upper lips. But he could have spared her more than a mere glance."

"Kiera, I understand what you're saying, but even if their marriage wasn't happy, even if he doesn't grieve her loss, that doesn't mean he killed her."

I backed away from him, crossing my arms over my chest. "I can't believe it. You don't believe me."

"It's not that. You're making some very serious accusations. We need to consider the matter carefully before we stir up a hornet's nest when there might be no reason for it. You said yourself that you were *almost* certain. Is that enough?"

I turned aside to stare up at the murky window. Was it? How sure was I that Lady Drummond had been killed by poison? Certain enough to stake my reputation and that of Gage?

"I liked her," I told him, my voice emerging softer than before. "I sincerely liked her." I knew he would appreciate the weight of those words, for I did not say them often. "And I suppose I could relate to her in ways I can't with other ladies." I glanced at Gage to find him watching me in quiet understanding. "I wanted to help her, but I didn't want to push her into telling me things I knew she wasn't ready for." Guilt squeezed my chest. "I thought she might be starting to trust me, you know. Yesterday morning. She asked if I was still assisting you with your inquiries."

"Really? Just yesterday?"

I recognized the hint of interest in his voice. I'd noticed that the more he suppressed his inflection, the more intrigued he was.

"Yes."

He moved a step closer. "Was this before or after he waved the letter in her face?"

I tilted my head, trying to figure out what he was thinking. "Before."

He reached up to push a hand through his cropped curls. He inhaled, seeming to come to a decision. "Let me make some discreet inquiries and find out if the physician has officially declared Lady Drummond's death to be from an apoplexy. He may have reconsidered the matter."

I knew he would not have, but I didn't argue. "Thank you!" I gasped, rising up on my toes to kiss his cheek.

His eyes gleamed as he caught me to him. "Yes, well, I think you can reward me better than that."

So I did.

CHAPTER 5

"My lady," Figgins said in astonishment as he admitted me to the town house. "Did his lordship's coachman forget to collect you from the Drummonds' household?"

"No, Figgins," I replied, passing him my satchel. "There were some unforeseen circumstances this morning." He didn't ask me to elaborate. A good butler never would ask more than he ought, and Figgins certainly excelled in his position. "Please let him know I won't be needing him to collect me."

"Of course."

I wearily removed my gloves and cloak. "Is Alana in the drawing room?"

"She's resting in her chamber, my lady."

I closed my eyes and heaved a sigh of relief. There would be no need to inform her of Lady Drummond's death just yet. But then I realized how rude my reaction to her absence must appear. My eyes darted to Figgins's face.

The butler merely hid a smile as he draped my cloak over his arm. "I imagine a lady's confinement must be trying for everyone."

"Er, yes," I said, grateful for his good humor.

"Shall I have tea sent up?"

"Not just yet."

He nodded, surveying my drawn features, but once again kept his curiosity to himself.

I trudged up the stairs to the drawing room and crossed to the large window that looked out on Charlotte Square. Only a handful of children played in the grassy garden at the center of the square on this blustery day, their governesses huddled together to the side, their shoulders hunched against the wind. My gaze strayed up to the gray sky as I sank down on the green settee Alana so often favored, restricted to the house as she was. The ivory blanket she draped across her lap was tossed carelessly on the cushions beside me. I unconsciously reached out to run my hand over the soft wool.

Gage had promised he would come to see me this evening with the information he had uncovered, but that was hours away and I had no idea how I would occupy myself until then. I had portraits to work on in my studio upstairs, so I supposed I should try to paint. Maybe if I could become lost in my art, then this hollow ache in my chest, this driving need to fix what was wrong however I could, would go away. At least, for a time.

I was summoning the motivation to stand and leave the room when Figgins entered with a package in his hands.

"My apologies, my lady. I neglected to inform you that this was delivered for you while you were out. Would you like me to have it taken to your room?"

I glanced at the brown paper in confusion. "I'll take it."

"Very good, my lady."

There were no markings other than my name and direction. I untied the string binding it and peeled back the paper. The box contained three jars. I lifted one to see the label read "Hinkley's Body Cream."

These were from Lady Drummond. She'd said she would send a note around to Hinkley's asking them to deliver the creams and other unctions for Alana, and she had. Was this the last missive she'd ever sent? Knowing what I did about her, it was fitting that it would be one written out of kindness.

I leaned forward, covering my eyes with my hands.

I wished I could go back to the day before and try harder to make Lady Drummond talk to me. Maybe if I'd just asked, she would have shared what was troubling her. I hadn't wanted to cause her more distress, but wasn't a little discomfort better than death?

I knew it was silly to blame myself for any part of what had befallen Lady Drummond, but I couldn't help thinking over and over again about our last interaction. Perhaps I shouldn't have stood up to Lord Drummond—maybe that had somehow escalated or precipitated matters—but I couldn't make myself regret doing so. Had I left the room when he asked and let him do whatever he intended to her, I would have repented it more. Besides, no matter what I'd said or done, I hadn't forced the killer to poison her.

If it was poison.

I rubbed my temples. What if I was wrong? What if she truly had died of an apoplexy?

Dr. Davis was correct. For all my late husband's enforced anatomical tutelage, I wasn't a physician. There could be numerous signs and symptoms of an apoplexy of which I was unaware. Maybe I saw his hasty diagnosis as suspicious because that's what I wanted to see.

The fact was, I didn't want Lady Drummond to be dead. She had been kind to me when so many others had not. To see her so full of life one day and then watch the light forever drain from her eyes the next was too difficult to accept. Strange as it might seem, it was easier to accept that someone had ended her life than that she had died of natural causes. I wanted someone to blame, and Lord Drummond was the likeliest candidate.

I didn't like him. He was brusque and unpleasant, and he clearly had not treated his wife well. But was I letting my memories of Sir

Anthony and his ill treatment of me affect my judgment? I couldn't help but think of my late husband when I saw Lord Drummond. There were too many similarities. But were there enough that I was allowing them to influence my logic and intuition?

"My lady."

I looked up to find the butler standing in the doorway. I didn't bother to hide my obvious distress this time. "Yes, Figgins?"

He took a single step into the room. "There is a Lady Rachel Radcliffe here to see you. Shall I tell her you're not accepting visitors?"

I perked up at this pronouncement. Lady Rachel was a close friend of Lady Drummond. I'd met her twice—once when she arrived at the Drummonds' town house just as I was packing up my supplies to leave, and a second time when she actually sat in during one of Lady Drummond's portrait sessions. I was accustomed to my portrait subjects having visitors. It did not bother me so long as they did not try to include me in their conversation or otherwise distract me, and as long as the person I was painting could remain calm and still.

I knew very little about Lady Rachel, but the regard and affection Lady Drummond displayed toward her said much in her favor. There was a comfort between the two women that could not be feigned, and a type of silent communication that only lasting friendships exhibited.

I wondered what Lady Rachel was doing here now. Had she heard about her friend?

"No, thank you, Figgins. Please show her up."

He bowed. "Very good, my lady."

I had my answer shortly, for when Lady Rachel appeared, it was evident she had been crying. Her eyes were ringed in red and her face drawn, but as always she was immaculately turned out in her usual monochromatic palette. Today she was dressed in shades of red, from the scarlet trim on her bonnet to the tips of her maroon satin slippers. It contrasted quite strikingly with her dark hair and eyes.

I stood to receive her as she reached out a hand to me. "I've just come from the Drummonds' town house." She hiccupped, pressing her handkerchief to her nose.

I moved aside the package from Hinkley's as we sat side by side on the settee.

"Oh, it's just dreadful. I don't think . . ." She broke off, squeezing her eyes shut as she turned away. Her throat worked several times as she struggled to master her emotions.

I had to look away, lest her anguish draw tears from my still dry eyes. I suspected at some point I might weep for the loss of Lady Drummond, for after all, she deserved my grief. But let it be later when I was alone, not here with this woman I barely knew, even if she had probably been one of the closest people to Lady Drummond.

Lady Rachel sniffed and patted at her nose. "I'm sorry. It's just all so sudden. I arrived at Drummond House expecting to have tea with my friend, and instead . . ." She choked. Drawing a calming breath, she settled her voice. "Instead, I find she's deceased." Her eyes, still dewy with unshed tears, met mine again. "But I'm sure you're wondering why I'm here."

I nodded.

"Jeffers told me you were there. That you . . . tried to help her."

"I did," I replied, wondering what else the Drummonds' butler had told her.

"The physician said she suffered an apoplexy?"

So Dr. Davis had not reconsidered the matter. I'd known he wouldn't, but apparently I'd been holding out some hope that he would. Then I wouldn't have to decide whether to push for an inquiry, or face so much difficulty if I did.

But none of this affected Lady Rachel. Not immediately anyway.

"That's what he said," I replied neutrally.

Her eyes searched my face and then flared wide. "I knew it," she exclaimed with vehemence.

I drew back in surprise.

"I knew there must be more to it. He killed her, didn't he?"

"But I didn't say . . ."

"I know you saw the way he treated her, the way she cowered in his presence. He finally grew tired of her and decided to kill her. Just like his first wife."

I hardly knew what to say. If Gage and I did begin an official inquiry into the matter, I couldn't divulge the details of it, nor could I share my thoughts on a suspect. However, this was the first I'd heard about his first wife's death being suspicious. I knew he had been married before. I had met his eldest daughter, the current Lady Drummond's stepdaughter, very briefly. She was perhaps fifteen, not quite out of the schoolroom.

"Lady Rachel, I can't . . ."

"Oh, I know you can't say anything. Not yet. But you have begun an investigation, haven't you? You and Mr. Gage?"

I floundered. Should I deny it? Tell her we were only beginning to look into the matter?

She patted my hand, offering me a tight, but satisfied smile. "I understand. You'll come to me with your questions when you can."

She rose to leave, taking several steps toward the door before I found my voice.

"Lady Rachel."

She glanced back at me.

"This is a private matter. Can I count on your discretion?"

"Of course. As far as I'm concerned, this conversation never happened." She waved her hand as if to make it disappear.

I nodded, hoping she could be trusted. For though I'd never said a word, somehow my intentions had been made clear, but it would be best for all if they didn't come to light so soon. Otherwise, this inquiry might be obstructed before it had even begun.

I stared after her, pondering how I was going to explain to Gage what had just happened.

My sister appeared in the doorway, staring over her shoulder. When she saw me, she asked, "Was that Lady Rachel Radcliffe?"

"Yes," I replied, watching Alana waddle across the room. She hated for her wobbling walk to be called that, but in her condition it truly was the best way to describe it.

"Why was she here?"

I waited for my sister to sit down beside me on the settee and swing her feet up. I settled the blanket over her legs and slid to the opposite end. She gazed across at me, her eyebrows raised expectantly.

"Lady Drummond died this morning."

She gasped. "Oh, no. That's terrible." She glanced back at the door with a frown. "Did Lady Rachel come to inform you? But I thought you had a portrait session with Lady Drummond this morning."

"I did."

I waited for her to grasp the implication.

"Did it happen while you were there?"

I nodded.

"Oh, Kiera," she murmured sympathetically. "Why does death seem to follow wherever you go?"

I knew she had not meant it so, but her comment stung. It was not my fault that I'd encountered so many deaths in the past seven months.

She seemed to realize what she had said and reached a hand out toward me. "Oh, dearest. You know I didn't mean to hurt you." She sighed. "My words seem to come out all wrong lately."

I wondered if she was referring to the argument I'd heard coming from her and Philip's bedchamber last night. I couldn't make out what was being said, nor did I want to, but it was difficult to ignore the raised voices coming through the wall my room shared with theirs.

I squeezed her fingers. "I know."

"So does this mean you and Gage will be investigating?" Her voice was resigned.

"How do you know it was murder?" I hedged. "Maybe she died of natural causes."

Her bright lapis lazuli eyes turned scolding. "I may be slower than normal, but I'm not daft. Why else would Lady Rachel have visited you? And why else would you be mincing your words, worried that I'll dissolve into hysterics?"

I offered her a sheepish smile.

"Between you and Philip, I think you'd like to wrap me in cotton padding and lock me in a room. I'm made of sterner stuff, Sister dear."

"It's only because we love you."

"That may be, but it doesn't make it any less annoying." She sank back against the pillow propped behind her. "Now, tell me."

I described what had happened at the Drummond town house that morning, and then relayed for her what Gage and Lady Rachel had said, though I left out the part about seeking Gage out at his lodgings. I didn't think Alana needed those details. She listened while absently rubbing her rounded abdomen.

"Well, I know nothing about poisons or apoplexies, so I'm afraid I'm no help there," she said regretfully.

My lips quirked upward in a smile. That my sister would apologize for not knowing something any lady shouldn't warmed my heart. I was the unusual one, but you wouldn't know it listening to her.

"However, I do know how keen your intuition is. In fact, I've never known it to be wrong." She leaned forward as far as her belly would let her. "If you think Lady Drummond's death is suspicious, then it undoubtedly is."

"Yes, but I've never encountered something like this before," I argued.

"How so?"

"What if I'm letting my own past cloud my judgment?" I dropped my gaze to my lap. "What if when I see Lord Drummond, I'm really thinking of Sir Anthony?"

From her silence, I knew she understood what I meant. We'd talked very little about what had happened during my marriage, but I knew she must have speculated. If Sir Anthony would threaten to break my fingers if I didn't sketch his dissections, what was to stop him from striking me when he was displeased?

"I think you're doubting yourself unnecessarily."

I looked up to find her watching me.

"Did you not worry that your own desire to escape suspicion would influence your opinion of Lady Stratford and her guilt or innocence? Did you not fret that your history with William would make it impossible for you to be objective about him?" she recited, naming just a few of the complications I'd encountered during the first two inquiries I'd worked on with Gage. "I think you're more conscientious than most people about your ability to be impartial during an investigation."

"So you think I'm right to push for an inquiry?"

She shook her head. "I can't tell you what to do about that. But I *do* know that if you choose to proceed, you'll do so fairly."

I nodded once, wishing I felt as confident as she did.

"And I can also tell you how Lord Drummond's first wife died, since it's obvious you don't know." Her eyes drifted to the ceiling. "She died in childbirth."

My chest tightened, hearing aloud the words we had all been avoiding for the last few months, even if they hadn't been directed toward Alana's condition.

"So I'm not sure why Lady Rachel tried to blame Lord Drummond. Though I suppose he did bear some responsibility for the fact that she was giving birth in the first place."

"Or she knows something we don't." I frowned, realizing Lady Rachel had been right. I would have questions for her. "I guess I'll have to visit her and ask."

CHAPTER 6

Later that evening, Gage confirmed what Lady Rachel already had. Lady Drummond's death had officially been attributed to an apoplexy. No one yet had raised objections. There wasn't really anyone to do so. Lady Drummond's parents had passed away and her brother was a diplomat living somewhere on the continent. It would be weeks before he even received the news.

"I gathered as much information as I discreetly could on Lord Drummond, which was not all that difficult as many people were eager to discuss his wife's sudden death." Gage tilted his head to see into my eyes better. "None of it pointed to anything nefarious or suspicious about the man. He does keep a mistress, though many gentlemen do. And he's known to be mulish when he does not get his way. But neither of those things give him motive for killing his wife, especially in such a calculated way."

I crossed to stare out the window of Philip's study at the shadowed mews beyond. Darkness fell later with each day we moved closer to summer, but in mid-March we still ate dinner by candlelight.

Gage was right. Had Lady Drummond been beaten, or stabbed, or taken a tumble down the stairs, it would have been easier to blame

Lord Drummond. But perhaps he had known that. After all, he'd been a naval captain. He must be far from dumb. And for his wife to be found murdered from any of those violent methods would immediately implicate her notoriously hot-blooded husband.

However, poison was far more difficult to detect, let alone prove, and the suspicion could fall on anyone should the source of Lady Drummond's demise come to light. Though poison indicated a far more devious and determined mind than a husband losing his temper. Did Lord Drummond have a strong enough motive to kill his wife in such a premeditated way? Or was this the work of someone unexpected, someone yet to come to light?

It rattled me to recognize that had I not been there that day, it was likely no one would have questioned the physician's findings. The murder would have gone undetected, and the killer would go free.

Of course, all of this was supposing that Lady Drummond truly did die from poison, which we had yet to prove. I supposed that was to be our first step if we were to embark on an inquiry into the matter. But I still needed to convince Gage it was necessary.

"What of Lady Drummond herself?" I turned to ask. "Did anyone have anything unusual to say about her?"

"I'm afraid not. Though that's not surprising. People rarely want to speak ill of the dead."

He moved closer to stand beside me as I mulled over the information we had obtained and my own perceptions. I was still quite new at all of this, and I had never pursued an inquiry where we weren't specifically asked to investigate. I didn't know how to proceed, or even if we should, but how could I just walk away? My conscience would not rest until I was assured either that Lady Drummond had died from an apoplexy or that her killer had been brought to justice.

I glanced up at Gage through my lashes, trying to decide how to convince him to begin an inquiry. I could tell he did not share the same doubts I did.

In the end, I didn't have to say a thing. He could read my thoughts in my eyes.

"You still believe her death is suspicious."

"Yes," I admitted, relieved to have it out. "It simply doesn't sit right with me. None of it does."

Gage frowned. "Because of her argument with Lord Drummond the day before?"

"Partly."

He turned aside, rubbing a hand along his jaw. "You do realize that you don't know what that argument was about. You don't even know what was in that letter. Lord Drummond may have been justified in his anger that day."

I folded my arms over my chest. "Maybe. But not in his treatment of her."

But he continued on as if he was not listening. "For that matter, we don't really know what was happening in their marriage. Maybe Lady Drummond had wronged him in some way. Maybe there was a reason for his harsh conduct."

I knew what the law and society's opinions were on the matter. I was intimately aware of just how little power wives had. They were to obey their husbands, to defer to their decisions, and when they didn't, they could be punished. A woman had very few options if her husband chose to mistreat her, regardless of her class or status. Regardless of whether she was a duchess or a whore, she was still subject to her husband.

But to hear Gage speak so callously made me go cold. After everything that had happened in my first marriage, I'd had a difficult time reconciling myself to the idea of marrying again. It was no small thing for me to willingly place myself under the authority of a husband. As a widow, I was considered to be under the protection of my brother, Trevor, and my brother-in-law, Philip, but their power only extended so far. I also knew I was safe with both of them. Neither of them would ever raise a hand to me no matter how I infuriated them.

I trusted Gage, too. Or I thought I did. But from time to time I still feared I was making a terrible mistake.

"Is that really what you think?" I choked out.

Gage must have heard the apprehension in my voice, for he turned to look at me. His pale blue eyes softened. "You know I don't."

I searched his face, seeing affection mixed equally with aggravation. I knew he must grow weary of my misgivings. He had been extraordinarily persistent with me as I adjusted to our engagement and upcoming nuptials, reassuring me time and time again of his devotion and reliability. There were still a few secrets he had yet to share with me, but I was trying to be patient in return, allowing him to decide when the time was right to confide fully in me.

He reached out to take one of my hands. "What I'm trying to say, rather clumsily, is that we cannot begin an inquiry believing Lord Drummond is the guilty party."

"Agreed."

"You have to be objective. To treat every suspect with equal weight until the facts begin to definitively point in one direction or another."

Annoyed by his lecture, I arched a single eyebrow. "As you did during the inquiry into Lady Godwin's murder at Gairloch Castle?"

We both knew that I had been his main suspect when we began our first investigation seven months ago at my brother-in-law's isolated Highland estate.

His mouth tightened. "Yes, you were an early suspect, but I was determined to be as impartial as I could. Otherwise, I never would have allowed you to assist me."

"Oh, I see," I drawled. "I thought you were just keeping me close, hoping I would betray myself."

Amusement lit his eyes. "Flirting with danger, then? Trusting you wouldn't kill me next?"

"Something like that," I replied stubbornly.

He reached out to toy with a loose strand of hair, making the skin on my neck tingle. "Actually, I knew you were innocent quite early on."

I looked up at him in question.

"In the chapel cellar. When you vomited on the floor."

I blushed in remembrance.

"If you were guilty, you never would have placed yourself in such a vulnerable position."

He was right. I had hated losing my stomach and my nerve in front of him, no matter how justifiable the reaction had been. Still. "I could have been faking," I challenged.

His smile was almost condescending. "You're not that good of an actress."

I narrowed my eyes. "Then why did you continue to treat me like a suspect?"

"Even if I knew the truth, the other guests were still convinced of your guilt. I had to seem unbiased or risk their cooperation." He tilted his head. "And once again, you're not that good of an actress. Had I told you I knew you were blameless, it would have been evident to the others."

I wanted to argue, but he was undoubtedly correct. The four days of our investigation had been torturous for me, constantly wondering if I would be blamed for the crime purely because of my scandalous reputation. Would I have been able to feign my extreme agitation, my sleepless worrying? Probably not.

Just as I couldn't fake my true feelings about Lady Drummond's death.

Gage rested his hand on my shoulder, running his calloused thumb over my collarbone. "You are determined to investigate?"

I nodded diffidently, and then with more assurance. "Something isn't right, Gage. I don't know if it's poison or something else, but I won't be able to rest unless we look into it." I pressed a hand to his navy frockcoat. "Haven't you trusted my instincts in the past? Haven't they usually been right?"

He sighed. "Yes."

"Do you think you can do so now?"

"If you truly believe Lady Drummond was murdered. Then, yes, I'll trust you."

I gave him a tight smile of gratitude.

"But we must proceed with caution. If our inquiry is made public before we want it to be, we may run into difficulties."

I bit my lip, recalling how easily Lady Rachel had been able to deduce that I was suspicious. I would have to do a better job of hiding my feelings or all of Edinburgh would know what I really thought by the end of tomorrow.

Gage's eyes hardened with determination now that the matter was decided. "I think our first task is to figure out if she was killed by poison as you suspect, and if so, what type. An autopsy is out of the question. Lord Drummond will never allow it, and without proof of any wrong-doing, no magistrate will overrule his decision. So we'll have to gather our information another way."

"I can research some medical texts," I offered. "Though I doubt it will be immediately apparent. Many poisons have similar symptoms, and they often imitate illnesses. Which is why they can be so difficult to detect, as in this case. As well as . . ." I hesitated, realizing that what I was about to say would be painful for Gage to hear.

But he already knew. "As well as my mother," he finished for me in a flat voice. She had been slowly poisoned to death, and it had nearly gone undetected because the symptoms mimicked her recent illness.

"Yes."

He swallowed. "Then I'll speak to Sergeant Maclean. He will know if there have been any other strange deaths or known poisonings in recent weeks. Between the two of us, we should also be able to question the local apothecaries and chemists to find out if anyone has received any suspicious requests lately. I assume you believe it was mixed into her food or tea."

"I honestly don't know, though that is the most common method of ingestion."

He frowned. "I wish we could speak with Drummond's servants. If Lady Drummond was poisoned by her breakfast, then someone among the staff was involved, whether directly or indirectly." His gaze turned distant. "Perhaps Anderley should become better acquainted with the staff at Drummond House."

I'd wondered how often Gage's dark-haired valet assisted with his investigations.

I smiled wryly. "If he's anything like his employer, I imagine he's quite successful with the female members of the staff."

He didn't try to deny how charming he was. "Anderley does quite well for himself."

I shook my head, not sure I wanted to know exactly what that meant. "I'll also speak discreetly with some of Lady Drummond's friends." Including Lady Rachel. "Perhaps they know something that could be useful to us."

I didn't tell him my planned destination the next morning, for I knew he would only object, and I had no intention of changing my mind.

The following morning I let Philip's footman rap on the Drummonds' door, which was swathed in black crepe, rather than stand out in the cold wind myself. I needed the footman's assistance for this errand anyway. I watched as Jeffers attempted to argue with Johnny, but I had told the footman not to be turned away. Eventually the butler relented with a fierce frown etched on his face. Johnny hurried down the steps and helped me descend from the carriage before following me into the town house.

"Jeffers," I murmured, not removing my cloak. I thought I might have better luck if I at least pretended this visit would be brief.

He gestured down the hall for me to proceed before him. "The canvas is still in the drawing room as you left it, my lady."

I swiftly surveyed the front hall and up the stairs, hoping Lord Drummond was absent, as he normally was during the midmorning when Lady Drummond and I had scheduled our portrait sessions. "I imagine the household is still in shock," I remarked.

"Yes, my lady. It's been difficult to accept."

"I'm sure. I can hardly believe it myself." I pressed a hand to my abdomen. "I can barely stomach a thing. Just the thought of what happened makes me nauseated." I lifted aside the canvas covering Lady Drummond's portrait to look it over. "Has anyone here been similarly affected?"

Jeffers hesitated before replying. "I couldn't say, my lady."

"Well, perhaps your cook is better able to tempt everyone into eating. I'm afraid the items on the sideboard at Lord Cromarty's town house this morning did nothing but turn my stomach."

I could feel Johnny staring at me. He had been in the dining room when I cleaned my plate and went back for seconds.

"Perhaps I might speak with her. Maybe she has some suggestions I could make to our cook."

Jeffers was definitely suspicious now. I was not accustomed to giving long speeches, particularly in front of any members of staff. Nor was it like me to be so rude, worrying about my appetite when this entire household, particularly the children, must be grieving horribly.

"I suppose I could see if she's available," he replied carefully.

"Who's available?"

I almost cursed when Lord Drummond strode into the room. He halted to survey the scene before him, looking well rested and not the least troubled by his wife's recent death.

"Mrs. Larkins," Jeffers responded after only a small pause. "Lady Darby wished to ask her about the best food to eat for a stomach complaint."

I grimaced at how ridiculous it sounded when put that way. Perhaps I should have invented another pretense for speaking to the kitchen staff.

Lord Drummond raked his gaze over me as if I was something particularly unpleasant stuck to the bottom of his shoe. "She doesna appear to me to be sufferin' from any loss o' appetite."

I stiffened at his disparaging remark. I'd regained some much-needed weight since my return to Edinburgh after an emotionally harrowing winter, but I was far from plump. If anything I was still underweight by a few pounds.

"No, Lady Darby doesna need to speak wi' Mrs. Larkins." He flicked his wrist toward the door. "Show her oot."

"Actually, I'm here to collect your wife's portrait," I announced before Jeffers could move to do just that.

Lord Drummond glanced back at me, a guarded look in his eyes.

"I thought I might finish it in my studio since . . ." I swallowed the grief that suddenly welled up inside me ". . . since there's no reason for me to work on it here anymore."

His gaze drifted to the unfinished canvas propped on the easel still covered by a sheet. For a moment, I thought I saw some semblance of pain cross his features, but then it was gone, like a mirage. "Dinna bother," he replied dismissively.

I was stunned. He didn't want me to finish his wife's portrait?

I watched as he picked up a stack of letters and began to flip through them, as if he hadn't just done something so cold and unfeeling that it left me speechless.

"But what of the children?" I argued. "Won't they want to have a portrait of their mother? I would think it would comfort them."

He didn't even look up. "Dinna worry, Lady Darby. You'll still receive your full fee."

Fury shot through me, hot and swift. "I don't care about my fee."

He flicked a glance at me.

"What I care about is preserving Lady Drummond's memory. So I'm going to finish her portrait whether *you* care or not. For I'm sure your son and daughter do."

He returned to his letters. "Do as ye like."

I was forced to bite my tongue lest I say something I would later regret. I couldn't believe his heartless demeanor, his callous disregard for his children's feelings about their mother's loss. The portraits of my mother still gave me comfort, and she had been dead for almost twenty years. What kind of man was he that he didn't care to be reminded of his wife's image or preserve it for their children?

But perhaps her portrait would only remind him of what he'd done. It would be difficult to bear her likeness staring down at him if he had hastened her demise. If so, I hoped it haunted him. I hoped it wracked him with so much guilt that his conscience would eat him alive.

I directed Johnny in how to carry the canvas and then followed him and Jeffers from the room. At the threshold, I couldn't resist darting one more spiteful glance over my shoulder at the baron, and was surprised to find him staring after us. The look on his face was one of extreme anguish, but of what kind? Grief or guilt?

He turned away before I could decide.

As I was crossing the hall, it occurred to me that I'd never seen a portrait of Lord Drummond's first wife either. Was that because there wasn't one, or because he didn't wish for it to be hung in his home? Of course, I hadn't been in every room in the town house. Perhaps it was hanging in one of the less public rooms out of deference to his second wife. Or maybe it graced the wall of his first daughter's room—a memento of her mother.

As if conjured from my own thoughts, I glimpsed a flicker of movement on the landing of the staircase. There stood the baron's first daughter, Imogen. Her long, golden curls hung down her back unrestrained. In her simple gown, she was the perfect image of innocent young womanhood, and yet her eyes told a different story. They were watchful and sad, as if she had seen much, and was afraid of seeing more. Or was that my fancy?

She gripped the banister tight beneath her hands. I considered going to her, for I suspected she had something to tell me, but then a voice called her name from above. Her head jerked toward the sound, and with one more backward glance at me, she lifted her skirts and scampered up the steps and out of sight.

I frowned, wanting to abandon all pretense of politeness and propriety and follow her. But Gage had warned me not to reveal our suspicions and intentions too soon and I had already risked much coming here this morning. Besides, Lady Drummond's body was likely laid out in her bedchamber above to be prepared for burial, and I had no desire to stumble upon it in my current state. So I stifled my impatience and forced my feet toward the door.

I waited on the steps as Johnny struggled against the wind, carefully sliding the canvas into the carriage and propping it against the backward-facing seat. Then he stood to the side, offering me his hand as I climbed the steps into the coach. Just as I was about to duck my head inside, I felt a prickle along my neck and looked behind me once more. A curtain in a room on one of the upper stories twitched shut.

"My lady?" the footman asked.

I smiled absently at him, and climbed the rest of the way into the carriage.

Who had been watching me—Imogen or someone else? And why? Did they have something to tell me? Or were they unnerved by my visit?

CHAPTER 7

I was still contemplating the matter when I followed Johnny carrying Lady Drummond's unfinished portrait into the town house on Charlotte Square. "Up to my studio, please," I directed as I stripped off my gloves to hand them to Figgins.

"My lady."

Hearing the note of tension in his voice, I glanced up.

"Dr. Fenwick is with Lady Cromarty."

He hadn't finished the words before I was hurrying toward the stairs.

"My lady, your cloak," Figgins called after me.

I pulled it off and thrust it at him before dashing up the steps. Johnny pressed himself to the wall as best he could, carrying the canvas, while I squeezed past.

Dr. Fenwick was not scheduled to visit Alana today. I would have known, for I sat in on every visit now that her lying-in was so close. So if he was here now, that could only mean something was wrong. Something urgent enough for the physician accoucheur to rush here, for I'd been gone for less than an hour.

I rapped on Alana's door only out of courtesy before opening it. She was propped up against her pillows, her face drawn in pain, as Dr. Fenwick gently prodded her abdomen. Her lady's maid, Jenny, stood silently next to the bed, waiting for instructions. I closed the door softly behind me and crossed to where Philip was wearing a hole in the rug pacing back and forth in front of the window, his hat still in his hands from riding to fetch the physician. He spun the brim round and round between his fingers.

"What's happened?" I whispered to him.

He did not reply, but glanced at his wife lying on the bed. She suddenly seemed so fragile. His silence unsettled me, but I didn't press him for answers. The physician would provide them soon enough.

Dr. Fenwick leaned over to speak to Alana, who nodded. Then he poured something into a glass of water and passed it to Jenny for her to help my sister drink.

Philip stopped pacing and eagerly turned toward the physician as he approached us.

"There's no way to be certain," Dr. Fenwick began to explain in a low voice. "But I suspect that the placenta is separatin' from Lady Cromarty's uterus. It would explain the pain she's feelin' and her bleedin'."

My stomach dropped sharply. "That sounds serious," I murmured.

"It is." His eyes were earnest behind his spectacles. "But the bleedin' was relatively minor and has stopped for the time bein'. I've given Lady Cromarty some laudanum to help wi' the pain, and explained to her that she must remain in bed for the remainder of her confinement. Too much movement could tear the placenta irreparably."

"And if she doesn't?" The question had to be asked, though Philip stiffened beside me.

"She could hemorrhage."

Which would almost certainly result in her death and perhaps that of the infant.

I nodded, glancing at Alana where she lay with her eyes closed. Her face looked dreadfully pale against the plum counterpane.

Dr. Fenwick followed my gaze. "Should she begin to bleed again, send for me immediately, but beyond that I'm afraid all that can be done is to keep her still, and calm, and comfortable. If so, the placenta may reattach itself."

"Thank you," Philip said, finally speaking up. His voice was tight with strain.

The physician gathered up his things, placing them in his satchel. I turned to look at Philip, but his gaze remained fixed on his wife's prone form. I thought maybe he would go to her, but his feet remained rooted to the spot.

"If there are no more questions . . ." Dr. Fenwick glanced at each of us.

Philip surged toward the door to Alana's room. "I'll show you out."

I frowned after him in confusion. It was not like my brother-in-law to abandon my sister when she needed him most. He had always stood steadfastly beside her, in sickness and in grief. He was the shining example of constancy and dependability. So why now did he always seem so eager to escape her presence?

I knew he had a seat in Parliament and estate matters to attend to, but more and more often of late that had been the dismal excuse for his absence, either closeting himself in his study or attending dinners about Edinburgh. In the past Alana had accompanied him, but since she had been restricted to the house, she no longer could. I wondered if Philip truly needed to be present at all of those events or if they were just another pretext for avoiding his wife's company.

I caught Jenny's eye, recognizing the same uneasiness furrowing her brow that I felt. Pushing it aside for the moment, I drew a chair up to Alana's bedside and reached out to clasp her hand in mine. She squeezed it lightly, letting me know she was aware I was there.

"Go to sleep, dearest," I crooned. "I'll be here when you wake."

· · ·

I moaned as I sank down on the seat in front of my dressing table later that evening. My temples throbbed with worry for my sister and my neck ached from when I'd fallen asleep in an awkward position in the chair in her room earlier. I reached up to rub the spot where it still twinged every time I turned my head to the left.

"Here, m'lady."

I opened my eyes and sighed in relief. "Oh, Bree, you're a gem." I took the cup of willow bark tea my maid held out to me and drank it. I was in so much pain I almost didn't mind the musty aroma, though the bitter aftertaste left something to be desired.

I watched her smile to herself in the reflection of the mirror as she folded my discarded shawl. "Nay. Just good at tellin' when someone's head is fit to split open. Canna blame ye wi' all yer worries this week, what wi' Lady Drummond dyin' in front o' ye like that, and then Lady Cromarty's scare this morn."

She was right. It had been a troubling few days.

"Do ye still plan to attend the ball at Inverleith House tomorrow evenin'?"

I stifled a curse. In all the upheaval, I'd completely forgotten about it. "I was supposed to visit Madame Avignon's shop today for my final fitting."

"I sent a letter roond earlier to tell her what happened. She said she's happy to send her assistant by on the morrow."

I spun around to face her. "Did I call you a gem? I should have declared you a saint." I sighed. "Thank you, Bree."

She brushed my grateful words aside and gestured for me to turn back around so she could start on the buttons up the back of my dress.

I considered her in the reflection of the mirror, still somewhat amazed at how easily we'd adapted to each other. I had never been completely comfortable with my previous lady's maids. The first had been too much under my late husband's thumb, whether out of fear or reverence, and I'd never trusted nor liked her. If I'd been allowed, I would have replaced her almost immediately. While Lucy, an upstairs maid from Philip's household at Gairloch Castle, had proved untrustworthy and far too naïve.

Bree, on the other hand, was perhaps more worldly-wise than even I was. I knew she had seen and experienced things she'd only hinted at, and I had to admire her resiliency and determined good cheer. And, of course, there was also the fact that she wasn't afraid of me and my scandalous reputation, no matter how unfairly it had been earned. I suspected not many maids would consider themselves lucky to be employed by me.

I wondered what would happen to Lady Drummond's maid now. Would she remain in the household, perhaps passed down to the stepdaughter, Imogen, as she came of age, or would she be forced to look for employment elsewhere? And if so, how long would Lord Drummond wait before he gave her a reference and sent her on her way? I suspected it depended on how much the girl had seen.

I wished I could have spoken to her. She could probably tell me more than any of the other servants combined. After all, she helped the baroness dress and bathe, took up her breakfast tray, attended her when she was ill, and a hundred other tiny, intimate tasks. She would know if Lady Drummond had hidden any bruises or if she had been feeling poorly of late. She might have also been witness to an altercation or two between Lord and Lady Drummond. And most important, she had been with Lady Drummond immediately before she suddenly became sick, collapsed, and died. She could tell me how the morning had proceeded, what the baroness had eaten, and who had visited her employer recently.

I felt an almost urgent need to talk to the girl before it was too late. The poisoner could begin to wonder, like me, if she had seen too much. Or Lord Drummond could send her away, whether he was the killer or not, because he worried what she might report if someone did start asking questions.

I supposed there was also the possibility she had been the murderer's accomplice, since she was so intimate with Lady Drummond and could easily slip her the poison, but I didn't think so. My instincts told me she was not involved. Her grief and upset at the baroness's passing were too genuine, and I had seen no fear or contention in the maid's eyes when she looked at Lady Drummond during the days leading up to her death.

If only there was a way I could interview the lady's maid and all of the Drummond staff without Lord Drummond knowing. I glanced again at Bree, who was now pulling pins out of my barely tamed hair. Her auburn curls were still neatly arranged after a fourteen-hour day of work.

"Bree, do you ever get an opportunity to converse with the lady's maids from other households?" I mused.

"I chat wi' some o' the maids in the houses next door oot in the mews from time to time. And if by chance we meet on our day off or oot runnin' errands." She glanced up from extracting a pin from a snarl in my hair, a curious look in her eye. She was smart enough to know I had not asked my question out of idle curiosity.

"So it's possible you could encounter a maid from another street or square, even maybe Hanover Street."

Her mouth curled in amusement at my obvious hinting. "It is."

"Is that something you would be willing to attempt if I asked?" I kept my tone neutral, not wanting to force Bree into doing something she wasn't comfortable with.

She tilted her head to the side and began pulling a brush through my hair. "I've been thinkin' that Lady Drummond's maid could surely use a shoulder to cry on, poor lass." Her eyes flicked up to meet mine in the glass. They twinkled with understanding. "What would ye like me to ask her?"

I lay in bed that night with my cat, Earl Grey, curled up at my feet, replaying my conversation with Bree. I simultaneously fretted that I'd both forgotten to tell her something to ask Lady Drummond's maid and just done something monumentally stupid by enlisting Bree's help. But I had no choice. The maid needed to be questioned. She potentially possessed far too much information that could help us make sense of her employer's death.

I'd almost drifted into sleep when I suddenly heard a loud thump and a muffled curse coming from the bedchamber next door. I guessed Philip must have stumbled into something in the dark, but then I realized the sound had come from the guest room at the back of the town house. What was someone doing in there? Had my brother, Trevor, come to visit? If Philip had thought to write to him after the scare over Alana's condition this morning, he might have just arrived from his home in the Borders region, but only if both he and the messenger had nearly crippled their horses.

I frowned, doubting anyone could ride that fast on the muddy March roads.

I grabbed my dressing gown from the bottom of the bed, tugging it out from underneath the bulk of my cat, who grumbled before settling back into sleep. I pulled it on and tied the belt as I opened my door. The light of a single candle gleamed through the open door to the guest room. I crossed the hall on soft tread, careful not to disturb Alana in the chamber at the front of the house. I hoped I wasn't about to embarrass myself unnecessarily in front of a stranger.

Barnes, Philip's normally gregarious valet, came bustling through the doorway. He stopped short at the sight of me and his eyes slid to the side. I wondered why.

"M'lady," he pronounced, bowing once before he hurried off.

I stared after him before turning to face Philip, who now stood in the doorway. He looked harried and exhausted, a state I'd seen him in more and more often of late. His dark hair had even begun to turn silver at the temples, something I would have expected Alana to lovingly tease him about, but she had yet to mention it in my presence.

"Is there something you need, Kiera?" His cravat was askew, as if he'd begun to take it off.

"I heard a crash."

He nodded. "That was me. I apologize. I'm not used to the arrangement of the furniture."

"You're sleeping in the guest chamber?"

He glanced to the side. "Alana needs her rest. I don't want to disturb her."

"Yes, but I don't think Dr. Fenwick meant you couldn't share the room with her."

"Maybe," he replied, still not meeting my eyes. "But I don't want to take any chances."

I frowned in confusion, not understanding why his answers did not feel so kind and considerate. "What did Alana say when you told her?" I couldn't believe she had taken his decision well. She always found comfort in her husband's presence, even if they were also prone to argue.

"I haven't."

The unsettling feeling that had been gnawing at me since my return to Edinburgh bit a little deeper. I stared at him, not knowing what to say.

He sighed wearily. "If you don't mind, Kiera, I'd like to go to bed. Perhaps we can talk in the morning."

I nodded, though I knew we wouldn't. He would be too busy with one thing or another—work on the new reform bill several members of Parliament were currently drafting, a leak in the roof at the London town house, a new horse he wanted to take a look at for his stables. Chances were that he would be gone before I even came downstairs the next morning.

"Good night," he said with a tight smile before closing the door.

I gazed at the hard wood a moment longer before turning toward Alana's door a dozen feet away. The space between them suddenly seemed much farther, and it was growing wider every day.

CHAPTER 8

I spent the next morning scouring the shelves of Philip's study for information on poisons and any other medical knowledge that might be pertinent to Lady Drummond's death. Unfortunately, Philip's collection of books in his Edinburgh home was not as extensive as his vast library at Gairloch Castle. I suspected I would have to make a visit to Dr. Renshaw at the Royal College of Surgeons of Edinburgh to uncover the information I sought. Dr. Renshaw had been my late husband's apprentice during the early months of our marriage, and had assisted Gage and me during an inquiry we conducted late the previous year. I hoped he would be willing to help me again, or at least grant me access to the Royal College's library so that I might find the answers I sought myself.

I decided it would be best if I approached the Royal College with a letter of introduction from Philip, in case I had difficulty gaining admittance to speak with Dr. Renshaw. I'd learned to be wary of medical men's reactions to me. Thanks to my famous and infamous late anatomist husband, most of them knew my name, and some, like Dr. Davis, did not respond kindly. Others, like Dr. Fenwick, bore me no grudge. I'd discovered there was no way of predicting how each physician or surgeon would react, but a letter of introduction from an earl always helped.

If only Philip were here to provide one.

As anticipated, he was absent this morning. I swallowed my worry and annoyance and jotted off a message to request the letter I needed, and left it on his desk for him to find when he returned.

Alana was asleep, so I decided it would be a good time to call on Lady Rachel Radcliffe. I hoped she might have some useful information for me, but if nothing else, the lively widow was sure to distract me from my other concerns.

And I needed distraction. Gage was out questioning chemists, while Bree, whom I'd ostensibly given the morning off, would be doing her best to arrange a chance encounter with Lady Drummond's maid. Between my fear over my sister's health, Philip's distant demeanor, and my anxieties over the investigation, it was no surprise I felt tense. Add to that the fact that I'd promised to attend the Inverleith Ball with Gage that night, when I dreaded most society events, and it was a wonder I hadn't retreated to my art studio and refused to come out.

I realized I was calling at an hour that was earlier than etiquette allowed, but Lady Rachel graciously agreed to receive me anyway, having her majordomo lead me up to the intimate parlor attached to her bedchamber. The room was decorated in shades of emerald green, ivory, and gold, from the gilded mirror over the hearth to the chintz upholstery on the furniture. With its rich fabrics and plush pillows, it was the perfect balance of cozy and sumptuous.

Lady Rachel rose from her fainting couch, still draped in a lavender blue dressing gown with a high collar and exquisite embroidery. Her hair was half-dressed, with dark ringlets pinned around her crown and falling down her back. I could appreciate the effort she was making to appear her normal elegant self, even though her eyes were puffy and rimmed in bright red and her skin was ashen and swollen from extensive crying.

"Lady Darby! How good of you to call on me." She took my hand, guiding me to sit beside her.

"Thank you for seeing me at such an early hour."

"But, of course." She turned to her servant. "Monahan, some tea, please."

The man nodded solemnly before backing out.

"Now, tell me what you've uncovered," she said.

"I'm afraid nothing yet," I told her, knowing there was no use in prevaricating about the reason for my visit. But that didn't mean I needed to admit all. "I'm hoping you might be in possession of some information that could be helpful to us."

"Of course," she declared. "Anything." She leaned back, draping one arm along the back of the couch.

"Well, to begin, can you tell me when you last visited Lady Drummond? We're trying to get an idea of the timeline of events in the days leading up to the morning she died," I explained.

"Let me see." She lifted her eyes to the ceiling and tapped her chin with a finger. "We had tea at our normal time on Monday afternoon around four, so I suppose that was it." Her face tightened as she turned to the side.

"And did you notice anything odd about her behavior that day?"

She pressed her lips together as she considered my question. "She did seem a bit more anxious than normal, I suppose. I assumed her husband had been particularly unpleasant. She got that way from time to time, usually after he'd raged at her for one thing or another." Her mouth twisted. "But perhaps in this case I was wrong. Maybe something else upset her." Her eyes saddened. "Maybe I should have asked her about it instead of presuming I knew the truth."

I felt that same twinge of guilt inside me that I saw reflected in her eyes. I waited for her gaze to meet mine again. "I noticed it on Tuesday during our portrait session, and I didn't say anything either. So if you failed her in this, you didn't do it alone."

Lady Rachel blinked rapidly and nodded.

Monahan returned with the tea tray, so we paused in our discussion while the aromatic brew was poured. Once we were both settled with a cup and the quiet servant had slipped out again as unobtrusively as possible, I waited for Lady Rachel to take a sip before I pressed her for more information.

"So you only noticed her anxiety on Monday? Not on the days leading up to that?"

She shook her head. "Though she did seem a bit distracted. I noticed it about a week before. She kept having to apologize for letting her mind wander while we were conversing. And other small things, like letting her tea grow cold before she remembered to drink it. I only noticed because it wasn't like her. She was normally so attentive."

I nodded. Lady Drummond had been alert and focused. In fact, I would have described her as being more vigilant. It was the natural characteristic of a woman who was ever watchful of her husband's mood, listening for the heaviness of his tread, or the slight edge in his voice, the dip of his brow. For her to have been distracted must have meant something significant was occupying her thoughts.

Or her brain was not functioning properly. My chest tightened. I had heard distraction listed as one of the many symptoms of an apoplexy. I shook it aside, reminding myself it could be the symptom of any number of things. That alone did not prove Dr. Davis's diagnosis.

"Do you know what she might have been distracted by?"

"I'm afraid not." I watched as she stirred her spoon around and around in her cup. "But I've heard that some women get that way when they suspect they're expecting, especially if it's unplanned."

She glanced up at me through her lashes and I wondered whether she was trying to tell me something. Perhaps something she'd been told in strict confidence.

"Do you think that was what it was?" I asked, not wanting to force her to betray that trust, even if it was a bond with a deceased woman.

She stared down at her tea again. "I honestly don't know. But . . . it's possible."

I nodded slowly, not sure I was grasping all of the ramifications of what she was saying. "Lord Drummond's?"

She did not immediately respond, and I felt my stomach dip in shock. "Lady Drummond had a lover?"

"I don't know that," she hastened to say. "I don't know anything for certain. But I know there were several men interested in her. One in particular. She mentioned him several times, though not by name. And . . ." her gaze dropped ". . . well, I encouraged her."

I stared at her in silence, hoping my expression was not openly disapproving.

Her dark eyes flashed. "You've witnessed what a brute her husband is. And Clare was still a beautiful young woman. She deserved a man who would treat her the way a man should. Her husband was incapable and unwilling to do so. She gave him his heir. Why shouldn't she have taken a lover?"

I supposed there was some justification in what she was saying. Lady Drummond had deserved a better husband, and that was unlikely short of Lord Drummond dying since divorce was nearly impossible, even with the husband's support. So her only other option for satisfying companionship was to take a lover. I allowed myself to wonder for a moment what I would have done had I met Gage while my husband still lived. Would I have attempted to conduct a liaison with him? Would I have risked it?

Would Lady Drummond have? She must have known how furious her husband would be if he found out. Is that what had happened? Is that what had been in the letter he had shaken in her face? And if she had gotten with child . . . I inhaled sharply. There was no telling what he might have done.

My expression must have been as grim as my musings, for the fight drained out of Lady Rachel. "Yes. Those were my thoughts exactly."

She set her cup aside and wrapped her arms around herself as if she'd suddenly caught a chill. "If Lord Drummond had discovered his wife was being unfaithful . . . well, that could be his motive for killing her. I knew he would not react well when I encouraged her, but, of course, I'd never thought he would go so far."

I studied her. "The other day you said he grew tired of his first wife, and I got the impression you meant to insinuate he may have done her harm. From what I understand, she died in childbirth. Do you know something otherwise?"

"Not for certain." She laughed bitterly. "I don't seem to know anything for certain. But Clare said she had learned his first wife had taken a tumble down the stairs. That was what sent her into labor early. Apparently, she and Lord Drummond had argued furiously just a few hours before. The entire staff had heard it. And he was upstairs when she fell." She shrugged one shoulder, allowing me to infer the rest.

The implication was sickening.

"But no one saw him push her?" I asked, wanting everything to be clear.

"No. That's why there was never an inquiry or serious scandal." Her gaze sharpened. "Nothing could be proved."

Only a dunce would fail to see the similarities, and they unsettled me. Unfortunately, Lord Drummond's behavior after his second wife's death made it all too easy for me to believe him capable of being so cruel and unfeeling. Perhaps murder had not been his real intention when he pushed his first wife down the stairs in such a delicate state, but that didn't change the fact that his actions had caused it. He must have realized he'd been lucky not to get caught, and so he'd planned his second wife's death much more carefully.

But of course, once again, this was all supposition. Damning though it might be, none of it could be proven. Yet.

"You know the physician has now officially blamed Lady Drummond's death on an apoplexy," I said.

Lady Rachel wiped a hand over her brow. "But you don't believe it." I didn't reply, and she glanced to the side at me. "I know. You cannot say," she muttered impatiently. "But I am not unobservant. And in any case, I also doubt it."

"Why?"

"Because she was young and healthy. Because her husband was a brute, and likely had more than one reason to wish her dead. Because . . . because I am not unfamiliar with apoplexies. My late husband died of one, and his heart was not good." Her eyes bored into mine. "In every way. And that she should have died in the same way as that bastard . . ."

Her words broke off and she turned away, pressing a hand to her mouth. Her shoulders began to shake.

"I'm sorry," I murmured. "I didn't know."

She inhaled audibly. "I know," she replied in a broken voice. "Not many do."

I didn't hear the door open or the majordomo enter, but suddenly he was leaning down to assist Lady Rachel. "My lady, are you unwell?"

She shook her head. "I . . . I just need a moment."

The man glanced up at me. "Perhaps I should see Lady Darby out?"

"No. There is no need." She sat straighter, accepting the handkerchief Monahan offered her. She dabbed her face and inhaled several steadying breaths. "I am well. Thank you. You may leave, Monahan."

He appeared as if he wanted to argue, but a well-trained servant would never do so in front of a guest, even if they were on intimate enough terms to do so otherwise. He bent to collect our tea things and excused himself.

"I apologize. I didn't expect to become emotional like that."

"It's understandable."

"You can appreciate why Lady Drummond's suffering at the hands of her husband so upsets me."

I nodded. It explained her and Lady Drummond's close friendship. But unfortunately, it also made her a poor judge of Lord Drummond and what he was capable of. Memories of her own abusive husband would undoubtedly cloud her opinion and reactions, and I had no way of knowing if she was capable of being objective. I fervently hoped that my at least being aware of a similar conflict within myself would make me more impartial than I might otherwise have been.

I thanked her for her help. I was leaving with more questions than answers, but at least we now had a potential motive beyond Lord Drummond's simply growing tired of his second wife. With any luck, Lady Drummond's other friends would be able to tell me more, though I would have to be careful. I couldn't ask them directly if the baroness had taken a lover, nor could I hint at our suspicion that she had died of anything other than an apoplexy. But I had watched society ladies imply and insinuate often enough that I hoped I was capable of emulating them.

I promised to keep Lady Rachel apprised of the investigation before being escorted from the house by Monahan. He did not overtly show his disapproval, but I was certain he was cross with me for upsetting his mistress, and more than happy to see me go. I wondered again at their close relationship, and then dismissed it from my mind. It was none of my affair what Lady Rachel did with her man-of-all-business. She was a widow, and I was sure he was more than capable of taking care of himself.

"Please give Madame Avignon my compliments," I told the timid slip of a girl the modiste had sent to finish fitting my gown for the ball that evening. She dipped her head shyly before following the upstairs maid from the room. I stared after the girl, wondering how young the rest of the dressmaker's seamstresses were. She looked to be no older than twelve or thirteen, but she was a deft hand with a needle.

I tightened the belt of my sapphire blue dressing gown around my waist and turned to watch Bree fidget with the pleats of the ball gown.

The deep rose color of the bodice and overskirt was a brighter shade than I normally favored, but Alana had insisted I could not always wear blue and purple in the evening, even if they did compliment my chestnut brown hair and the lapis lazuli shade of my eyes. She had ordered Madame Avignon to use this fabric, and I had deferred to her opinion, though now I wished I hadn't. The pale cornflower blue I had wanted to use would have been far less . . . shocking.

Bree must have read the growing horror on my face, for she gave me a bright smile. "It looks lovely on ye, m'lady. It truly does."

"It doesn't make my skin look too pink?" I asked anxiously.

"Nay. Actually, the opposite. Makes ye look as pale and creamy as a pearl."

I crossed my arms over my chest and paced toward my dressing table, uncertain whether to believe her, and frustrated that I cared. Before Gage it had mattered very little to me what I wore, so long as it didn't interfere with my painting, but now I was afraid I would embarrass him. He was the charming golden boy of the ton, always impeccably turned out, and devastatingly handsome no matter what he wore. I knew they didn't understand how he could be attracted to me—an eccentric, scandalous outcast. I'd heard there were bets being placed even as far away as London on just how long our engagement would last before Gage found some way of ending it. I was sure no one would blame him if he did, even though it would be a horrible breach of promise and protocol.

I glanced once again at the rose confection with white underskirt and lace trim, and then decided to put it from my mind, at least until I had to wear it. "Were you able to discover anything this morning?" I asked Bree, reaching out to fiddle with the hair brushes on my dressing table.

She set aside the pair of slippers she was holding up to the dress and crossed the room toward me. "I didn't find Lady Drummond's maid. Aileen's her name. But I did happen upon one o' the footmen."

I looked up into her bright eyes. I could tell from the tone of her voice she had something to say to me. "Oh?"

"He said Aileen's been right broken up by her mistress's death—burstin' into tears in the middle o' dinner. And the whole house is in a bit o' a dither. One o' the maids left wi' oot given notice, and several o' the other members o' the staff are threatenin' to quit as well."

"Did he say why?" I asked in surprise. Everything had seemed quiet and calm when I'd visited the morning before, but perhaps that was only in the public rooms. Who knew what had been happening belowstairs?

"I gather they're scairt. At least the maids are. The others seem concerned he'll marry his mistress, and apparently she's no' fit to fill Lady Drummond's place."

My eyes widened. "Who's his mistress?"

Bree shook her head. "He didna ken. But his lordship visits her every Tuesday, Thursday, and Saturday in some house on Cumberland Street near St. Stephen's Church."

"This footman is quite chatty and relatively well informed," I replied.

She smiled impishly. "Dinna ye ken? Servants always ken the best gossip. There's no' much else to blather aboot."

I frowned, pondering what I should be worried she was telling the rest of the staff about me.

Her expression softened. "Dinna worry, m'lady. I'm the soul o' discretion. I ken better."

I turned to the side, not wanting to see the empathy in her gaze. "Did he have anything else to say?"

"No' that would be helpful to you."

I narrowed my eyes as she ran her hands over the bright yellow skirts of her dress. If I wasn't mistaken, her cheeks had turned a little pink. I wondered if I should be concerned. After all, my previous maid had essentially been seduced into sharing information about me. But Bree was different. She wasn't some sheltered Highland lass who had never been farther than five miles from home. I suspected if Bree wished, she would lead this footman on a merry chase, not the other way around. Maybe Gage's valet, Anderley, was not the only one handy at uncovering information from other people's servants.

There was a knock on the door, and Bree went to answer it. It was Alana's maid, Jenny.

"Lady Cromarty's awake now, my lady," she informed me. "You asked me to let you know."

I followed her from the room and down the hall to Alana's chamber, where she held the door for me. My sister was propped up on her pillows, her head turned to the side to look out the window. From her vantage, I didn't know if she could see much more than the gray sky, but she didn't seem to be admiring the view anyway. She was lost in thought, and whatever she was contemplating did not seem to be happy.

I shook my head as I spotted the gray lump of fur curled up next to her side. Alana's hand periodically stroked over the fur. Leave it to my cat, Earl Grey, to find the warmest, coziest place in the house.

"When did he sneak in here?"

Jenny smiled at the gray tabby. "I don't know, but the rascal was in here when I brought up her ladyship's luncheon a few hours ago."

Earl Grey was a mouser from our childhood home, Blakelaw House, where I had spent the winter with our brother. For some reason, the cat had attached himself to me, finding his way back into my art studio or bedchamber even when he'd been chased out. I had eventually accepted and even welcomed his presence, and now thought of him as my pet, bringing him with me to my sister's home in Edinburgh.

"Ring if you need me," Jenny said before closing the door behind her.

Alana glanced up as I crossed the room to her. I watched as she visibly made an effort to appear cheery. "Good afternoon, dearest." Her mouth smiled, but her eyes were tired and her complexion pale.

I glanced significantly at the cat curled into her side. "Is he bothering you?"

Her smile turned into something more genuine as she looked at the feline. "No."

Earl Grey opened one of his golden eyes as if to say, *Who would be bothered by me?*

I rolled my eyes at him and settled into the same chair I had occupied the day before. I clasped Alana's hand where it rested on the counterpane. "How are you feeling?"

"Exhausted," she sighed. "So no different than before."

I appreciated her attempt to make a joke, knowing it was more for my benefit than hers.

"Growing a baby takes a lot of effort," I murmured, staring at the mound of her belly beneath the blankets.

"It does. And it seems to get more difficult with age." Her eyes drifted to my flat stomach. "So you and Gage better start soon."

I flushed at the idea of carrying Gage's child, at the thought of the act that would create it. "I don't think we're in a great hurry," I replied. "And anyway, I don't even know if I'm capable."

"Because you and Sir Anthony never had a child?" Alana scoffed. "I don't know what the man made you believe . . ."

"He never said anything about it."

Her eyes searched my face. "Then he must have known it was his fault you never conceived, because he never showed you any kindness otherwise."

That was true, but still. "He . . . never really made much of an effort." I blushed brighter.

"Well, there you have it." Her eyes hardened. "At least he spared you that."

I stared down at our joined hands, uncomfortable with thinking about those moments let alone discussing them. My sister seemed to sense this and let the matter drop.

"Did you decide whether you would rather have the daffodils or the larkspurs?"

"Oh, Alana, I haven't even thought . . ."

"I still think the larkspurs would look best with the forget-me-nots," she hurried on to say. "But I know you've always loved daffodils, and they do mean 'chivalry.'"

I squeezed her hand. "Alana, slow down. There's no need to rush." I released her hand to brush a stray tendril of hair back from her face. "You need your rest. Just focus on that. The wedding plans can wait."

"No, they can't," she insisted.

I frowned.

She sat up higher on her pillows, jostling Earl Grey, who blinked open his eyes and then closed them again once she settled. "Kiera, all I've been doing is thinking about rest! Or rather how I'm supposed to be resting, and how I'm not supposed to think of anything distressing. But without something to distract me, all I *can* think about is the baby, and whether I'm bleeding again, or if I'm moving too much, or if I'll even live to hold him."

I grabbed hold of her hands. "Alana, don't talk like that. Of course you will."

"But you understand my point. I *need* something to distract me." Her eyes were wide with pleading.

I nodded slowly, supposing I did. I'd implored our brother, Trevor, in a similar manner just a few months ago to understand why I needed to be involved with the investigation at Dryburgh Abbey. Though I had needed to distract myself from my grief over a friend's death, not my own precarious health and that of my unborn child. How much more distraught must Alana be?

Her shoulders slumped in relief. "I want your wedding to be so beautiful. Everything it should have been the first time. Especially now that you're marrying the right man."

I smiled tightly. Alana had never understood why I had wed Sir Anthony in just a small private ceremony in a chapel in London. Her wedding to Philip had been an elaborate affair, as big as the joy she had felt on that day. That my sister should know me so well and yet not fully comprehend how nervous large events made me, particularly when I was the center of attention, puzzled me. But I knew she meant well. She wanted me to also have a celebration as big as my joy. She just didn't realize I would rather savor that joy and give a larger portion of it to those I truly loved than spread it far and wide.

Her eyes softened with a sheen of tears. "You've been through so much. I want to do this for you, my only sister. To know that it will be special." Her lips curled into a bittersweet smile. "Just in case I'm not there to see it myself."

I shook my head, feeling my own tears threaten. "You will be. You will be. Don't say that." I punctuated each phrase by hitting the coverlet with our combined hands.

She didn't try to argue with me, just continued to smile.

"Alana," I exhaled, feeling sick with the fear I had refused to completely acknowledge until now.

"We'll see," she said softly. "It's in God's hands now, isn't it?"

I sniffed and nodded, releasing one of her hands to dash away a tear that had escaped to trail down my cheek. "But that doesn't mean you can give up. I won't let you."

"I know. I haven't. I'm just preparing for all eventualities."

I still didn't like the sound of that, but I remained quiet. How would I react in her situation? Would I want to know I'd left everything and everyone as well prepared as I could, or would I obstinately refuse even to contemplate it?

"Now," she declared, as if the matter was settled. She inhaled deeply, composing herself, and then pointed toward the top of her dresser. "Bring me that stack of papers." She stroked a hand down Earl Grey's back. "We have just enough time to choose your invitations before you dress for the Inverleith Ball."

CHAPTER 9

The short ride to Inverleith House just north of Edinburgh passed quickly as I informed Gage first of Alana's health, and then to distract myself from my fear, of all of the things Bree and I had uncovered about the Drummonds. Whether any of this gossip was true and contained a viable lead was up for some debate, but Gage had to admit that things were looking worse and worse for Lord Drummond. We were now aware of two potential motives for him killing his wife, and the fact that his staff was in such tumult said something to his character.

However, before that information even mattered, we needed to prove Lady Drummond had, in fact, been murdered. Gage had not had any luck in questioning the chemists and apothecaries in New Town. Those who would talk to him had denied selling anyone any poisons that would cause such a reaction, while the others were close-mouthed and affronted by the very insinuation. I inherently distrusted these men who were so reticent. They sold poisons every day to help people combat an infestation of rodents or bugs. What was to keep someone from using those substances for a darker purpose?

I still had hopes that Sergeant Maclean had uncovered something from the chemists in Old Town, but I was beginning to suspect I might have to pinpoint a specific poison before we made any real headway in the matter. I made a note to redouble my efforts to schedule a visit with Dr. Renshaw at the Royal College.

I peered through the curtains as the carriage slowed to a stop. We sat in the darkness of the long drive, surrounded by trees and shrubs, as we waited in line to be delivered to the door. I knew that part of the estate had been purchased by the Royal Botanic Garden Edinburgh so that their collection of flowers and plants could be moved farther away from the filth and contamination of the city. I'd never had occasion to visit, but Philip was acquainted with Dr. Robert Graham, the society's Regius Keeper, and he had dined with us on occasion. In addition to his interest in botany, for which he was the chair at the University of Edinburgh, he was also a physician to the Royal Infirmary of Edinburgh, and one of the rare medical men who did not dismiss me as foolish or unnatural because of my scandalous history with my late husband's anatomy research. He was forthright in his opinions, but kindhearted and curious, which made him far more tolerant of someone like me.

Of the hundreds of guests who would be here tonight, he was one of the only people I was looking forward to seeing.

"Is Lord Drummond likely to attend?" I asked, as always making a list of people both to seek out and avoid.

"I don't know," Gage admitted, leaning closer to see out the window. "I would wager he was invited, though courtesy suggests he should excuse himself given that his wife died just two days ago."

I was interested to see if he would bow to protocol, in an effort to court society's favor if not out of respect to his late wife, or if he would defy convention and attend. The baron seemed little interested in the ton's good opinion, but if he wished to remarry, and to do so well, he would need to remain in the good graces of the matrons who ruled over society.

It was needless to say, I was certainly not regarded favorably. Though Alana had kept them from tossing me out completely, I remained on the fringes. Or at least I had until Gage had openly begun to court me and then asked me to marry him. From the spiteful glances the matrons sent my way, I was certain they thought I'd bewitched him in some nefarious manner.

"I'm going to seek out a few more of Lady Drummond's friends this evening to see if they will speak to me. Maybe one of them will know something that could help us."

Gage glanced down at me. "Would you like me to approach Lady Willoughby de Eresby?" he asked, clearly reading my thoughts.

Lady Willoughby de Eresby was perhaps the most coldly correct of society's matrons, and definitely the most surprising of Lady Drummond's friends. Her family had originally held the barony of Drummond, but they had lost their titles and lands after supporting the Jacobite rebellion in 1716. Though some of their previous rights and property had eventually been restored, the title of Drummond had been given to a distant cousin, the current Lord Drummond, for his services to the Crown during the wars with France. That Lady Willoughby de Eresby had willingly befriended Lady Drummond I could only attribute to either Lady Drummond's appealing nature or Lady Willoughby de Eresby's calculating one.

"Would you? I certainly don't relish an encounter with her. And you're far more likely to charm her into giving you information than I am."

"Of course," he replied with a smile. "Though I have a favor to ask of you in return."

"Oh?"

He pulled me closer and for a moment I thought this favor was going to be of the sensual variety.

"You recall I'm investigating a small matter for my father?"

I blinked, making myself focus on his words rather than the proximity of his lips. "Yes."

"I believe I'm close to solving it, and then I can devote my full attention to the matter of Lady Drummond. But first I need your opinion."

I felt something warm spread through me that had nothing to do with Gage's body pressed along my side. "You do?"

He tilted his head to look at me more closely. "You're very perceptive. Even more than I am. And though I feel almost certain I'm right, I would be more comfortable if our findings were in agreement."

"Go on," I urged.

"Do you recall when I asked Philip about Lord Kirkcowan over dinner last week?"

I nodded.

"He recently reported the theft of several items of jewelry from his town house here in Edinburgh. Well, I discovered that Lord Kirkcowan has something of a gambling problem. At first I thought he might have sold the jewelry to pay off his debts and then reported the theft to pacify his wife."

My lips twisted. "I'm sure he wouldn't be the first. Though why wouldn't he just have replaced them with paste?"

"I had the same thought."

"Maybe he was too lazy," I suggested.

Gage's eyes lit with excitement, as they always did when he was close to solving an inquiry. "I now think Lady Kirkcowan took them."

I frowned in confusion. "But they're her own jewels?"

"Yes, but if she's aware of her husband's proclivity for the gaming tables, then she may have hidden them away as future assurance."

"In case he bet and lost everything on a hand of cards," I added, finishing his thought.

"Precisely."

I tipped my head to consider his hypothesis. "I could see myself doing something similar if you ever became enamored by lady luck."

He pulled my close again. "The only lady I'll ever be enamored of is you."

I smirked. "I made that too easy for you, didn't I?"

His eyes twinkled with amusement. "You did. So will you speak with Lady Kirkcowan tonight? Be direct if you must. I just want you to get a sense of whether she's hiding something."

"If she did take the jewels, what do you plan to do? Are you going to tell her husband?" I hedged.

"As far as I'm concerned, they would still be in the hands of their owner, and my involvement would no longer be necessary. There's no need to expose Lady Kirkcowan's precautions."

I arched my eyebrows in skepticism. "Would your father accept that answer?"

A frown formed between his brows. "No. But I've fobbed him off before. I can do so again."

I smiled at his chivalrous spirit. Relations between Gage and his father were strained at best, and yet he was still willing to risk the consequences of defying him to do what was right by Lady Kirkcowan. His unobtrusive gallantry was definitely one of the reasons I had fallen in love with him. Rather than wait for him to do so, I leaned forward and kissed him.

"Not that I'm complaining . . ." he murmured in a deeper voice as I pulled back ". . . but what prompted that? I want to be sure to repeat it."

I felt my cheeks turn pink. It was true, I rarely initiated our kisses, but not out of lack of desire. I was simply not used to the fact yet that Gage was mine to kiss whenever I wanted.

I began to tell him so when the door suddenly opened. In our distraction, we'd failed to realize our carriage had reached the front of the queue. I pulled my wrap tighter around me and allowed the footman to help me from the coach. Gage descended behind me and took my arm to guide me through the door.

In terms of architecture, Inverleith House would never win any prizes. Its grandeur and appeal lay in the gardens surrounding it, not in the manor home itself. Its exterior was the epitome of Georgian simplicity and order, built in a solid block of sturdy stone and symmetrically placed single windows. The only nod to anything unconventional was a rounded section in the middle of the façade connected to the small portico entrance.

Gage and I passed through this door, passing our outer garments to a pair of footmen waiting to take them. I twitched the overskirt of my rose-colored gown into place and tried to tug discreetly at the deep V of the bodice, which was lower than I was accustomed to. I knew I was not in danger of spilling out, but that did not make me feel less exposed.

I forced a tight smile to my face as Gage turned to me and paused. His eyes immediately swept up and down my figure.

I glanced down at myself. "Is something out of place?" I whispered, smoothing my hand over the decorative detail at the center of my cleavage and down over the white lace belt.

Gage reached out to still my hands. "No. You look lovely. I'm just not used to seeing you in pink."

I inhaled shakily. "Alana convinced me to choose it." I bit my lip, glancing to the side at the throng of people passing us. Nonsensically, I felt the backs of my eyes begin to sting. "I knew I should have insisted on the cornflower blue."

"No, you shouldn't have."

I looked up, surprised by the conviction in his voice. His pale winter blue eyes looked decidedly warmer than their normal crystalline quality. That sight steadied me.

"You're sure?"

His gaze traveled over me one more time, leaving a heated trail everywhere it touched. "On second thought, I don't want you questioning anyone tonight. You're going to remain firmly affixed to my side."

I smiled.

"I'm serious," he told me, pulling me closer. "I already want to plant a facer on every man who walks by and looks at you in that dress."

I pressed a hand to his chest. "Gage, no one is looking at me."

His eyebrows arched. "You truly don't know," he replied in incredulity.

I frowned in confusion and his lips curled into a tiny smile.

"Come," he murmured, linking my arm through his and tucking me in close to his side.

After being greeted by our hosts, the Rocheids, we threaded our way through the crowd, pausing periodically to exchange pleasantries with one person or another. At first I thought nothing of it when the wife of one of Gage's acquaintances stared down her nose at me. I'd grown accustomed to being subjected to unfriendly looks since the scandal broke over my involvement with my late husband's anatomical studies. It was true, these snubbings had occurred less and less often in recent months, but they had never really stopped. But as I encountered three more hostile glares, and then a gaggle of women who all turned to whisper to one another as I passed, I began to wonder at the return of their coldness.

I glanced at Gage out of the corner of my eye to see if he had noticed, but his expression revealed nothing but bored politeness. Perhaps I was imagining things, allowing my own insecurities to influence what I saw. It would not be the first time I'd done so. So taking my cue from Gage, I squared my shoulders and tried my best to be as charming and unaffected by the swirl of people surrounding us as he was. If my smile was a shade too tight or my voice modulated a bit too high, I assured myself that few would notice. Most of society was perpetually self-absorbed, and terribly unobservant of anything but clothing and potential disgrace. If the bright pink of my gown distracted them from the rest of my appearance, then perhaps it had not been such a poor choice after all.

When Gage paused to speak to a man who had hailed him, I

spotted Mrs. Fitzhugh, a friend of Lady Drummond's, just a few steps away. I excused myself and began to cross to her, but at that moment she turned away, though I could have sworn she'd seen me coming. I stumbled to a halt, unsure whether I should still approach her and force a conversation if necessary or return to Gage.

Fortunately, Gage's friend Mr. Knighton, being true to his surname, came to my rescue.

"Lady Darby, how nice to see you," he murmured, offering me a genuine smile. "You look enchanting this evening." He glanced around him. "How on earth could Gage let you out of his sight?"

I couldn't help but smile at his outrageous flattery. "Don't be alarmed. He's nearby."

He gestured to the man at his side. "Are you acquainted with Dr. Graham?"

"I am," I replied in delight. "You must be quite pleased with the turnout this evening. It's an absolute crush."

As if to illustrate my point, Mr. Knighton moved closer to allow a couple to pass behind him deeper into the room.

"I am," Dr. Graham proclaimed. "So kind of the Rocheids to lend their backing to our cause. The remainder of our plants are scheduled to be moved here in April and May, depending on the weather."

"That must be a relief."

"Oh, indeed, indeed." He reached up to straighten the front of his hair, a nervous habit of his I'd noticed before.

"I've yet to visit the collection that is here, but I hope to soon."

"Oh, yes, please do. Though you might wait until later this year. In addition to our exotic species, we're cultivating a section exclusively of Scottish flora." He rocked back on his heels in pride. "Filled with both rare specimens, like the Scottish primrose, the twinflower, and the Shetland mouse-ear, as well as common—the spear thistle, of course, devil's cap, and even the harebell."

"I will," I promised him. Then seeing Gage weaving through the crowd, looking left and right, I excused myself. He was so tall, it was much easier to spot him and his golden curls than it would be for him to find me.

"There you are." His eyes twinkled. "I'd begun to think some disreputable man had run off with you."

"Only Mr. Knighton and Dr. Graham."

His eyebrows lifted. "Really? Well, then I might have to have a talk with my old friend then."

I darted a glance over my shoulder. "I believe they're still near the middle of the room, if you wished . . ."

My voice trailed away as I caught the way he was looking at me, an amused smile curling his lips. "What?" I asked in confusion.

"I take it Mr. Knighton didn't accost you?"

"Of course, not! Why?"

He stared at me expectantly.

"Oh," I murmured, finally apprehending his meaning. "You were jesting. Because of my gown."

Seeing my abashment, he smiled broadly and pulled me close. "You are remarkably observant, but there are times when you can be delightfully obtuse." He leaned down so that his nose almost brushed mine. "It's quite reassuring to those of us with duller wits."

I couldn't not smile at a compliment like that, especially when we both knew very well that Gage's faculties were quite sharp. "Balderdash," I teased back. "If your wits are dull, then the rest of this assembly must be positively blunt."

"Mr. Gage," a strident voice called out.

We both turned as one to see Lady Willoughby de Eresby swishing her way toward us wearing an enormous feather headdress. I expected the plumage to flop forward over her face at any moment, but remarkably it stayed in place. I could only guess that it had been starched, much like the gentlemen's shirt points and cravats, to remain smooth and upright.

"I've been meaning to speak with you," she harrumphed.

"I'm flattered, my lady," Gage replied, pouring on his usual charm. "How may we . . ."

"Alone," she demanded, turning her back so as to all but cut me dead.

My mouth dropped open in shock. Though common during the month I remained in London after Sir Anthony's death, it had been six months or more since anyone had snubbed me with such ferocity. I knew now that I had not been imagining the pointed whispers and narrowed eyes directed at me; however, I had no idea what had heralded their return. Had the rumors regarding my scandalous past resurfaced, or was there some new infraction for which I was being shunned?

I glanced at Gage, anxious that he would be embarrassed by her ladyship's behavior, but instead I saw outrage stamped across his features. Knowing we still needed information from Lady Willoughby de Eresby, and worried his defense of me might create an even bigger scene, I pressed a restraining hand to his arm. He did not look at me, but I could see him visibly inhale, calming himself.

"Allow me a moment to fetch *my fiancée* a bit of refreshment, and I shall be content to speak with you," he replied, not completely banishing the edge to his voice, though I was sure it was done purposely. I felt a flush of pleasure at his emphasis of our relationship, and grateful to him for still finding a way to defend me even under difficult circumstances.

"I would be happy to escort her," Mr. Knighton chimed in, having inched closer to us at some point during the confrontation. "It would be my privilege."

Gage shared a significant look with his friend, and then nodded. "I shall join you both shortly."

He transferred my arm to Mr. Knighton, taking an extra moment to squeeze my fingers before he let him lead me away. His eyes were still flat with repressed anger, but I could feel the reassurance he was trying to convey to me in his touch.

I did not look back, though I wanted to. I suspected the crowd had filled in behind us anyway, eager to eavesdrop on what Gage and Lady Willoughby de Eresby had to say.

Mr. Knighton led me out of the drawing room and across the hall to the quieter and cooler dining room, where a spread of food had been laid out. Conscious of those who might have followed us in order to overhear our conversation, he waited until our backs were to the room.

"I gather you need something from her ladyship," Mr. Knighton said as he served us each a glass of punch. When I didn't immediately respond, having been surprised by this speculation, he looked over at me. "Otherwise no amount of interference on your part would have kept him from rebuking her for her treatment of you." He took a sip of his punch and narrowed his eyes at those in the room around us. "Most people think of Gage as an amiable, charming gallant, and that's the way he prefers it, but he can be feral, especially when he's riled. I went to Cambridge with him. I watched him defend his mother when fellow students made disparaging remarks about her."

"They ridiculed his mother?"

"Mostly her illness." He tipped his dark head. "And Gage for living with her instead of in a room at the university."

Gage had told me about his mother's sickness, and how his grandfather had obtained special permission for him to live in a cottage with her near Cambridge. It had been the only way he would consent to attend, having refused to leave her alone in their home near Plymouth. His father had been away at sea almost fifty-one weeks out of the year, manning the blockade versus Napoleon and France and transporting supplies to the troops on the continent.

"He has always been protective of the women he cares for," Mr. Knighton mused. "Sometimes to his own detriment."

I glanced at him, uncertain exactly what he meant. I didn't think he was referring to me. Then a thought formed in my mind. "You mean in Greece?"

"Yes."

My heart began beating faster at this confirmation that there had been a woman involved in whatever had happened to Gage in Greece. He had yet to explain the events that had transpired there to me. All I knew was that it had something to do with the Greeks' fight for independence from the Turks. Gage had remained closemouthed about the rest, promising to tell me when the moment was right.

But apparently Mr. Knighton knew something about the incident. I considered pressing him for more information, but then decided it was not his to share. When Gage was ready to tell me, he would. However, that didn't mean I wouldn't use this new bit of knowledge to further attempt to persuade him. Gage did not share things easily— something I understood, being the same way myself—so sometimes he had to be coaxed into revealing more.

"Does he still wear his pistol tucked into the back of his trousers?"

I glanced at Mr. Knighton in surprise. "Most of the time, yes."

He nodded.

"But I thought that was because of the nature of his business?"

He turned to meet my gaze with his emerald green one. "I'm sure it is." I could see him debate whether to say more. "But that's not why he began doing so."

My eyes widened.

"He hasn't told you, has he?"

I shook my head. "Not all." Not most.

Mr. Knighton's countenance turned haggard and he looked away. "Well, I don't know everything either. I just happened to be with him on a night not long after his return from the continent when he got too deep in his cups."

An image of Gage in such a state—too lost to the world to care about guarding his secrets—formed in my mind, and my chest tightened. I had never seen him so despairing and I hoped I never would, no matter how anxious I was to uncover all of his mysteries.

We stood surveying the room a moment longer, and then Mr. Knighton linked my arm though his again and we moved off in the direction of the parlor, which had been set up as a gaming room. I was so wrapped up in my own thoughts that I almost overlooked the sight of Lady Kirkcowan hurrying out of it, a harried expression stamped across her porcelain features.

"Would you excuse me a moment?" I told Mr. Knighton, remembering my promise to Gage. I followed her progress toward the back of the house with my eyes.

"Of course."

I wove through the guests lining the hall, catching up with her just as she paused to consider whether to go left or right. "Lady Kirkcowan."

She turned to face me, struggling to master her feelings. "Lady Darby, I'm afraid you've caught me at . . ."

"I need just a moment of your time," I interrupted before she could dismiss me entirely. "Please."

She glanced about her and then sighed and nodded, lifting the skirts of her lavender gown.

We moved a few steps to the side of the hall, into the shadow cast between two wall sconces.

"You want to ask me about Lady Drummond," she guessed.

"I've been told you were friends," I replied obliquely. When she didn't respond, I pried further. "Had the acquaintance been long?"

"Since we both made our curtseys at court. I tripped over the hem of my dress, but rather than titter behind her fan at me like the other debutantes were doing, she came over to see if I was well."

That sounded like Lady Drummond.

"Did you remain close?"

She regarded me thoughtfully with her golden eyes. "We called on each other at least once a month. But if you mean, did we share confidences, I'm afraid the answer is no."

"When did you see her last?" I murmured in a lower voice, knowing the answer was likely to cause her some pain.

She dropped her gaze and twitched at her skirts. "She called on me last Tuesday."

"And did she seem . . . well?" I asked, opting for the vague term so that Lady Kirkcowan could interpret it as she wished.

"Yes. Perhaps a little more tired than usual, but nothing to be alarmed about."

I nodded.

Her eyes searched mine. "Is it true then?" she whispered.

I leaned closer. "Is what true?"

She looked at the group of ladies standing closest to us, as if to be sure they weren't listening. "That you and Mr. Gage are investigating her death?"

I stiffened in shock. "Where did you hear that?"

"I . . . I don't recall exactly. I think I overheard someone in the ladies' retiring room talking about it."

I pressed a hand to my suddenly swirling stomach and glanced about me. How had news of our inquiry become so public? It was true, we had questioned several people, both members of the ton and apothecaries, and any number of them could have shared our actions, but I was still surprised at the speed at which it had spread. Or perhaps people were only making assumptions based on the fact that I had been there the day Lady Drummond died.

Whatever the reason, Gage was not going to be happy our inquiry was no longer so private.

"It's true then?" Lady Kirkcowan implored. Her brow furrowed. "Because if it isn't, it should be."

"Why do you say that?"

She glanced about her once more. "Because it seems awfully convenient for Lord Drummond that his wife is suddenly deceased since her dowry is spent and he's about to be floating up the River Tick. Unless he can find a wealthy new bride, that is."

A situation that sounded like it struck remarkably close to home for Lady Kirkcowan given her husband's gambling problems. I couldn't stop my eyes from dropping to the diamond and sapphire necklace draped around her neck.

She reached up to finger it. "It's paste."

Her gaze turned challenging, almost as if she dared me to say something about it. At first I wondered if it might be her pride I was in danger of wounding, but the longer I continued to meet her stare, the more apparent the fear behind her defiance became. Gage had been right. She was hiding something, and it was most likely the jewels her husband believed were stolen.

I opened my mouth to tell her something reassuring when a deep voice spoke behind me.

"Lady Darby."

Lady Kirkcowan stiffened and I turned to see who had so unsettled her.

At first I was puzzled by the hard glare of the man standing before me, and why it was directed at me, but as I studied him, his features slowly became more familiar. I knew that cleft in the chin, that strong jawline. I knew that determined frown, and that twist of the curls on the forehead, even if this man's hair was now gray instead of golden.

"Lord Gage."

CHAPTER 10

I tried my best not to show how shocked I was, but I was certain Lord Gage could tell anyway. Had Gage known his father was coming to Edinburgh? That he was here this evening? I wanted to look around for him, but something told me it would not be wise to break eye contact with the man before me, that to do so would mean I had already failed some kind of test.

I locked gazes with him, reminding myself I'd faced far worse things than the iron stare of my future father-in-law. As a retired naval captain, he was accustomed to others bowing to his will. That was why he and Gage had clashed so fiercely these past few months, even if only from a distance through letters. Gage was tired of following his father's dictates, and Lord Gage was not willing to allow him the freedom to make his own decisions. I'd gathered that the struggle between them had steadily been escalating, and had finally come to a head over Gage's refusal to wed the debutante his father had chosen for him. Instead he'd announced his engagement to me. Gage had not shared his father's reaction to the news, if in fact he even knew it, but knowing the little bit I did about Lord Gage, I could guess what it had been.

And apparently, the matter had been serious enough for him to travel all the way to Edinburgh to address in person.

"I see my reputation precedes me," he pronounced in precise, clipped tones. It was a style of speech someone perfected rather than developed naturally. His eyes swept up and down my form, and it was obvious he found me lacking. "As does yours."

His disapproval stung even though I had been expecting it. Society had been judging me and finding me deficient even before the scandal following Sir Anthony's death. The difference was that I cared little for much of the ton's opinion, but I was anxious for Lord Gage to like me, at least for his son's sake.

"Actually, I recognized you because your son looks so much like you. Just younger." I tilted my head. "Except your eyes. He must have inherited those from his mother."

"Indeed," he bit out, and I wondered if it was possible to lace a word with more disdain. His eyes pivoted to skewer the woman I had just been speaking to. "Lady Kirkcowan."

She curtsied stiffly. "Lord Gage." Rising, she pressed a hand to my shoulder. "Please, excuse me. There's a matter I must see to," she murmured.

"Of course," I replied, but she was already moving off before I could finish the words. Lord Gage watched her make her hasty retreat with narrowed eyes.

"I was asking her about her lovely gown," I said, trying to distract him. "I think my sister would be eager to have something similar once she's through her confinement. We expect the baby any day now."

"Do not paint me the fool, Lady Darby." His eyes blazed angrily. "I know exactly why you were speaking to her. And I expect my son asked you to do it."

"Yes," I hissed with a forced smile. "But I didn't think you wanted it known publicly." I glanced out of the corner of my eye at the people surrounding us, inching ever closer to hear our conversation.

Lord Gage turned to glare at a woman who was actually leaning our way. She flinched and moved away. He inhaled and his shoulders dropped as he seemed to settle himself.

His gaze turned calculating. "Or were you questioning her about another matter entirely? A recently deceased friend, perhaps?"

I stiffened in surprise.

His lips quirked haughtily.

I fumbled for what to say next. What did Lord Gage know of the matter? Or was he only speculating based on the rumors circulating the ball? I was suddenly suspicious of the connection between Lord Gage's arrival and society's renewed animosity toward me. Gage had said his father could be ruthless. Would he go so far as to rekindle the scandalous rumors surrounding me in hopes that it would upset and embarrass his son enough to persuade him to break our engagement?

"Father?"

I was saved from making a reply by Gage's appearance. He halted next to us and stared at his father with a mixture of alarm and frustration. "Sir, when did you arrive in Edinburgh?"

Lord Gage stared up and down at his son's faultless appearance. "This afternoon. I called at your rooms, but I was informed you were here." The tone of his voice made it clear that he had been displeased by this.

Gage's jaw tightened, but he did not make the sarcastic remark I knew he longed to. Instead he turned to me and reached for my hand. "I see you've met my fiancée." He offered me a reassuring smile. "Isn't she lovely?"

"Mmm, yes," his father replied in a voice that conveyed the exact opposite. He arched his eyebrows significantly. "She was speaking to Lady Kirkcowan."

Gage's posture was as straight as a poker. "I see. Well, they are acquainted."

"Is it a long-standing friendship or newly formed?"

"I'm not certain. Does it matter?"

I felt my eyes widen as the contentious conversation bounced back and forth between father and son. It was like watching a fencing match, overtly polite and correct, but barbed underneath.

Lord Gage shifted closer to his son. "It does if they were discussing a matter which I expressly forbid you to involve her in."

Gage's fingers tightened around mine as if in unconscious reaction. "Perhaps this is a conversation we should have elsewhere."

Lord Gage studied his son and then nodded shortly.

"I will call on you tomorrow." Gage turned to me, pulling my arm through his. "If you don't mind, my dear, I think I should like to retire."

"Of course."

"There's no need for that," Lord Gage interrupted. "I shall accompany you now."

Gage stared at him. "That's not necessary."

"Oh, but it is."

The pent-up hostility between the two men fairly made the air quiver. I felt the hair along my arms stand on end. I glanced about me, knowing I couldn't be the only who had noticed.

"Perhaps we could go *now*," I whispered, wanting to escape the avid gleam in the eyes surrounding us.

Gage did not look at me, but he did wrap a protective hand around mine where it lay on his other arm. As we pushed through the crowd, who parted in the face of Gage's angry stride, I did my best to keep my head held high. I could hear the sharp click of Lord Gage's tread following us, and it was like a hammer to my already fragile composure.

Our outer garments were quickly fetched, and then we were climbing into Gage's carriage. The night air was cold and I was grateful for the press of Gage's warm body along my side as he settled into his seat. I stared out the window as Lord Gage sat across from us and the door was latched. The coach rocked as the footman climbed onto the back and then we were rolling forward.

I blinked as Lord Gage reached over to twitch the window curtain shut.

"Sebastian, what is the meaning of this?" he demanded. "I arranged a politically advantageous marriage for you. One I went to great lengths to cultivate, mind you. And not with just some snub-nosed chit, but with the most charming and beautiful debutante in all of England. But instead of the grateful and dutiful arrival of my son in London, I receive a letter telling me you *refuse* to wed Lady Felicity. And to complete the outrage, in her place you've chosen to wed this . . . this butcher's wife." He gestured toward me with disgust.

It was an epithet I hadn't heard in some months, referring to the years I had spent sketching the dissections made by my late husband, an anatomist and surgeon, occupations commonly derided as butchers and sawbones. So to hear the words hurled at me from my fiancé's father was like a bucket of ice water being flung in my face. I flinched at the impact.

"Do not call her that," Gage snarled.

"What? The truth?"

"She is my future wife. Your future daughter-in-law . . ."

"We'll see about that."

Gage appeared momentarily flummoxed by his father's certainty, and then his complexion flushed bright red. I didn't think I'd ever seen him so furious. "There is no 'we.' I *am* marrying Kiera. I don't care about any ridiculous rumors about her past. Regardless, if *someone* decides to dredge them up again . . ."

So he'd had the same suspicions about his father.

"I already know the truth. The rest is just nonsense." He turned to take my hand. "Kiera is loyal, beautiful, intelligent, and talented. And perhaps the most perceptive person I've ever met. She's become a gifted investigator in her own right."

I felt a warm glow inside me hearing his praise, and I couldn't help but smile even under the tense circumstances.

"Ah, so that's why you're marrying her. You can't handle the inquiries on your own," Lord Gage snarled.

I gasped at the nasty comment.

"Is that why you had her speak with Lady Kirkcowan against my wishes?"

Gage spoke slowly, biting out each word. "I had her speak to Lady Kirkcowan because I wanted a second opinion. As I said, she is very perceptive, and I wanted to be certain my suspicions were correct."

"She's guilty. I could *perceive* that in two seconds," he scoffed.

"Guilty of what?" Gage argued, ignoring the barb. "You can't steal your own jewels."

"They aren't her jewels. They all belong to her husband."

"Who will only gamble them away," I couldn't resist interjecting.

"A point that could be argued," Gage insisted. "For he gave them to her as gifts. When a gentleman gifts his mistress with jewelry, it's hers to keep once she's been given her *congé*."

"Yes, but unlike his wife, a gentleman does not own his mistress."

I stared at Lord Gage in astonishment. While everything he was saying was strictly true, to state it in such an arrogant, callous manner infuriated me. "Do you have no heart?" I demanded. "What is Lady Kirkcowan to do when her husband finally impoverishes her?"

"That is not our concern." His eyes narrowed. "Just as the Drummonds are not yours."

I glanced at Gage in surprise, wondering how he already knew.

"Oh, yes," Lord Gage drawled. "I've already heard about your ridiculous accusations."

"We've accused no one of anything," Gage argued far more calmly then I could manage. "But what do you know of it?"

Lord Gage sat back, crossing one ankle over his other knee. "When I was leaving your lodging house, I happened upon Lord Drummond, who, you may not know, is an old friend of mine. We served together for five years as lieutenants on the same ship, and were both made captains within six months of each other." His gaze swung to mine. "So you can imagine how disturbed I was to discover my son's . . . fiancée . . ." the word sounded distasteful on his lips ". . . had tried to convince him there was some sort of foul play involved in his wife's death."

"The circumstances surrounding Lady Drummond's death *are* suspicious," Gage defended me.

His lips curled into a sneer. "Why? Because the *perceptive* Lady Darby says they're so? You are to stop this preposterous inquiry at once," he ordered me. "Lord Drummond is a worthy, honorable man; a decorated war hero. You will not sully his reputation or distress him further by making these baseless allegations."

"They aren't baseless," I argued. Gage pressed a restraining hand to my wrist, but I did not heed. "You friend is a brute. Lady Drummond was terrified of him."

"Of course she was. She was his wife."

My mouth dropped open in shock, and I felt Gage jolt beside me.

His father scowled at him. "Do not look at me like that. I rarely lifted a hand to your mother. I didn't need to." His eyes swiveled to me. "Lady Darby, on the other hand . . ."

Gage actually surged forward in his seat. "Do not even finish that sentence."

For a moment I thought the two men were going to come to blows, but Lord Gage held his tongue, albeit begrudgingly from the way he glowered at his son. Gage slowly sat back just as the coach rolled to a stop in front of the Cromarty town house on Charlotte Square.

I felt nothing but relief to escape the confines of the carriage and the hostility between father and son. Perhaps I should have been concerned about the vitriol Lord Gage was certain to continue to pour in his son's ears, but as irate as Gage was, I knew there was little chance of him heeding his father's words. And while I was distressed by the extreme dislike Lord Gage had taken of me without even giving me a chance to prove the rumors wrong, I was wise enough to understand when retreat was better than confrontation—for my own wounded self-esteem and for his heated temper.

I did not wish him a good evening. From the look on his face, I knew he didn't want me to, so I happily obliged. Gage helped me out of the carriage and escorted me up the steps to the door.

"Kiera, I'm so sorry," he leaned close to tell me.

"It's not your fault."

"No, but I should have at least prepared you. My father is a cold and difficult man when he is crossed."

Figgins opened the door to admit us, but before he could take my shawl, Gage requested a moment of privacy. He nodded and disappeared toward the back of the town house.

"Did you know he was coming to Edinburgh?" I finally asked, as I'd wanted to since the moment Lord Gage appeared before me.

He sighed. "Not definitively. But I had my suspicions when I did not receive a reply from him after I wrote to announce our engagement," he admitted. "I knew he would never let the matter rest. It's simply not his way."

So that was where Gage had gotten his hardened determination. In that, at least, he emulated his father.

"And Lady Willoughy de Eresby mentioned something about seeing him," he added with a grimace.

"What did she wish to speak with you about?"

I could tell from his expression that he did not want to reply.

"She expressed much the same opinions of our engagement as my father."

His words pinched me in my chest even though I knew it was silly of me to care what the fussy society matron thought. "Not surprising."

"Yes, but of no consequence. And I told her so." He leaned forward to press a warm kiss to my forehead just below my hairline. "Do not fret. Father will not prevail in this."

I nodded.

He caressed my shoulders. "I'll call on you tomorrow." Then after dropping a quick kiss on my lips, he was gone.

I stared at the door as it closed behind him, feeling oddly cold and bereft. It was a sensation I had grown accustomed to in the years following my marriage and subsequent widowhood. I realized then that it had been weeks since I'd felt it. Not since accepting Gage's proposal almost two months ago. It was unsettling to feel it again.

"My lady?"

I turned to see Figgins had reemerged.

"Is everything well?"

I offered him a tight smile. "As well as it can be for the moment."

He nodded solemnly, though he couldn't have known what I was talking about.

I turned to allow him to help me remove my shawl. "Is Lord Cromarty in?" I asked, deciding now was as good a time as ever to speak with my brother-in-law. Whatever his response, I doubted it could sour my mood further.

"In his study, my lady."

I thanked him and pattered down the hall to the dark-paneled room at the back of the house.

"Come in," he called out at the sound of my knock. He was seated at his desk, his head bent over a sheaf of papers while he massaged his right temple. From the lines radiating across his forehead and the dark circles under his eyes, I could tell he had not slept well the night before and was likely suffering from a headache.

I waited for him to look up.

"Kiera," he sighed, finally taking notice. "My apologies." He gestured to the stack of papers in his hand. "They bungled the wording on this again." His brogue had deepened, as it normally did when he was tired. "Did ye need something . . . ah!" He set down the papers to dig through the detritus on his desk. "I saw your note." He located the letter of introduction I'd requested and held it out to me.

"Thank you." I moved forward to take it.

Philip nodded absently, already becoming absorbed in his documents again.

I watched him a moment longer, trying to decide whether to broach the topic of Alana's health and his increased absence. When he never again looked up and resumed rubbing his temple, I decided the matter could wait.

I slowly climbed the stairs toward my room, feeling the weight of my worries. My body craved the cushion of my soft mattress, but my head was spinning with the night's revelations. Seeing the light under Alana's door, I crossed the hall to rap on it softly, and then opened it to peer inside. My sister looked up from the book propped against her rounded belly.

"Kiera." Her face brightened. "Come in. Save me from this dreadful novel and tell me about the ball."

I smiled at her as I crossed the room to sit in the chair next to her bed. "If the book is so dreadful, why don't you send Jenny to fetch you another?"

"Oh, it's not the book," she sighed, closing it and setting it aside. "It's me. I simply can't concentrate."

"That's understandable."

"Yes, but not helpful." She tipped her head back and groaned. "I've only been confined to this bed for a day and a half and I'm already restless. And yet I'm terrified of moving about, lest the bleeding start again." Her face was drawn with fear and unhappiness.

My chest tightened at the reminder of how precarious her situation was.

Her eyes drifted to the opposite side of the bed, where her husband normally lay, and I felt a stirring of anger that Philip could not read his parliamentary business in bed, keeping her company. But then would they both be worrying that his movements would harm the babe?

She grimaced suddenly and lifted her hands to gently rub her belly.

I sat forward in alarm. "Are you in pain?"

"No. It's my skin. It's so dry, and then the baby kicks and stretches."

"Well, I think I may be able to help with that," I replied, suddenly remembering.

She glanced at me in confusion as I rose to exit the room.

"One moment."

The package from Hinkley's was still perched on top of my dresser. I carried it to Alana's room, setting it on the bed next to her.

"What's this?" She leaned over to peer inside.

"Lady Drummond's last act of kindness."

Alana glanced up at me in surprise.

"I know it sounds morose, but it's quite possibly true." I perched next to her and began pulling out the jars. "During our last portrait session Lady Drummond told me how much these creams helped ease her discomfort during her confinements, and she thought they might help you as well."

She examined one of the jars. "That was generous of her."

"The package arrived two days ago, but in all of the excitement, I forgot about it."

I could tell from Alana's expression that she did not know what to make of the gift.

"Alana, I'm sorry," I gasped, realizing how insensitive it was to offer her a gift from a dead woman when she was facing that possibility herself. "I should have thought. If it distresses you, I'll take it away."

"No, no," she argued. "I just . . . I barely knew Lady Drummond, and for her to make such a considerate gesture . . ." Her words trailed away into tears.

I reached for the handkerchief on her bedside table and handed it to her, having grown accustomed to her emotional displays. My sister was more weepy than normal when she was expecting a child. I suspected many women were like that.

She sniffed. "I wish I could thank her, that's all." She placed the jars carefully back in the box and I transferred them to the table. "How was your evening?" she asked as she dabbed at her eyes.

I moved over to the chair, firmly affixing a smile to my face as I launched into a description of Inverleith House and the guests. With all of Alana's current troubles, I simply couldn't burden her with more. If she knew how society was whispering about me again, how Lord Gage had treated me so abominably, it would only upset her. And given how protective my older sister was of me, that could be dangerous for her and the baby. So I kept the night's indignities to myself, and prayed that in this, at least, I was a better actress than Gage claimed.

When Alana's eyes had drifted closed, I tiptoed out of the room. I rang for Bree, who helped me out of my evening gown. But rather than slip into my nightdress, I donned an old woolen gown that buttoned up the front. My maid said nothing, having grown accustomed to my midnight forays to my art studio. When I could not sleep—which occurred more frequently than I wished—I painted. It quieted my mind and allowed me to momentarily forget what was bothering me. Though that night, as I worked on Lady Drummond's portrait, I was reminded it was far more difficult to forget when the person you were painting was the very one whose death so disturbed you.

CHAPTER 11

The next day dawned wet and dreary. The rain had begun sometime in the middle of the night, pattering on the roof as I painted in my studio, and it showed no signs of letting up. I sat alone in the dining room and picked at the remainders of my breakfast while I gazed out the window at the leaden skies. The scrape of my fork was the only accompaniment to the steady drum of rain and the clock ticking away on the mantel. It seemed as if I could be the only person in the world.

The garden at the center of the square was deserted—the weather keeping all of the governesses and their charges inside—and it had been over a quarter of an hour since I'd last seen a carriage. I'd already dismissed the footman, feeling it was silly for him to stand at the sideboard with only me to serve. I suppose I could have attempted to converse with him, but I always felt awkward trying to speak with someone standing across the room at attention while I tried to eat. In any case, I wasn't feeling very chatty. My mood was much more suited to silent contemplation.

I didn't know where Philip was, and I didn't ask. Alana was confined to her room, and the children were in the nursery three floors above me. So the home I always thought of as lively and filled with sound was suddenly neither of those things.

I stared down at my half-eaten sausage and toast, wishing I could shake this melancholy that seemed to have descended over the entire house. It was as if we were all holding our breaths, waiting for something terrible to happen, but hoping and praying it never did. Coupled with my grief over Lady Drummond's death, the lack of real progress in our investigation, and Lord Gage's treatment of me the night before, it was amazing I'd bothered to roll out of bed this morning.

I should visit the nursery. The children were undoubtedly in need of some reassurance. They couldn't help but notice how somber the house had become since their mother had been ordered to stay in bed. And I could use a bit of their indomitable energy and cheer. Philipa and Greer at least were still young enough to trust that when you said everything would be all right, it would be. However, Malcolm was at the age when he was just starting to realize that everything adults told him might not be true. He was eight. The same age I was when I lost my mother.

The thought permanently soured my stomach, and I pushed away my plate.

I glanced up as Figgins entered the room, holding out a silver tray. "My lady, this just came for you."

"Thank you." I took up the letter, expecting it to be from Gage, but the handwriting was far more feminine than his almost illegible scrawl. I opened my mouth to ask Figgins who had delivered it, but he had already quietly exited the room. Picking up my knife, I split open the seal and unfolded the missive. My eyes went immediately to the bottom, where I saw with a start that it was from Lady Stratford.

My heart stuttered as memories from my first investigation flooded back to me. Seven months ago a viscountess had been murdered during a house party Alana had hosted at their home in the Highlands, Gairloch Castle. Lady Stratford had been framed for the murder, but because of my persistence, we had uncovered that it was her husband who was the real culprit. The Earl of Stratford had then kidnapped his wife, her maid, and me, and nearly succeeded in sending us to our watery graves.

Though Lady Stratford had initially despised me, believing the rumors about me, she had eventually apologized and even extended a tentative offer of friendship. Knowing what she'd been through, I had not held her previous treatment of me against her, and had even felt a certain kinship with her. But I'd never expected to actually hear from her again, let alone be invited to join her for tea, I discovered as I perused the letter.

She would still be in mourning for her malicious husband, who had suffered the fate he'd intended for us after being shot during our rescue, so her activities would still be restricted. Personally, after what her husband had tried to do, I thought she should have refused to grant him the courtesy of observing full mourning. I had not remained in my widow's weeds for as long as dictated after Sir Anthony's death, and for all his sins, he had not framed me for murder and then tried to kill me. But then, I had been hiding away at my sister's isolated castle, where no one but family and their servants saw me. Upon leaving Gairloch Castle, Lady Stratford had gone to stay with her great-aunt near Glasgow, and now she was apparently in Edinburgh, where there was a great deal more of society to encounter.

I considered ignoring the missive, but then I decided it would be silly not to accept. I had no immediate plans for the day, except stewing in my own gloom. If the visit turned out to be awkward, I could always decide not to return. Besides, I didn't have many friends outside of my family. It would be nice to have someone to talk to. Just because I was not gregarious by nature did not mean I didn't long for companionship. My marriage to Sir Anthony and the subsequent scandal had made it difficult to make and keep friends, but that was no reason to have given up on the prospect entirely.

So several hours later, after spending some time in the nursery with the children and then changing my clothes after one-year-old Greer smeared snot across the shoulder of my dress, I found myself being ushered into a town house off St. Andrew Square on the opposite end of New Town. Lady Stratford was still staying with her great-aunt, Lady Bearsden. They had simply relocated to Edinburgh for the spring.

Lady Stratford appeared as lovely as ever, perhaps even more so, as she shook out her black bombazine skirts and rose to greet me. Widowhood, or more accurately, escape from her late husband's philandering and insults, seemed to agree with her.

"Lady Darby, I'm so glad you could come." Her smile was warm, and her cheeks flushed a pale shade of pink.

"Thank you for inviting me," I replied, sitting on the pearlescent blue settee she indicated. "I hadn't realized you were in town."

"We only just arrived earlier this week, and, of course, I cannot go many places." She gestured to her mourning gown. "Have you been introduced to my great-aunt, Lady Bearsden?"

I turned toward the older woman perched on a chair near the crackling fire. Her hair was an almost shocking shade of white, as pure as snow. "I have not. How do you do?"

"Very well, thank you." Her voice was bright and musical. "I'm so pleased to finally meet you. I've wanted to thank you for what you did for my darling Charlotte." She gazed at her great-niece affectionately. "When I think of what might have happened had you not been there . . ." She shuddered.

I squirmed in my seat, unaccustomed to such gratitude. "It was the least I could do."

"No! To put yourself in danger like that. Why, I'm not sure my dear Lumpy would have been willing to do what you did, and he loved me." Her eyes widened in emphasis. She had a way of speaking that stressed every second or third word, making it difficult to tell if she was being serious or sarcastic. I suspected it was the former, given that Lady Stratford was listening to her so calmly.

"Her husband," she clarified, though I'd suspected just that. I couldn't help but imagine what a man nicknamed Lumpy had looked like.

"Well, I'm glad I did," I said, not knowing what else to say. At the time, I'd only done what I thought was right. And now, looking back, I could honestly say I wouldn't have chosen differently, even knowing the danger I would face.

"Good." Lady Bearsden nodded.

Lady Stratford smiled at me again and changed the subject. "Allow me to offer my congratulations on your engagement to Mr. Gage."

"Oh, thank you."

"I have to say, I'm not entirely surprised. The way he cradled you in the boat after they pulled you from the loch and you passed out and his urgent stride up to the castle were very telling."

I felt a blush burning its way up into my cheeks. I hadn't realized Gage had held me in the boat. No one had ever told me. I, of course, remembered how he jumped into the loch to save me, and the way he had first kissed me while we floated, waiting for the boat to reach us. And Alana had informed me that he'd carried me into the castle and up to my room. But the time between was an empty void. Apparently one filled with Gage's embrace. Even knowing how cold I was and how much pain I had been in, I almost wished I could remember it.

There was a glimmer of teasing in Lady Stratford's eyes. "I only wonder why it took him so long to propose." She tilted her head. "Or did it take you this long to accept?"

I fumbled for a reply, unused to this side of Lady Stratford. There had been no light banter between us at Gairloch Castle, but then again, she had been facing much more difficult circumstances. I was glad to see how much happier and serene she seemed. I was curious whether this was how she had been during her London season when she had been a diamond of the first water, plucked up by the rakish and elusive Lord Stratford, who had hidden his darker side very well. I made a note to ask Alana, who had debuted the year before her.

Her mouth softened sympathetically. "You don't have to say. I'm just pleased for you. Mr. Gage is a good man."

I smiled in return, knowing she might be one of the few people who truly understood what it meant to find someone like him after such a horrible first marriage. "Yes. Yes, he is."

"Is he related to a Captain Gage?" Lady Bearsden asked, leaning forward over a cane that was propped between her legs.

"Yes. Mr. Gage is his son. And Captain Gage is now Lord Gage."

"Is he now? Given the title for his service during the war, I suppose," she mused, settling back in her chair.

"Among other things," I replied. Namely some delicate inquiry he'd conducted on behalf of King William a few years ago. I wasn't privy to the details.

Her gaze turned wistful and her fingers tapped the gold figurehead on the top of her cane. "Oh, I remember how he set all the ladies aflutter when he first came to London. Such a charmer, and so handsome. I don't suppose his son is anything like him?" Her eyebrows lifted hopefully.

I hid a grin. "Very much so."

"Well, then you must bring him by the next time you call."

I glanced at Lady Stratford, who appeared equally amused. "I'm sure he would be eager to meet you." Especially when I told him what a character she was. "And actually, Lord Gage is in Edinburgh as well."

Lady Stratford's eyebrows lifted.

"Then you must bring them both," the older woman proclaimed. "It would be good to reminisce. Didn't he marry the Earl of Tavistock's daughter?" Her eyes brightened. "Oh, yes. I remember. They discovered she'd been murdered. By her maid, if I recall correctly."

Her great-niece appeared shocked by this news, but I had already heard the story from Gage. It was one of the things he had first confided in me to explain some of his actions at Gairloch Castle.

"Yes, that's right," I said, my voice more subdued.

Lady Bearsden shook her head. "So sad. And now I hear Lady Drummond may have been murdered as well."

Lady Stratford's already perfect posture stiffened further. "What?"

"Where did you hear that?" I asked hesitantly. How were our suspicions spreading so quickly when Gage and I had made such an effort to keep them quiet?

"I believe it was Mrs. Oakley next door who told me. And she said she had it from a very reliable source."

"I'm sure."

I could feel Lady Stratford's eyes on me, but I did not look at her, choosing instead to stare at the landscape painting of a cliff-backed beach hanging over the fireplace.

A maid entered at that moment, carrying the tea service as well as a plate filled with delicious-looking sandwiches and small cakes.

"Well, if you'll excuse me, I believe I'll go lie down for a time," Lady Bearsden said, pushing herself to her feet with the aid of her cane. "It was lovely to meet you, Lady Darby."

"And you as well," I replied.

"Mary, if you would?"

The maid slid Lady Bearsden's arm through her own and helped guide her from the room.

"Sleep well, Auntie," Lady Stratford called after her.

"Your great-aunt is delightful," I told her after the pair had disappeared from sight.

She leaned forward to pour the tea. "She's incorrigible, is what she is. But yes, thank you. I'm terribly fond of her. She helped raise me, you know. After my mother died in childbirth. My father was an old bachelor with no idea what to do with a young girl. So his favorite aunt stepped in."

"That was good of her."

"She was never able to have children of her own." Lady Stratford paused, staring at the delicate china cups, and I knew she was thinking of her own barren state, proved so cruelly by her late husband when he got one of her closest friends with child. "So she always calls me her little changeling." She looked up at me through her lashes. "You know the myth?"

"That fairies will secretly take a human child and leave one of their offspring in the baby's place? Yes."

"She said the fact that I was so fair and beautiful only proved the matter."

I smiled, imagining Lady Bearsden saying just that.

Lady Stratford passed me my tea and then took a sip of her own before carefully setting her cup back in its saucer. "Now. What's this about Lady Drummond being murdered?"

I brushed a piece of lint from my plum skirt, avoiding her gaze. "What do you mean?"

"Do not play coy with me. If there is suspicion of murder, I know you and Mr. Gage must be involved somehow." She ran a finger around the rim of her cup. "Especially since I know you were painting Lady Drummond's portrait."

I looked up into her soft gray eyes, realizing there was only one way she could know that. "You were friends."

"Yes," she confirmed. "Though not as close as we once were. The truth is, we hadn't seen each other in years." She glanced toward the dainty writing desk in the corner of the room. "We corresponded regularly. I sent her a letter on Tuesday asking her to call on me, and I received her reply that afternoon. She promised to visit this week, but . . ." her face paled ". . . she never got the chance."

Lady Drummond had died on Wednesday morning, which meant her note to Lady Stratford just might have been the last missive she ever wrote. From the tightness around Lady Stratford's eyes, I could tell she was conscious of this.

A thought suddenly occurred to me.

"Were you acquainted with her husband?"

"Not well. Lord Drummond was quite a bit older than his wife." She hesitated slightly, her posture and expression becoming more rigid, as I remembered it from seven months ago. "Like Lord Stratford was. So we had that in common. And though she never went into details, she did say that he was also a bit controlling." As Lord Stratford had been.

"Would he have any reason to disapprove of his wife's acquaintance with you?"

Lady Stratford's eyes drained of all emotion.

"My apologies," I leaned forward to say, realizing I had misstepped. "I'm not explaining myself well. You see, Lady Drummond received a letter on Tuesday that her husband became very angry about. He confronted her about it during our portrait session, and I was just wondering if it could have been the note from you. I didn't mean to imply . . ."

She held up her hand. "Please. I understand." Her lips compressed into a tight smile. "I'm afraid I'm still a bit touchy. I find I'm not used to being considered a social pariah because of what my late husband did."

I nodded, wondering how much more difficult it must be to fall from the ton's graces when you were one of their darlings. Would Gage face a similar downfall once he wed me? Would he resent me for it?

"Have they snubbed you?" I asked gently.

"Some people have." She tilted her head to study me. "But I suppose, if nothing else, this whole experience has shown me who my true friends are. And maybe I needed to learn that." She sighed. "But to answer your question, I don't know how Lord Drummond felt about me. Lady Drummond never said. But it's quite possible he believed I was too scandalous for our association to continue."

So the letter Lord Drummond had waved in her face could have been from Lady Stratford. Though it seemed an extreme reaction to have over such a small thing. After all, Lady Stratford was still in mourning, and as yet unable to move freely about society. It was unlikely their friendship would be noted or commented upon.

Lady Stratford squeezed her hands together in her lap. "You were there when she died?"

"Yes."

She glanced down and then up again. "Did she . . . was she in a lot of pain?"

I didn't know how to answer her. I couldn't tell her yes, and yet I didn't want to lie. But in the end, my silence spoke for me.

She nodded and tears filled her eyes.

"It was over quickly," I said through the tightness in my throat, hoping to alleviate some of her distress.

She sniffed into a lace-edged handkerchief she'd pulled from her sleeve. "And . . . and you believe it was murder, not an apoplexy?"

Once again, I hesitated, and she lowered her handkerchief to look at me more closely. "I don't know," I finally admitted. Revealing my misgivings to Lady Stratford suddenly felt very different than speculating on them to Gage or my sister, or even Lady Rachel, who had held suspicions of her own. Would they seem ridiculous? Would they only hurt her more?

When Lady Stratford continued to stare at me, I pressed a hand to my forehead, feeling confused and uncertain. "There's no proof that it was murder. It could very well be an apoplexy. That's what everyone seems to think." Including Gage's father.

"Yes. But everyone is not you," Lady Stratford replied with quiet certainty.

I looked up in surprise.

"And proof is not always clear. Did not the proof in Lady Godwin's murder all point to me? And yet you knew something was not right. You believed in my innocence before you had evidence of it." Her steady gaze brooked no argument. "So if you believe that Lady Drummond's death was not so straightforward, if you think something is wrong, I trust you're right. I would be a fool not to."

A warmth flowed through me at the surety in her words. Her

confidence bolstered something inside me that had been floundering, something that even my sister's belief had not repaired. But before I could thank her for it, she pressed me with another question.

"What does Mr. Gage think?"

I placed my teacup on the table. "He is willing to support me." I frowned, reaching up to finger my mother's amethyst pendant. "Or at least, he was. I'm not sure what he thinks after his father scolded us last night for our idiocy in pursuing such an investigation."

Lady Stratford took a dainty sip of her tea. "I thought relations between Mr. Gage and his father were strained?"

My hand tightened on my pendant. "Is that commonly known?"

"How could it not be? You must have seen the way they bristle when they are near each other."

"Like two hedgehogs fighting over a snail."

This surprised a smile out of her. "Quite."

"Do you know Lord Gage well?"

"No," she said, drawing out the word. "But I am aware he's a terrible snob. And determined to see his son rise to even greater heights than he has."

"I gather Gage's mother's family did not approve of the match."

She laughed dryly. "Not in the least." Her eyes narrowed in consideration. "But then not many respectable members of the ton dream of having their children marry into the notorious Roscarrock family."

"Roscarrock?"

"Lord Gage's mother was a Roscarrock from Cornwall. Apparently they're infamous. Smugglers and rogues, barely able to call themselves gentlemen."

This was the first I'd heard of Gage's maternal ancestors. Like so many things, he had been reticent to share much about them.

I turned to stare at the fire crackling in the hearth. "Well, Lord Gage seems to have conducted himself honorably enough," I said, wondering if and when Gage would finally share all of himself with me. Maybe he was waiting on me to ask, but when I had in the past, he'd always turned the conversation. Of course, I hadn't been his fiancée then.

"Yes. Which is why he's determined for his son to continue in the same vein. Even if that means making him unhappy."

"Would it?"

"Yes."

I glanced at Lady Stratford, realizing I'd actually voiced my question aloud. Her gaze was perceptive and her mouth set in a determined line.

"I don't know Mr. Gage well, but I do know him well enough to be sure of this."

"Even though I'm completely hopeless in social situations?" I could hear the pleading whine sneak into my voice, and I hated it. But still I craved reassurance. Even from such a tentative friend as Lady Stratford.

Her eyes softened, but her voice still scolded. "You know he doesn't care about that, or else he wouldn't have proposed marriage."

I did know this. Or at least I should have. But recognizing you should believe something and actually believing it were two very different things.

"But . . ." she added. "If you wish to feel more competent among society, I might be able to help." She smiled wryly. "I'm currently an outcast, but I do still know how to charm and mingle."

"It would be nice to feel less awkward," I admitted. I doubted I could ever become comfortable with the whirl of society, but if Lady Stratford could help me feel even a fraction more capable and relaxed, then it was worth a try. Perhaps Gage was not concerned with my ineptness, but I was concerned for him. Especially now that his father was in Edinburgh.

CHAPTER 12

I left Lady Stratford with a promise to call on her again soon, and set off to visit a home around the corner on St. Andrew Lane. After the kindness the countess had shown to me, I knew what I needed to do. Gage and his father might be cross with me for intervening, but only if they found out.

Lady Kirkcowan did not hide her surprise or her wariness as her butler ushered me into her drawing room. I did not waste time by mincing words as we settled into a pair of Hepplewhite chairs near the front bow window.

"Lord Gage knows it was you who stole your jewelry. Though how you can steal something that is rightfully yours, I don't know," I added, not bothering to hide my aggravation.

"I don't know what you're talking about," she replied stiffly, even though her panicked expression would fool no one.

"Mr. Gage and I tried to convince him to remain quiet, but I'm afraid he's intent on informing your husband." I leaned forward to stare into her eyes. "I'm telling you this so that you can do something about it before he does so."

She swallowed. "Perhaps they've been miraculously found?"

"Exactly. Accidentally stored in the bottom of a trunk. Or . . . or fallen behind your dresser," I suggested. They were inane excuses, but without implicating a servant and further complicating the matter, there weren't many places they could have disappeared.

She pressed a hand to her abdomen. "What if Lord Gage tells him anyway?"

I considered the matter. "If he hasn't already, then maybe a letter from your husband saying the matter is resolved will keep him from doing so. We can hope."

Her eyes strayed to the window, watching a carriage drive by. "Yes. I suppose that's my only choice." Her shoulders sagged with the weight of my revelation, and undoubtedly the realization that the gems were once more at risk to her gambling husband.

"I'm sorry," I murmured, wishing there was something I could do.

"It was silly to even try, wasn't it?"

"I don't think so."

She sniffed. "You don't?"

"No. Better to try something than nothing."

She nodded and offered me a tight smile.

My heart was heavy as I rose to leave. At the door, I glanced back to find her still staring out the window. Fear tightened her features, and I knew it was not just for herself, but for her three young children. I wished there was some way I could help her.

The ring of church bells filled the air, momentarily holding me and Gage silent as we crossed the street to the garden at the center of Charlotte Square. The dome of St. George's Church soared above us on the west side of the square, reverberating the peals of its bells. I knew better than to attempt to speak before the midday chimes had finished, but Gage attempted to talk over the ringing. I shook my head, refusing to raise my voice, at least not for this particular conversation, and Gage looked up to frown at the copper dome.

The rain from the day before had blown east, leaving behind the low-hanging gray clouds Edinburgh was so known for. However, unlike on most March days, periodically the sun would peak through, teasing us with its warmth. It was enough to tempt us outside, away from the stifling atmosphere of the house. Gage had not remarked upon it, being already acquainted with the source of the majority of our tension, but I could tell from the way he had rolled his shoulders when we had escaped into the chill air that he had noticed.

Our steps slowed once we entered the garden to cross toward the other side. I noticed we weren't the only ones enjoying the weather. Children dashed about playing games under the watchful eye of their governesses, while other couples meandered down the paths or perched on the benches spaced throughout. A pair of spinster sisters who lived in the town house two doors down from Philip and Alana sat closest to us, darting disapproving glances at the man in shabby clothes lurking under a tree in the corner trying to look unobtrusive.

I smiled and shook my head. "If Bonnie Brock is going to continue to send his men here, he really needs to do a better job of teaching them to blend in," I murmured as the sound from the last bell ring died away.

Gage's mouth tightened at my mention of the notorious criminal. "He still has men watching your town house?"

"From time to time."

His expression grew angrier.

"Did you honestly think he would heed our orders for him to stop?" I asked.

"How can you find this so amusing?" he demanded instead.

I tilted my head in gentle chastisement. "Because there really is no other option."

At first I had been infuriated and alarmed by the men Bonnie Brock

Kincaid repeatedly sent to shadow me, but since they never approached me or attempted to do me any harm, I learned to see the humor in the situation. The men he was sending to watch over me were clearly not the cleverest or keenest in his band of merry thieves and grave robbers. They were becoming increasingly easy to spot, and I had begun to suspect that tailing me had become a sort of training exercise for new recruits to his criminal gang or a way to occupy his dimmest underlings. There was really no other reason for him to continue to keep watch over me.

We had first encountered the rogue a few months before during an investigation into the body snatching of bones from old graves. I no longer feared or particularly disliked Bonnie Brock, but I knew better than to trust him. He was a hard and ruthless man. Gage, on the other hand, despised him.

"Something really needs to be done about him," Gage ruminated. His eyes narrowed in challenge.

"That is the job of the city police, not you," I reminded him. "Besides, you know as well as I do that if he is ever convicted, someone else will rise to take his place. Someone we are not acquainted with, and who might not listen to or agree with our reasoning." I squeezed his arm where it linked with mine. "I know how much you loathe him, Gage, but I say better the devil we know than the one we don't."

Gage did not argue, though I could tell he wished to. But he did sneak one last angry glare at Bonnie Brock's minion. I hoped the man would not report that back to Bonnie Brock. I was sure he would only find Gage's displeasure entertaining.

We painted on neutral expressions to nod to a passing couple.

"How is your sister faring?" Gage leaned closer to ask, turning the conversation to a more amicable, though not more cheerful, topic.

I inhaled and exhaled deeply. "Well enough, I think. She seems to be sleeping a lot. Which is good, for both her and the baby. She can't worry when she's resting," I contemplated, staring down at the russet brown silk of my skirt peeking out from my forest green pelisse with ecru trim.

"And how is Cromarty?"

"I wouldn't know," I muttered.

Gage turned to me in surprise. When I failed to elaborate, he began to speculate himself. "He did seem a bit distracted when I came to see you yesterday."

"Well, the half hour you spent with him waiting for me to return was longer than I've spoken to him in weeks." I looked up at him out of the corner of my eye, wanting to tell him my concerns over Philip and Alana's increasingly strained relationship, but it somehow seemed like a betrayal of their trust. In any case, Alana had not yet spoken to me about it. I wondered if my brother-in-law had been as silent.

"Did he . . . confide anything to you?" I asked, trying not to sound as curious as I was. Gage had needed to leave before I arrived home, so I'd not had a chance to quiz him then about their conversation.

I felt Gage's eyes studying my profile. "About Alana's condition?"

"About anything."

"Not really. Unless you're referring to his frustration at the Tories in Parliament."

My brow furrowed. "No."

"He did say that Alana seems determined to continue our wedding plans. That it appears to be a welcome distraction for her."

It was a relief to hear that Philip at least knew this much. "Yes. I told her not to concern herself, but she insisted."

Gage led me through the gate on the opposite side of the garden. "Is she asking for your input?"

I could hear the concern in his voice and paused to look at him. "Yes. Though you know I'm not very well versed in such things." I pressed a hand to his other arm in reassurance. "If it makes her happy to plan our nuptials, then I'm happy, too. I . . . I just want to marry you. It doesn't really matter to me how it's done. Big and lavish, or small and intimate."

His pale blue eyes warmed and the corners of his mouth curled upward in that affectionate smile he seemed to reserve only for me. For once, my acting seemed to have fooled him, hiding the nerves that fluttered in my stomach every time I thought of the grandiose affair my sister was planning.

He pulled me closer. "Then I will say no more, for it does not matter to me either. I will be content when I know that I can finally call you mine." His eyes dipped to my lips, and I knew that if we were not standing on the street in broad daylight with two dozen onlookers, he would have kissed me.

I swallowed. "What of your father? Do you think he'll attend?"

A line formed between his eyes. "I do not know. And the truth is, I don't really care."

But I knew he was lying. I could see it in the pain reflected in his eyes. He did care. Perhaps not enough to bow to his father's wishes, but enough that his absence would leave a permanent scar. I ached for him.

My father had never tried to dissuade my interest in art. And when I'd determined to continue my training and even seek out portrait commissions, he had supported me wholeheartedly even though such things were simply not done by a gentlewoman. The fact that I did not do it for the money at that time did not matter. I was still courting scandal by pursuing such a course.

From what I had witnessed, Gage did not have that kind of love and support from his father. He was to do as he was told. Return to London when he was ordered, not hang about in Scotland. Investigate the inquiries assigned to him, not seek out his own. Marry the woman chosen for him, not fall in love with an eccentric outcast.

The irony was, for all of Lord Gage's dutiful expectations, it was obvious he would never respect his son if he meekly submitted. He wanted his orders followed, just like when he was captain of a ship in the Royal Navy, but he would never really be pleased with such obedience from his own flesh and blood. This conflict within his father made it impossible for Gage to please him. Even to try was to fail.

We resumed our stroll, turning up Charlotte Street toward the castle, hovering dark and forbidding high on the hill overlooking the city.

"Did you speak with him about Lord Drummond?" I asked, pressing a hand to my bonnet as a gust of wind pushed against its brim.

"I did. And he's still insistent that our inquiry into Lady Drummond's death is foolish, and he remains adamant that we stop."

I sighed, even though I hadn't expected to hear anything different.

"He maintains that Lord Drummond is incapable of murder." Gage's voice turned cynical. "Even though this opinion is based on his friendship with the man fifteen years ago."

"What do you think?"

He frowned, considering my question. "I don't think it matters what I think. We've established that there are numerous potential motives for him to have murdered his wife. What we haven't proved is that Lady Drummond was actually murdered. And until we do that, all of this speculation is for naught."

"You're right," I admitted. "Still no luck in questioning the apothecaries and chemists?"

"I'm afraid not. But maybe Sergeant Maclean has been more successful in Old Town." He dipped his head toward me. "I've arranged a meeting with him at his sister-in-law's tea shop for tomorrow morning after Lady Drummond's funeral." His eyebrows lifted. "I assume you wish to join us?"

"Of course."

He nodded once. "After we've spoken to Maclean, we can decide how to proceed."

We fell silent as a gentleman walked past us huddled in his coat. He tipped his hat to me politely. I glanced behind us to watch as he hurried away, wondering if I knew him. Perhaps he was an acquaintance of Philip's.

"Kiera, you know I have the utmost faith in your instincts," Gage said, seeming to take extra care with his words. I lifted my eyes to meet his anxious gaze. "But if Sergeant Maclean doesn't have any information for us tomorrow, I'm afraid there may be nothing we can do."

"I understand." And I did, even though the thought of halting the inquiry tore a hole inside me. Without facts, without proof, my instincts were useless in bringing Lady Drummond's killer to justice, particularly if a man like Lord Drummond was involved.

"I'm sorry," Gage murmured, and I could see that he thought he was failing me.

I gripped his arm where it twined with mine. "You did what you could. That's all I can ask. We've been impeded at nearly every turn."

"I know. But it *frustrates* me to admit defeat, especially when it matters so much to you to uncover the truth."

"What of the servants? Maybe one of them knows what really happened."

"But will they ever admit it?"

"What about the kitchen maid who quit?"

"Anderley found her."

"He did?" I gasped, feeling renewed vigor spread through me. "Where? What did she say?"

"She was working as a scullery maid in a pub off Canongate."

A significant step down from her position in the household of a baron.

"From what he could understand in between her heaving sobs was that she feared for her life because Lord Drummond was furious with her. Apparently she dropped a crystal dish that held Lady Drummond's sugared plums and it shattered. I guess they were her ladyship's favorite treat, and the maid had been ordered to toss the remainder of them out."

My eyes widened. "I'd forgotten about those. She would nibble on them during her portrait sessions sometimes." I looked up at him. "But isn't that . . ."

"Suspicious?" he finished for me, but in a far more subdued voice. "Yes. But since there are no sugared plums left to examine, we can't prove there was anything wrong with them."

My shoulders slumped, knowing he was right. "Still, it sounds like Lord Drummond overreacted if he became so irate over such a small thing that the girl was afraid he would do her some harm."

"Yes, but we have only the maid's word that he responded so strongly. He may have merely snapped at her and the girl heard it as a roar," Gage pointed out. "Anderley said she was a timid slip of a girl. That she jumped at every order the proprietor barked, even if it wasn't aimed at her."

It was possible. One of the maids on Sir Anthony's staff was like that, and no matter how hard I tried to put her at ease, she always slunk about the house like a whipped dog. She had started to make *me* feel uncomfortable just being in her presence.

"We're also forgetting that the man had just lost his wife. No matter our suspicions or the face he shows the world, he might still be grieving. Perhaps the maid's clumsiness simply occurred at a time when he was contemplating her death. Or maybe that dish was sentimental to his wife, or him, because he associated it with her. And so he reacted harshly."

"You're right, of course," I admitted. "I should know better." I lifted my skirts to step down off the walkway to cross Princes Street. "Do I not hide behind a mask, often to my own . . ."

"Look out!" someone shouted just as I became aware of the rumbling of a speeding carriage's wheels careening toward me.

I turned to see a pair of dark horses bearing down on me. I gasped in terror and closed my eyes, bracing for the impact. But then an arm wrapped around my waist and pulled me backward with enough force to expel the breath from my lungs. We landed hard on the pavement.

I lay gasping for air, trying to come to terms with what had just happened. Gage rolled over to look down at me, a golden lock of hair draped over his forehead. "Kiera, are you hurt?" His hands began to run carefully over my arms and shoulders. "Kiera."

I shook my head, still unable to breathe normally, let alone speak.

A small crowd began to gather around us. "Blasted scoundrel," one older man cursed. "I cannot abide these young men and their racing carriages," a woman screeched.

Gage ignored them all, carefully helping me to sit up. His brow was furrowed in concern. "Are you certain you aren't injured?"

"I don't think so," I finally managed to say. "At least . . . no more . . . than a few bruises," I stammered, still winded from the fall.

I clutched my side where I had fallen as Gage pulled me to my feet.

"I say, excellent timing," the older man praised him. "If you hadn't been so quick, she would have been trampled by that rapscallion."

"Did anyone see who it was?" Gage asked.

One woman thought it'd been a young man with dark hair, while another said the fellow had looked much older, possibly with graying hair. Ultimately, no one could agree.

I pressed a hand to Gage's arm, simply wanting to be away. "It doesn't matter," I told him. "He may have been driving too fast, but I wasn't paying attention."

I could see from his expression that he was far from satisfied with such an explanation, but my weary smile convinced him to cease his questions and escort me home. My hip ached as we walked, and I could feel a knot forming on my leg, but otherwise I felt fine. Perhaps a little shaken, but that was to be expected.

He was especially vigilant on our walk back to the town house, as if he thought another carriage might attempt to run me down. I did not say anything, merely leaned on his arm and enjoyed the sensation of being cherished and protected. It was not a feeling I was accustomed to. Philip and my brother, Trevor, had done their best to care for me in the nearly two years since Sir Anthony's death, but it was not the same. And I knew I would never take it for granted.

CHAPTER 13

Sergeant Maclean was waiting for us at the same table near the back of the tea shop as the last time we had met him there. The brawny police officer rose from his chair to greet us, and as before, I was taken aback by the man's size. I had only seen a bear once, in a menagerie at a nobleman's house, but that was the image that immediately came to mind. However, his demeanor was restrained and his movements carefully controlled, as if he was ever conscious of how much space he took up.

"Mr. Gage," he said, shaking his hand. His burly fist nearly swallowed Gage's. "Always good teh see ye. Though I mun wonder if ye ever take a break. Ye do ken you're a gentleman, dinna ye?" he teased.

"Yes, but don't you know gentlemen hate to be afflicted with ennui," he jested back. "Some men gamble, and some race phaetons or chase lightskirts." He flashed a bright grin. "I solve murders."

Sergeant Maclean tipped his head back and gave a hearty laugh. "And I see ye've brought Lady Darby this time." He offered me a short bow. "Allow me teh offer my congratulations, m'lady." He flicked a glance at Gage. "It's aboot time someone caught this rogue in the parson's mousetrap."

I smiled. "Thank you. I think."

The sergeant's sister-in-law, Mrs. Duffy, emerged from the back of the shop carrying a tray. I sighed in delight as I spied the plate of scones dotted with sultanas next to the teapot and a bowl of clotted cream. I'd not been able to stomach much breakfast earlier that morning, thinking of Lady Drummond being interred in the cold, hard ground. Out of deference to the ton's belief that ladies could not handle the rigors of a burial, and a desire to avoid causing a scene should Lord Drummond protest my presence, I had not attended the funeral. However, Gage had gone and reported nothing abnormal in the behavior of the other mourners. But now my appetite seemed to have emphatically returned.

Mrs. Duffy dimpled at my reaction. "I remembered how much ye enjoyed them the last time ye were here."

"Oh, they're heavenly," I replied, breathing in the herbal aroma of the tea and the sweetness of the scones.

Mrs. Duffy disappeared back into the kitchen while I poured for each of us. The shop looked much the same as it had two months prior; dark wood paneling covered the walls and floor, while each of the eight tables was draped with a pristine white tablecloth. However, in the place of the tiny bud vases that had graced the center of each table before sat a tiny pot filled with fresh mint.

"How charming," I remarked.

Sergeant Maclean grunted. "'Twas some banker's wife's idea. I guess she always puts mint in her tea. Dinna ken why. She isna a cow."

I nearly sprayed tea all over the tablecloth. I forced the drink down, nearly choking on it, and then started to cough.

Gage reached over to pat my back. "Are you well?" The twinkle in his eye told me he had also appreciated the sergeant's wry humor.

I nodded.

Sergeant Maclean set his cup back down on its saucer. "Noo, did ye have any luck wi' the chemists in New Town?"

The light in Gage's eyes dimmed. "No. Most of them refused to talk, and those who did could not tell me anything of use. A few said they would tell me what they could if I returned to ask about a specific poison."

He nodded. "Those I talked to had the same complaint. Said there were too many substances that could kill a person if taken in the wrong amount. Though I did have half a dozen admit they'd sold rat poison recently, which contains arsenic." He looked to me hopefully.

"It's very common," I confirmed. "And unfortunately, it's possibly the most popular poison because it's so easy to obtain with little suspicion." I frowned, discouraged.

"Could Lady Drummond have been killed by arsenic?" Gage asked me.

The one time I had encountered poison in a cadaver, it had been arsenic. For all Sir Anthony and I had known, the poisoning had gone undetected, but my late husband found evidence of its presence during his dissection. I remembered asking if he should notify the local magistrate, but he had told me it was not our concern, and threatened me to keep quiet. I had suspected then that that particular corpse had been purchased from a body snatcher, but I had held my tongue, too afraid of Sir Anthony to do more than obey.

"It's possible." I sighed in frustration. "Hundreds of people have probably purchased arsenic in some form or another in the past six months. If that was what killed Lady Drummond, it will be almost impossible to prove. Arsenic might have been detected during an autopsy, but Lord Drummond refused the suggestion before and there is no way he would allow it now."

I scowled at the scone on my plate. The lingering taste of my last bite suddenly turned to ashes in my mouth.

Sergeant Maclean shifted awkwardly in his chair, making the wood groan. "Well, maybe it isna arsenic. Maybe it's something else."

"Weren't you going to speak to someone at the Royal College?" Gage prodded gently.

"Yes." I made an effort to rouse myself from my irritated stupor. "If the poison was not arsenic, perhaps there is still some chance of finding proof."

The two men glanced at each other and I knew what they were thinking. Even if we could connect the purchase of a particular poison to the Drummond household, it did not necessarily prove guilt. There were many more factors involved, but it would at least be a start.

I took another sip of tea, refusing to let their doubt crush my renewed hope.

Sergeant Maclean fidgeted in his chair again. At first glance, I thought perhaps he was simply uncomfortable in the tiny chair on which he perched, but after taking a closer look at his face, I could tell there was something else on his mind. Something he was wrestling with.

"There is still one other option," he murmured, frowning into his tea.

Gage and I glanced at each other, curious about the police officer's reticence.

He considered us each. "But before I say more, I mun' ask. Are you sure aboot this? Are ye certain Lady Drummond was murdered?"

I opened my mouth to argue, but he held up his hand to stop me.

"I ken why ye suspected it. Mr. Gage has relayed most of the details to me, and I mun' admit, I find it all rather suspicious, too. Though most people dinna want the city police in their homes." He scowled. "They still think we're petty thieves and bumblin' idiots. So Lord Drummond's refusal to let us investigate is no' surprisin'."

He leaned toward us, resting his arms on the table. "But ye've no' been given access to the body or the house. The physician has said her death was caused by an apoplexy, and unless ye can show he was bribed teh say so . . ." his expression said that was doubtful ". . . then that's likely to stand. Even if ye do discover that Lord Drummond or someone in his household bought poison, ye are no' likely teh prove they used it on her ladyship."

I sank back in my chair, knowing what he said was true.

His expression was grim, but not without sympathy. "Ye face a long, hard battle, and it could all be for naught."

"That may be," I replied solemnly. "But I have to try. Lady Drummond deserves that much."

Sergeant Maclean continued to study me, and then as if he'd judged my intentions to be true, he nodded and turned to Gage in question.

Gage's lips curled up at the corners. "Whither she goes, I follow."

Sergeant Maclean gave a gruff laugh. "Aye, well, that's good enough for me." His expression grew serious and a line formed between his brows. "There's rumors o' an underground chemist workin' doon near Grassmarket and West Port."

I stiffened at his mention of the area where the notorious criminals Burke and Hare had prowled for their victims—plying them with drink, and then suffocating them and selling their bodies to the anatomists at Surgeons' Hall. They had only been discovered and tried for their crimes a little over two years ago, so the events were not so far from the minds of the citizens of Edinburgh. There was still some fear that other resurrectionists had turned from the risky and labor-intensive practice of body snatching to the relative ease of murder in order to obtain fresh corpses to sell. Even as far away as London, there was panic at the prospect. I knew this intimately. It had played into the scandal and horror of the discovery of my involvement in my late husband's work.

"What exactly does that mean?" Gage asked.

Sergeant Maclean sat back in his chair, crossing his arms over his chest. "They say he's willin' to mix up any potion, any poison for the right price."

"So he might be the man we're looking for? He could have mixed the poison for Lord Drummond or whoever the murderer is?"

He didn't appear so certain. "Aye, maybe. If he really exists. And if ye can find him."

"Maybe Bonnie Brock knows."

Gage's face tightened. "You are not contacting Bonnie Brock."

"Why not?" I turned to him to argue. "If anyone knows who this chemist is and how to reach him, it's probably Bonnie Brock. And besides, he owes me a favor."

His eyes grew hard. "You are *not* contacting Bonnie Brock."

I frowned. "Be reasonable. He can help us."

"Maybe I don't want his help."

"Because he gave you a black eye?"

"Because the man is not to be trusted."

I crossed my arms over my chest. "Even I know that."

His nostrils flared. "But you're going to ask him to find this chemist anyway?"

"The man is a criminal, but he does have his own code of honor. And returning the favor I did him would be part of that."

He turned away with a grunt of frustration. "No, Kiera."

He never called me by my given name in public, so for him to have forgotten and done so now must have meant he was furious. But I didn't care. He was being unreasonable.

"I canna tell ye what teh do," Sergeant Maclean said. His gaze darted back and forth between us. "But if ye truly want teh find this chemist, you're gonna need help from someone who kens Edinburgh's dark and seedy corners better than I do." His brow lowered. "I dinna like Bonnie Brock Kincaid. I've seen too much o' his handiwork, and watched him slip oot o' the hangman's noose too many times. But Lady Darby is right." He nodded to me. "He does have his own code o' honor. 'Tis why his hold on the city is so tight. People ken he'll keep his word so long as they do right by him, and that suits most o' 'em just fine."

He leaned toward me. "Just a word o' warnin' should ye choose to take this path." Perhaps it was the way the light fell on him, throwing his crooked nose and the scars from his days as a pugilist into relief, but suddenly his face looked almost menacing. "Dinna cross him. Ye willna like the result."

I swallowed and nodded.

"It doesn't matter," Gage retorted. "Because we are not going to contact him." His eyes bored into mine. "We'll locate the chemist another way."

I narrowed my gaze in resentment.

He turned away, ignoring me as he asked Sergeant Maclean about another matter.

I sipped my now tepid tea and stewed. He was being obstinate. I thought his high-handed protectiveness had ended, but apparently I was wrong. This infuriated me because I'd proved myself to be more than reasonable, and perfectly capable in precarious situations. In fact, it had been my brother, Anderley, and I who had saved Gage from peril during our last inquiry. If this was how he intended to behave during our marriage, then I was not pleased, and I let him know so as soon as we returned to his carriage.

"So this is how it will be?"

He turned to me as the carriage rolled forward. "How what will be?" he asked, though he must have had an inkling, for his expression was still rigid.

"Our marriage. Our investigations. You'll tell me what to do and I shall fall in line," I sneered.

His eyebrows arched condescendingly. "That is the way it usually goes."

I glared at him, furious he would say such a thing when he knew how frightened I was of that very paradigm. Husbands held all the power in marriage. Sir Anthony had illustrated that to me very clearly. They could hurt you and force you to do terrible things, and there was nothing you could do about it. I had sworn never to marry again for this very reason.

But then the unexpected had happened. I'd met Sebastian Gage and fallen in love. Even then, I'd resisted him, turning down his first offer of marriage because I feared to place myself completely in another man's power. Until I accepted the truth, that Gage was different. Or so I thought.

My stomach dipped and I felt as though I might be ill. I turned aside, pressing my hand to my mouth. Had I been wrong? Was I making a mistake? The prospect made the blood in my veins run cold.

I felt the warm press of Gage's hand on my shoulder and nearly shrank away from it.

"Kiera. Kiera, look at me."

I shook my head.

"Kiera," he murmured more gently, making me face him. His eyes had softened in remorse. "I apologize. I shouldn't have said that."

"But it's true," I bit out.

"For most marriages," he admitted. "But that is not the way it will be for us. At least, not most of the time."

"But some of the time."

"I cannot promise I will never try to forbid you from doing something, but I promise that my reason for doing so will always be good."

I lifted my chin defiantly. "And when I think you're wrong?"

His brows snapped together. "I'm not Sir Anthony. How many times do I need to remind you of that?"

Guilt pressed down on my chest. He was right. I did give in to my fears far too often. But I wasn't about to admit it.

Instead I snapped back. "How many times do I have to ask you to tell me about Greece?"

His mouth flattened and he turned away.

"Mr. Knighton said he thought it had to do with a woman. Someone you cared for."

He sighed in annoyance.

"Is it true?"

"Contrary to what he thinks, Mr. Knighton doesn't know everything," he muttered under his breath.

"But was he right about this?" I pressed, unwilling to be deterred yet again.

His reply was terse. "I'm not going to discuss this now."

"You never want to discuss it. You tell me to be patient, and I have been. But eventually even a saint's patience runs thin."

He turned to glare at me. "I will tell you when I'm good and ready."

"Which is never." I sank back against the squabs and turned to stare out the window, seeing that we had already pulled into Charlotte Square. I gathered my pelisse around me and sprung from the carriage as soon as the footman lowered the step. I knew I risked spraining my ankle descending so fast, but I couldn't bear the strained silence in the carriage a moment longer. Whether Gage even noticed, I didn't know, for I didn't look back. I hurried up the steps to the town house, biting back tears I refused to let fall.

The shadows of late afternoon had just begun to gather when Bonnie Brock's sentinel finally arrived. I knew he hadn't been there sooner, for I would have spotted him. Like the day before, he stood out sharply among the usual residents frequenting the garden, but it appeared that today he had at least made some effort. He had donned a cravat and his jacket was buttoned, but no amount of scrubbing was going to remove the stains from his trousers, although a bath would not be remiss.

I watched him through the drawing room window as he took up his post, leaning against a tree. My foot tapped an agitated rhythm on the floor, undecided what to do.

I understood what I risked. I remembered the menace I had seen in Bonnie Brock's eyes when he lounged in the seat of Philip's carriage across from me the evening he abducted me. Even when I had pointed a gun at him, I had recognized he was still the one in control. And the night he had intercepted me as I walked home and trapped me against the fence surrounding the garden, I recalled his words to me. "If ye wander into my territory, ye willna leave again." I would be a fool to be swayed in any way by the gentleness I'd witnessed him exhibit toward his sister when we returned her to him six weeks ago, after her ordeal. Or the obvious affection between the siblings when Maggie had clung to him and cried. So the man wasn't completely heartless. That didn't mean he would hesitate to harm me or someone I loved if I crossed him.

However, even knowing all the risks, even knowing what I was considering would infuriate Gage, I couldn't dismiss the idea. My mouth quirked wryly. Or perhaps Gage's anger wasn't a deterrent. Every time I thought of his defiant glare, my muscles tensed, ready to march across the square. But I didn't want my only reason for doing this to be to spite Gage. It couldn't be about flouting his orders. It had to be about Lady Drummond.

The image of her lying on the floor, her eyes desperately pleading with me as she writhed in pain, haunted me. I knew she hadn't died of an apoplexy. It simply didn't make sense. But if I didn't do something, the world would never accept that. Her killer would never face the consequences. And quite simply, I didn't think I could live with myself if I didn't do everything in my power to uncover the truth, wherever that might take me.

My decision made, I walked quickly from the room, snatching up my shawl where it was draped over the back of a chair. My feet pattered down the steps and out the front door. I glanced about as I hurried across the street to the green space. I could feel Bonnie Brock's henchman's eyes on me, but I did not look at him. Not until I was almost upon him.

He startled when I fixed my gaze on him, halting a few feet away. I couldn't resist arching a single brow haughtily. Had he honestly thought he'd gone unnoticed?

"I need you to deliver a message to Bonnie Brock."

He didn't speak, but I could tell from the panicked look in his eyes he understood what I was saying.

"Tell him I need to meet the chemist working near Grassmarket. And remind him he owes me a favor. He'll know what I mean."

The man swallowed, but still did not respond.

I sighed and rolled my eyes before walking away. I trusted he would do as I asked.

One of the spinsters who lived two town houses east of Philip's stood at her window staring down at me. Her eyes were narrowed in suspicion, and for once I was in no mood to ignore it. I glared back at her in challenge and she shrank away from the glass.

The ever-unflappable Figgins appeared to open the door. "My lady," he intoned, revealing not even an ounce of surprise, though he must have been curious why I was out in the square with just a shawl to keep me warm.

"Figgins," I replied.

I felt his eyes on me, but when I looked back, they were carefully averted.

A letter was waiting for me on the table the next morning as I sat down to breakfast. I glanced about for the butler, but he wasn't there. Normally Figgins handed us our correspondence or left it sitting on the silver salver in the hall. I flipped the missive over to see the seal. It was stamped with the crest of a castle with an arm rising out of it brandishing a sword, and the words *This I'll Defend*. I arched my brows, recognizing it as the Kincaid clan crest. I wondered just whose finger Bonnie Brock had stolen the signet ring from that bore this mark.

I looked around me again, pondering just how this had been delivered. The footman stood at attention by the sideboard, avoiding my gaze, but then he always did that.

Breaking open the seal with my knife, I unfolded the letter to find a short message written in a far neater hand than I'd anticipated. But for the arrogant slant of the letters I would have thought it was written by a female.

Wednesday. Nightfall. Castlehill. Don't be late. The Chemist waits for no one. And neither do I. Even bloodthirsty wenches.

P.S. Do not bring Mean Maclean.

I refolded the letter and turned toward the window. A bloodthirsty wench. That was what Bonnie Brock had called me when I threatened to do what I was rumored to be capable of should he or his men harm Gage. I didn't know why he was harking back to that, but knowing Bonnie Brock, I was sure it had been done with intention.

A trickle of uneasiness ran down my spine.

Whatever the reason, there was no turning back now. If I didn't show, Bonnie Brock would demand to know the reason why, and I, or Gage, would suffer the consequences of trifling with him. For better or worse, I would be descending into the dark wynds and closes of Old Town tomorrow night. I only hoped I would emerge again.

CHAPTER 14

"I know Alana wishes she could have come tonight," I said.

Philip looked up from his silent contemplation of the dark streets of Edinburgh. He'd been staring out the window ever since we'd pulled away from Charlotte Square. It was obvious he wasn't ignoring me. I knew him well enough to realize he was organizing his thoughts, preparing to debate with some of the other members of Parliament who would be at the dinner tonight. After all, that was why we were going.

But I couldn't help but feel tense, wanting to broach the subject of his and Alana's relationship, but knowing now was not the time. I would need to bite my tongue until after the event, when a disruption to my brother-in-law's concentration would not matter so much. However, I couldn't continue to sit in silence, feeling the nerves that had tightened my stomach ever since I received Bonnie Brock's note grow tauter with each passing hour. Tomorrow night could not come quickly enough, and yet part of me wished it never came at all.

Philip smiled. "Yes. She does enjoy these sorts of gatherings, more than me or you." His eyes strayed back toward the window. "I shall miss her this evening." His eyes darted back toward me. "Not that *you* are not also a lovely companion."

I grinned at his concern that he had hurt my feelings. "Oh, hush, Philip. It's only right that you should miss your wife. Besides, I know I'm probably the least advantageous woman in all of Edinburgh to attend a political dinner with. In fact, I would say I'm more of a liability." It was my turn to look away as I muttered under my breath, "I hope Gage realizes that."

"He does."

I looked up in surprise at Philip's response. His eyes matched the warmth in his voice.

"Are you sure about that?" I couldn't help asking, feeling the familiar anxiety stir in me.

"Yes." He shifted to face me more fully. "I won't say that won't be a frustration at times. But he knows exactly what your limitations are in that regard and accepts them. Just as you accept that the fellow can be dashed secretive at times. Like pulling teeth to get information out of that one. Used to frustrate the lot of us at Cambridge. Especially when it was something we truly needed to know."

Except I'd pressured him yet again to tell me what had happened in Greece. I felt like I'd swallowed a helping of guilt chased by a serving of frustration. Because Philip was right about one thing. His secretiveness was exasperating. I didn't know when to push and when to be patient. Where was the line between being nosy and interfering, and being a fool for not demanding the truth sooner? For I knew one thing—Gage would never reveal a thing if he was not forced to.

Philip's gaze turned shrewd. "Though I daresay, if anyone can understand his guardedness, it's you. A more uncommunicative pair I've never seen, at least about yourselves."

I didn't argue. I'd always been a bit quiet and reserved, preferring to observe rather than be observed. It wasn't so much the lack of a desire to socialize, but the fact that I didn't understand the point of small talk. So much time at gatherings and soirees seemed to be wasted on discussion about the weather and compliments on one's clothing, and the other half was spent in gossiping. My marriage to Sir Anthony and the resulting scandal from his death had only made matters worse.

Gage, on the other hand, was different. He was charming and self-assured. A true master at the art of trivial conversation. His presence was always sought after at any event. Or at least it had been. I didn't know whether our recent engagement had changed that. I suspected not, the novelty of such a shocking match being as much a draw as Gage's good looks and charisma.

The carriage slowed and Philip leaned forward to see farther out. "No comment?"

"It's true," I finally replied. "I can't refute that."

He lifted his eyebrows in gentle chastisement. "Then stop questioning Gage's powers of perception. He knows what you are and what you aren't capable of."

The carriage finally rolled to a stop. Philip helped me out and then escorted me up the steps and into the town house. Mrs. Pimms was coolly polite as she welcomed us to her home, and then I was left to my own devices as Philip separated from me at the door to the drawing room. I edged around the room in the opposite direction as he approached a small cluster of men gathered near the sideboard. I stiffened at the sight of Lord Gage standing on the fringes of the group, chatting with a viscount. If he was here, then I wondered . . .

"Fancy meeting you here," a deep voice drawled in my ear.

I turned to find Gage looking down at me, a hesitant smile quirking the corners of his mouth. I was beginning to doubt I would ever cease being dazzled by his attractiveness. He was flawlessly turned out in his dark evening kit with a roguish blond curl draped over his forehead, artfully arranged by Anderley, no doubt.

It took me a moment to find my voice. "I didn't know you would be here," I said softly. I hadn't forgotten that our last meeting had ended in an argument with me fleeing his carriage. And I was nervous that tonight would end the same way.

"I didn't either." He flicked a glance across the room. "My father believed I needed to socialize with a certain set of people."

I followed his gaze to the men gathered with Philip and lifted a hand to finger the gold trim of my Prussian blue gown. "I suppose one day you will be taking his seat in Parliament."

"Yes. I suppose I will," he replied, though he didn't sound particularly enthused about it.

"Philip has become remarkably absorbed with it all," I said, making awkward conversation.

"Yes. The reform bill. Among other things." He leaned closer to me, waiting for me to meet his gaze. "I'm sorry for yesterday," he murmured remorsefully. "I shouldn't have allowed things to end the way they did."

I flushed, still unsettled by the anger that had overcome us both, and keenly aware I was only going to make matters worse when I told him what I'd done. "I'm sorry, too."

His hand brushed against mine. "Perhaps we . . ."

"Mr. Gage," a smooth feminine voice crooned. "How lovely to see you."

He swiftly masked the annoyance I saw flare in the depths of his eyes with one of his carefully cultivated smiles, and swiveled to bow over Lady Jane Humphries's proffered hand. "A pleasure, as always."

She tittered and I rolled my eyes.

Gage's pale blue eyes twinkled at me, letting me know he'd seen my reaction. "You've met my fiancée, Lady Darby."

Lady Jane's mouth pressed into a thin line. "Of course. Though I'm surprised you showed your face here." Her large eyes blinked innocently. "I wouldn't have the nerve." When I stared at her in confusion, she leaned closer to mock whisper, "You know Mr. Pimms is great friends with Lord Drummond, and Mrs. Pimms used to be his paramour."

Only among the upper classes could two such contradictory things be uttered in the same sentence.

"And now you're accusing him of murdering his wife." Lady Jane's eyes were lit with spiteful glee. "It's positively shocking."

"I've done no such thing," I retorted. At least not publicly.

"Where did you hear something so absurd?" Gage bantered, but I could hear the tension in his voice.

"Oh, I don't know." Lady Jane brushed his question off as if it were inconsequential. "But it's all anyone can talk about."

I noticed now the cluster of women seated by the windows at the front of the house. They were all leaning together gossiping, and every once in a while one of them would throw a disapproving glance my way.

I couldn't stop my gaze from sliding toward Lord Gage. Our eyes locked, letting me know he was aware of my presence. Was he the one stirring up trouble for me? If so, why do it in such a way? Did he honestly think his son would fail to leap to my defense when he was just as involved in our inquiry into Lady Drummond's death?

He crossed the room to join us, showering Lady Jane with flowery compliments while he offered me only the tersest of greetings. Gage's eyes drilled into his father, but Lord Gage paid him no heed.

Instead he added fuel to the fire of Lady Jane's avid curiosity by raking his gaze over me and remarking, "I didn't know you were permitted in such circles. But I suppose having an earl for a brother-in-law covers any number of deficiencies."

"Sir," Gage snapped.

"Lord Cromarty has been very good to me," I replied calmly, unwilling to let him intimidate me or goad me into behaving poorly, especially with Lady Jane looking on.

"Yes, he has." Lord Gage's face screwed up as if he smelled something foul, and I silently wished it would freeze that way. "I suppose that's why he's pushing for a separate anatomy act, to make changes to the current laws. I imagine it would . . . relieve his conscience."

My eyes strayed toward where Philip was deep in conversation, his brow furrowed in concentration. "I didn't know he was pursuing such a thing. I thought he was focused on the reform bill."

"Oh, he is. But little good he does being all the way up here in Edinburgh while they're debating and voting on it in London." His tone was harsh.

I hadn't realized how torn Philip must feel at the moment. I knew he would never even think of leaving Alana in her condition to travel to London, no matter the existing tensions in their marriage. But he still must feel some anxiety to fill his seat in Parliament at such a crucial time. I knew how strongly he believed in the need for election reform. He discussed it often enough.

"You know very well why he's in Edinburgh, sir," Gage interjected before I could respond. "Let's not make an issue of it."

Lady Jane turned to Lord Gage, her bright eyes expecting him to do just that.

"Yes, he's pandering to his wife." Lord Gage sniffed in disapproval. "There's a reason men are not involved in such things. He can hear of his child's arrival just as easily by letter. It's not as if he's expecting his heir."

Rage spiked through me, but before I could defend my sister and brother-in-law, Gage stepped between us.

"I happen to find Lord Cromarty's devotion to his family quite commendable." His eyes turned hard. "It's too bad there aren't more men like him. Willing to sacrifice as much for their hearth and home as they would their country and their own petty pursuits."

If I had not been looking at him, I might have missed it, for Lord Gage had the same ability to disguise his thoughts with a mask of indifference as his son, but I saw the lines tighten around his eyes as he internally flinched from the blow of Gage's words. So the man did have a heart after all, for if he could be wounded, he could bleed. His gaze twitched to mine and then narrowed, displeased to discover I had witnessed his moment of weakness.

"Now, if you'll excuse us. There's a portrait I know Lady Darby would like to see," Gage intoned blandly, making it clear that he wasn't so much eager to show me the painting as escape our present company.

Nevertheless, he guided me down a flight of stairs to the hall beyond the dining room. The portrait was of little consequence and only mediocre quality, so I knew immediately that the true appeal was its location, far enough from the others to be private, but still in view of enough guests not to be improper. He stared up at it with his arms clasped behind his back and I joined him in his feigned inspection, waiting as he marshaled his emotions.

I shook my head at the painter's poor shading and sloppy arrangement of folds in the clothing. Rather than falling about her naturally, the skirt of the woman in the portrait looked as if it had been wadded up like a dirty handkerchief.

"I must apologize for my father yet again," Gage said. "That was abominably rude of him."

"You don't need to do that, you know."

He glanced sideways at me.

"Apologize for him," I clarified, rocking back on my heels. "I know you don't share his opinions."

He turned to face me more fully. "Yes, but I feel responsible for him." His tone turned sardonic. "Or at least for inflicting him on you."

I tilted my head, anxiety fluttering in my abdomen. "Well, consider that when you hear what I'm about to tell you."

His expression lost what little humor it had. "What is that?"

I cleared my throat. "I'm going to the Royal College of Surgeons tomorrow morning should you wish to join me, and then tomorrow night . . ." I braced for his reaction ". . . Bonnie Brock has agreed to take me to see the Chemist."

Red suffused his features and his jaw clenched. When he was able to speak, his voice was low with fury. "You contacted him even when I asked you not to."

I scowled and crossed my arms over my chest. "You didn't ask. You commanded. I might have responded better to a request."

He turned back toward the painting. His expression was so black that had the woman depicted been alive, she would have surely cowered.

My muscles tensed, waiting for a blow that rationally I knew would never come. But apparently the body does not quite so easily forget what the mind can reason away.

Gage saw it, and instantly his shoulders relaxed. A bleak bewilderment softened the anger snapping in his eyes. "You believe I would hit you?"

I shook my head, forcing myself to breathe deep. If I'd ever needed confirmation that I was right, his expression in that moment told me all.

"No. No, I don't." My voice trembled. "I . . . I don't know why I recoiled. Habit maybe."

As he studied my face, a tenderness I was still not accustomed to filled his eyes. He reached out slowly to take my hand, pulling me a step closer. "You still haven't told me all that Sir Anthony did to you, have you?"

I swallowed. "No. And quite honestly, I don't know that I ever will. You know the worst of it already."

He nodded in comprehension. "Then I won't ask, unless I don't understand. But if you ever want to tell me anything, I will listen."

"I know."

He ran his calloused thumb over my fingers. "Now then. I suppose it's too late to tell Bonnie Brock his assistance isn't necessary."

I grimaced.

"Right." His expression turned resigned. "Well, I guess we'll just have to meet him tomorrow night and pray he doesn't intend us harm, for I don't know if I can defend us both once he leads us into the dregs of Edinburgh." He must have seen the look on my face for he stopped me before I could argue. "Do not think for a moment that I'm going to let you go alone." His eyes narrowed on me. "But you knew that, didn't you? That's why you told me."

I shrugged one shoulder. "Maybe I just felt guilty."

"Perhaps. But you're also far from foolish." He looked chagrinned. "Sometimes I need to remind myself of that."

Which was all I'd wanted him to realize when he'd ordered me about in such an overbearing manner the day before.

We could hear the people above moving toward the staircase. Apparently dinner was ready to be served.

Gage laced my arm through his. "We shall do it your way then. But do not forget your pistol." His brow furrowed. "It may come in handy."

I nodded, though I didn't need the reminder. Since escaping near death twice in the last year, I'd taken to carrying my Hewson percussion pistol with me always. One never knew when one would be kidnapped from the theater by criminals or forced to ride out and save one's fiancé from bandits.

"I believe we'll be unharmed. This time," I added in a lowered voice now that the other guests were moving closer. "Bonnie Brock understands we saved his sister. His honor will demand he sees us safely to the Chemist and back." Or else I wouldn't have asked.

Gage didn't sound so confident. "I hope you're right."

I pressed a hand to my swirling stomach. I hoped so, too.

CHAPTER 15

Surgeons' Hall was located in High School Yards, not far from the old town walls. I had never visited, not having been eager to encounter any of the medical men who had known my late husband so well. Some were his colleagues, while others, like Dr. Renshaw, were former students and protégés. Sir Anthony was still viewed by some to have been a great anatomist, contributing much to his field of study, while others spoke of him with censure. The comprehensive textbook he had slaved away at so feverishly, and forced me to sketch the anatomical drawings for, had ultimately besmirched his reputation once my involvement became known, much like Dr. Robert Knox's standing had suffered because of his connection to the body snatchers-turned-murderers Burke and Hare.

A new and grander building was being constructed on Nicolson Street for the Royal College of Surgeons, but for now they were housed in the cramped confines of this brick building. The façade was lined with two rows of windows, and the uneven texture of the masonry would have perhaps seemed crude and stark if not for the softening effect of the landscaping surrounding the building. That and the lovely houses on either side gave the small square an elegance that belied the events happening inside its buildings.

My insides quavered as we approached the door. It has been nearly two years since I'd crossed the threshold of Sir Anthony's private medical theater, and I hoped I would not have need to enter a medical theater here now. But first, we had to gain admittance to the College.

Gage squeezed my hand where it rested on his arm, and I offered him a small smile of gratitude. I knew he understood my trepidation, even if I could not voice the words.

Our presence was met with disapproval, but we were allowed entry. Philip's letter had proved its worth, silencing the dean who was called to admit us. He ordered a student to lead us to where Dr. Renshaw was finishing a lecture.

My stomach roiled at the pungent odors of lye, ethanol, and decay, and I had to swallow hard to keep what little breakfast I'd eaten from reemerging. I pressed my handkerchief to my nose and inhaled shallowly. Too many painful memories were tied to that smell, and I was forced to battle them back with each step we took deeper into the building.

"Are you well?" Gage leaned down to ask in concern.

"Yes. Let's . . . let's just keep moving."

A group of young men spilled out of a room on the left, carrying stacks of books and papers. They stared at me in avid curiosity, even glancing back at me as they continued down the corridor. We waited for the room to empty before we stepped inside.

Fortunately, it was not an anatomy theater, but a sparse lecture hall, smelling mostly of old wood and ink. Dr. Renshaw stood hunched over a book, his pale sandy hair still a shade too long, curling awkwardly upward at his neck and ears. When he had been Sir Anthony's apprentice, I had forever been teasing him about his absentmindedness when it came to his appearance. His cravat had been perpetually half-tied, as if he'd forgotten what he was doing in the midst of fastening it, and his jaw often sported a strip of stubble he'd overlooked while he was grooming himself. These minor quirks had only made me fonder of him—a bit of much-needed humor in my dark world.

We were almost upon him when he finally looked up from his text, and his eyes flared wide in recognition. "L-Lady Darby," he stammered, almost dropping his book.

"Dr. Renshaw. It's good to see you," I said, hoping to set him at ease.

"Y-you as well." He clutched the book under one arm, wiping the palm of the other on his trousers. "I read about the closure of Larkspur Retreat. I hope what I was able to tell Lord Cromarty was helpful." His eyes darted to Gage and back again.

"Oh, yes. Thank you. It was. But that's not why we're here."

"Oh." He glanced at Gage again. "It isn't?"

I looked up at Gage, noticing for the first time that his expression was not exactly friendly. I recalled then how angry Gage had been when I'd told him about Dr. Renshaw. How he had been the only witness to Sir Anthony forcing me to sketch his dissections. And how he'd essentially taken a bribe from my late husband to remain quiet rather than report what was happening to a magistrate. I'd never held it against Dr. Renshaw, having accepted there was nothing he could have done. Sir Anthony's word would have been believed over that of a lowly assistant, and so Dr. Renshaw would have sacrificed his career while I suffered my late husband's wrath. But Gage had not been so forgiving.

I'd worried Philip had taken his revenge on the poor man when he visited him in October to gather information about a surgeon managing a lunatic asylum, and apparently Gage was now intent on at least intimidating him.

I elbowed Gage in the ribs. "No. It isn't." I smiled cajolingly. "I need access to the Royal College's library, and I thought you might be able to help me with that. We need to find information on poisons."

He snuck another glance at Gage. "For an inquiry?"

"Yes."

He licked his lips and nodded. "I . . . I will try."

I smiled brighter. "Thank you."

His cheeks reddened to a fiery hue and he bowed his head. He approached slowly, passing us on my side. "Is the poison mineral or organic?"

I met Gage's eyes as we followed him from the room. "We don't know. Will that make it more difficult to detect?"

"I couldn't really say. Though I read a fascinating journal article recently about new methods to chemically analyze mineral compounds found in remains."

I noticed his voice grew stronger when he was discussing things he was more comfortable with.

"But if the poison was organic, I was going to recommend you speak with the chair of the university's botany department."

"Dr. Graham?"

He stopped and turned to me. "Are you acquainted?"

"Yes. He's dined at Lord Cromarty's home several times," I explained.

He bobbed his head as if this made sense, and then turned to resume his stroll down the hall in short, quick steps. We had to hurry to keep up.

The library was like many studies in private homes, all warm wood and heavy furniture. Thick tomes lined the shelves alongside thin, well-worn volumes and rolled parchments. The scents of dust, paper, and leather warred with the aromas of past dissections and the harsh cleaners used to scrub away what they left behind, which issued from the rest of the building. Half a dozen men were scattered about the room, seated at the tables and in chairs, perusing the books. All but one, who appeared engrossed in a tome with yellowing pages, looked up to stare at us.

It was difficult to ignore them as Dr. Renshaw guided us toward the far corner at the end of the room. A man who looked too young to even grow facial hair shifted to the side as we approached.

"I think you'll find the information you're looking for here," Dr. Renshaw said, gesturing toward the lower three shelves. "Unless you have a specific book in mind."

Out of the corner of my eye I could still see the student staring at me. "Uh, no specific book, but we're hoping to uncover any poisons whose effects mimic the symptoms of an apoplexy."

Gage leaned down to examine the titles.

"Did you need my assistance?" Dr. Renshaw asked, rocking back on his heels eagerly.

"Well, if you have the time, we would welcome it," I replied, absurdly not wanting to disappoint him. In any case, three people could work faster than two, and a surgeon might know better what we were looking for, even if he specialized in the brain and not poisons. "But if not, we understand."

His eyes lit with pleasure. "For you, I would be delighted."

I returned his smile, though it was halfhearted at best.

Over the course of several hours, the three of us were able to winnow the list of potential culprits down to six likely candidates. Most of them were organic, so a visit to Dr. Graham would not be remiss. However, that would have to wait for another day. Time had gotten away from us, and I had promised Malcolm and Philipa I would spend some time with them this afternoon before my and Gage's rendezvous with Bonnie Brock. I suspected they had been feeling neglected of late, with their mother not being able to visit the nursery and their father distracted by business. They were allowed to visit their mother every day for a quarter of an hour, but most of that was spent in careful hugs and cuddles, answering questions their mother posed to them in an overly bright voice. A bit of fun would do them good, and hopefully distract them from their sadness.

In any case, I had enough information to quiz the Chemist intelligently, and to also be certain I hadn't wasted my favor from Bonnie Brock. I now knew specific substances to ask about, and should the Chemist prove unhelpful, Gage and Sergeant Maclean would also be able to better question the apothecaries throughout Edinburgh.

I thanked Dr. Renshaw, who declared himself ready to assist should we ever need him, and then we excused ourselves. The library had become suspiciously crowded in the hours since our arrival, but I noticed how carefully they cleared a path for me and Gage as we exited. I clung to his arm, disliking the sensation of being a specimen in a jar.

I inhaled deeply as we escaped through the front door and crossed the square toward Gage's waiting carriage.

"Better?" he asked.

I nodded. "That place. It just reminded me too much . . ."

"I know," he said, sparing me from having to finish my statement.

I exhaled, trying to brush aside the memories that had stolen into my brain like creeping vines overwhelming the exterior of a building. I lifted my arm to sniff the sleeve of my dress and shuddered. It was as if the scents of decay still clung to me. I would have to order a bath after I returned to the town house, or else I would never believe I'd washed the stink away. It would follow me into my dreams tonight, and those were nightmares I preferred not to relive. They had been bad enough after I witnessed Lord Drummond's ill treatment of his wife. Sometimes I felt I would never be free of Sir Anthony. I would wake in the middle of the night and still feel his hands around my throat and hear his foul-smelling laugh in my ear. Or I would struggle to emerge from a dream where I was standing next to his dissection table, unable to close my eyes or turn away as he pulled organ after organ from the chest cavity in an unending autopsy.

"He's sweet on you, you know."

I blinked up at Gage, realizing he had not followed me into my darker thoughts and I had lost the train of our conversation. "Who?"

He arched his eyebrows in gentle reproach. "Dr. Renshaw. He's besotted with you."

I frowned. "No, he isn't."

"Oh, come now. He was practically tripping over himself to please you, and the man dissolved into a stammering mess whenever you so much as brushed his arm while we were scouring those books."

"I'm sure he merely felt guilty for failing to help me four years ago," I protested. "And . . . I alarm him."

"Not in the way you mean." He held his hand out to help me up as we reached the carriage, but before letting me enter, he squeezed my fingers, and added, "You know the difference."

He was right, of course. I might have been inexperienced in romance and attraction, but I wasn't completely oblivious to such things. At least when it came to exhibiting signs as obvious as Dr. Renshaw's. I'd known he nursed a bit of a *tendre* for me all those years ago when he was apprenticed to Sir Anthony. It had been gratifying to my bruised and battered self-esteem.

It had also made it easier to accept his decision to take Sir Anthony's bribe. I'd rationalized that he must have realized how much worse it would be for me if he filed his allegations, only to see them dismissed by the magistrate when the official almost certainly sided with Sir Anthony over him. I still believed that, regardless of Gage's and Philip's opinion that he'd taken the easy way out.

"Well, don't hold that against him as well," I told Gage as he settled beside me.

He turned to me with a surprised laugh. "Now, why would I hold that against him? If anything, it speaks well of him." He leaned toward me to add in a lower voice. "He has excellent taste."

I dimpled shyly, still unused to being looked at or complimented in such a way.

Fortunately, he delighted in making me blush. He chuckled and captured my lips in a kiss.

It was a very pleasant interlude. And when I climbed out of the carriage at Charlotte Square, I realized how thoroughly he'd helped me banish those disturbing recollections brought on by our visit to the Royal College. I sniffed. Though I was still determined to bathe.

. . .

Gage and I arrived on Castlehill just as the leaden sky over Edinburgh faded to deepest charcoal. Ahead of us beyond the Esplanade we could perceive the massive silhouette of Edinburgh Castle. Its craggy stone was but a shadowy blur, felt more than seen, as it dominated the narrow cobblestone street. The buildings on either side leaned inward, seeming to close in on us as if they arched overhead to form a tunnel instead of stretching upward into the darkness.

It was surprisingly quiet. I had expected to hear the normal sounds of the inhabitants packed cheek by jowl in the tenements of Old Town sitting down to dinner or preparing for bed. From time to time we did hear a raised voice or the crying of a baby, but it was mostly the noise of Gage's horses snuffling or the jangle of the reins that broke the silence.

I had dressed in a slate gray cloak to avoid drawing attention to myself and tucked my pistol into the pocket sewn into my midnight blue woolen skirts. My eyes were the only spot of bright color in my appearance, and those could not be helped. Gage must have had similar thoughts, for he had worn a dark greatcoat and breeches tucked into his riding boots. He had even eschewed his fashionable tall hat for a shorter one with a wider brim.

We stood side by side next to the carriage, not speaking. His expression was thunderous because I had refused to remain in the coach. I had argued that Bonnie Brock might not approach if he did not see me. In actuality, I was more worried he would try something dastardly if he saw I was not standing next to Gage, such as to "mistakenly" shoot him.

I was just beginning to worry he had lured us there under false pretenses when a voice drawled next to my ear. "If ye were wantin' to poison yer fiancé, all ye had to do was say the word. I woulda brought the foul brew to ye."

I swiveled to see Bonnie Brock leaning against the black lacquer of the carriage, his arms crossed loosely in front of him. A wide unrepentant grin stretched his face.

Gage tensed and moved closer to wrap a protective arm around my waist. Bonnie Brock's eyes went cold as they shifted to him. I could feel the weight of their mutual animosity like the thickness of the air just before a thunderstorm. Matters were not helped by the three large men who emerged out of the shadows to surround us.

"How kind," Bonnie Brock murmured mockingly. "Did ye bring him along so I could take care o' him for ye? I'd be sure there wasna a drop o' him left to find."

Gage's fingers tightened around me.

"No," I told the criminal, narrowing my eyes. "And well you know it," I declared, determined not to show him any weakness. "I'm not a fool. I knew better than to come alone." I lifted my chin. "You wouldn't let me bring Sergeant Maclean, so I brought Mr. Gage."

A smirk curled the corners of Bonnie Brock's mouth upward. "I see. Then I suppose your note wasna a poor excuse just to see me after all."

I felt the stirrings of alarm, but tamped them down. "You said you would take us to see the Chemist."

He turned the full force of his gaze back on me. "*You*. I said I'd take *you* to see the Chemist."

Gage raised himself up to his full height. "She goes nowhere without me."

Bonnie Brock's mouth pressed into a tight line.

I lifted a hand to intervene before he ordered one of his men to stick a knife in Gage's ribs. "He helped to find your sister as well," I reminded him. "It seems only fitting that he should share in the favor."

Bonnie Brock's head tilted to the side, making his overly long, tawny hair fall over his shoulder. "From what I hear, he needed rescuin' as well."

His men chuckled at the jab.

He watched Gage for any sign of a reaction, but when Gage gave him none, he pushed away from the coach. "But I suppose we willna quibble. Ye willna need that." He gestured over his shoulder at the carriage.

I hesitated to follow, questioning one more time whether I was about to do something incredibly imprudent. Once we descended into the unruliest part of Edinburgh with its most notorious criminal, there was no turning back. And no way of knowing whether we would reemerge.

Bonnie Brock noticed, pausing to look at me. "But ye will need to stay close. I canna control everyone. But no one within ten feet o' me will harm ye." His voice turned hard. "The rest risk my wrath to their own detriment."

I swallowed and shuffled forward a step before I was able to even out my stride into something more confident and sure. Gage hovered just beyond my shoulder, cupping my elbow.

Bonnie Brock motioned with his head and one of his men moved up the street ahead of him. He turned to follow, not bothering to see if Gage and I fell in line. Presumably, his other two men brought up the rear.

We moved quickly but carefully on silent feet, darting around the corner into the dark channel-like passage of one of the closes that ran between the buildings. This particular close was more like a long slope than a lane, plunging ever downward at such a steep angle that it was like descending into the abyss. In some spots the buildings pressed so tightly together that only a single person could pass between. I glanced upward, but in the darkness I could not see the narrow slice of sky that I had to remind myself was above.

I wrinkled my nose against the musty, gut-churning stench. The rough stones were slick with any number of foul substances that I forbade myself to think about. I only hoped no one opened their windows above and decided to toss something out in those moments when we passed below. I braced for the shout of "gardeloo" that was supposed to proceed such an action. This was why New Town had been built—to alleviate overcrowding in the disease-ridden, packed houses of Old Town—but from all I had seen, the only thing the north section of town had provided was a more illustrious address for the upper classes.

We turned left and right and left through a series of fast turns, until I was no longer certain in what direction we were walking except that we'd continued downhill. Every once in a while we would cross a wider street and hear the sounds of raucous merrymaking coming from one of its establishments. At the third such street we traversed, I slowed my steps, trying to read some of the signs adorning the shop fronts to figure out where exactly we were. However, Bonnie Brock either did not want us to recognize our surroundings, or was in too much of a hurry to allow me to dawdle, for he grabbed my hand and towed me behind him into the next close.

I pulled against his grip, but he did not release my hand. Instead he murmured something to his man in front of him, who suddenly raced on ahead. Bonnie Brock also increased his pace, dragging me through another series of fast, sharp turns. I had to nearly run to keep up. By the time we reached a straighter stretch and I was able to glance behind me, I could no longer see Gage.

My heart pounded even faster in alarm and I opened my mouth to protest. But before I could speak, Bonnie Brock tugged me into a dark recess on our right. One hasty glance around me revealed that it was the opening to a small courtyard surrounded by buildings.

"Where is Gage?" I gasped.

Bonnie Brock lifted his hand and pressed it against the wall just over my head. He leaned negligently against it, crowding into my space. "Oh, is he no' wi' us? I did tell ye both to stay close."

I drew my pistol from the pocket of my skirt and cocked it. Pressing it into Bonnie Brock's midsection, I arched my chin upward. "Let's try this again. Where is Gage?" I bit out.

At the hard press of my gun, he didn't even flinch. "It's nice to see ye havena lost your bloodthirstiness," he drawled. "Though I did warn ye . . ." In one swift move, he gripped the barrel of my pistol with his left hand and pointed it up in the air and wrapped his right hand around my throat. He lowered his face so that it was mere inches from mine. There was no indolence about him now, only restrained violence. He growled in a cold voice. "Dinna threaten me unless ye mean to follow through."

CHAPTER 16

I swallowed, unable to nod or speak. The pressure he exerted did not cut off my air, but it was more than enough to frighten me, particularly as I'd never seen it coming. I blinked my eyes, fighting a wave of terrified tears, and prayed he would let me go. The darkness around us was so deep that even though I could feel the gust of his breath against my face, I could not read his expression to see how angry he truly was. His hand loosened around my throat, but he did not release me, instead backing me harder against the wall.

"Release her."

My heart leapt in my chest at the sound of Gage's voice. Out of the corner of my eye, I could see his silhouette. He was standing at the ready with his pistol aimed at Bonnie Brock.

Bonnie Brock slowly turned his head to look at him, still unfazed by yet another gun being drawn on him. "Ah, I see you've decided to join us," he murmured in his deep burr.

"No thanks to you," Gage snapped back.

"And ye were worried," he said to me with a tsk. "Ye should have more faith in him if ye mean to marry him."

My eyes narrowed at this provoking pronouncement.

"Stumps, Locke," he barked.

The two men that had been following Gage moved forward, flanking him.

"Noo, why dinna we all sheath our weapons. We've kept the Chemist waitin' long enough."

Gage hesitated, and for one breathless moment I was worried he was furious enough to do something rash. But then I heard the click of his pistol uncocking and he lowered his arm to his side. Bonnie Brock released my throat and stepped back, though he retained his grip on my gun barrel until he heard me release the hammer.

He turned to walk into the court as if nothing extraordinary had happened. And perhaps for him it hadn't. Maybe he faced down death every day.

For me, it was a different matter. I inhaled deeply, trying to calm my nerves, but my hand still trembled as I slipped the pistol back into the pocket of my dress. Gage pressed a steadying hand against the small of my back, as if he'd known I needed it, and we moved forward as one, following Bonnie Brock toward the far side of the court.

It wasn't until we were almost upon it that I saw the stairway leading downward into a shop in the cellar of one of the buildings. Much like Gage's workshop, there were windows lining the wall at ground level to let some light into the space. However, unlike Gage's, which were relatively clean despite the sawdust, these windows were grimy and coated with soot built up at the corners.

Bonnie Brock led us down into the shop, which I noticed had no sign to signify what it was. Stumps and Locke did not follow, but instead faded into the shadows nearby. I smiled wryly. If Bonnie Brock had men of this type in his employ, capable of disappearing at will, then clearly watching my movements was not a high priority. I found I was both relieved by this and annoyed that he still even bothered.

Inside, the shop looked like any other apothecary, just more poorly kept. Large jars lined the shelves on the walls to our left and our right, some empty and some filled with an assortment of herbs and other substances, none of which I would have trusted were fresh. A long counter stretched across the back of the room, blocking access to a door leading to what was likely a storeroom. Was that where the man kept most of his supplies? Was the front of the shop merely for show? Or did the man throw together concoctions made from the rotting flora displayed before us? If so, I doubted our ability ever to pinpoint exactly what substance had killed Lady Drummond.

A stoop-shouldered man hobbled out of the door to the back room. His hair was nearly all gray but for a few oddly spaced streaks of darker hair dispersed throughout. However, it was his eyes that were his most startling feature—wide and dark as pitch. Though as he came closer, I saw that it was his pupils that made them look that way, for they were dilated so much that only a thin sliver of dark brown could be seen around them.

"Mr. Kincaid," the man exclaimed. "So good teh see ye." His voice lowered. "Did ye need some more o' me special elixir to rid yerself o' another pest?" His eyelids dipped to half-mast. "Or perhaps yer here for yer sister again. How . . ."

"Nay. We're here for information this time."

"Oh," the Chemist replied, glancing at me and Gage as if he'd just noticed us. His eyes widened again as he studied us, though their expression remained curiously blank. I squirmed as his gaze dipped insolently down my form. "Ye need to rid yerself o' a bairn," he guessed, turning back toward his counter.

"No!" I exclaimed, before he could say any more.

Bonnie Brock's eyes twinkled in amusement, and I felt a blush rise to my cheeks.

"It's not that."

"Oh." The Chemist turned to look at us again. "Then it mun' be you, lad," he said to Gage, his gaze dipping low. "Canna make . . ."

"We need information about one of your clients," Gage interrupted sharply. "Someone who may have ordered a poison recently."

The Chemist glanced at Bonnie Brock, who nodded. "You'll have teh be more particular than that. There's a lot o' people wantin' me expertise wi' that."

Gage and I glanced at each other.

"They probably would have visited you early last week or the week before. Though I suppose it could have been earlier than that," I added, discouraged. Lord Drummond or whoever the killer was might have been planning to kill Lady Drummond for some time. I approached the counter next to where the Chemist stood and pulled out of my pocket the sheet of foolscap I had jotted our list of potential poisons on. I smoothed out the paper and laid it on the counter. "We think the poison was made from one of these substances."

The Chemist looked back and forth between me and the paper, but made no move to take it.

"He canna read, lass," Bonnie Brock told me.

"Oh. I'm sorry. Um, well, then . . ." I picked up the page ". . . arsenic?"

His head bobbed enthusiastically. "Me best blend. Like teh cut it wi' soot," he proclaimed proudly.

"Do you sell a lot of it?" I wondered if this man understood he was helping people to kill. He spoke of his product as if it were a special blend of tea or a precisely distilled whiskey.

"A few times a week. Sometimes twice a day."

My eyebrows shot skyward. I hoped some of those purchases were made to kill rats.

In any case, that was a large number of potential clients to sort through, and I had little hope they would have stood out to this man. "Then, what about May lily?"

He tilted his head. "If ye mean Our Lady's tears, nay. Isna the season."

I glanced over my shoulder at Gage. I hadn't thought of that. It was March, after all. Not all organic poisons would be in season, or made from parts of plants that could be stored for a long time. I wanted to kick myself. We might have been able to narrow this list down further ourselves.

I studied the remainder of the list. "I don't suppose monkshood is? Or . . ."

"No' the flower. But it's the leaves and roots that do the trick. I mixed up a nice batch o' devil's cap just the other week and sprinkled it into some cream. Scented it like flowers."

The hairs on the back of my neck stood on end. "Cream? You mean skin cream?"

"Aye. 'Twas in a fine jar. I woulda liked teh keep it for myself, for my collection, but the man insisted it had teh stay in that container."

"Can you describe the jar to me?"

"Aye. 'Twas aboot yay high . . ." he illustrated with his hands ". . . and had white flowers on each side of the writing."

I glanced back at Gage, curious if he recognized the jar like I did. "And you dosed it with devil's cap?" I wanted clarification.

"Aye. Or monkshood, friar's cap, bane o' the wolf . . ." he gestured impatiently ". . . whatever you high flyers call it."

I paused to stare at him, wondering if he meant to insult me, or if he just didn't understand what the term "high flyer" meant. I suspected it was the latter, for in my dowdy dress and cloak I clearly was not dressed like a strumpet.

"This man who had you put monkshood in the cream. Did he give you a name?"

The Chemist shared a look with Bonnie Brock and smiled. "Naïve, this one is? Nay, lass."

"Then can you describe him?"

"Canna do that either."

I narrowed my eyes. "Can't or won't?"

"Canna. He wore a hood and hid his face. But I can tell ye he was as bland as toast, and he spoke like a nob."

"So he was a gentleman?"

He shrugged. "Mayhap."

Or a gentleman's servant. Either way, it could have been Lord Drummond.

I thanked the Chemist and hurried up the steps ahead of Gage and Bonnie Brock, anxious to be on our way now that I knew how the poison had been administered.

"Ye have what ye need then?" Bonnie Brock asked, curiosity shining in his eyes.

"Yes." I began to turn away, but then stopped to add, "Except safe passage back to Gage's carriage." I arched my eyebrows in expectation, not trusting that the man wouldn't abandon us here if I didn't specify.

His lips quirked in amusement.

Our motley band resumed our trek, this time headed toward Castlehill. My legs burned from the exertion of walking uphill. I could tell little about our journey except that I was almost certain we were taking a different route than the one we'd taken earlier, and Bonnie Brock seemed particularly vigilant, pausing at each juncture with another lane or close. By the time we reached the long slope, my breathing was more like pants. At the top, I nearly collapsed, leaning against the wall behind me. Gage moved to take my arm.

Bonnie Brock stood to the side, his face in deepest shadow. "Noo we're even," he declared in a firm voice.

I started to nod, but just that quickly he had vanished. One second he was there, and the next he was gone. I knew he had merely dipped back into the close or turned into another wynd or passageway, but I still half expected to peer around the corner and find nothing there.

Gage helped me across the street to where his carriage still waited. We didn't speak until we were seated safely inside. However, when he instructed his footman to tell the coachman to return to Charlotte Square, I protested.

"No. Hanover Street."

Gage turned to me in surprise.

"I'll explain on the way. But we need to go to the Drummonds' town house. Now."

"As she says," he told his footman.

The door shut and we heard the hushed conversation of the servants just before the carriage rolled forward.

He reached up to turn the interior lamp brighter. "I take it you recognized that jar of cream our queer chemist described to you."

"He did seem slightly mad, didn't he?"

His eyebrows arched upward. "To say the least."

"Likely from all the poisons he's been handling. I doubt that back room of his gets much fresh air, and if he's handling substances like arsenic and aconite . . . monkshood," I clarified, "then he's risking exposure. Some of my pigments contain those things, which is why I always mix my paints in a well-ventilated space while wearing gloves, and sometimes a mask." I shook my head at the man's risky behavior. I knew of too many painters who had not bothered with such safety precautions and had poisoned themselves.

"But to answer your question, yes. I would wager quite a large sum that that jar of skin cream came from Hinkley's. Which is the type of cream I know for a fact that Lady Drummond used. She had them send a jar of it and some of their other ointments to Alana to help with her dry skin." I frowned, not liking the idea of my sister using the same product that had been used to murder Lady Drummond, even though I knew the poison had been added to the unction later, and so was not a risk to Alana.

He frowned. "I thought you believed she'd ingested the poison with her breakfast or by eating some of her sugared plums."

"I did, but if you'll recall we also read that monkshood, or devil's cap, as the Chemist called it, could be absorbed through the skin. That, in fact, there had been many incidences of people accidentally poisoning themselves by handling parts of the flower with bare hands." I paused, feeling something tug at my memory. "Devil's cap. Now where have I heard that name recently?"

Gage shook his head.

I sat up straighter. "Dr. Graham. I heard him mention them as being part of the new exhibit at the Royal Botanic Garden." I stared blindly at the window. "But how that relates to any of this, I don't know, except to say that the plant is indigenous to Scotland and obviously available nearby."

"I'm guessing you wish to see if a jar of Hinkley's cream is still among Lady Drummond's things," he said, leaning forward to catch my eye. "Then what do you propose to do?"

"Well, confront Lord Drummond with it, I suppose. And insist we have it tested. I'll steal it if I must."

"And if it's not there?"

"Then someone removed it, and there would have been no reason to do so unless that person was trying to cover their tracks." He opened his mouth, but I cut him off. "*And* it would mean that person has access to Lady Drummond's room. If the killer were someone from outside the house, I doubt they would have chanced sneaking back in to retrieve it, especially knowing that Lord Drummond has forbidden an investigation."

"Yes, but, Kiera, how are you going to prove any of that?" He pointed out.

"I don't know," I snapped in annoyance. "But we need to at least *try* to secure that jar of cream."

"You're right," he admitted. "But let me do the talking once we get there. I have a feeling we're going to have a hard enough time just gaining admittance to that house."

In the end it was not as hard as he'd predicted. Apparently, butlers rarely expected respectable members of society to rush past them. I admit, even I was caught off guard when Gage greeted Jeffers with his normal cordiality and then grabbed my hand and pushed past him into the house.

We hurried across the hall toward the stairs, with Jeffers calling after us. The sounds of voices and the clinking of billiard balls in a room on the right made Gage skid to a halt.

"Go on," he told me. "I'll divert them."

I watched as he turned to intercept Jeffers, and then I picked up my skirts and dashed up the stairs. At the top, I hesitated, uncertain which door led to Lady Drummond's bedchamber. The layout of this town house was different from Philip and Alana's. There were four doors on this floor instead of three. There was nothing to be done but to try them all.

The first door on the left led to a guest room, pristine and empty. I pushed open the door next to it, and startled the person lying on the bed inside. The light from the hall lamps fell across Imogen, Lady Drummond's stepdaughter, who stared at me with wide eyes.

"My apologies," I murmured, closing the door.

I ran to the door across the hall. Lady Drummond's chamber had to be this room or the one next to it. I only hoped that the voices and clinking below had meant Lord Drummond was still awake, and that I wasn't about to disturb *his* slumber.

Without even looking, I could tell as I opened the door that I'd found the right room. The scent of Lady Drummond's perfume wafted out with the swing of the door, and I halted, half expecting to find her inside, waiting for me to join her for tea.

Forcing myself to ignore the grief swelling up inside me, I crossed the room toward her dressing table. The surface was littered with bottles and jars of numerous shapes and sizes—perfumes, salves, balms, ointments, and even creams, but I could not find the particular jar I was looking for. I frantically searched the contents of the table again, clinking the glass bottles together as I shuffled them and knocking her hairbrush to the floor.

"What are ye doin'?"

I glanced up in the mirror to see Lord Drummond standing in the doorway behind me. His face was cast in shadow by the light behind him, but I didn't need to see it to know he was furious. I swiftly examined the last of the jars on top of the table, and then whirled around to face him as he advanced into the room.

"Get oot o' my wife's chamber!"

"Where is it?" I demanded, unleashing my own anger.

He glared down at me, his hands shaking in fists at his sides.

I suddenly remembered that this was a man who felt no qualms about hurting a woman, however he could, and here I stood challenging him as perhaps he'd never been challenged before. I caught a glimpse of Gage over Lord Drummond's shoulder, moving into the room, and that steadied me.

"Where is your wife's jar of Hinkley's cream?" I asked again, pointing toward the dressing table.

"What?" He shook his head, his brow furrowing in what looked to be genuine confusion. "What are ye talkin' aboot?"

"Where is the jar of Hinkley's cream?" I reiterated. "It's not here. Would your wife have kept it somewhere else?" I narrowed my eyes. "Or did you get rid of it?"

"The woman is talking nonsense," another voice proclaimed, and I realized for the first time that Lord Gage was also present. He must have been with Lord Drummond in his billiard room when we arrived.

"No, she's not," Gage defended me, never removing his eyes from Lord Drummond as he turned so that he could see everyone. "Answer the question, my lord."

"A jar o' cream? I dinna care for such things," he growled derisively. "And what does it matter?"

"It matters a great deal," I bit out. "And well you know it."

"We've received confirmation that Lady Drummond was poisoned by a substance mixed into her usual jar of skin cream," Gage explained.

Lord Drummond's pupils widened.

"A jar that has now gone suspiciously missing."

He shook his head. "It's a lie. She died o' an apoplexy."

"Then produce her jar of Hinkley's cream."

Lord Drummond looked at Lord Gage, who was watching the confrontation with a stony expression. "I dinna ken anything aboot creams. Ask her maid." He stomped toward the door to bellow, "Jeffers!"

The butler appeared almost immediately, making me suspect he'd been standing in the hall listening. "Yes, my lord."

"Find my wife's maid."

Jeffers moved off and Lord Drummond's gaze swung across the hall. Imogen stood in the doorway to her room, her pale blond hair hanging over her shoulder in a long plait. It almost appeared white in the light from the hall sconces. Her eyes were wide and fathomless, and I couldn't tell if this was because she'd already known her stepmother had been poisoned, or because sleeping in the room across the hall she'd already seen and heard too much ever to be surprised.

"Go back to bed," her father roared and she jumped.

She scurried backward and closed the door.

"Where did you get this confirmation?" Lord Gage questioned his son. "From a reputable source?"

Gage's jaw clenched. "Do you think I would have barged in like this had it not been?"

His father shrugged and turned his glare on me. "She might have convinced you to do anything."

"*She* convinced me of nothing. I do have my own mind, sir. Much as you'd like to forget." He muttered the last under his breath.

"Well, it's a damn foolish one," Lord Gage snapped.

Gage advanced on his father. "Watch your language in front of the lady."

Lord Gage's mouth clamped shut and he scowled at his son. He didn't apologize to me, but he also didn't argue, and I counted that as a victory. I'd anticipated some scornful comment about my lack of gentility, but apparently a title was still a title. Otherwise, where did that leave him?

"My lord."

We all turned as one to look at Jeffers. His face was paler than it had been just a minute before, and he seemed to be having difficulty speaking.

"What is it?" Lord Drummond snapped.

"The maid. Aileen. She's . . . gravely ill, my lord."

CHAPTER 17

I sprang forward, having a horrible premonition. "Take me to her," I commanded. "And if you haven't already, send for a physician. Not Dr. Davis." I glanced over my shoulder to glare at Lord Drummond. "Send for Dr. Robert Graham."

Jeffers turned right toward the back of the house and then, as if recalling who was following, began to make an about-face.

"It doesn't matter. Whichever way is quicker," I told him.

He turned about again and opened the door hidden in the paneling to reveal the stark servants' staircase. We climbed quickly past the floor where the younger children rested in the nursery to the servants' quarters in the attic. Aileen had her own tiny room, barely bigger than a closet, at the front of the house. One of the other maids kneeled next to her, but had not touched her.

I shooed the girl out of the way. She reached for the chamber pot next to Aileen's head as she rose, but I ordered her to leave it. It smelled acrid and foul as all vomit did, but it might contain clues that Dr. Graham would need should monkshood prove not to be the culprit. A trickle of additional vomit pooled next to Aileen's mouth as if she had been unable to raise herself to reach the bowl that one last time.

"Bring washcloths, soap, and a basin of water," I told the other maid. "It doesn't need to be warm."

Speed was of the essence. Aileen's face had yet to fix itself rigidly, for she grimaced in pain, clutching her abdomen.

I glanced up at the small table next to the girl's bed. Two bottles and two jars decorated the surface, one of them being the container of Hinkley's cream.

"Aileen," I said. "Aileen, can you hear me?"

She groaned.

"Did you take that jar of cream from Lady Drummond's chamber?"

She groaned again and then panted.

"You're not in trouble, but I need you to tell me now," I demanded in a firm voice. "Did you take that jar from Lady Drummond's chamber?"

She nodded.

I exhaled, wishing I knew what to do. Dr. Graham likely would not arrive for at least half an hour, maybe longer.

"I know it burns," I told her. "But try to stay awake. Help is on the way."

The maid returned carrying the items I had requested, having to push past the men, who huddled in the doorway watching us.

"Help me bathe her. All of her." There was no way of knowing where exactly she had applied it or if it had been transferred by her hands and clothing to other parts of her body. "The poison was rubbed into her skin."

The maid stared at me with wide eyes, but did as I ordered. I took up a washcloth and began on Aileen's right arm and hand, while she started on the left.

When I reached up to begin unbuttoning her dress, I glanced back at the door expectantly. "Gentlemen. Some privacy, please."

They cleared their throats and shuffled backward.

"Gage, take the jar." I flicked a look at Lord Drummond. "We don't want it disappearing again."

I didn't wait to see how the baron would react. I handed Gage the jar of cream and then resumed my ministrations, scrubbing Aileen's skin pink.

By the time Dr. Graham finally arrived, we had cleaned every last inch of her and lifted her up onto the bed. Her pulse was thready, and I had no idea if our efforts had done her any good. I hastily explained our suspicions to the doctor, who listened in shocked silence, and then I stood back as he examined her.

I thanked the maid who helped and sent her off to find herself a cup of tea, promising I would remain until she returned. If Aileen survived, someone would need to sit with her all night, and the maid was going to need some kind of fortification to do so.

I paced in a tiny circle in front of the door, feeling my anger build. Now that the rush to do something was over, I could focus on the fury I felt that this should have happened. If Lord Drummond had allowed us to investigate earlier, then we might have discovered that the cream was the culprit, and this innocent maid might not be lying here near death. He obviously hadn't wanted us to find it and be able to prove his guilt.

But then why hadn't he removed the cream from his wife's room after the deed was done? Or had he worried it would have been noticed missing?

I scowled and rubbed my temples with my fingers. I could feel a headache building behind my eyes, and it was not helping me to think clearly.

I looked up as Dr. Graham sighed and closed his medical bag. "Will she live?"

He glanced back at his patient one more time. "Only time will tell. But the fact that she's still breathing is a good sign. The effects of the poison should wear off further with each passing hour."

"So it appears that it *is* monkshood poisoning?"

"Its symptoms mimic other things, but if you believe there was monkshood in that cream she put on, then it's likely the culprit." He tilted his head. "Did I hear you correctly? You believe Lady Drummond was murdered by using the same jar of cream?"

"Yes." I explained the symptoms Lady Drummond had exhibited that I had witnessed and those that had been relayed to me by the servants.

The furrow between his eyes grew deeper and deeper with each second. "That certainly sounds like monkshood. Though it's quite rare for a person to absorb enough of the poison through their skin to kill them. But not impossible, I suppose." He tipped his head to the other side. "It's much more likely she ingested water that the flowers or stems had been crushed or soaked in. It could have been poured into her tea or drizzled over her food."

The book we had read at the Royal College had not explained this. "So she might have been poisoned by more than one method?"

He shrugged his broad shoulders. "Perhaps the cream wasn't working fast enough or she wasn't using a large enough amount. If her exposure was minimal, she may have only felt mild skin irritation, slight nausea, or a headache." His eyes moved to where I was rubbing my temples again. "Speaking of which, did you wash your hands thoroughly after assisting the maid?"

"Yes," I insisted. "My head is just pounding from all of these new discoveries."

"Understandable."

"The devil's cap you mentioned at Inverleith House. Those are a type of monkshood, aren't they?"

He nodded. "*Aconitum napellus*. Native to Scotland." He frowned. "And now that you mention it, we had a handful of our clippings at the Royal Botanic Garden go missing. I wonder if it could be related."

I had a hard time believing it wasn't. But who had taken them? The mad Chemist or Lady Drummond's killer?

The maid returned, and I excused myself as Dr. Graham explained how best to care for Aileen, and what to do if she grew worse.

I followed the light shining through the open drawing room door and paused at the threshold. Lord Drummond paced back and forth behind one of the settees while Lord Gage perched on the window seat on the opposite side of the room. Gage leaned against the wall by the fireplace with his arms folded over his chest and one ankle crossed over the other—a stance I was not the least bit surprised to find him in as he seemed to favor it whenever he was observing a suspect. To the less perceptive he appeared carefree and relaxed, but if you looked closely, you could see the watchful intensity in his eyes and the restrained vigor in his muscles.

I flicked a glance at Lord Gage again, noticing he displayed the same vigilant readiness. I wondered if Gage had learned this particular trick from his father.

They all looked up at me as I advanced into the room. "Dr. Graham thinks she shall live. She didn't absorb enough of the poison to kill her."

Lord Drummond's body went rigid. "But it was poison?"

I turned to look him in the eye, daring him to flinch from my angry gaze. "Yes."

He remained upright, his posture as stiff as a pole, but I got the impression that were I to approach him and push him with my finger, he would topple over.

"And it might behoove you to know," I continued in a hard voice, "that Dr. Graham believes that because of the manner in which Lady Drummond died, she likely also ingested the poison in some fashion, in her food or drink. All of which you conveniently ordered be tossed out during the hours following her death."

"That is enough," Lord Gage proclaimed, rising to his feet. "We shall take it from here."

My eyes widened in shock. Of all the nerve! Less than a week ago the man had derided me as a fool and ordered me to stop investigating, but now that I had proved I was right, that Lady Drummond had in fact been murdered, and just as I said, by poison, he wanted to step in and take over. I began to advance toward him to tell him exactly what I thought of his insufferable demeanor, but Gage spoke first.

"It's only fair that she remain. After all, she's the one who suspected murder."

"It would be highly inappropriate," Lord Gage argued. "Lord Drummond may be implicated, out of form, but he is also a peer of the realm and a man who served the Crown with distinction. I'm not going to make him suffer the indignity of being questioned by a female."

"Perhaps it isn't your friend's feelings you should be considering at the moment," Gage bit out.

Lord Gage reached up to straighten his already flawless cravat. "Be reasonable, Sebastian. Lord Drummond is far more likely to be forthcoming with the two of us than with Lady Darby. It's also clear that Lady Darby was far too attached to the victim to be objective. Send her home." His eyes lifted to stare at his son. "Or I'll insist that you both leave."

Gage jolted as if he'd been physically struck.

"I would suggest I'm the *only* one being objective," I disputed loudly, having difficulty restraining my temper. "Lord Drummond is your friend, and you've been protecting him since the moment you arrived in Edinburgh. I would hardly call your behavior impartial."

Lord Gage didn't even acknowledge my comment, but simply continued to gaze at his son with cold eyes. Gage's hand wrapped around my elbow, and I whirled around, pulling it from his grasp. The mask of indifference I so hated had dropped over his face, and I wanted to scream at him to remove it, for I knew what it meant.

His voice was soft when he spoke. "Perhaps you should leave."

"You cannot be serious?" But I could see from his expression that he was. "*None* of this would have come to light if I had not pursued it." I gestured broadly. "You all were happy to accept Dr. Davis's rushed diagnosis. To let her killer go free."

Gage lowered his voice, moving closer. "Kiera, please."

I lifted my hands to ward him off and stepped back. I could not believe he was bowing to his father's demands, after everything that had happened. It felt as if he'd stuck me with a knife, and each pleading look only twisted the blade in farther.

I whirled away and stomped from the room, slamming the door as hard as I could.

B y the time I returned to Cromarty House, my temper had abated, but not vanished. I stood in the middle of my chamber, clenching and unclenching my fists while my thoughts chased furiously around my head. Which was how Bree found me when she entered the room. She took one look at my face as I turned, and she hurried over to take my cloak.

"No luck?" she murmured.

I exhaled gustily. "Actually, we had plenty of luck. Perhaps too much of it," I added bitterly. Maybe then Gage and his father wouldn't have forced me out of the interrogation.

I filled Bree in on the night's discoveries and the state of poor Aileen. Clearly, Aileen had no idea what had befallen her mistress, or she would not have taken the cream and used it. I didn't blame the girl. Most of the jars and bottles on Lady Drummond's dressing table would be discarded. Normally there would be no harm in confiscating an item for yourself, though I doubted she had permission to do so.

"Poor lass," Bree echoed my thoughts. "One thing's for sure, I can promise she'll no' take something from her mistress's chamber again."

I nodded absently, still thinking of Gage's dismissal of me. Bree searched my face, but didn't press, though I knew she must have wondered just what had made me so angry.

"How are things here?" I asked, shaking myself from my fuming stupor.

"Your sister has been askin' for you." She picked up my discarded boots, wrinkling her nose at the smell emanating from them.

"Is she well?" I swiveled around to ask in alarm.

"Aye. As well as can be. I told Jenny I'd send ye to her when ye returned." She paused at the door to look me up and down. "I'll scavenge up somethin' in the kitchen for ye as well. Somehow I doubt ye stopped for a bite amidst all the excitement."

As if in answer, my stomach growled.

She arched her eyebrows in emphasis.

I knocked softly on Alana's door, worried that as late as it was, she might be asleep.

"Come in," she called.

I peered around the door to find her lying in bed, her hands crossed over her chest above the mound her belly created under the blankets. From the heaviness of her eyelids, I guessed she had almost been asleep.

"Dearest," she murmured. "Come sit beside me."

I closed her door softly and crossed the room to the chair positioned by her bed.

"Where were you? With Gage?"

I knew she was asking out of curiosity, not censure, but guilt tightened my chest anyway. Here she was, confined to bed, and I was gallivanting about the city with my fiancé, even if our excursions had been for a good cause.

"Yes." I briefly explained the events of the evening, leaving out any mention of our descending into Old Town with a notorious criminal or the danger we had faced. Thankfully, she accepted my whitewashed version of our meeting with the Chemist, and didn't ask for the details of Aileen's poisoning. I was also careful not to mention which cream had contained the monkshood or my rage-inducing dismissal by Gage and his father, but Alana was not unperceptive.

"So what did Lord Drummond say when you questioned him?"

"We're going to speak with him tomorrow," I muttered before

changing the subject. "Bree said you wanted to see me. Did you need anything?"

The lines at the corners of her eyes deepened, but she allowed me to distract her. "I wanted to ask what you thought of hiring a string quintet for the wedding instead of just having the organ. I know how much you love the Mozart quintets."

I felt the familiar stirrings of anxiety that surfaced whenever she mentioned the wedding. I forced a smile. "That would be lovely."

Her face fell. "Did I get it wrong? You do like the Mozart quintets, don't you? Or am I confused?"

"No. You're right. I do like them. Particularly Number 3. I just hadn't given it much thought."

She gazed at me fondly. "You were anticipating the same dry music. Not for this affair. Something much more lyrical is called for."

I turned away, lest she see how nervous her plans were making me. Seeing a drawing on the bedside table, I picked it up to examine it.

"Philipa said you were helping her with it this afternoon."

"Yes. She wanted to do something to cheer you." The picture depicted their family on a trip to the park—with father and mother, Malcolm, Philipa (with an overlarge bow in her hair), Greer, and the new baby. She had also included me with what looked to be a sketch-book tucked under my arm. I chuckled. "For a six-year-old, she's really quite good."

Alana smiled. "She says she wants to be like her aunt Kiera and draw people's pictures."

A warmth flooded through me, but I arched my eyebrows in humored skepticism. "We'll see how long that lasts. She also wants to be a mother. It's all she ever wants to play."

"Yes, Malcolm complained of the very same thing."

I set the drawing back on the table. "Has Philip seen it?"

"No. He's out." Her brow creased. "Or at least he was. Perhaps he's returned."

I could see the worry reflected in her eyes, and it made the fury I had only recently banked flare back to life. I vowed, no matter his protests, I would force Philip to talk to me tomorrow. This had to stop. His odd behavior was causing Alana more harm than good, and no matter his distance of late, I knew my brother-in-law did not want that.

I noticed her rubbing a hand over the side of her belly in fast, anxious strokes. "Does it hurt?"

She stopped, as if she'd only just realized what she was doing, and then resumed. "No. But it itches. Although that cream Lady Drummond sent me has helped immensely." Her eyes dimmed. "I wish I could thank her."

I smiled tightly. I'd considered telling her to stop using it, but if it was helping, then it seemed wrong to ask her to discard it just because the thought of her using it made me feel uncomfortable.

She yawned and I rose from the chair to excuse myself. Like a small child, she protested she wasn't the least bit sleepy, but I could see the drowsiness dragging down her eyelids. I leaned over to kiss her forehead, and then slipped out.

True to her word, Bree had left a tray of bread and cheese and an apple on my bedside table. I sat in the chair by my hearth and ate. However, rather than making me drowsy, as expected, I suddenly felt more alert. I doused my lamp and climbed the stairs to my studio. If I wasn't going to sleep, then I could at least be productive. Lady Drummond's portrait was almost finished, and I hoped by concentrating on it, my mind might be free to ponder our inquiry. I was always worried there was something I'd missed, some crucial observation, and ironically, distraction seemed to be the best way of uncovering it.

CHAPTER 18

I was still in my studio the next day when Gage finally came to see me, though I was no longer working on Lady Drummond's portrait. Sometime around sunrise I'd finished it and slunk back to my room to rest for a few hours. Upon waking, I'd realized I would drive myself mad if I didn't do something to occupy my mind while I waited for Gage to call. So I climbed back up to my studio to continue working on a painting I'd begun months ago.

However, as the day stretched on and I watched the sun rise and then begin to sink in the sky, the anger I had suppressed began to build again. Perhaps Gage didn't intend to show himself. Perhaps, like his father, he had dismissed me from the investigation entirely. By the middle of the afternoon I was so furious that I had to set aside my paintbrush. I was too consumed with hurt and resentment, which made my movements stiff and jerky.

Instead, I threw open my window, ignoring the chill in the March air, and set about preparing a batch of new canvases. The exertion of stretching the fabric over the frames and then coating them with an emulsion of gesso and linseed oil was just the mindless activity I needed. When Gage did arrive, I was making such a clamor that I didn't even hear him until he spoke.

"That smell is awful," he declared, burying his nose in his sleeve.

"Of course, it is," I snapped. "It's animal glue, chalk, and linseed oil. It's not meant to smell good."

He stared at the new canvases arrayed before me with a sickened look on his face.

I sighed in exasperation. "Either go or come. But shut the door. I don't want the fumes wafting down to the nursery at the other end of the hall."

He wrinkled his nose and shut the door. "Can't we talk somewhere else?"

I turned back to the task I was performing. "We could have. Had you arrived six hours ago when I expected. Or better yet, we wouldn't even need to have this discussion had you not expelled me from the Drummonds' town house like an errant child." I swiped my brush across the canvas in front of me in broad strokes.

"That's not what I did," Gage argued.

"Oh, excuse me. I meant to say, like an errant *wife*."

"That's not fair. You heard my father. Had I not asked you to leave, he would have ejected us both. He does not jest when he makes threats."

I rounded on him. "And just how was he going to eject us? Physically? Your father might still be healthy, but he's at least sixty, and no match for you." I set aside my jar of gesso emulsion and dumped the brush into a glass of linseed oil. "You bowed to his will, Gage. You fell in line and hopped to his orders just like you were one of his sailors. You did exactly what you said you refused to do."

"That is not what happened," he bit out.

"Isn't it?"

"No. We needed information from Lord Drummond, and I recognized that the fastest way to get it was by listening to my father. He was right about one thing. Lord Drummond is not comfortable around you."

"Because I actually stand up to him."

He exhaled in frustration. "I don't know that he would have told us anything had you been there."

I gave him a bitter smile. "I guess we'll never know."

He turned to the side, raking his hand through his hair. "I don't know what you want me to say, Kiera. I made a judgment call. Maybe it was wrong, maybe it was right. But what's done is done."

"So this is what I can expect when we're married? That I'll come second to your father's wishes."

"Don't," he ground out. "Don't make this another excuse for you to be afraid of marriage. You know that's not what happened."

I stared at him with pain pressing down on my heart. "All I know is that you could have supported me," I said in a quieter voice. "Your father has been despicable to me, and he and everyone else have been calling me a meddlesome ghoul for insisting that Lady Drummond was poisoned. Last night proved them all wrong, but instead of standing by me, you sent me away."

His face softened as if he seemed to finally grasp what I had been trying, but apparently failing, to say. I inhaled a shaky breath and turned away to clean my brush. The last thing I wanted was to break down in tears. With everything that was happening, I wasn't sure I would be able to stop.

I heard Gage shuffle a few steps closer. "Do you want to know what Lord Drummond told us?"

"Yes. Did your father let you press him about the suspicious information we uncovered?"

"Not as hard as I would have liked," he muttered crossly. "But enough to get some answers. I think he wanted to know what his responses would be as much as I did. It is *freezing* in here," he exclaimed, breaking off.

I glanced up to find him staring at the open window. "I am aware. But those fumes you were complaining about earlier would have been strong enough to make me ill had I not opened the window." I laid the brush down to dry and turned to look at him, leaning against the table. "The cold is easy enough to bear when faced with the other prospect."

"Well, are you finished? Can I close it now?"

I nodded. "But leave it open about two inches. The gesso emulsion isn't finished drying, so there are still vapors to smell."

I watched as he reached up to push the window down, admiring the breadth of his shoulders and the dashing figure he cut. As he turned to face me, I whirled around to carry my supplies back to their shelves in the special storage unit Gage had built for me. If I was as bad an actress as he claimed, the moment he saw my face, he would know what I had been looking at, and then I might never get him to answer my questions about their interrogation of Lord Drummond.

"So what did Lord Drummond have to say for himself?"

Gage leaned back against the wall beside the window with his arms crossed indolently over his chest. "He claims that he didn't know anything about it. That he truly believed his wife had died of an apoplexy like Dr. Davis pronounced."

"So he's claiming he's innocent?"

"Yes. When I asked him why he'd so readily accepted the physician's diagnosis even though it had been made in such a hasty manner, he argued he had no reason to doubt it. I'm afraid we can't dispute that." He scowled. "Though I would like to question Dr. Davis about it."

I removed my painting apron. "What of the allegation that he needed money and had already spent Lady Drummond's dowry?"

"He scoffed at the suggestion, as did Father. In any case, it's easy enough to verify. And I intend to."

I reached up to hang my apron on its peg on the wall. "Did he know if his wife was expecting?"

He shook his head. "Once again, he claims that if she was, he didn't know anything about it. I suggest we ask her maid." He paused. "If she survived."

I stiffened at the reminder. "I hope they would let us know if she hadn't." I frowned. "Or would they have alerted your father? And we already know how easily he shares information."

"I suspect they would send word to you before Father." He pushed away from the wall and cleared his throat. "Let me rephrase that. I suspect Jeffers would send word to you before Father." He skirted my table and the easel where the painting I had been working on was propped. "You were not with us in the drawing room while we waited to hear the fate of Lady Drummond's maid, but I noticed how much the Drummond butler disliked my father. He could have put some of the butlers I've encountered in London to shame with his display of haughty disdain."

"Really?"

Gage nodded, turning to study the portrait.

"I've never seen Jeffers behave that way, and I've been at the receiving end of more than my fair share of condescension from butlers," I muttered dryly. Servants, especially those of higher rank, were oftentimes far more snobbish than their masters.

"Well, then. I like him even more." He turned to me. "Do you think we could tempt him away? After all, we're going to need a butler for our own household."

This startled a short laugh out of me. "You want to poach Lord Drummond's butler?"

"Why not?" He shrugged, moving closer. "I'd like to know the staff I have installed in our house are loyal to not only me, but my wife. And the fact that he dislikes my father doesn't hurt." He stared down at me almost eagerly. "What do you think?"

I tilted my head. "I *think* you're straying from the topic."

He didn't look the least chagrinned, and I wondered if these playful comments were meant to distract me.

"So we need to question Aileen. Did you ask Lord Drummond whether his wife had a lover?"

"No."

I frowned.

"Given the answers we still needed to find elsewhere, it didn't seem necessary."

"Didn't seem necessary?" I repeated. "His reaction could have told you a great deal. Was he jealous? Secretive? Angry?"

Gage scowled. "Father would never have allowed such a question, so it seemed fruitless to ask. It would only have given Lord Drummond time to plan his response if it should come up again."

"Which, I suppose, means you didn't ask about his brutal treatment of his wife, or how his first wife died?"

"No. Because, once again, Father would not have allowed it. And the answers to the true cause of his wife's first death are better found elsewhere. If he'd had anything to do with it, he simply would have lied."

I reluctantly conceded that. "Well, did you at least find out whether he has a mistress?"

"Yes. And I can assure you there is no danger of her becoming the next Lady Drummond."

"Why? Is she already married?"

"No."

"Then how do you know?"

His expression grew wary. "Let's just say, she's not the type of woman a man of Lord Drummond's stature would wed."

I realized then what he meant. "You can't know that for sure," I argued. "After all, the Duke of Lancaster married an opera dancer."

"Allow me to phrase it this way: my father is more likely to marry a dairy maid than Lord Drummond is to wed his current mistress." Gage lifted his eyebrows in emphasis.

This silenced me for a moment, but then I couldn't help but ask. "Is she that disgraceful or is Lord Drummond that supercilious?"

His lips quirked. "A little of both, I imagine."

I nodded, wondering who this woman was.

He clearly sensed my curiosity, because he dipped his chin to say, "I'm not telling you any more."

I couldn't help but smile. He'd accompanied me into one of the darkest corners of Edinburgh the night before, and yet he was attempting to shield me from the scandalous activities of a member of the demimonde.

"I imagine I could discover her name in a quarter of an hour if I really tried," I teased.

"I'm sure you could. But it's not her name I'm worried about."

"What? Do you think I'll call on her?"

His eyes hardened in scolding.

My eyes widened. "You do. Well, perhaps I will at that," I declared, folding my arms over my chest. "I'm sure her conversation would be enlightening."

He stepped forward to stand over me and I arched my chin to stare him directly in the eye. "I know you jest. But seriously, do not visit this woman. She's not some misunderstood society miss."

I narrowed my eyes, not liking to be told whom I could and could not befriend, but I didn't argue. I understood how the rules of decorum worked. Women of quality did not socialize with courtesans and doxies, no matter how cultured they might be. Their husbands could discreetly do as they wished with them, but their wives were supposed to ignore their existence. Not that I was worried Gage was regularly mingling with such women. Sir Anthony had kept a mistress, but in his case I had been quite happy for him to take his attentions elsewhere. I hoped Gage would never decide that was necessary.

He left soon after, leaving me to contemplate how satisfied I was with his explanations, as well as the manner in which he and Lord Gage had questioned Lord Drummond. I still felt unsettled by Gage's easy dismissal of me the night before, but I was also tired of thinking about it, so I did my best to push it to the back of my mind and focus on our investigation.

I didn't believe they had pressed Lord Drummond very hard for answers, and I blamed Lord Gage for that. He still seemed intent on sheltering his friend. I scoffed. And he claimed *I* was the one who wasn't being impartial.

I paced back and forth in front of my easels. I wished I had been there. Even if Lord Gage had insisted I remain quiet, I could have at least observed Lord Drummond's reactions. They often told me far more than the words a person said.

My eyes strayed to the easel on the left draped with a cloth. I reached out and carefully pulled back the cover to stare at Lady Drummond's likeness. Critically, I knew it was not the best portrait I had ever painted, but it was still quite good. I thought I had done well to capture her essence. And when I looked into her eyes, I could almost imagine she was staring back at me, listening to what I had to say and forming a careful response, just as she had in life.

The portrait was not completely dry, and wouldn't be for almost a week, but I suddenly apprehended exactly what I needed to do. I was certain that if Lady Drummond had been alive, she would have been willing to risk this image of her likeness for the truth.

CHAPTER 19

"Lady Darby," Jeffers intoned, not looking the least shocked to see me despite my ignominious exit the night before. His gaze drifted over my shoulder to where the footman Johnny stood, balancing the large canvas in his arms.

"Lady Drummond's portrait is finished," I told him bluntly.

"I see." He stepped back to allow us to pass. "Lord Drummond is in his study."

I could tell from the shrewd look in his eyes that he knew exactly what I intended to do, and the slight curl of his lips at the corners told me he approved.

"Thank you," I replied, marching farther into the house with my head held high.

Jeffers closed the front door and then turned to lead us, but I held up a hand to stop him.

"First, how is Aileen?"

His eyes softened. "Improving."

"Good."

He dipped his head in response and then guided us down the corridor to the room I knew to be Lord Drummond's study. He knocked once and then opened the door without waiting for a response. I sailed inside, stripping my gloves off as I searched the room for the baron. I found him slouched in a coffee leather wingback chair before his hearth. One glance at the half-empty whiskey decanter on the table at his elbow told me all I needed to know.

"Over there," I directed Johnny, pointing toward the fireplace.

Lord Drummond pushed himself upright as I advanced toward him with Jeffers and Johnny in tow. "What are ye doin'?" he demanded.

Ignoring him, I stopped a few feet from the mantel to survey the ugly hunting scene holding prime place there. "Jeffers, would you mind removing that atrocious piece. I hesitate to call it a work of art." I screwed my face up in distaste.

"Of course, my lady."

Lord Drummond sat dumbfounded as his butler pulled down the painting and then assisted Johnny in hanging Lady Drummond's portrait in its place. There were two small areas in the intricate folds of her skirts that had smudged, but the rest of her appeared unscathed. I decided I could live with that.

Lord Drummond's eyes widened at the sight of his dead wife. "Noo, see here . . ." he began, but I disregarded him again.

"Thank you," I told the two servants, dismissing them. "I'll be but a few minutes," I added to Johnny.

He nodded, his eyes straying toward the inebriated baron. "Are ye sure ye dinna need me to stay?"

I smiled, appreciating his concern. "I'll call for Jeffers if I need anything."

Johnny looked to the butler and then, as if finding this acceptable, nodded.

Once the door clicked shut, I turned back to glare down at Lord Drummond. "Now," I declared, setting my gloves on the table at my elbow, and shrugging off my cloak. I draped it over the chair opposite him and settled into the seat. "We're going to have a little chat."

"And if I dinna want to?" he argued in a gruff voice.

"You really don't have a choice," I replied with an arch smile.

He scowled as his eyes drifted back up to his wife's portrait. I was stunned as the man seemed to crumple before my eyes.

"I failed her, didna I?" he blubbered, his Scottish accent becoming even thicker in his distress.

I was still so astonished, I didn't know what to say.

He bent forward, almost spilling the amber liquid in his glass, and cradled his head in his other hand. "I was her husband. I was supposed teh protect her." He rocked back and forth. "But she was murdered. An' in my own house." He gestured in emphasis. "An' then wha' do I do, but accept the diagnosis o' tha' imbecile, an' fail her yet again, lettin' her murderer go free."

Between the brogue and slurring, I had to concentrate to understand what he was saying. But in spite of it, or perhaps because of it, I thought I was finally hearing the truth from him. "Why *did* you accept his diagnosis?"

He waved his arm in a circle. "Because . . . because if she was murdered, then it was proof."

"Proof of what?"

"That I was a rotten husband," he snapped. "Do ye want me teh say it? I was a terrible husband. I was mistrustful, an' mercurial, an' I accused her o' awful things. Things I had no right teh." His eyes took on a faraway cast, as if looking into the past. "But I ken I always kept her safe."

"From everyone but yourself," I muttered.

"But if she was murdered . . ." His voice trailed away.

"Then you failed at that as well," I finished for him.

He nodded despondently, and lifted his gaze toward his wife's portrait again. I could see now that he had loved his wife, in his own warped, possessive way. Which didn't mean he wasn't capable of having killed her. Love was often an even stronger motive for murder than hate. But in this case, much as I was reluctant to admit it, I was starting to believe he had not been responsible for her death.

It was easy to cast Lord Drummond in the part of the villain. He was mean, violent, and bad-tempered, and quite frankly, I despised him. But his emotion was too genuine to be feigned, and his excuse for listening to the physician also made sense, even if I didn't like it.

Moreover, the solid evidence I had been building up against him in my head had already been shaken by another insight. When given more time to contemplate the events of the night before, I had realized that if Lord Drummond had been the killer, he almost certainly would have gotten rid of the poisoned cream at the same time that he instructed his staff to discard his wife's breakfast and sugared plums. It was the work of a moment to order that her room be cleaned and the oils, creams, and unguents covering her dressing table be tossed out. It was far more likely that the culprit did not live at Drummond House, and so could not easily return to retrieve the tainted jar.

I scowled, frustrated that we'd been forced to waste all of this time proving Lady Drummond *had* been murdered when we could have been searching for her killer. "You realize that because of you, the murderer has now had over a week to conceal his actions."

His brow lowered. "Had I believed she was murdered, I wouldna have hindered ye." His gaze fixed on his wife's portrait. "Who'd want to kill my sweet Clare? She never hurt nobody."

"You," I stated baldly.

He stiffened, but did not attempt to argue. He couldn't. He'd just admitted himself how he mistreated her.

"Why were you so terrible to her?" I asked, needing to try to understand. "She was kind, considerate, and had a wonderful sense of humor, despite everything. What could she possibly have done to make you so cruel to her?"

"Nothing," he admitted. "I . . ." His voice shook as he raised his hand to rub his eyes. "I couldna stop believin' she was like my first wife. Everyone admired Clare so."

And by "everyone," I could tell he meant men.

"She was beautiful and amusing and lovely. And whene'er I saw her smile at someone else, I worried it was happenin' again."

I watched him wrestle with how ludicrous that sounded, and all of a sudden I understood something I'd been puzzling over since the moment I met him. When first he had contacted me to request I paint his wife's portrait, I thought he was like most of society, more interested in my notoriety than my talent. A portrait by Lady Darby, or K.A. Elwick—the pseudonym I had begun using after my husband's death—was now fashionable. Which baffled me, for I couldn't comprehend how I was too scandalous to be tolerated one moment, and then desirably infamous the next. But I quickly realized that Lord Drummond did not approve of me, nor was he the least interested in my notoriety, which left me mystified as to why he wanted me of all artists to capture his wife's likeness on canvas.

It was because I was a woman, plain and simple. He couldn't tolerate the thought of another man spending so much time with his wife, much of it alone. He was irrationally jealous, and I suspected, if pressed, he would lay all the blame for that at his first wife's feet.

"Your first wife was unfaithful?" I phrased it as a question, but I already knew the answer.

He nodded, staring at the floor. "I dinna even ken if Imogen is really mine, and she was born ten months after our wedding."

"I understand your first wife died in childbirth following a fall down the stairs. Did you assist that?"

His red-rimmed eyes lifted to meet mine. "I ken she was carryin' a bastard, but I dinna kill her. Even if I woulda liked to."

I studied his face, trying to tell if he was being truthful. I noticed he had phrased his answer very carefully. He hadn't denied pushing her down the stairs, only killing her. This left room for interpretation.

Though whether he was capable of such deception in his current state, I didn't know. But I still wasn't certain of his innocence in his first wife's death. I supposed we would never know, for if a servant hadn't come forward already, they probably never would.

I arched an eyebrow imperiously, determined to draw this conversation to a satisfying conclusion. "Are you going to continue to impede our inquiry?"

"Do what ye must," he muttered in resignation, closing his eyes. "I'll no' stop ye."

I gathered up my things and left, hoping he meant what he said and would not conveniently forget our conversation the next day.

Johnny searched my face as I descended the steps toward him and the carriage. I appreciated his protective instinct. I would have to suggest to Philip that he should be assigned to assist Alana in the future.

Taking hold of his hand, I was about to step up into the carriage when I felt a creeping sensation along my neck that told me I was being watched. Night had fallen while I was inside Drummond House, and though the streetlamps had been lit, there were still pools of shadow all around. I glanced over my shoulder to the floor above, but unlike the week before, I could see no immediate signs of anyone observing me. In the bleak darkness it was not so easy to detect. I scoured the windows for any hidden vantage points, until I began to realize that the prying eyes were not scrutinizing me from above, but farther down the street.

I looked up and down the thoroughfare, but could see nothing outside the bright circles of lamplight. I frowned. Maybe it was merely one of Bonnie Brock's men. In these conditions, it would not take very much skill to remain concealed.

"My lady," Johnny said in concern.

I apologized with a tight smile and climbed up into the coach. As we turned the corner onto George Street, I twitched the curtains shut, but the unsettling feeling would not go away.

. . .

Upon my return to Charlotte Square, I was still distracted by the evening's events. So preoccupied, in fact, that I almost walked past Alana's maid, Jenny, without acknowledging her.

"Oh, Jenny. I'm sorry. I didn't see you there." I smiled at her, but then the import of her waiting here at the base of the stairs struck me. Panic streaked through me. I reached for her arm. "Alana . . ."

"Is resting now," she assured me. "But my lady was feeling sharp pains earlier, so Dr. Fenwick was sent for. He gave her some medicine and they subsided."

"And the baby?"

"Was kicking when my lady was in discomfort. Dr. Fenwick said there is no way to know for sure how healthy he is until he's born."

I inhaled, steadying myself now that I knew the immediate danger was past. "And you said she's asleep?"

Jenny nodded. "Dr. Fenwick said that was the best thing for her now." Her face paled. "He told me her delivery might be long and difficult, and that I should do my best to see she's as well rested as possible when the time comes."

I squeezed the maid's arm where I still grasped it, sharing her concern. "If she fights you on this, you let me know. And when the time comes, I don't care where I am or what I'm doing, send for me at once. We'll get her through this." Desperate determination constricted my voice.

She blinked back tears and nodded in understanding. Feeling an answering emotion well up inside me, I sent her off to find some nourishment. It simply wouldn't do for me to start weeping in front of the servants.

I stood, staring at the floor while I stuffed all my worries back down deep inside me. The house around me was silent, save for the occasional scuffle and clatter coming from the servants' floor below. I had missed dinner again, I realized. I wondered if Philip had been home to enjoy it, or if once again the dining room had sat empty.

My gaze was drawn to the light shining across the gleaming wooden floor from beneath his study door. I squared my shoulders, deciding it was high time we had the discussion I'd been putting off. I rapped once and then twice, and when he still didn't answer, I opened the door anyway.

At first I couldn't find him. A fire crackled in the hearth, but no lamps had been lit, steeping much of the room in shadow. He was not working at his desk or in either of the two chairs positioned before it, or searching the bookshelves that stretched from floor to ceiling. Nor was he at the window, staring out at the mews. It wasn't until I heard the clink of a glass that I found him stretched out on the settee in the corner to my left, half-hidden by the contents of the sideboard.

"Philip, we need to . . ." I began, moving in his direction, but the full impact of him brought me up short.

His jacket had been discarded somewhere and the sleeves of his shirt were rolled up to reveal the dark hair on his forearms. His cravat was draped carelessly over the back of the settee. One knee was bent so that his leg fell back against the cushions. His shoulders were wedged into the corner of the settee so that his head remained upright on the arm. The better to pour whiskey down his throat, apparently.

He was attempting to unsteadily pour from a bottle into his glass, which rested on the floor, though it appeared more liquid ended up on the wood than in his tumbler. He set the bottle down with a thump and nearly knocked it over reaching for the glass. I recognized the label as being a single malt from his family's Matheson Distillery.

First Lord Drummond and now Philip. What was happening tonight?

I watched as he drank a third of the glass seemingly in one swallow. "What are you doing?" I gasped in shock.

"What's it look like, lass?" he drawled in a brogue deeper than I'd ever heard him use.

I stomped across the room, lifting my skirts to step over the growing puddle of amber liquid. Snatching up the bottle, I was shocked to feel how light it was. "How much of this did you drink?" I demanded, shaking the bottle at him.

He shrugged, drinking more of his whiskey.

My insides quavered seeing him behave in such a manner. This was Philip. Strong and steady and dependable. Even during that long, awful night when we had both feared losing Alana while she struggled to deliver Greer, he had never wavered. The slovenly, thoughtless, reckless man before me was *not* my brother-in-law.

"What if Alana should go into labor?" My voice rose shrilly. "What if she should go into distress? She'll need you."

His face, which had been flushed red with drink, visibly paled, but instead of speaking, he tipped back his glass and drained it.

My hand flexed around the bottle. I wanted to throw it at the wall over Philip's head. Maybe that would knock some sense into him.

His arm fell back into his lap, heedless of the cup tipping sideways and spilling the last drops of whiskey on his trousers. "Go away," he moaned, covering his eyes with his other hand. The mournful note of his voice cut at something deep inside me, making my anger drain away, and replacing it with dread.

"Philip, what is going on?" I pleaded in a calmer voice.

He shook his head.

I moved around the puddle to the settee, perching on the edge beside his still shod feet. "Philip, talk to me. I . . . I want to help. I want to understand. Please."

I waited for him to respond, but he lay still and silent, and I felt the distance between us growing ever wider.

Until a soft snore issued from between his lips.

My shoulders dropped. It appeared he'd found the oblivion he was seeking. I lifted the bottle, considering drinking the last two inches myself. I grimaced and thunked it down on the sideboard behind me instead.

I rang for Philip's valet, Barnes, and stood over Philip with my arms crossed, watching the slow rise and fall of his chest as I waited. The problem between Philip and Alana appeared not to be lack of feeling, but perhaps the opposite. For it had not escaped my notice that the night my brother-in-law had decided to dip too deep was also the night his wife had suffered sharp pains. For all of his warmth, Philip was generally quite a stoic, but this hardship might have proved too much for his enduring nature. How could I make him talk to me? How could I make him understand? Before it was too late.

CHAPTER 20

The next morning I climbed into Gage's carriage only to find Lord Gage glaring down his nose at me. I turned to Gage, who was settling into the seat beside me, in surprise.

He grimaced in response. "Father was with me when your message arrived last night."

I had jotted off a quick note, letting Gage know that Lord Drummond had agreed to let us proceed with our investigation as we saw fit. I had suggested we start by questioning Lord Drummond's servants this morning. When Gage arrived to collect me, I thought his unhappy look was because I'd gone behind his back and visited Lord Drummond on my own. I'd been prepared for an admonishment once we were alone in his carriage, but it appeared I was wrong, or at least in part.

I would wager that some of Gage's displeasure was directed at his father. And that Lord Gage was going to scold me just as much, if not more, than his son was.

"Is this how a lady behaves?" Lord Gage demanded to know. "Disobeying orders, accosting gentlemen in their homes. *Alone*," he emphasized.

I rolled my eyes. As if he was truly worried about my reputation.

But he wasn't finished. "Making demands." His eyebrows arched. "Associating with criminals."

I glanced at Gage. Apparently, he'd told his father about the Chemist and possibly Bonnie Brock.

Gage merely shrugged.

"I'm sure it's not how London debutantes are taught to behave," I replied. "But it's how a lady investigating a murder does."

Gage spluttered and began to cough.

Lord Gage's eyes darted to him in irritation before returning to me. "What did you do? Show up on Lord Drummond's doorstep and demand entrance?" His gaze flicked back toward his son. "Or did you just barge in as you did the other night?"

"No. I simply delivered Lady Drummond's finished portrait," I answered calmly, with my hands crossed demurely in my lap.

My answer seemed to surprise Lord Gage, for he fell silent. Gage, meanwhile, was not fooled. Out of the corner of my eye I could see him looking at me. He knew there was more to my visit to Lord Drummond than that, but he didn't ask me to elaborate in front of his father.

Lord Gage narrowed his eyes, not ready to admit defeat. "And Lord Drummond just happened to give you his blessing to investigate?"

I smiled at him sweetly. "Yes."

He glowered at me a moment longer, and then harrumphed and turned aside.

When we arrived at Drummond House, Jeffers directed us straight into Lord Drummond's study. But before I could follow his father inside, Gage pulled me aside.

"You are magnificent. I've never seen my father routed so soundly." He leaned toward me, almost touching our foreheads together. "I wish we were alone. Then I could properly express my admiration."

My breath caught at the gravelly tone of his voice, but I was not going to allow flattery to distract me from the fact that there was still much unresolved between us. "Remember that later," I told him, before tossing him a cheeky grin and whirling away.

He caught my arm, pulling me back against his hard chest. "I will." His words blew warm against my ear.

I pulled away before all my resolve dissolved into a puddle.

Lord Drummond reclined on a sofa with a hand covering his eyes, much as Philip had looked the night before. The sight brought me up short and made my chest tighten in remembrance. I'd tossed and turned much of the night in worry, arguing with myself about what I should do. Part of me wanted to share my anxiety with Gage, while the other part cringed at revealing such an embarrassing episode. Philip was a private man, and I knew he would hate for me to share his foibles with others, even if it was only Gage. But for the moment my decision had been made for me as Lord Gage's presence had left no opportunity for such a private discussion.

Though disconcerting, Lord Drummond's pose was not surprising, as I'd seen how much whiskey he had already drunk when I arrived, and suspected he had imbibed more after I left. Lord Gage's stance, however, was somewhat of a shock.

He stood in the middle of the Aubusson rug seemingly transfixed by Lady Drummond's portrait above the fireplace. I crossed the room toward him, wondering what had so captivated his attention, but I hesitated to speak when I saw his expression. Perhaps it was a trick of the light, but his skin, which was rough and perpetually bronzed from his years at sea, now appeared quite pallid, and the firm line of his jaw almost sagged, as if weighed down. Meanwhile, his eyes scoured the image, as if absorbing every detail.

When he caught me observing him, he scowled blackly.

"Did you know Lady Drummond?" I couldn't help but ask.

"Of course," he replied gruffly, turning away.

"Stood up wi' me at our wedding," Lord Drummond mumbled.

I glanced at Lord Gage again, whose back was still to me, and then his son. "We'd like to question your staff. Perhaps we could begin with the maids."

Lord Drummond waved his hand. "Do as ye please."

Lord Gage suddenly pivoted in a precise turn. "Now, don't be so hasty," he urged his friend. His eyes narrowed on me. "Lady Darby might take you at your word. Sebastian and I will begin questioning the servants. Perhaps Lady Darby can sit here and sketch you."

My hands tightened into fists.

"Don't be ridiculous, Father," Gage argued. "Lady Darby has every right to join us. In any case, she will probably be able to get more information from them than we will. They know her. They trust her. And I don't intend to waste my morning talking to a bunch of stammering maids too frightened to string their words together properly. They'll be far more comfortable with another woman present."

My heart lifted at his defense, but Lord Gage was not so pleased. His face hardened in anger—mostly, I was sure, because he knew his son was right. Gage might have exaggerated, but the Drummond staff was at least accustomed to me, if nothing else. I had been a visitor here almost every morning for weeks.

Maybe it wasn't very noble of me, but I quite enjoyed Lord Gage's silent rage at being foiled, and from the manner in which his eyes twitched, I could tell he knew it.

I sank down to perch on the edge of a chair. "Before we begin, I do have one question for you, Lord Drummond."

He parted his fingers, to stare between them at me. "Just one?" he drawled sarcastically.

"Which you don't have to answer," Lord Gage had to say.

I arched my eyebrows at him, wondering if he was this intent on spiting me, or if he truly didn't want us to solve Lady Drummond's murder.

"The letter Lady Drummond received. The one you waved in front of her face that day during her portrait session," I clarified, not bothering to bite back my disapproving tone. "Who was it from?"

He didn't immediately answer me, though I could tell he understood. His body had tensed, I hoped in remembrance of his reprehensible behavior. Lord Gage remained silent for once, I assumed because he'd known nothing about this note.

"It was from a physician," Lord Drummond finally replied. "A Dr. Abercrombie."

I sat taller. "What did it say?"

"She'd asked to meet wi' him at his office, and he was informin' her of an acceptable time."

I wished he would lower his hand so that I could see his face. If I questioned the clandestineness of such an appointment—away from her own home with an unfamiliar physician—then I knew he had, and I wanted to gauge his reaction. "Did you speak with her about it later?" I held my breath in anticipation of his answer.

"Yes." He swallowed. "I accused her o' bein' unfaithful. I assumed that was the only reason for her secrecy."

My stomach twisted. I did not regret speaking up to stop his angry tirade during that last portrait session, but I had wondered whether it had done her any good. Hearing Lord Drummond now, I suspected not. I gripped my hands together in my lap to keep from leaping across the space and slapping him. "And what did she say?"

"She denied it. But when I demanded to know why she had asked for a meeting wi' the man, she refused to tell me. She insisted she couldna."

I wondered if Lady Drummond had lied to her husband, or if she truly had been harboring some other secret. One she'd been determined to keep, even facing her husband's wrath. But what could it have been?

Perhaps there was some clue in the note itself.

"Do you still have the letter? May I see it?"

His lips flattened. "I burned it."

I sighed. Of course he had.

"If there's nothing more," Lord Drummond said, swinging his legs off the sofa, "I'd like to retire to my chamber." His face, when I finally saw it, looked like it had aged ten years in one night. None of us tried to stop him as he hobbled out.

We decided the study would be the ideal place to question the staff, one by one, positioning them so that whenever they looked up, they would see Lady Drummond's portrait. Perhaps it would work on their conscience, if need be. Unfortunately, none of the servants informed us of anything new. Several of them voiced their hesitant suspicions about one person or another, but none of them had good reasons why. I suspected the murder had become popular conversation in the servants' hall and each of them wanted to be the person who had stumbled upon the real culprit first—because of a feeling a particular lady had given them, or a look a tradesman had sent their way. It was tedious and obstructive.

Thanks to Jeffers, who had a prodigious memory, we were able to compile a complete list of guests Lady Drummond had received both in her bedchamber and in the drawing room in the weeks prior to the murder. There were also a few of Lord Drummond's guests to contend with, and, of course, any number of servants had passed in and out of the rooms. In the course of describing her usual weekly schedule, Jeffers also told us that Lady Drummond had taken tea in her chamber with her stepdaughter, Imogen, several mornings each week, and the governess every Friday.

All in all, we were left with a list of almost thirty names. Lady Drummond had many friends, which spoke well of her, but not of our ability to wrap up this inquiry quickly.

When our interviews with the house staff were finished, we opted to climb the stairs to the attics to speak with Aileen before venturing out to speak to the coachman and stable lads, in their quarters above the carriage house. I was pleased to see she was seated upright, leaning back against her pillows with a book in her lap. Her eyes widened at the sight of us, and I held up a restraining hand before the men could follow me inside the tiny room. Gage and his father remained in the hall while I sat on the edge of the ladder-back wooden chair wedged next to her bed.

"You look much improved," I told her. "How are you feeling?"

"Well, my lady," she murmured softly. Her accent was English, and I guessed she had come to Edinburgh with Lady Drummond upon her marriage. "Thank you for asking. And thank you for saving my life."

"Oh, I don't know that I did that much. But I'm glad I was here to help."

She nodded. Her eyes were wide and serious.

"Do you feel well enough to answer a few questions?"

She glanced toward the door anxiously. "I suppose." Her voice was hesitant, and I realized that she was worried she was in some sort of trouble.

I offered her a reassuring smile. "We don't care that you borrowed her ladyship's beauty creams. I'm sure Lady Drummond would have liked for you to have them rather than them being thrown in the rubbish bin. But I'm sure you understand now that the jar of Hinkley's cream was poisoned."

Her large brown eyes blinked back tears. "That's what killed her?"

"Yes, at least partly." I looked to Gage, who watched from the doorway. "We're trying to figure out who did it. But we need your help. Do you know how that jar of cream found its way into Lady Drummond's bedchamber?"

"I unpacked a jar of cream the store had delivered a few weeks ago."

"Did Lady Drummond open a new jar the morning she died?"

"No, my lady. She had been using the same one since it was delivered. It wasn't even half gone."

I tilted my head. "Was the jar you used filled about the same?"

She nodded.

So the cream had not been delivered tainted, but swapped at some point.

"Tell me about that morning. The morning Lady Drummond died."

She crossed her hands over her lap. "Her ladyship woke up at nine, like she always does . . . did." Her face tightened in pain. "An . . . and I took up her breakfast."

"What did she eat?"

"Tea, eggs, toast, and kippers. Like every morning."

"Really? An Englishwoman who liked kippers for breakfast?"

Aileen scrunched up her face in revulsion. "I never knew how she could eat them. They're so slimy. And they smell horrid."

I bit back a smile. "What next?"

"I readied her clothes for the day and drew her bath."

"Sometimes I like to scent my baths with rosewater. Did Lady Drummond ever ask you to put anything in hers?"

She nodded. "She used rosewater, too. And if her wrist or hip was bothering her, I would pour in a bit of lavender oil."

I frowned. "Did she injure herself?"

Her expression went blank. "She fell once," she replied vaguely.

I bit my tongue, knowing exactly what that meant.

"Did you put anything in her bath that morning?"

"Yes. The lavender oil."

I began to turn to Gage, but then stopped and looked at Aileen's table instead. "Is it still in her room?"

Her cheeks flushed a delicate pink. "It should be."

"On my way," Gage said, already anticipating my request.

"Then what happened?" I asked.

"She bathed and slathered on her cream, and then I helped her dress." Her face paled. "I was gathering up the linens to take them belowstairs when I heard her retching."

"Did she show any signs of illness before that?"

"She did look a bit flushed, but I thought it was from the bath." Her eyes widened. "And she kept scratching her skin, especially her hands. She actually rubbed some more cream into them." She fell silent, pressing a hand to her mouth. "I didn't know."

"You couldn't have," I assured her. "It's winter. The air is dry. You had no reason to believe her skin itched because she was rubbing poison into it."

She nodded, but I was sure my assertions meant nothing. She blamed herself, and would go on doing so for some time no matter what I said.

I glanced toward the door, wishing Lord Gage were not hovering there at this moment. "I have a somewhat delicate question to ask you," I began.

Aileen's gaze lifted to meet mine, but there was no hint in her eyes that she knew what I implied.

"Was Lady Drummond expecting?"

Her brow furrowed. "A child?"

I nodded.

"I don't think so. And I should have noticed if she was. I was the first to suspect it with Master Freddy, and I knew within a week with Miss Victoria."

I believed her. It was a lady's maid's job to notice even the most subtle changes in her mistress, and to make whatever alterations were necessary to keep her looking her best. They often knew when their mistress was ill, or increasing, or low in spirits long before their husbands.

"One more question. And I'm sorry to be impertinent. I assure you I wouldn't ask if it wasn't necessary. Did Lady Drummond have a lover?"

Her eyes widened. "Not that I knew of. Though . . ." She squirmed uncomfortably. "I did hear her discussing it with Lady Rachel Radcliffe. I . . . I think she was considering it."

I thanked Aileen for her help and then we left her to rest. Gage was standing in the hall with his father when I joined them. He held up a vial of clear liquid.

"The lavender oil?"

He nodded. "Our Chemist friend failed to mention it."

"Maybe it's not the other source of the poison."

He looked doubtful. "Maybe. But we still need to test it."

I agreed. "I'm sure Dr. Graham will be happy to help. Though, once again, it's absorbed, not ingested," I pointed out.

"Yes. But between the oil and the cream, that's a heavy dose being absorbed all at once."

"True."

"And she may have ingested a few drops of the tainted water while she bathed. It would be easy to do."

I nodded, though I questioned whether it was enough. Gage could tell.

"I'll ask Dr. Graham what his opinion is, and if he thinks we're still missing something, we'll keep looking."

"Except the food has long since been thrown out," Lord Gage interjected unhelpfully.

I sighed. "Either way, we may never know for certain. But it's a start."

I joined the men as they questioned the stable lads in the tack room of the carriage house, but it swiftly became evident I was only hindering matters. I wasn't sure whether the boys were aware of my reputation, but it was clear they were not used to speaking to ladies. They stumbled over their words, trying to answer without using inappropriate slang—most of which was harmless if somewhat coarse and confusing. I suspected someone had been coaching them on suitable language to be used in front of gentlewomen, but in their excitement they had difficulty employing it. Though commendable, these efforts only wasted our time.

So I left Gage and his father to finish questioning the outside staff while I returned to the house. I'd thought of something else to ask Jeffers and gone in search of him. When I couldn't locate him in the front hall, I decided to pull the bell rope in one of the nearest rooms and wait for him to appear. I ducked into the study and was crossing toward the cord when I saw the room was occupied.

Imogen stood in the middle of the rug, much as Lord Gage had, staring up at the portrait of her stepmother. Her head was tilted to the side, making her long, wheat blond hair fall over her shoulder. She stiffened as she heard me enter and turned to glance over her shoulder at me. Tears glistened on her lashes. At the sight of me, her shoulders relaxed, and I could only surmise she had been worried I was her father.

I slowly approached her, feeling somehow that if I made any sudden movements I would unnerve her and send her scurrying from the room. She reminded me of a fawn, with her sad, dark eyes surrounded by long lashes, her pert nose, and her petite bone structure. She was dressed all in black, which only diminished her frame even more.

I didn't speak, merely moved forward to join her in her contemplation of the portrait. Though, truth be told, I think we were both contemplating each other more. I watched Imogen from the corner of my eye, catching the looks she continued to send my way. Remembering the way she had stared down at me from the stairs and the window that day when I collected the portrait, I suspected she was working up the courage to speak, so I waited patiently.

And was rewarded when she asked in a timid voice, "She was murdered, wasn't she?"

I turned to look at her.

"I . . . I heard the servants talking. They said you proved it was murder."

I nodded. "I'm sorry."

Her composure, already so fragile, crumpled further. "Do you know who did it?"

"Not yet. That's what we're trying to find out."

She swallowed and her gaze fell to my neck. "I may know something important."

The skin along my arms prickled. "Yes?"

She gazed up at me through her impossibly long lashes. "I take . . ." Her face scrunched up in pain. "I took tea with my stepmother every Monday and Thursday, and as I was leaving her chamber on Monday, I noticed she had another visitor." Her voice dropped to almost a whisper. "I'm almost certain it was my father's mistress."

"Why do you think that?"

"Because I heard two of the maids discussing it in the hall. They didn't know I was there. The one maid was scolding the other for sneaking the master's doxy up to see her ladyship. She said she deserved to lose her place."

"And how did the girl respond?" I asked, wondering why I hadn't heard any of this from the servants themselves.

"She offered to split the money she'd earned for sneaking the woman up." Imogen began to run her hands over and over a strand of her hair. "Do . . . do you think she was the one who put poison in her cream?" Her voice trembled at the end.

"I don't know. But I'm going to find out," I assured her. "Thank you for telling me."

She sniffed and nodded, looking up again at the portrait of her stepmother in longing.

"You loved her," I said, having wondered at the relationship between them. I knew Lady Drummond well enough to predict she had loved Imogen as her own, but the stepdaughter was largely unfamiliar to me.

"She was kind to me," she responded simply.

"And not everyone is?" I guessed.

She wrapped her arms around her torso and shook her head.

I hesitated, not knowing how to ask what I needed to, but ultimately I could not remain silent. "Your father. Does he . . . hurt you?"

Her face flushed. "Like he did my stepmother? No." Her eyes dipped again. "I think he prefers to believe I don't exist."

As painful as that must have been, I couldn't help but wonder if it was better than the alternative.

"There you are!"

Imogen jumped at the boom of Gage's voice. He took in the scene at once, tempering his expression. But the fawn had already been startled.

"Please, excuse me," she murmured, fleeing the room with her head bowed as she edged through the door past Lord Gage.

"What was that about?" Gage asked once she was gone.

"I'll explain in the carriage."

CHAPTER 21

O n the carriage drive to Dr. Abercrombie's home, which we quickly discovered was on Henderson Row, Gage and his father informed me of what little information the coachman and stable lads had been able to provide, and I told them what Imogen had confided in me.

When I had finished, Lord Gage turned to his son with a grim expression. "Then I suppose we shall have to pay a visit to Mrs. Dubois."

Anticipating an argument, I didn't say anything then, but I was not about to be left out of their conversation with Mrs. Dubois, no matter how scandalous it would be.

Surprisingly, no one fought my attending the interview of Dr. Abercrombie. Whether it was because of my background or the fact that I was a female, I was not about to question Lord Gage's acquiescence. Nor did I make the mistake of believing he had finally accepted my assets as an investigator. I was just glad to be included without having to battle for it.

Dr. Abercrombie was closeted with a patient in his study when we arrived, so we were shown into his drawing room to wait. We passed a quarter of an hour in uncomfortable silence. I'm certain we all should have liked to discuss the inquiry, but we were ever conscious that we were in a stranger's home and we had no way of knowing whether the physician's staff was eavesdropping.

I tried to occupy my time by identifying the species of each of the porcelain bird figurines decorating the surfaces of the room. They were quite lovely, if a trifle excessive. The collection was delicate and feminine, and almost certainly his wife's, except that I knew Dr. Abercrombie to be an old widower. I couldn't decide whether they were actually his, if he'd left them out for sentimental reasons, or if he simply couldn't be bothered to redecorate.

Dr. Abercrombie himself was a rather large man, with just the beginnings of a rounded stomach. His grizzled facial hair was thick and prodigious and his spectacles crooked, leaning toward one side of his face. I hid a smile. He reminded me a bit of my rather absent-minded uncle who lived in southern England, buried in his books much of the time or blundering about the countryside.

Once the introductions were made, Gage explained the reason for our visit. "You received a letter from Lady Drummond, we believe, requesting an appointment with you. Do you recall?"

"Why, yes," he declared, seeming to expand in his chair as he talked. "Verra brief, it was. Wanted to meet wi' me aboot an urgent matter, but made no mention of what that was."

"Not even a hint?" Lord Gage interjected.

He shook his head. "Nay. But ye can see for yourself, if ye wish."

Gage said we would. "But first, can you tell us, do you have any prior acquaintance with Lady Drummond?"

"Nay. I may have heard her name, but I dinna ever recall meeting her. It's hard to forget the nobility."

I shifted in my seat, frustrated with the lack of answers we were uncovering. Gage saw it and tried one more line of inquiry, even though it was dubious.

"Can you speculate on why she might have contacted you?"

Dr. Abercrombie leaned against the wooden arm of his chair, which creaked. "Well, lad, I can speculate all ye wish, but that's no' goin' to give ye any answers."

He was right. It was a futile exercise. She could have been hiding an illness, or gathering information for a friend. She could have wanted a second opinion on something Dr. Davis had diagnosed for her. Not all of the potential reasons for her coming here were in any way scandalous or nefarious, and there was no way to know whether it had anything to do with her murder. Just because she had been guarded, and her husband had grown angry upon his discovery of her appointment, did not mean it was connected to her poisoning.

We thanked the physician for his time and, after collecting the letter, departed.

Gage sighed and passed me the missive. "He's right. It's short and to the point."

"And worthless to pursue further," Lord Gage added, dismissing it from his mind. "Shall we return Lady Darby to Charlotte Square and venture to Mrs. Dubois's?"

I refolded Lady Drummond's letter. "I believe I'll accompany you."

Gage scowled. "You cannot be serious."

"I am," I answered calmly. "I think a woman's point of view could be beneficial for this interview."

"Yet highly inappropriate."

"I'm well aware. But you can't tell me that given Mrs. Dubois's profession, she isn't a gifted actress, particularly adept at manipulating men. She wouldn't be so successful if she was not."

Gage's brow lowered. "Are you implying that she will bamboozle us?"

"Of course not. I'm merely suggesting that a woman will see things differently than a man. And since our murder victim was a woman, it might be useful to observe how she interacts with another female." I stared at him with wide eyes, daring him to argue.

Lord Gage startled us both when he gave a bark of laughter. "Oh, let her come. She already associates with criminals. Meeting a courtesan can hardly tarnish her reputation further."

I didn't know whether to be grateful for his interference on my behalf or apprehensive of his intentions in giving in. Given the way he had treated me since his arrival in Edinburgh, I chose the latter. But I remained silent, hoping Gage would be too stunned to argue further.

In the end, his father didn't allow him time to object. He rapped against the carriage wall at the back of his head and shouted an address up to the coachman.

"How do you know where Mrs. Dubois lives?" Gage eyed his father suspiciously.

His father didn't reply, instead turning to stare out the window at the passing town houses, resting his hands one over the other on the head of his cane.

"You're acquainted with her." Gage spoke in a flat voice. When his father still did not answer, he snapped, "You might as well tell us. We're about to find out."

Lord Gage's jaw tensed. "Yes. I am *acquainted* with Mrs. Dubois. Or more accurately some of her . . . friendly neighbors."

I blushed at the implication.

"You've been in Edinburgh for barely a week," Gage leaned forward to hiss.

Lord Gage finally turned to look at him. "Oh, don't be such a green lad, Sebastian."

I could tell Gage was biting back hot words, for the vein in his temple throbbed.

Before he could formulate a calmer response, the carriage rolled to a stop before an unobtrusive little town house. The street was quiet. Quaint, even. Not the sort of place I had expected members of the demimonde to live. But, of course, I knew very little of these women's lives. As Gage had said, it was inappropriate for gentlewomen to speak of them or be spoken to about them, so everything I'd gathered had been through idle gossip.

I knew that many gentlemen kept mistresses, and that their wives were supposed to accept it as inevitable and learn to overlook it. Some wives were even afforded the same liberty to conduct an affair with another gentleman, after they had given birth to the requisite two male children, of course—an heir and a spare. And society basically approved this behavior, so long as everyone involved was discreet. It was when one of the parties involved overstepped themselves or behaved too conspicuously that scandal resulted.

Philip and Alana's loving, committed marriage unfortunately seemed to be in the minority among the members of the upper class. And now even that seemed uncertain. I glanced at Gage as he pulled my arm through his and guided me up the stairs to Mrs. Dubois's door. Was a loyal, lasting marriage even possible? Or was every relationship doomed to fail at some point or another? It was a distressing thought. And one I did not have the leisure to contemplate at the moment.

A rather normal-looking butler opened the door and nodded as if two gentlemen and a lady came to call on Mrs. Dubois every day. He showed us into the drawing room, and offered us tea or something stronger, before leaving to inform his employer of our presence.

I hesitated at the threshold, somewhat taken aback by the room's décor. I could only assume Mrs. Dubois was a fan of ancient Egypt, for the room was a shrine to the now dead empire. The walls and the tables were covered in sculptures and busts of gods and other bizarre creatures in gold and ebony. I leaned closer to examine a statue of what looked to be a lion's body with a man's head in a long headdress. Except it was all fake. Cheap imitations of what I assumed were real Egyptian treasures.

However, the dark furniture with gold inlay was certainly authentic. As were the delicate linens and silks draped over fainting couches and cascading from the ceiling to create private little nooks in the corners of the room.

I allowed Gage to lead me toward where Lord Gage had already taken a seat in a spindly-legged chair. I perched on one of the sofas adjacent to him, unable to stop myself from craning my neck to see everything in the room. It was overwhelming and yet fascinating all at once.

We did not have to wait long for Mrs. Dubois to appear. Given the room's outlandish décor, I expected her to be a gaudily dressed, flamboyant woman. Instead, I encountered a softly beautiful woman, not many years older than Alana, clothed in an amethyst silk morning gown. The material draped and clung to display her figure to the best advantage, but it was neither vulgar nor distasteful. I'd seen many women of the ton wear things far more revealing. A simple amethyst teardrop adorened her neck and I reached up to wrap my fingers around my own amethyst pendant. Mine was smaller in size, but being my late mother's, of great sentimental value.

"What a lovely surprise," she proclaimed with a melting smile. Her eyes surveyed each of us quickly, but she did not reveal by even the flicker of an eyelash that she was in any way shocked or alarmed by our presence. One would have assumed that she entertained inquiry agents and gentlewomen every day.

Gage and Lord Gage rose to greet her, as was polite, even if she was not, strictly, a lady, while I reserved my prerogative as a woman of higher rank to remain seated.

Gage bowed very shortly and correctly. "Thank you for seeing us on such short notice."

"But of course," she replied and then turned to his father. "Lord Gage, I am glad to see you again looking so well."

He smiled his charming smile, the one Gage had inherited from him and often employed among the ladies of the ton. "Likewise. I didn't think it was possible for you to look even more beautiful, but you have proven me wrong once again."

Mrs. Dubois batted his arm playfully, before turning to me.

Gage performed the introductions without a hint of irony. "Lady Darby, allow me to introduce Mrs. Dubois. Mrs. Dubois, my fiancée, Lady Darby."

"The pleasure is all mine," she demurred.

I offered her a tight, but not unfriendly smile. "It's good to meet you."

I had to give her credit. She had assessed the situation and played her role to perfection. She had recognized that too much flirtation toward Gage would only discomfort him, rile me, and vex his father. Instead she'd chosen to pour the flattery on Lord Gage, and treat me and Gage with precise properness. She was deferential, but not groveling, and I could see that this had relaxed Gage and even me, to a certain extent, even though I was aware of her shrewd calculation.

Her eyes brightened with humor as we continued to regard one another, and I realized she was aware that I had seen her cunning. My smile became more genuine as we shared a moment of amusement.

Lord Gage offered his hand to help her to her seat just two steps away. She lifted her skirts and gracefully arranged herself on the white and gold fainting couch to best advantage. I realized this was her throne, of sorts, from which she charmed and beguiled guests. If not for the honey blond shade of her hair, styled in a simple Grecian knot, I would have likened her to Cleopatra receiving her subjects, or perhaps the Romans. Was that why she'd chosen this room's outrageous décor?

The corners of her mouth quirked upward in a smile. "Ridiculous, isn't it?" she asked, seeming to read my thoughts. She gestured to our surroundings. "My first protector insisted that it be decorated so. And later I discovered that men seem to expect to be entertained in such extravagant surroundings, so I left it." She glanced up at the large bust of some Egyptian god perched on a shelf behind her. "Someday, when I retire, I look forward to ripping this all out and replacing it with something less . . . preposterous." Her eyes laughed.

"So . . . you own this house?" I asked in disbelief. I knew few women who owned property. It all went to their husbands, or fathers, or brothers, or sons. All of us, even duchesses, were beholden to the men in our lives for a roof over our heads.

"Yes. It was gifted to me. As were my clothes and jewelry, and any number of other things." Payment for services rendered. She did not say this aloud, but her eyes did. Services that wives rendered for free, though that wasn't the way they were supposed to be viewed.

Gage squirmed beside me, likely uncomfortable with the inappropriate direction our conversation had turned.

"But I don't think you came to speak with me about my property," Mrs. Dubois proclaimed lightheartedly. "Now, to what do I owe the pleasure of this visit?"

Lord Gage cleared his throat. "I imagine you are aware of Lady Drummond's recent death?"

Mrs. Dubois effortless cheer faltered appropriately, but also genuinely, I thought. "Yes. Yes, I am."

"And . . ." he cleared his throat again ". . . we have been made aware that Lord Drummond is your current protector."

"Was," she declared.

Lord Gage blinked in surprise.

"We ended our arrangement almost two weeks ago."

I glanced at Gage, who frowned. "But you furtively called on Lady Drummond last Monday."

At first I thought she would deny it, but then she sighed and shook her head. "I knew that little maid would talk."

"Actually, someone else saw you."

She considered the matter, and then nodded. "The stepdaughter." She smiled self-deprecatingly. "I hoped she wouldn't recognize me."

"So you admit you visited your former protector's wife in her home?"

"Yes. Though why that should matter to you, I don't know.

Unless . . ." She gasped, seeming to recognize the import of our presence. "You think I killed her?"

Gage eyed her suspiciously. "How do you know she was killed?"

She arched one eyebrow imperiously. "I'm not unobservant. You *are* three inquiry agents."

"Then why did you think we were here?" I asked in confusion, ignoring the warm glow I felt at being described on equal terms with Gage and his father.

"I thought Lord Drummond murdered her. That you'd come to ask about him."

"Why do you think that?" Lord Gage leaned forward to inquire.

"Because . . ." She heaved a sigh. "Well, to start with, the man has a vicious temper. One that he has no qualms about unleashing on women. Not me," she clarified sharply. "Unlike his wife, I was free to sever our arrangement at any time." She shook her head in bewilderment. "But why would you think I killed her? She died several days after I called on her."

"She was poisoned," Gage explained. "By something slipped into her bedchamber. The room where you visited her."

Mrs. Dubois's mouth puckered as if she'd swallowed something unpleasant. "I see."

"So why did you call on her? And why did you end your relationship with Lord Drummond if not because of his temper?"

Her eyes dropped to the floor, considering the matter. From the looks of the fierce frown on her face, she seemed to be debating something. When finally she looked up, it was to examine each of us closely. "So long as what I have to say does not impact your investigation, may I rely on your discretion?"

Gage, his father, and I all looked at one another in silent communication.

"If it does not impact our investigation, yes," Lord Gage said, speaking for us all.

Mrs. Dubois did not seem entirely satisfied with this response, but she nodded anyway. I watched curiously as she shifted in her seat, for the first time not looking completely self-assured.

"I went to see Lady Drummond because . . ." her mouth twisted ". . . her husband infected me with clap."

Her eyes darted between us, trying to see how we had all taken this pronouncement. I did my best to hide my shock.

She swallowed. "I didn't trust Lord Drummond to tell his wife, and I thought she should know." Her eyes blazed angrily. "It's also why *I* ended our arrangement."

"A letter . . ." Lord Gage began, his nose wrinkled in unconcealed disgust.

"Can be ripped up or discarded," she snapped. "I had originally intended to inform her in such a manner, but then I realized that since I'd threatened to do just that, Lord Drummond would be looking for it. I knew I wasn't obligated to tell her, but . . . it seemed cowardly not to."

"How do you know Lady Drummond didn't give it to her husband?" Lord Gage asked.

We all turned to look at him in undisguised skepticism. That was not likely, even if she had taken a lover, as Lady Rachel had intimated.

I turned back to Mrs. Dubois in sudden comprehension. "That's why you thought he'd killed her. You thought she'd confronted him with the venereal disease he'd given her and he'd flown into a rage."

She nodded. "Something like that."

"So you haven't been harboring hopes of becoming the next Lady Drummond." Gage phrased it as a statement, but the question was still implied.

She actually laughed. "Goodness, no. The man was tedious enough as a lover."

It was easy now to guess how that particular rumor started. One of the other servants had probably seen Mrs. Dubois in the house, or heard the two maids discussing her visit, and the maid had lied and said Mrs. Dubois had wanted to see the furnishings or some such nonsense. It was impossible to know exactly without the maid admitting to it, but it was a close enough guess.

In any case, now that her visit to Lady Drummond had been explained, Mrs. Dubois was no longer a suspect. She had no motive. And frustratingly, this left us with little to go on.

A list of visitors to the Drummond household in the days leading up to the murder. A mystery lover that Lady Drummond may or may not have taken. And an odd letter she'd written to an unfamiliar physician, which now seemed to be explained. If Lady Drummond had feared her husband had infected her with a venereal disease, she might have sought treatment from Dr. Abercrombie. Though why she didn't visit her normal physician, Dr. Davis, I didn't know, especially since the ailment was her husband's fault. Regardless, none of these clues was substantial. I only hoped that further interviews would turn up something useful, because at that moment, Lady Drummond's murder looked like it would go unsolved.

CHAPTER 22

I returned home late that afternoon, just as Philip was leaving. He paused at the base of the stairs when he saw me in the entrance hall divesting myself of my outer garments. A wary look crossed his features.

"Good evening, Kiera," he said politely. "Had a productive day?"

"Yes . . ." I sighed ". . . and no."

"I'll take that to mean, many questions were asked, but none of the answers have moved you closer to solving Lady Drummond's murder."

I smiled tightly. "Precisely."

"Well, I'm off to Rothschild's for the evening." He tilted his head down to speak to me conspiratorially. "You're lucky to miss this one. The man is as dull as a spoon, but we need his vote."

"Philip," I said, interrupting his feigned joviality. "Do you have a moment?"

He looked as if he wanted to say no, but good manners prevented it. "Of course."

We moved down the hall a short distance toward his study, and away from Figgins and the footman standing by the front door.

"What is it?"

I searched my brother-in-law's face, seeing the dark circles under his eyes and the pale pallor of his skin. "Philip, is everything all right?"

"Of course."

"Really? Because it doesn't seem like it."

He tilted his head as if in fond exasperation. "If you mean last night . . ."

"For a start."

His brow flexed in annoyance before he smoothed it out. "I apologize if it upset you. I just had a bit too much to drink, that's all."

"But why were you drinking?"

This time he didn't attempt to hide his irritation. "Do I need a reason?"

"When you decide to get so disguised you need to be carried upstairs? Yes."

"Everything is not a mystery to be solved, Kiera. Sometimes a man simply chooses to enjoy a few glasses of whiskey." He turned away, dismissing me.

"Yes, but you weren't enjoying it."

His steps faltered.

"If I'm not mistaken, you weren't even tasting it. You frightened me, Philip." I let him hear the distress in my voice. "You still are."

He turned back toward me.

"Please, tell me what is wrong."

He stared at the wall, allowing me to see only his profile as he spoke in a calmer voice. "Nothing is wrong. I'm sorry I frightened you. It won't happen again."

And with that, he was gone, striding across the hall and out into the evening.

I trembled as I did my best to swallow back my emotions. They made my stomach ache.

Trudging upstairs, I thought to speak to Alana before changing for dinner, but the children were with her, and I didn't want to interrupt their limited time with their mother. I could hear their bright voices talking over one another as my sister tried to respond to them all. Greer's words were half babbles, but Alana seemed to understand her just as well as her two older children.

I paused with my hand on my doorknob, imagining the scene they must make. Was my sister right? Would I have children of my own? Would I one day be surrounded by their excited voices and sticky hugs?

Even as quiet and calm a child as I had been, I still remembered eagerly competing with my older sister and brother for my mother's attention. She would gather us up on her enormous bed and pull me in close to her sweetly scented body while Alana and Trevor bounced up and down relaying their adventures. I would brush my fingers through her soft, chestnut brown curls, and listen to her tinkling laughter. Until I tired of waiting my turn and jumped into the fray, tugging at her sleeve to hear whatever my accomplishment had been for the day.

I always tired before my sister and brother, and often subsided to lie against my mother's shoulder. There was many a time when I fell asleep that way and had to be carried to bed by my father or one of the footmen. The next morning I would awake surrounded by her scent and the memory of her arms around me.

There were some nights when I still awoke with the feel of her hair on my fingertips and the smell of her perfume in my nostrils. It always left me feeling disoriented and heartsick.

Would Malcolm, Philipa, and Greer feel that someday remembering these times? Would my own children?

I turned away from my door and descended the stairs, suddenly needing fresh air the same way Philip had needed his whiskey the previous evening.

As the evening light faded, somehow I found my steps had led me to the town house Lady Bearsden had rented for herself and her great-niece. I knew it was a terribly inappropriate time to call, but I also knew Lady Stratford, being still in mourning, would be at home. So before I could reconsider my actions, I climbed the stairs to her door.

I was ushered into the drawing room, where Lady Stratford jumped up from the settee.

"Is everything all right?" she asked in alarm.

"Yes. I'm sorry," I stammered, now feeling silly for having given in to the impulse. "I know this is an odd time to call. I just . . ." I grimaced in embarrassment. "Perhaps I should go."

"Of course not," she declared. "Please, come sit with me. I'm glad of the company," she assured me, pulling me down on the settee next to her. "Mourning is tedious. I must tell you, sometimes I feel I shall go mad from the boredom and silence."

"Where is your aunt?" I asked.

"She's gone to the theater this evening. She's a dear, always keeping me company. But there's no reason she should be made to suffer alongside me." She leaned closer with a twinkle in her eye. "Besides, I know she's dying to hear all of the latest on-dits."

I smiled. "Then she will hate to have missed me."

"Oh?"

I instantly sobered. "Lady Drummond was murdered. We've confirmed it."

Lady Stratford closed her eyes, clasping her hands tightly to her bosom.

"I'm sorry."

"I expected it. But I find that isn't making it any easier to hear." She exhaled and opened her eyes to look at me. "Poison?"

"Yes. Mixed in her skin cream and perhaps her lavender oil."

"How dreadful." She stared off into the distance, as if contemplating the matter. A moment later, she shook herself. "Is this why you came to see me?"

"Maybe."

She looked at me quizzically and I smiled sheepishly.

"To be honest, I'm not exactly sure how I ended up here. My steps just found their way to your door."

She reached over to touch my hand. "Then I'm glad they did."

And I suddenly was, too.

A maid carried in a tray of tea and little cakes, and Lady Stratford set about preparing us each a cup. I glanced around at the comfortable furnishings and muted décor. It was bland, but cozy and inoffensive. The perfect style for a rented home. And the desirable address more than made up for any deficiencies.

In a way, Lady Drummond had been similar. She had not been an exciting woman, but she was kind and lovely. Not strikingly beautiful, as Lady Stratford was, but definitely above average. She was exceptionable enough to be admired, but not envied. And yet someone had murdered her.

"Why?" I muttered.

"Why what?" Lady Stratford asked as she handed me my tea.

"Why would someone want to poison Lady Drummond? She was gentle and well liked, and as far as I know, completely harmless. Why would someone plan so carefully to kill her? What could she possibly have done to drive them to such an action?"

"I take it you've ruled out Lord Drummond as the culprit."

I scowled. "Unfortunately, yes."

She nodded and took a sip of her tea. "Perhaps they weren't striking at her, but her husband. Maybe this was someone's way of hurting Lord Drummond?"

I narrowed my eyes, considering the suggestion. "Except it almost went undetected. If not for my insistence, we would all still believe she died of an apoplexy."

"Maybe that was an accident."

"Maybe," I said doubtfully. "But I still think if someone wanted to send a message to Lord Drummond, they would have done it in a more obvious manner. Poison is a very passive form of murder. Devious and calculated, but far removed. Whoever killed her had no desire to see it happen. It was enough for it to be done. They didn't need to witness it."

I looked up as Lady Stratford's cup clattered against her saucer. Her thoughts seemed troubled. She lifted her eyes, catching me watching her. "There is one possibility I can think of."

I arched my eyebrows in encouragement.

"Clare and I did not debut together, but I remember her telling me about one particular suitor she had spurned who had been particularly furious when she turned down his proposal. He had even tried to insinuate she was damaged goods by spreading rumors about her."

"Clearly he didn't take rejection well."

She shook her head. "And it was made even worse by the fact that he actually wagered with another gentleman that she would say yes. Clare found out about it when a cousin of hers saw it written in the betting book at one of his clubs."

I screwed up my face in disgust. Gentlemen and their stupid wagers. "It certainly sounds like he had a reason to despise her then, even though he only had his own foolishness to blame for making such a bet. But that was more than a dozen years ago. Why would he exact his revenge now?" I was skeptical that anyone would do something so drastic for such a silly cause.

"Because my great-aunt told me he'd recently made a new wager. One that Clare's death would have prevented him from losing."

I sat straighter, lowering my cup of tea. "He's here in Edinburgh."

She nodded.

"What was the wager?"

Her lips puckered in distaste. "That Clare would not take a lover before midsummer's eve."

My first impulse was to roll my eyes, but then I remembered what Lady Rachel had told me. If Lady Drummond was considering taking a lover—if she hadn't already—and her former suitor found out about it, then that could give him a powerful motive to stop it. Though, once again, murder seemed a rather extreme solution.

"Who is this suitor?" I asked.

"Walter Kirkcowan."

I nearly dropped my tea. "Lord Kirkcowan?"

She tilted her head. "Yes. He did ascend to his father's title, didn't he?"

I scowled. I didn't know why I was so surprised. If Lord Kirkcowan was capable of paupering himself and his family by gambling away his property, he was certainly capable of making ludicrous bets. What I found most curious was that Lady Kirkcowan could be friends with Lady Drummond even knowing her husband had once courted her. But maybe she didn't know. Or maybe she wished now that the other woman had said yes and saved her the heartache.

Regardless, it was worth questioning both Lord and Lady Kirkcowan. We had no better suspects, and people had committed murder for stranger reasons.

CHAPTER 23

Gage's carriage slowed to a stop, and I lifted the curtain aside to see outside. We were still several blocks from the Assembly Rooms, and I could only assume we were waiting in the line of coaches queued up to deliver their passengers at the doors. Closing my eyes, I relaxed back into the cushions, grateful for the momentary reprieve.

Gage and I had spent all afternoon calling on those who had visited Drummond House in the weeks leading up to Lady Drummond's murder. It had been an exercise in futility, as no one we had seen thus far had anything of value to tell us. And perhaps worse, none of them struck either of us as a viable suspect. Though there had been a few I wouldn't have minded accusing of such a horrible act simply because of their rudeness.

I had returned to Charlotte Square with barely enough time to bathe and dress before Gage came back for me. Originally we had not planned to attend tonight's assembly, but when we realized how long each of these individual interviews was taking, we decided we could proceed faster if we went to a place where a large portion of the Drummond House visitors, as well as Lord and Lady Kirkcowan, were known to gather.

But now, feeling a headache building behind my eyes, I wished we'd elected to enjoy a quiet dinner at Cromarty House instead. Although, with Alana confined to her bed and Philip sure to be absent, such an intimate meal would not have been strictly proper. I frowned, remembering my and Philip's conversation, or rather, lack of conversation, the prior evening. I had not seen him since then, but I had heard him moving about in the guest room the night before when he returned from his dinner.

"Kiera."

I blinked open my eyes to find Gage looking at me in concern.

"Is something wrong? You were scowling."

"Was I? Just a headache." I let my head sink back again.

"Are you sure? You've seemed a bit distracted all day." His mouth flattened. "Even before Mrs. Coon snubbed you."

I studied his handsome face, debating whether to say anything. At first, I had elected to remain quiet, out of respect for Philip, but after last night's dismissal, I was no longer certain that was the best course. I didn't want to betray my brother-in-law or his privacy, but I was troubled, and apprehensive that if I didn't find a way to intercede, things would get worse.

"You've known Philip a long time?" I began tentatively.

"Since university. Why?"

I ran a hand over the folds of my claret red gown with black braid. "Did he often get deep into his cups?"

"Occasionally. But all young men do. It's almost a rite."

"And later?"

"Well, he was something of a rakehell when we first went up to London. But you know that. Your sister teases him about it often enough."

I nodded. "How she reformed him."

Gage shifted in his seat, adjusting the tails of his coat. "I don't think there was really much she needed to reform. Cromarty always had the makings of a devoted husband and father; he simply needed to meet the right woman. But yes." He studied my face more closely. "Why are you asking this? What is going on?"

"What about in the last year?" I asked, ignoring his query. "Have you known him to get foxed?"

"No." His response was drawn out.

I wrapped my arms around my middle. "I thought not."

"Kiera, has Philip been drinking heavily?"

I pressed my lips together, still hesitant to say, and then plunged in. "Just the once. The other night. I . . ." my voice lowered to a whisper ". . . I've never seen him that way before. He . . ." I pressed my lips together again.

Gage's brow furrowed. "Did he hurt you?"

"Oh, no," I assured him. "No. He . . . he seemed so despondent. I didn't know what to do. He scarcely spends any time with Alana now. He's always busy with political matters or attending meetings and dinners. He moved into the guest room because he said he's afraid of jostling or disturbing her and the baby." Once I began to speak, it all seemed to come pouring out. "I can see how much it hurts Alana, but I don't know what to say or do to fix it."

Gage had taken hold of my hand sometime in the middle of my speech, and he squeezed it now. "There may be nothing you can do."

"But why is he doing this? Why is he turning away from her?" I pleaded.

His eyes dropped to where our hands were linked, and he ran his thumb gently over the back of my fingers. "I think Cromarty may be frightened."

"We all are," I protested.

"Yes, but as painful as it would be for you to lose your sister, think of how much worse it would be for him to lose his wife. His wife whom he adores, who's given him three, and now four children." His eyes stared into mine earnestly. "If I were in his place, watching you struggle to birth our child, I would be terrified, too. Especially in Cromarty's situation. He was warned his wife shouldn't have any more children. He must wonder if he could have taken better precautions."

This silenced me. I hadn't thought of it that way. Philip always seemed so strong, so sure, but of course he would be frightened. However, it didn't excuse his actions. "But he was so calm and steady when Alana struggled to give birth to Greer. He's faced this before," I pointed out.

"Yes, but that was a shock. He didn't have time to contemplate what it would mean if your sister died. This time he's had months to do so."

I frowned. "Then why isn't he spending every available moment with her? Why is he avoiding her?"

Gage's lips curled in a tight, humorless smile. "I suppose he thinks it will make it easier should the worst happen."

I considered what he said. "That's stupid. He's going to feel worse when he realizes he squandered his last few weeks with her. That he essentially abandoned the woman he loves when she needed him most."

He did not scold me for my display of temper. "I agree. Do you want me to talk to him?"

I heaved a sigh. "No. I should." I scowled. "And give him a swift slap on the head to go with it."

The carriage inched forward another few feet, and I lifted the curtain to see we were just a half a block away. I turned to see Gage staring out the opposite window. His hand still clasped mine. "Thank you."

He looked at me in question.

"For listening. For explaining." My eyes dropped. "I don't always understand when it comes to matters of the heart. I guess at some point I stopped wanting to. It was easier that way. So I'm a bit behind in my education."

Gage squeezed my fingers. "I'm happy to educate you anytime." His voice lowered as his gaze dipped to my lips. "About anything."

"We're almost to the door," I gasped softly. "The footmen will see."

"Let them."

And so I emerged from Gage's carriage for the second time that year with a flushed countenance and bright eyes, the first having happened during our investigation in January. The footmen employed at the Assembly Rooms were going to begin to think I was suffering from some sort of illness. One I was happy to have contracted.

Gage and I climbed the wide sweeping stairs inside as if marching into battle. We'd elected to divide and conquer, agreeing to separate and approach the witnesses on our own. Those who would not talk to us here, or in my case, at all, we would pay visits to at a later date if necessary. The one exception was Lord Kirkcowan, whom Gage had agreed to corner and bring to me so we might both question him.

I circulated through the rooms on the left while Gage moved right. I did my best to ignore the titters and poorly disguised gossiping that followed in my wake, but it was impossible not to see them. Whoever had renewed the rumors about me had clearly done their best, and I was starting to doubt it had been Lord Gage. Not that he wasn't capable, or even motivated. This just seemed much more of a woman's game. Thus far all of Lord Gage's other attacks had been direct, and this was far more cunning.

I circled the rooms, gathering very little useful information until I stumbled upon Lady Kirkcowan. She smiled politely when we crossed paths with one each other in the hall outside the room where couples were dancing, a contrast to her begrudging reception at Inverleith House. Her skin was paler than the last time I'd seen her, her eyes sadder. Her gown was a beautiful shade of gold just slightly deeper than her eyes, but rather than enhance her handsome looks, it outshone her, as well as the strand of pearls around her neck.

I wanted to ask her about her jewelry, whether she'd found a way to make it miraculously reappear, but I could tell from the wary look in her eyes that was the last thing she wanted to talk about. So instead I turned to the topic for which I'd sought her out. I knew it might be just as painful, but it couldn't be helped.

"You've heard?" I murmured. Our steps turned toward the window at the end of the hall, away from the crowd.

"That Lady Drummond was poisoned? Yes."

I had known that once Gage and I began questioning potential witnesses and suspects that afternoon, word of the baroness's murder would spread like wildfire. The entire assemblage here tonight probably already knew. This should have brought me vindication, but I had learned not to count on society's conscience.

"Then you realize Mr. Gage and I are investigating."

She nodded. "Though I don't know what else I can tell you."

"I'm afraid we have few suspects," I began carefully. "I know you believed Lord Drummond capable of it, but from everything we've uncovered, it appears unlikely. So we're forced to turn elsewhere, to pursue every possible motive."

We had reached the end of the hall and she turned to face me. "You're speaking of how my husband courted Lady Drummond before me, aren't you?"

I searched her flat golden eyes for any sign of nervousness or distress. "Partially."

"We were friends, so of course I knew about it," she readily admitted. "And to be honest, I don't know that I would have been at all interested in him if it hadn't been for the fact that Lady Drummond had considered him for a potential husband. Yes, yes, I knew about his silly wager." She frowned. "Or, at least, that's how he categorized it to me then. Just a folly of youth." She sighed. "I wish I'd known better."

"I was told he treated Lady Drummond rather poorly when she refused him."

"He did. But later he offered her a very pretty apology. And when he first began to pursue me, she gave me her blessing, saying she trusted he'd learned from his mistakes." Her brow furrowed, obviously thinking of how false this statement had proved to be.

I wasn't surprised by how forgiving Lady Drummond had been. It seemed just like her.

"Did you resent her for any of this?"

Lady Kirkcowan looked up at me in surprise. "Not in the least. It's not her fault Lord Kirkcowan married me for my dowry." A little pleat formed between her brows. "I'm the one who should have known better when he confided in me that the only reason he'd courted Lady Drummond was for that exact reason. He meant to flatter and appease me, and I was easily blinded by praise." She turned to stare down the hall at the milling crowd not so far away, their voices providing a humming accompaniment to our conversation. "As far as I know, the only things my husband has ever truly cared for are cards and horses, and anything else he can bet on," she muttered.

"Speaking of which," I interjected, glad for the opening she'd provided, "were you aware that your husband recently placed another bet regarding Lady Drummond?"

Her eyes widened in genuine surprise. "About?"

"Whether she would take a lover before midsummer's eve. Apparently he wagered she would not."

Her gaze dropped to the floor and she pressed her fingertips over her mouth as if she might be ill.

"Lady Kirkcowan?" I said in concern.

"I . . ." she swallowed ". . . I may have let slip that she was considering doing so."

"What do you mean?"

"We were arguing. I made some threats about taking a lover so that I could have some nice things again. He . . ." her voice shook ". . . he said some rather nasty things back to me. And I said that even paragons like Lady Drummond considered such things."

So once again Lord Kirkcowan had been in danger of losing a wager he had placed on Lady Drummond.

"Did your husband react?"

She shook her head. "I don't know. I was so angry, I don't think I really paid attention." She paused to consider. "He did leave the house soon after. But I don't know where he went."

I reached out to still her pleating hands. "Do you think your husband would have been capable of murdering Lady Drummond just to win a bet?"

Her eyes were troubled. "I want to say no. It's so completely ridiculous. But . . . we don't have much left." Her voice dropped to a hushed murmur. "He lost our house in Ayrshire just last week. There's going to be nothing left for my son to inherit but an empty title." I could hear the panic in her voice she was struggling to contain.

I clenched my fists in anger. "Has he sold your jewels?"

"Not yet."

But it was only a matter of time. He would need something to wager next.

An acquaintance of Lady Kirkcowan's saw us and called out her name. We both pasted on fake smiles. The other woman chatted away, seeming oblivious to the strain behind Lady Kirkcowan's eyes that seemed so obvious to me. Or perhaps her friend simply didn't wish to see it.

I excused myself, promising to call on Lady Kirkcowan. More than ever, I was determined to do something to help her, though what that was, I still didn't know.

Lord Kirkcowan proved not as easy to converse with as his wife. Gage had to almost forcefully drag him away from a game of *vingt-et-un*, even though he'd waited for nearly an hour for Lord Kirkcowan to come back from a deficit and break even.

"Now, see here," I heard him snarl as Gage pulled him into the alcove where I sat waiting for them. "I was about to be plump in the pockets. You just cost me an untold amount of blunt."

"I just *saved* you from losing what brass you have again," Gage snapped, releasing his arm with a shove. "The little good that will do. You're determined to have pockets to let."

Lord Kirkcowan reached up to swipe at his sleeve, straightening it. "What do you want?"

"For you to develop some common sense," Gage drawled, looking him up and down like he was an insect. "But as that's not likely to happen, we'll be satisfied with your answers to our questions."

He scowled and then glanced about, seeing me for the first time. "Is this about my wife's jewelry? I already told your father she found it. *Apparently* she'd forgotten she hid it in her dresser the night our butler was ill and she didn't want to disturb him to open the safe."

A plausible excuse, though it appeared her husband didn't believe it.

"No," Gage replied in a hard voice. "It's about Lady Drummond's murder."

"Oh, yes. I heard someone nattering on about that. What's it to do with me?"

"It seems you made a wager many years ago when you were courting Lady Drummond that she would agree to marry you, and when she declined, you lost a significant amount of money."

Lord Kirkcowan's jaw tightened. "I remember."

"Well, it's come to our attention that you recently made another wager. This one also concerning Lady Drummond. That she wouldn't take a lover before midsummer's eve. And we've discovered you knew you were about to lose that bet. Except she was poisoned before that could happen. Convenient, yes?"

Lord Kirkcowan's lips twisted into a nasty sneer. "Ah, but you're missing one crucial piece of information. I made a second bet. This one for double the amount I wagered before. But this time I bet that she *would* take a lover." He nodded toward the gaming room. "Ask Mr. Pimms. He's still trying to collect, even though the lady is dead. If anything, I've lost money from her being murdered, not gained."

I bit back a curse. I despised Lord Kirkcowan. He was a mean, selfish oaf. But that didn't make him guilty of murder, no matter how much I would have liked to see him detained. Lady Kirkcowan and her children would face scandal, but at least they would be able to keep the remaining property they had.

"Now, if there's nothing else you'd like to accuse me of . . ." He squared his shoulders and marched out of the alcove.

Gage didn't try to stop him, though I could tell he wished to do the other man some kind of bodily harm. "We're back to where we started," he muttered in frustration.

I sighed.

CHAPTER 24

I decided to call on Lady Rachel again the next day in hopes she might be able to point me in another direction. There seemed no better option, except to continue our interviews of the visitors to Drummond House, something I was not the least enthused about.

At first Lady Rachel was resistant to consider anyone else but Lord Drummond. "You're certain it wasn't him?" she demanded, lounging on the ivory fainting couch in her upstairs parlor. Her eyes were sharp with persistence.

"Nothing is certain." I leaned toward her. "Believe me, I don't like the man any more than you do. So the fact that I'm confident enough of his innocence to search for other suspects should say something. Otherwise I wouldn't be wasting my time."

She heaved a heavy sigh. "I know. It's just . . . I was so sure it had to be him." She shook her head. "Who else could it be? Everyone else *adored* her."

"Maybe someone was jealous. Or frustrated . . ." I felt like I was grasping at thin air. I couldn't begin to guess the motive, so I turned to what I could deduce. "What of the man who was interested in pursuing a liaison with her? The one you said that Lady Drummond mentioned several times?"

Lady Rachel lifted her hand from her brow to gesture wildly in frustration. "Yes, but I don't know his name."

"Can you guess it?"

Her dark eyes turned to me with interest.

"Surely you must have some idea," I argued, knowing I had her attention. "You were her closest friend. If anyone knew, it was likely you."

"But if I'm wrong . . ."

"We shall find that out quickly enough, and he will have suffered nothing more than a few pointed questions."

She tapped her fingers against her rouge-stained lips. "There is one man I felt certain Clare was attracted to. I saw them chatting at a ball once, their heads bent together. She was so happy. Her face looked as if it had been lit from the inside." Her eyes turned sad. "I never saw her look that way with Lord Drummond. She should have had a husband who made her feel that much joy."

Her words pinched me in my chest. She was right. Lady Drummond had deserved that.

"Who was he?"

She pressed her lips together, hesitating for one more moment before relenting. "Lord Henry Kerr."

"The Duke of Bowmont's youngest son?" I asked in some surprise.

She nodded.

I had to admit, I knew very little about Lord Henry, except that he was the youngest of six children, five of whom were boys, and that his mother, the duchess, had been notoriously unfaithful after giving birth to her second son. It was widely accepted that Lord Henry, his sister, and two of his brothers had been conceived on the other side of the blanket, though the duke had agreed to claim them as his own.

Probably because he claimed more than his own fair share of bastard children begotten by his mistresses.

"Thank you," I told her. "Even if he turns out not to be a suspect, even if they were not lovers, perhaps he knows something that could be helpful to us."

Her smile was doubtful as she shifted forward in her seat, as if to rise.

"I do have one more question, if I may?"

She settled back. "Of course."

"It has come to our attention that Lady Drummond wrote a letter to a physician, a Dr. Abercrombie . . ." Her eyes flared wide and I paused. "Do you know him?"

"No," she replied and then hastened to explain. "I'm just aware that Dr. Davis is her normal physician, so this is certainly out of the ordinary."

"She asked for an appointment with him, to discuss an urgent matter, but nothing else was said. Do you know why she would have done such a thing?" I hoped Lady Rachel could confirm our suspicions that it was in regards to the venereal disease her husband may have given her, but she shook her head in bewilderment.

"The only thing I can think of is that she suspected she was carrying a child, and it was not Lord Drummond's. That's something I would definitely want to find out privately first, so I could decide how to tell my husband." She tilted her head. "If at all."

I grasped her implication, but I doubted Lady Drummond would have even contemplated such a thing. Though I supposed if she had been scared enough of her husband, anything was possible.

"Her maid said she wasn't enceinte. And without an autopsy, I would trust her word over anyone else's."

Lady Rachel's face was grim. "Yes. Aileen would have known. How is she, by the way?"

"She's doing well. Dr. Graham believes she shouldn't suffer any lasting effects."

"Good." She swung her knees around to sit straighter, effectively ending my questions. "I'm sorry I couldn't be much more help in naming potential suspects." She shook her head. "I just don't see how anyone would want to hurt Clare." Her voice almost pleaded with me, as if she was asking me to explain.

"I'm encountering the same problem."

"Maybe one of her acquaintances from the past will have some suggestions. I'm afraid our friendship has been relatively brief in the scheme of things. Just four or five years. But I imagine the ladies she made her debut in London with might know things I don't."

I opened my mouth to tell her I'd already been pursuing that very same angle when she said something that made me pause.

"Perhaps Lord Gage has a better idea of who would wish to harm her."

I considered what she'd said. "You mean because he's such an experienced inquiry agent," I guessed, though it had been an odd way to phrase it. "He hasn't . . ."

"No," she interrupted, sounding confused now herself. "Because he knew her. I was told he actually courted her for a time when she was a debutante. Am I wrong?"

I felt like I'd been punched. Lord Gage had failed to mention any of this. From the way he had been behaving, I had believed he was only acquainted with her through her husband. Though if he had once held her in regard, it explained his strange reaction to seeing her portrait.

If it was true, then Lord Gage must have pursued her not long after his wife, Gage's mother, had died. It must have been but a year or two later. I wondered how serious the courtship had been, and if things had ended amicably between him and Lady Drummond. And what of Lord Drummond? Was he aware of the prior connection between his wife and his old naval colleague? And if so, had this knowledge affected their friendship?

Either way, I found it curious that Lord Gage had not said a word about this. For a man so concerned with objectivity, he had certainly failed to practice it himself.

However, it seemed bad form to let Lady Rachel know any of these thoughts, not to mention embarrassing to me as an investigator and the future daughter-in-law of the man who had refused to be so forthcoming. So instead, I smiled and said, "Of course."

I wasn't sure this fooled her, for her expression remained puzzled, but she didn't press me further.

In light of the lovely weather—such a rarity this early in spring—I had elected to walk back to Charlotte Square. The coachman, who was normally a rather disapproving fellow, had not even batted an eyelash when I informed him this after he delivered me to Lady Rachel's door. Apparently, even he could appreciate a rare display of March warmth.

Unfortunately, the sun and crystal blue sky of the morning did not last into the afternoon. I emerged from Lady Rachel's front door to a sky full of heavy clouds and the first gusts of a sharp breeze that heralded the arrival of rain. I sighed and wrapped my cloak tighter around me. And I had so been looking forward to some warm sunshine on my face.

"Shall I send for your carriage, my lady?" Monahan, Lady Rachel's majordomo, asked from behind me.

I turned and smiled. "No. I think the rain will hold off for a bit yet, and it's only a few blocks. I could use the exertion."

"Very good, my lady," he intoned with a bow. So staid. So proper.

I set off down the street at a relatively fast pace. The rain would hold off, but not forever, and I had no desire to be caught out in it.

The one advantage to the return of the clouds was that I had the pavement all to myself. There were no promenading ladies and gentlemen to impede my progress, just the occasional passerby going about his normal business. I smiled and nodded to a gentleman carrying a leather satchel and then turned the corner onto a quiet street. The uniform gray stone town houses seemed to hunker together beneath the lowering sky. The only spot of color was a single cheery red door on one of the homes across the street. I smiled at the bright floral print curtains I could see in the front window of the same house.

It was only then that I realized I wasn't alone. My shoulders inched upward in alarm, and then just as swiftly fell when I discovered who was keeping pace with me. His hands tucked into his pockets as if out for leisurely stroll, Bonnie Brock flashed me his blinding white grin as I turned to glare at him.

"Isn't there a better way of approaching me?" I asked.

"Well, I can hardly march up to yer brother-in-law's door and ask to see ye, noo, can I?"

I grimaced. That was true.

"So unless ye want me to abduct ye again . . ." His eyebrows arched hopefully.

"No," I told him repressively.

His eyes twinkled in amusement. "Then I'm afraid an afternoon constitutional is our only option. Gage willna be jealous, will he?"

I didn't even dignify that with a response. "So to what do I owe the pleasure?" My voice twisted with sarcasm. I knew better than to think Bonnie Brock had sought me out just for the pleasure of my company.

He shrugged. "Perhaps I merely wished to harass Gage."

I could believe that, but I knew that was not the reason he'd gone to the trouble to come to New Town himself to shadow me. But if he wanted to dither about telling me, who was I to argue. In all likelihood, he wanted something from me, and I was in no hurry to find out what that was.

"How is your sister?" I inquired, changing subjects until he worked his way around to whatever he'd come to say.

He did not respond and I turned to see that his brow had lowered in concern. "She's no' the same."

"I suppose that's to be expected. Maggie has been through an ordeal."

Even though the sixteen-year-old girl had left Edinburgh willingly with one of the men who used to be employed by her brother as a body snatcher, she had only done so because he'd promised to marry her. Unfortunately, he'd done nothing of the sort, instead abandoning her in a shack in the wilds of the Cheviot Hills during the freezing cold of winter, while he and his colleagues rode about the countryside committing crimes. She'd been trapped in a horrible situation until Gage and I had caught up with the men and rescued her. She'd suffered some frostbite, and I suspected she'd been used terribly by at least one of the men. We had cleaned her up as best we could, treating what wounds we could see, and escorted her back to Edinburgh.

"Has she talked to you about it?" I ventured to ask, wondering how much he knew.

"Nay." His eyes were troubled when he turned to look at me. "Did she tell you anything?"

I shook my head. That was the truth. Maggie had been solemn and silent for much of the time she was in my care. But the fear in her eyes and the marks on her body told their own story. One I wasn't about to reveal to her brother unless she gave me permission to.

But it appeared he'd deduced at least some of it.

"She . . . she lost a bairn a few weeks ago." His voice was raw with pain, and I had to swallow to hold back a swell of answering emotion.

Though it had been too early to tell the last time I saw her, I had known there was a real possibility the girl was carrying a child.

"I'm sorry," I murmured.

He scowled. "I ken it's for the best. A bairn would only have reminded her o' the father's devil-spawned soul. But she seemed to have wanted it. I've ne'er seen her weep so. Even when our mam died."

I shook my head in sadness. Poor Maggie. She'd been through enough hardship. It seemed horribly unfair that she should have had to face more.

Bonnie Brock's body suddenly bristled with violence. "I wish ye'd sent my men back to me instead o' takin' 'em afore a magistrate," he growled. "I'd o' administered a more fittin' justice than the men in Berwick." His eyes narrowed. "I still might."

"I thought about it," I admitted. Out of the corner of my eye I could see him glance at me in consideration. I shrugged. "It did seem a fitting retribution. But I wasn't the only person chasing them. And in the end it was easier to secure their imprisonment at Berwick than try to transport them north to Edinburgh."

We turned the corner onto Charlotte Street, and I huddled deeper inside my cloak as a sudden gust of wind swept down the street, making me shiver.

"Yer bein' watched," Bonnie Brock announced without preamble.

I looked up at him in surprise. "I know. I've seen your man at Charlotte Square."

"No' just by my men."

My steps slowed to a stop. "What do you mean?"

He arched a single eyebrow impatiently. "Just what I said. My men noticed someone followin' ye twice noo. But when they tried to confront him, he slipped away." His scowl turned black. "It willna happen a third time."

I blinked up at him. "Your men?"

His mouth curled into a cocky grin. "Ye didna think I'd only posted Rosy to watch ye noo, did ye?"

That's exactly what I'd thought, but I didn't tell him so. I lifted my chin. "What did this man following me look like?"

He shook his head in frustration. "He was too well covered. Middling height and build. That's all my men could see."

I turned to stare up the street, wondering why this man was following me. Did it have something to do with the inquiry? But what? Was it a witness too scared to approach me? Or did he have more nefarious purposes in mind?

"I'm only warnin' ye that ye may have made an enemy. I canna tell ye more until my men catch the sneak."

I nodded. Bonnie Brock's long, tawny hair whipped around his head, and for the first time afforded me a better look at his face. Normally concealed by the fall of his hair, a puckered scar ran from his hairline down across his temple to his left ear. This mark was far worse than the ridge of scar tissue running along his nose that stood out white when he was angry. I stiffened in shock and then tried to hide it, but from the hard look that had entered his eyes, I knew he had seen my surprise.

"I'll be careful," I told him, trying to pretend I wasn't intensely curious about his scar. It definitely painted his sobriquet in a different light. I was certain there was a story behind it, but I wasn't about to ask. The last thing I wanted was to anger him. If he took such pains to conceal it, then there was a reason, and I suspected it wasn't simple vanity.

We resumed our walk, and I wondered how far he would escort me. I had expected him to peel away as soon as our conversation was done, but he remained by my side as the trees of Charlotte Square came into view. A lone figure stood huddled under the branches.

"Why do you call him Rosy?" I couldn't help but ask.

"Because he sure dinna smell it," Bonnie Brock pronounced drolly.

I laughed, ever appreciative of Scotsmen's irony. At least with nicknames like that, you knew what to expect of a man. With gentlemen, it wasn't so easy.

I paused before crossing the street, staring ahead at the castle high on its hill. He waited, perhaps knowing I was coming to an important decision.

"You have men who specialize in larceny, don't you?"

He didn't answer immediately, and I turned my face to the side to look up at him.

"I think ye ken the answer to that. What's the snatch?"

"Jewelry."

I could tell I'd piqued his interest, for he shifted a step closer.

"Whose?"

"An imprudent baron's."

He tilted his head. "How much?"

"Enough to make it worth your while."

"Yer proposal?"

"I can give you the layout of the house, the position of the safe, and even a few guesses as to the combination. A percentage of the gems go to you, while the rest go to my . . . client."

We eyed each other shrewdly.

"And *no one* is to be harmed. But your men have to make it obvious there was a robbery."

Bonnie Brock's eyebrows lifted toward his hairline. "That's an odd request. But easily done." He narrowed his eyes. "But I would no' have branded ye a procuress. You're full o' surprises, Lady Darby."

I turned to stare up at the castle again, hoping I wasn't doing the wrong thing trusting such a task to him and his men. They were, after all, criminals. But that's why they were so perfect for the job in the first place. I frowned. "Some situations call for a little improvisation."

CHAPTER 25

My conversation with Lady Rachel had given me much to think on, so before I spoke to Gage, I decided it would be best if I confirmed her assertions about Lord Gage's courtship of Lady Drummond. After all, she had admitted she hadn't known Lady Drummond then, so perhaps she had gotten her facts wrong. I knew Lady Kirkcowan had debuted with Lady Drummond, but in light of my and Gage's contentious conversation with Lord Kirkcowan at the Assembly Rooms and the plan I had set in motion with Bonnie Brock, I thought it best not to be seen at her house. Since Alana knew nothing about it, that left Lady Stratford as the only person I could trust. Though I hoped she would have told me about it before.

Her brow puckered as I relayed the information Lady Rachel had given me. When I finished, her gaze dropped to the blue cushions of the settee and she sighed. "It's true."

I felt almost numb upon hearing her answer. "She told you?"

"Yes. She never intimated that it was serious," she hastened to assure me. "Though I don't know what Lord Gage's feelings were on the matter. It bothered Clare that he already had a son who was older than her. Yes, I know Lord Drummond is almost as old, but his only child was just three years old at the time, and a girl. A marked difference. And Lord Drummond already had his title, while Lord Gage, though a war hero, was still merely a mister."

I knew it was a gentlewoman's duty to note such things when considering a future spouse, but it rang hollow to hear Lady Stratford speak so. For despite all of their husbands' supposed assets, she and Lady Drummond had both suffered horribly in their choice of mates.

"Why didn't you tell me before?" I asked guardedly, trying to understand why she wouldn't have shared such an important piece of information.

She pleated her hands in her lap. "I considered it. But then it seemed so clear that Lord Drummond was guilty. And I knew you were having difficulties with Lord Gage, and with your engagement to his son. I didn't want to cause you further trouble."

"But what about after I confided that Lord Drummond was no longer a suspect? Why didn't you tell me then? Don't you think this is something I should have known?" I inhaled, trying to settle myself. My voice had risen with my frustration, and my sense of betrayal.

"You're right. I . . . I should have said something. I just . . ." She shook her head. "I only wanted to prevent further strain between you and Gage, but I was wrong. I'm sorry."

I nodded, accepting her apology, though I still felt discontented. I could appreciate that she had been trying to save me from a confrontation that might have proved unnecessary, but in doing so she had also hindered our investigation and made me question whether she was keeping other pertinent information from me. Perhaps I was being too hard on her, but I'd had few friends in my life, and most of those had eventually proven themselves disloyal and untrustworthy. I was wary of such a thing happening again.

We ended our conversation cordially, but I began to wonder how long our newfound rapport would last.

. . .

"Do you see him?" I leaned over to murmur.

Gage continued to survey the elegantly dressed ladies and gentlemen seated in the private boxes across from ours. "Not yet." I hoped Lady Bearsden's information had been correct. Otherwise our trip to the Theatre Royal would have been a waste of time. Not that I minded spending the evening with Gage. To the contrary, I would have loved to enjoy a quiet evening curled up beside him before the hearth in Philip and Alana's drawing room. But I was also anxious to see this inquiry finished, especially now that I knew I was being followed.

Gage's brow creased in frustration. "Are you sure Lady Bearsden is reliable?"

"Lady Stratford's great-aunt is a notorious gossip, and apparently friends with the Dowager Duchess of Bowmont." I nodded toward the Duke of Bowmont's large box. "From the crowd in their box, it at least appears Lady Bearsden was right about the dowager wishing to celebrate her eighty-first birthday at the theater." I frowned. "But I suppose it's possible Lady Bearsden only assumed the dowager's grandson would put in an appearance."

I glanced about at the number of eyes that were fastened on our box instead of the play on the stage. Our presence in Philip's box had not gone unnoticed, and neither would our conversation with Lord Henry Kerr, if he decided to attend. We would have to proceed carefully.

"There he is," Gage announced.

"Where?"

"The level above his family's box and two to the left."

I followed his directions to the private box with two ladies seated at the front and a trio of gentlemen standing behind them at the back near the curtains. "Which one is he?"

"The man on the left with auburn hair."

I narrowed my eyes. "The one in the striped waistcoat?"

"Yes."

It was difficult to see from such a distance, but I thought I could understand the appeal. Although I suspected his personality had more to do with Lady Drummond's attraction to him than his handsome face.

"How do you suggest we approach him?" I asked, ever conscious of being observed.

Gage flipped through the playbill in his lap. "Let's wait a few more minutes until just before the interlude. Perhaps we can catch him as he leaves that box."

I nodded, trying to settle in to enjoy the play. But my eyes and my thoughts kept straying toward the opposite side of theater to the man who may or may not have been Lady Drummond's lover. Had he known how her husband was treating her? Had he cared enough to try to stop it? Or was she just a convenient flirtation? Whatever she meant to him, I knew that if Lady Drummond had embarked on an affair with him, it had been one of the heart. Had he reciprocated her emotions? Had they grown dark with possessiveness and jealousy?

Sensing my distraction, Gage reached over to take my hand in his warm one below the balcony edge, out of sight of the prying eyes of the ton. His thumb danced over the tops of my knuckles, and I returned the favor. My skin tingled with each pass of his thumb. It never ceased to amaze me how such a simple, innocent touch from him could arouse so much feeling in me, even through my glove. My pulse quickened as his little finger dipped inside the opening at my wrist to swirl over the delicate veins there.

I had never felt this excitement, this intensity, about anyone before. It was like a tide coming in, first lapping at my toes and then the tops of my feet and then my ankles. I could feel it pulling me deeper into the sea, and I wanted to let it, to allow Gage to do and show me what he wished. That we had to wait until our wedding night was a delicious torture, but one that at least I knew would eventually end.

But if I were in Lady Drummond's shoes, if I had still been wed to another—a man like Lord Drummond or Sir Anthony—I could understand the temptation. Particularly because it wasn't just a physical desire to connect, but a mental and emotional one as well. That Gage knew and accepted and loved me was an elixir even headier than his touch.

When the time came, and Gage pulled me to my feet, I found I was very anxious indeed to meet this Lord Henry. But not anxious enough to pull away when Gage dragged me into the small alcove at the back of the box, shielding us from the theater beyond, and thoroughly kissed me. By the time he stepped back, I'd nearly forgotten why we'd risen from our seats in the first place.

He smiled down at my bemused expression with masculine satisfaction. "I may have rumpled your . . ." He gestured toward my head.

I reached up to feel that a few strands of hair had fallen from their pins to stray down my back. "Oh," I murmured, repinning them as best I could.

By the time we reached the boxes on the other side of the theater, the interlude had already begun. We wove through the people streaming out, trying not to draw attention to ourselves. Fortunately, the box where Lord Henry had been standing was near the front of the theater, so there were few people milling about on that end of the hall. Which made it easy to spot Lord Henry when he strolled out of the box with his hands clasped behind his back, a serious look on his face.

"Lord Henry," Gage addressed him quietly.

He stopped short upon seeing us, and then his shoulders dropped, almost as if he'd been resigned to this happening.

Gage glanced around to make sure we weren't drawing too much attention. "Could we have a moment?"

He nodded and we stepped farther down the hall to stand in the shadows of the long drapes flanking a window.

"You know why we asked to speak to you?" Gage asked, having also noted his reaction.

The anguish that flashed in Lord Henry's eyes for just a moment before being masked said volumes more than his words. "Lady Drummond."

But was he pained because he cared for her, or because he'd been responsible for her death?

Gage studied the other man. "We have reason to believe the two of you were lovers." His words were implacable, but almost gently spoken.

"Not lovers. Not . . . in that sense." His brow furrowed as if recalling something painful. "But, yes. We were . . . close."

"You understand we're investigating her murder?"

Lord Henry flinched at the word.

"So you'll appreciate we have to ask some difficult questions."

He nodded.

Gage tilted his head. "How long had your liaison with Lady Drummond been going on?"

He frowned. "It wasn't a liaison. It wasn't like that."

Gage arched his eyebrows, waiting for the answer to his question.

Lord Henry sighed. "Nine months. Maybe longer."

That long? And Lady Drummond had been able to keep it secret from even her dearest friends?

Gage seemed to have the same thought. "And you had not yet become intimate? Who resisted?"

"She did. She . . ." He pushed a hand through his hair. "She didn't want to betray her marriage vows." His face became hard. "Even though her husband was a rotten blackguard."

"That must have made you mad?"

Lord Henry shook his head, staring off into the distance. "Not mad. Frustrated, yes. But not mad. How could I? It was one of the many reasons I loved her." His expression tightened, and he seemed shaken by either the confession or the realization that she was gone.

"So you didn't poison her in a fit of jealous rage because she wouldn't leave her husband?"

I turned to look at Gage, surprised by the blunt casualness of his comment.

Lord Henry scowled, but did not rise to the bait. "No," he answered firmly.

Gage scrutinized the man and then nodded. "Then do you have any idea who might have wanted to harm her?"

His mouth twisted. "I suppose you're already investigating Lord Drummond."

"His name has been mentioned one or two times," he replied vaguely, but tellingly. "Did he know about his wife's relationship with you?"

Lord Henry's expression turned grave. "I hope not."

There was no need to elaborate. We all knew how Lord Drummond would have reacted.

"Not that I'm surprised, given your reputation, but may I ask, how did *you* find out about us? We were so discreet." His eyes were stark. "We couldn't risk it."

Gage glanced at me.

"Lady Rachel Radcliffe thought there might have been something between you," I told him.

His mouth tightened. "Of course."

Gage's eyes met mine.

"Why do you say that?" I asked.

"Because Lady Rachel was perhaps Lady Drummond's closest friend. And yet, Lady Drummond insisted we be cautious around her. Maybe it was my imagination, but it seemed almost as if she was as worried about Lady Rachel finding out as she was her husband."

That was curious. "Do you know why? Was she afraid Lady Rachel wouldn't keep your secret?"

He considered my question. "I don't know. But I sensed her friend was privy to other confidences, so that doesn't seem right." He inhaled as if he had a sudden thought. "I did notice that things seemed to be strained between them during the week or two before . . ." He swallowed.

"Strained how?"

"Just small things. Little hesitations. Tight smiles." He paused as a couple strolled passed us. The interlude must have been nearing its end. "I don't think I would have noticed if I hadn't been so attentive to Lady Drummond's every word and action." He shrugged. "Maybe it was just a small disagreement. The type friends have all the time. But I did note it."

"Thank you," Gage told him. "Even the littlest things can some-times help solve an inquiry, but we won't know until the full picture is formed."

Lord Henry nodded, waiting once again as a trio of ladies walked by, observing us with undisguised interest. Once they had passed out of hearing range, he leaned in closer to Gage. "You will catch whoever did this, won't you?" His eyes burned with intensity. "You will see that they pay for what they did to Lady Drummond?"

He nodded. "We will do our best."

Lord Henry looked as if he wanted to argue, but in the end he simply bobbed his head and turned away.

We stood for a moment, watching him go.

"If Lord Drummond had been the one poisoned, we would be having the exact opposite problem," Gage muttered. "Far too many suspects. And I would have put him at the top of the list."

"But he didn't harm Lady Drummond," I stated.

"No. He didn't do that," Gage agreed. His attention shifted to me. "Did you wish to see the rest of the play?"

I thought of the pleasant interlude we'd enjoyed in the box before venturing out to find Lord Henry. But there were far less public places for us to appreciate each other's company. My cheeks became flushed in anticipation. "No."

A twinkle entered Gage's eyes, letting me know he suspected where my wayward thoughts had gone. "Then let's go. We can discuss the inquiry and . . . other things better elsewhere."

He took my arm and we began to weave our way toward the exit against the flow of audience members returning to their boxes and seats. He was right. We did need to discuss the inquiry first. In particular, I still needed to tell him what I'd learned about his father. Though I suspected after I told him, he might not be so eager to return to other pursuits. But he needed to know. Lord Gage had to be confronted, sooner rather than later.

I debated the best way to tell him as we descended the stairs toward the lobby and went to collect our outer garments. Gage was helping me into my pewter gray cloak to match my tarnished silver dress when one of the porters hurried toward us, his heels rapping against the floor tiles.

"Lady Darby?" he asked.

"Yes, that's me."

He sighed in relief and held out a letter. "This was delivered for you."

I stared at it a moment, feeling alarm race through my veins. I snatched the letter out of his hand.

"Thank you," Gage told him as I broke open the seal. "What is it?" he asked, leaning over my shoulder to try to read. "Your sister?"

It took me a moment to respond, for that was exactly what I had thought the missive was about. "It's . . . from Bonnie Brock."

He reached out to take it from me, reading the same words I had.

Maggie is in trouble. Come to the White Hart Inn at Grassmarket. My men will meet you.

> *BB*

"Well, of course we aren't going."

I glared at him. "Of course we are." I pulled the letter from his hands and refolded it.

"Don't be foolish, Kiera," he reasoned, following me across the lobby. He threaded his arm through mine, slowing my steps. "You owe this man nothing."

"No," I agreed. "But if he was desperate enough to send me a note, then his sister must truly be in distress. I'm not going to just ignore that."

He ducked his head against the wind, holding his hat on his head. "But why on earth should he send for you? The man isn't to be trusted. He may mean you harm."

I waited until the footman had helped me up into Gage's carriage and Gage had settled in beside me before I replied, "Because Maggie recently lost a baby."

He opened his mouth to argue, but then stopped as he grasped the implications.

I straightened my skirts, tugging at the pleating. "He admitted he's concerned for her. She's been low in spirits and health. If he thinks I can help, then I'm not going to turn away."

Gage's eyes narrowed suspiciously. "When did he tell you all of this?"

I ran my hand over the embroidery, trying to decide whether I could lie, and if I should. I sighed, electing for honesty. "He came to see me yesterday."

"Kiera," Gage growled in a low voice.

"I was walking home from Lady Rachel's and he appeared out of nowhere," I snapped. "What was I supposed to do? Scream for help?"

His expression was thunderous. "You should have told me."

I turned to stare out the window at the darkened street. I knew he was right, but I didn't want to admit it.

"How often does he take you for an afternoon stroll?"

I scowled at his sarcastic tone. "Now who's being ridiculous?"

"I don't know."

I huffed. "Think what you want. But I'm going to Grassmarket with or without you." I glowered at the seat in front of me, before grudgingly adding, "But I would rather you come with me."

Gage was silent a moment longer, and then thumped the roof of the carriage with his fist.

I inhaled in relief as he gave directions to his coachman. Much as I wanted to be sure Maggie was well, I didn't really want to descend into that part of Old Edinburgh alone. Grassmarket, which ended on the west side at West Port, had been the haunt of Burke and Hare, and was currently the hangout for any number of criminals.

We rode in silence as the carriage turned left to climb up the hill to Old Town and then sharply descended toward the Grassmarket. Grassmarket sat in a hollow directly below the south side of the castle. The shambles stood at the west end of the market where traders and cattle drovers gathered, while the remainder of the wide street was lined with inns, taverns, and lodging houses.

The smell was something to be avoided at all cost, a mixture of the caustic scents of pitch and hemp and dye, and butchered animals. I journeyed here from time to time on market days to purchase linseed oil and other paint supplies, and always left as quickly as I could. But aside from the other night, I'd never ventured into this part of the city after dark. From the grim look of anticipation on Gage's face, I suspected he had.

He ordered his carriage to let us out at the east end of the market and wait for us there. As I climbed from the coach, he tugged my cloak tighter around me, hiding my gown, and instructed me to tuck my mother's pendant down my bodice. I did as I was told, even removing the jeweled comb from my hair and placing it inside the inner pocket on my cloak. Once he was satisfied I looked as inconspicuous as possible, he pulled me close to his side and we set off down the street.

"Stay close," he leaned down to murmur. "And avoid eye contact."

I nodded, dropping my gaze from a man who hobbled past.

The sliver of the waxing moon was shrouded with clouds, making the deep shadows at the edge of Grassmarket vast caverns of darkness. From these caves emerged guttural sounds and bursts of raucous laughter, and the occasional groan of satisfaction. Even the better-lit establishments contributed a higgledy-piggledy of noises to the night, many of which I had no desire to investigate. The cobbles were broken and uneven in many places, making us mind our steps even more than usual.

It felt absurd to admit how relieved I would be once we found Bonnie Brock's men, but I knew that while we were under his protection, nothing would happen to us that he had not sanctioned. I wondered how we would recognize them, and then I realized they would see us long before we would spot them, even with a description. My cloak and gown might be dark-colored, but they were still obviously high quality, and Gage might be wearing black, but the stark white of his shirt and the height of his hat would reveal him as a gentleman from twenty feet away.

Out of the gloom, the sign for the White Hart Inn suddenly emerged, swinging in the wind. We picked up our pace, and were but a few paces from the door, when a voice shouted out of the darkness.

"Oy, that's Lady Darby, the butcher's wife."

I stiffened at the coarse voice's pronouncement. Our steps halted as a pair of large men stumbled out of the inn, blocking our path as they turned to look at us. I felt the hairs on the back of my neck stand on end as an untold number of eyes peered out of the darkness at me.

"She mun' be gatherin' fresh meat for the sawbones up in High School Yards," another voice accused.

As aware of the growing danger as I was, Gage tried to guide me around the two ruffians standing in front of the entrance to the White Hart Inn, but they would not allow us to pass. So instead he swung me around, trying to hustle me back toward the carriage. I looked about, wondering where Bonnie Brock's men were. Or was this them, calling out allegations sure to incite the crowd? But I couldn't understand why Bonnie Brock would do such a thing. It made no sense.

Our way was swiftly obstructed by a brute with a cauliflower ear and his scrawnier companion. "Noo, where do ye think yer goin'?"

"Prowlin' our streets for easy pickings?" another man charged.

"Mayhap we should show 'em what we did to the last fellow."

Gage pulled me in another direction, shoving aside the hand of a man who tried to grab me. But we were thwarted again by a growing crowd of people, their faces red with anger and too much drink.

I clutched tightly to Gage's arm, looking all around me, searching desperately for a way out. This was one of my worst nightmares come to life. Being surrounded by a mob that believed the vicious rumors that had circulated about me after Sir Anthony died. Rumors that I roamed the streets at night, luring fresh victims to their doom on my late husband's or another anatomist's dissecting table. That the tales about me were so close to the truth about Burke and Hare did not help my case, particularly in this part of Edinburgh, where the notorious criminals had prowled.

An older woman clawed at my arm and Gage reached over to push her back. Suddenly someone shouted, and a large man ripped Gage away from my side. I dug in my reticule for my pistol, remembering it too late as a pair of arms grabbed me from behind.

CHAPTER 26

I screamed as a gun fired to my left.

"Hush, lass," a familiar voice murmured in my ear.

I swung about to see Bonnie Brock's face hovering over mine, his arm wrapped around my back. He towed me into the shadows at the edge of the street.

"Gage," I gasped, resisting.

"We've got him, too. Noo, move."

We darted between two buildings and then right and then left again into the Vennel leading steeply uphill. I hurried along beside him as fast as I could, even though I quickly developed a stitch in my side. At some point we slipped into another close and then through a door and up a dark flight of stairs.

In the room at the top, Bonnie Brock released me and crossed to the dusty window to peer down at the Vennel below. He murmured to one of his men, who stationed himself at the other window, pistol drawn.

I stood bent over, gasping for air as I clasped my side. When a hand came to rest on my lower back, I glanced up sharply, and nearly crumpled in relief to see Gage staring down at me.

But my respite was short-lived.

"What the bloody hell were ye thinkin'?" Bonnie Brock rounded on us to demand. His finger shot out to point in the direction of the stairs. "Those people woulda tore ye to shreds."

"You *told* us to meet your men there," I snapped back in between breaths. "So if anyone's to blame, it's you."

"*What?* You've gone daft, lass. I dinna tell ye to meet me anywhere."

I whipped out his letter from the pocket inside my cloak and held it out to him.

He scowled over the few lines and then crushed the paper in his fist. His eyes, when they lifted toward me, burned bright with a restrained violence that made the skin along my arms bristle. "I dinna send this to ye," he said in a low voice.

I glanced at Gage, who watched the man with a furious frown.

"Then who did?" he demanded.

"I dinna ken." His eyes narrowed. "But I mean to find oot." His gaze focused on me again. "Who delivered it?"

"I don't know. The porter at the Theatre Royal said someone had delivered it for me. I didn't ask for details. I didn't know I needed to."

"Dinna fash yerself. *I* will."

I reached out to grab his arm. "Don't harm him. He was only doing his job."

He looked as if he wanted to disagree, and I squeezed tighter. He relented with a sharp nod.

"What of Maggie?" I searched his face. "Is she well?"

He grimaced. "As well as can be." He lifted his hand clutching the crushed missive. "She's no worse."

"Now that we have that cleared up." Gage stepped between us, pulling me closer to his side. "How are we going to return to my carriage?"

For a moment, I was worried Bonnie Brock was going to take out his wrath on Gage by punching him, or worse. Gage must have sensed it, too, for his muscles braced, as if ready to spring back at him. But Bonnie Brock audibly inhaled and exhaled, and the tension passed.

"One of my men told yer driver to move to Greyfriars Kirk. I'll take ye there when we're sure the way is clear." He waited a second, as if expecting Gage to argue, and then returned to the window, peering through the dirty glass.

Periodically we could hear shouts outside, and I wondered if the crowd was still searching for me or if general mayhem had broken out. Many of them had already been foxed, or at least half-sprung, so I didn't suspect it would take much to rile them into a frenzied mob intent on bedlam.

I wrapped my arms around my middle, grateful for Gage's steady hand at my back. I felt like such a fool for falling for whoever's ruse it had been to lure me to Grassmarket. The note was clever, but if I'd paused long enough to think, I would have looked closer at the seal and realized that Bonnie Brock would never sign his name, even with simple initials.

I watched as he conducted a hushed conversation with a few of his men. If he hadn't arrived when he did . . . I shivered in remembrance of the woman's clawing hands. I didn't need much of an imagination to envisage what would have happened next.

Shaking aside the frightening thought, I glanced about me for the first time at the sparse furnishings and dirty floor. It looked like a room in a temporary lodging house, for there were few personal possessions I could see. I had been curious where Bonnie Brock kept his lodgings, but this did not seem to be the place. It wasn't befitting his image as the head of a large criminal gang, nor did it reflect the comfort I suspected he enjoyed.

Two of his men crossed the room to the door while he turned to tell us what they had decided. "Stumps and Locke are gonna cause a distraction doon at West Port. Give 'em a few minutes." He propped his foot up on a rickety chair and leaned into it, seemingly oblivious to the way it swayed.

"Did your men inform you we'd come to Grassmarket?" I couldn't resist asking, pondering the providence of his being there just when we needed him.

"Nay. I happened to be nearby conductin' a bit o' . . . business."

What this business was, I wasn't about to ask. Especially not when the amused lilt to his words suggested he wanted me to.

"I thought this part of the city was under your control?" Gage challenged. "From where I'm standing, it sure doesn't look like it."

I frowned up at him, not understanding his belligerent tone. Did he *want* to fight with Bonnie Brock?

"No one controls the mob," he responded with a hard glare. "'Specially no' an Edinburgh one. Unless yer bent on violence. But then ye'd better be careful it dinna turn back on ye." He turned his head to the side, shielding his face from our view with the fall of his hair. "But dinna worry. They'll hear o' my displeasure tomorrow. And whoever started it willna be capable of doin' so again."

One of his men stationed near the window grunted something unintelligible, but Bonnie Brock seemed to understand him.

"Come," he ordered, moving toward the door.

My stomach swirled anxiously, and I glanced back at Gage for reassurance before following Bonnie Brock down the stairs. We paused at the bottom for a few seconds before finally plunging out into the street.

He led us down a series of back lanes, darting between buildings as we wove our way toward the church. From time to time, shouts rang out in the distance, but most of our journey was accompanied by only the scurry of our feet on the cobblestones. At an intersection with one of the wider lanes, two of Bonnie Brock's men peeled off to confront a pair of men standing a few feet away. We did not wait to see the results of the scuffle, but from the movements of one of the men, I suspected a knife was involved.

When finally we darted through the gate leading into the grounds of Greyfriars Kirk, deftly picked by one of Bonnie Brock's men, I noticed, I breathed a sigh of relief. However, it was prematurely done. Bonnie Brock pulled me into the shadows clinging to the wall to the right of the gate. The stone at my back was cold through my silk gown and cloak.

"Watchmen," he told us simply.

I nodded, aware of the precautions the burying grounds near the anatomy schools in Edinburgh, Glasgow, and London had taken to protect the bodies of the recently deceased from resurrectionists. Being so close to Surgeons' Hall but a few blocks away, Greyfriars Kirkyard had been one of the most frequently raided cemeteries in all of Scotland.

We hunkered against the wall for what felt like a quarter of an hour, but what must have been only a minute or two, before a man walked by a few feet in front of us. I held my breath until he disappeared back into the gloom. Then Bonnie Brock sprang into action.

"Quick, noo," he ordered us.

We hurried down the path that circled the church to the right, past the Gothic-arched windows, their glass oily black in the dim moonlight. At the corner of the building we paused once more, but only for a few seconds before dashing across the open space between the front of the building and the eastern gate. My heart pounded in my ears, conscious without being told so that this was the most vulnerable part of our flight. When finally we dived back into the shadows along the wall, I inhaled sharply, feeling the darkness wrap securely around me like a blanket.

The gate creaked as it was opened just wide enough for Gage and I to slip through.

I touched Bonnie Brock's shoulder. "Thank you."

I couldn't see his face, but I felt the warmth of his breath as he exhaled. "Go," he snapped impatiently.

I slithered through, and waited for Gage to follow. He grabbed my hand and we ran down the short lane to the carriage waiting in the street at the end. We didn't stop to see if there was anyone watching.

The footman was still perched at the back so Gage threw open the door and boosted me inside before following suit.

"Go!" he shouted in an unconscious imitation of Bonnie Brock moments before. He slammed the door and tumbled sideways onto the floor next to me.

We lay there breathing heavily as the coach slowly rolled forward and then turned before finally gaining speed. I closed my eyes, never so grateful to be in a moving carriage in my life. My forehead rested on my hands, and I turned to the side to see Gage propped up on one elbow, staring at the ceiling. As I watched, he turned to regard me, and though it was too dark to see the expression in his eyes, I felt a barrier there that had not existed just an hour before. Some of the relief that had been coursing through my veins vanished.

He pulled himself upright to perch on the seat and then reached down to help me up, which proved not to be an easy endeavor with my legs tangled in the voluminous fabric of my skirts. When finally I was seated across from him, doing my best to straighten my rumpled appearance, he spoke.

"We were lucky Bonnie Brock was there." His voice was flat and emotionless.

I gave up on fixing my hair, pushing the strands that had fallen behind my ear. "Yes," I agreed cautiously, unsure which direction this conversation was headed.

"If he hadn't been there, I'm not sure I could have gotten us to safety."

I tilted my head, wishing I could see his face. "Gage," I began and then fumbled to a stop. I didn't know what to say. What he said was true, but confirming that hardly seemed like the reassurance he needed. "I knew you were doing your best to protect me," I told him. "It was you who fired your pistol, wasn't it?"

"Yes. But little good one bullet could do versus a mob of people." He turned to stare out the window with his arms crossed.

"Gage," I gently scolded.

"The truth is I failed to protect you," he retorted more loudly. "Yet again. And this time I was right next to you, not an estate or a village away."

I frowned. "I was the one who insisted we respond to Bonnie Brock's letter. Or what I thought was Bonnie Brock's letter. That's not your fault. There was nothing you could do."

His head suddenly snapped around to look at me. "Exactly. There was *nothing* I could do. I'm your fiancé. It's my *duty* to protect you. And yet I couldn't."

I realized then how furious he was, though that anger was directed at himself, not me.

I leaned forward to grab his hand, clutching it between mine. "I know you were doing everything you could to keep me safe. That's all I can ever ask."

"Yes, but it wasn't enough." He pulled his hand from mine. "It wasn't nearly enough."

I sat straighter, feeling stung by his dismissal. I was trying to reassure him, but he didn't want to hear it. "And what about me?" I demanded. "How do you think I feel knowing that when you charge off on one of your inquiries, I can't always be there to watch over you? I was terrified when those criminals captured you during our inquiry in the Borders."

He scowled. "That's different."

"Because you're the man, and I'm the woman. I know. But that doesn't make it any easier to endure."

He stared across the short distance between us. His face was still in shadow, but I could feel the weight of his gaze. When next he spoke, it was with quiet certainty. "I'm never going to be able to be confident you're safe. It's impossible."

"Who of us is ever completely safe? Just look at Lady Drummond." I gestured. "Harmless and beloved, and yet she was poisoned. Or

Alana, confined to her bed. She . . . she could die in childbirth," I stammered and then swallowed, wanting to bite back the words, even though they were true.

"Yes, but they don't insist on joining their husbands in investigating dangerous matters."

"They also don't have husbands who occupy their time as gentleman inquiry agents. But we are who we are."

The carriage rolled over a jarring bump, and Gage leaned to the side to peer through the curtains. He rapped on the ceiling with this knuckles, and turned to shout his instructions to the driver through the slat that slid open in the wall behind him.

"We're going back to the Theatre Royal?" I asked him once he'd finished.

He raked his hand through his hair. "We need to question that porter before Bonnie Brock gets to him. I don't trust him not to scare him so badly he leaves town."

I nodded in agreement, and then realized he probably couldn't see it. "Sadly, that's probably true."

Whoever had chosen to impersonate Bonnie Brock by sending that letter had just made a ruthless enemy, and even though it was likely the porter had done nothing more than deliver the message, Bonnie Brock would not see it that way. Especially if the porter could not give him the answers he wanted.

As frightening as this evening had been, at least we knew one thing. Someone was intent on silencing me, and there could be only one reason why. We must be getting close to uncovering Lady Drummond's killer. Which meant I had almost certainly already met them, had probably questioned them, and yet I had not detected their guilt.

It made me anxious to locate this man who was following me. Had he been looking for an opportunity to do me harm, observed my conversation with Bonnie Brock, and decided he'd found the perfect chance? And what of that carriage that nearly ran me over? Had that been an accident or his first attempt to get rid of me? If so, he'd been working against me for far longer than I had even been aware of him.

Or perhaps not.

I glanced at Gage, who was still quietly stewing over what he saw as his failure to protect me. "Where was your father this evening? I thought he would have insisted on following us to the theater."

"I don't know," he replied shortly. "I don't keep track of his movements."

Something I was sure he counted on. Was this a fatal error on our part?

"When did he say he arrived in Edinburgh?" I tried to make the question sound casual, but Gage must have heard something in my voice.

"Friday the eighteenth. The day of the Inverleith Ball. Why?"

I shrugged it off. "Just thinking."

"Thinking what? Kiera."

I hesitated, not sure how to tell him what I needed to, or if I even should.

A light suddenly flared to life and I flinched away from it. "Gage," I scolded in annoyance. "You could have warned me." I blinked open my eyes, watching as he lit the lantern and then closed it before setting the tinderbox aside.

"I know that tone of your voice." His eyes brooked no argument. "What are you thinking?"

"Just that your father has no wish to see us wed, and every reason to wish to be rid of me."

His brow furrowed. "You think my father sent us to Grassmarket tonight?"

"Me. The note was for me," I reminded him.

"Yes. But he had to know I would insist on accompanying you."

"Maybe." I paused. "But that's not all." I told him what Lady Rachel had told me about his father's courtship of Lady Drummond, and how Lady Stratford had later confirmed it.

Gage remained silent, his gaze fixed on the carriage floor. He seemed stunned.

"I'm sorry," I told him. "I'm sure it's not what you wanted to hear. Especially since I know your mother must have been dead only a year or two."

"Less than that."

My chest constricted, hearing the pain in his voice. "But he needs to be questioned. It seems far too convenient that he neglected to tell us."

"And presents a potential conflict of interest," he added, lifting his eyes to look at me.

I smiled humorlessly. So he'd noticed how his father had accused me of just such a thing while ignoring it himself. "Yes. So you understand why I wondered when he had actually arrived in town. We need some straight answers. No more . . ."

"I'll talk to him." His jaw flexed.

"Yes, but wouldn't it be better if we *both* talked . . ."

"No, Kiera," he cut me off. "I know my father. If we both try to confront him, he won't tell us anything."

"Because he dislikes me."

Gage sighed and shrugged. "Partly."

I crossed my arms over my chest. "Well, I don't care what he likes or dislikes. He's been lying to us, and we deserve answers."

He leaned toward me. "You're absolutely right. But if we want any, then we have to do this my way."

I scowled at him skeptically.

"Please, Kiera," he pleaded. "Will you just trust me on this? This is going to be a difficult conversation. It will be hard enough to get him to talk to me. I . . . I need to be the one to confront him. Alone." He looked deep into my eyes. "Will you let me do that?"

I wanted to say no, to insist I come with him, but I couldn't. Not knowing he was probably right, and that he didn't really need my permission. He could do as he pleased and I would just have to accept it. The fact that he was at least asking for my agreement salved my pride at being required to step aside again.

I nodded. "But you'll come to me with what you uncover? As soon as you can?"

"I will. This is our inquiry. I'm not going to deny you access to any relevant information, despite my father's wishes."

I stared into his handsome face, so clearly troubled and yet so open to me. I lifted my hand to touch his cheek. Stubble rasped against the delicate silk of my glove. He pressed his face deeper into my hand, before turning to the side to place a kiss in the center of my palm. His breath feathered across the exposed skin of my wrist, making my pulse beat faster.

Suddenly the carriage skidded to a halt, throwing me forward into Gage's lap. He braced me, keeping me from tumbling onto the floor, and then glanced up at the sound of his coachman shouting at someone. Once I was seated again, he lifted aside the curtain to see what commotion had forced us to stop. The lights from the Theatre Royal blazed before us, along with all of the carriages waiting to pick up the patrons as they streamed through the doors. Our coach had nearly collided with one of them.

Had the play truly just ended? It seemed we had been gone for half the night, not just a little over an hour.

We fought our way up to the theater and into the lobby, ignoring the suspicious looks over our rumpled appearance, only to discover that the porter could not be found. His manager stammered apology after apology as they searched for him throughout the building, but it seemed he'd vanished. Another freckle-faced porter admitted that he thought he'd seen his coworker leave early, but he couldn't be certain. No one admitted to knowing where the young man lived, so we were forced to leave empty-handed.

"You don't think Bonnie Brock could have gotten to him already?" I asked doubtfully.

Gage's face was creased in a fearsome frown. "No. I think it more likely that he was either part of the scheme, or he was tipped a very large sum of money to deliver that message and left early to spend it."

I tilted my head in thought. "He did seem awfully eager to give it to me, and I've never known the porters to be so zealous. But the rest of the staff knew him, so he couldn't have been positioned there simply to deliver the message."

"No. He was a regular employee. I'll have Anderley drop in to try to catch the fellow tomorrow when he comes to work. But if he doesn't come back to the theater, it may not be easy to locate him."

"Perhaps Bonnie Brock will have better luck. I don't expect he'll give up easily."

Gage was silent as he helped me up into his carriage—this time using the step. But once he'd settled onto the squabs beside me, he spoke in a carefully indifferent voice. "Will he let you know what he uncovers?"

"I don't know. I suppose it depends on what he finds out. And what he proposes to do to the perpetrator," I added cynically.

"Well, for once I hope the scoundrel does interfere," he groused.

I wisely kept my own counsel.

CHAPTER 27

Fatigued both in body and spirit, I dragged my feet up the stairs to my room. It was well past midnight and I expected the rest of the house to be fast asleep, but a light still shone beneath Alana's door. I considered ignoring it, but then I thought of all the lonely hours my sister had been wiling away this past week, with nothing but her own worrisome thoughts to occupy her. I rolled the tension from my shoulders before crossing the hall to tap on her door.

She was lounging in bed as ordered with her head tilted toward the window even though the drapes were shut. At my entrance, she turned her head on the pillow, but she did not smile. I crept closer to see that tears glistened on her cheeks in the soft light cast from the bedside lamp.

"Oh, dearest," I murmured, dropping my cloak on the chair and ignoring protocol to crawl into bed beside her. I was careful not to jostle her stomach as I gathered her head into my chest as a mother might a child. She whimpered and then began to weep as I ran my hand through her lovely chestnut brown hair. I did not try to speak, just held her. Words weren't needed anyway. I knew how nervous and frightened she was, because I felt those things, too, but to a lesser degree.

When finally her tears were spent and the sniffles began, I reached into my dress to hand her my handkerchief. I waited as she dabbed at her cheeks and eyes. Earl Grey watched us from the bottom of the bed. I was pleased to see at least someone was keeping my sister company regularly.

"I'm sorry," she began. "I just . . ."

"No apologies," I told her, gently cutting her off. "You're under a tremendous amount of strain. You wouldn't be human if you didn't cry at least a little."

She swallowed another sob and nodded.

"Do you want to talk about it?"

She shook her head, and then proceeded to speak anyway. "It's just . . . I'm so scared." Her voice trailed away to a whisper. "Do you know what Philipa asked me?" She turned to me with wide eyes. "She wanted to know if I would be here for her birthday next month. I told her yes. But what if I'm not? What if I lied?"

"Alana." I tried to comfort her, but she rushed on without listening.

"And this baby." She caressed her rounded abdomen. "What if I'm not here to take care of him? What if I abandon him before I even get a chance to hold him?"

"Alana, stop this. You are not abandoning him."

"He may never know me." She broke down into wracking sobs, soaking the fabric of my gown. I'd never seen her so upset.

"Alana. Alana," I said more loudly, gripping her shoulder. "You must stop this. It's not good for you or the baby. Please. If you want him delivered safely, you must gain control of yourself." It was the only thing I could think of to calm her, harsh as it sounded to my ears, but fortunately it worked.

She inhaled shakily and closed her eyes. I massaged her shoulder as she struggled to compose herself. It seemed to help when she rubbed her stomach, as if soothing the life inside her as well as herself. When her breathing evened out, I took the handkerchief she clutched in her hand and turned it inside out before dabbing at the tears wetting her cheeks.

"You cannot give in to despair," I told her firmly. "It does you no good." She blinked open her eyes to look up at me. "You are *going* to deliver this baby safely, and you are *going* to live long enough to see their children, their grandchildren. So stop this nonsense. I won't hear any more of it."

She sniffed and reached up to take the handkerchief from me. But before I relinquished it, I demanded an answer. "Do you understand?"

"Yes," she replied in a hoarse voice.

"Good."

She shifted her head back onto her pillow and blew her nose. I sat with my back propped against the headboard, my ankles crossed, and waited for her to finish. As if sensing this was now the time to ask for attention, Earl Grey sauntered up the bed to sit beside me, waiting for me to scratch his chin. I obliged.

A few moments later, I heard Alana draw breath to speak, but I cut her off. "*Don't* apologize." I glanced down at her and could tell from her expression that's exactly what she had been about to do.

"Well, then at least let me say 'thank you.'" She sniffed. "I've been sitting here all evening feeling sorry for myself. I needed someone to correct me."

"I never said you couldn't feel sorry for yourself," I explained. "Just don't wallow in it."

"Point taken. As Grandmother used to say, 'We're not pigs. We don't wallow in our filth. We soldier on.'"

A smile curled my lips. "She did have a way with words."

"Yes." Alana stared up at the ceiling, and I thought she was remembering our eccentric Irish grandmother. But then a small crease appeared between her brows. "Kiera, at the risk of wallowing a bit more, may I ask you a question?"

"I suppose."

Her bright lapis lazuli eyes gleamed like jewels, as mine always did when I had been crying or terribly angry. "Do you think Philip has a paramour?"

The question caught me so unawares that at first I couldn't formulate a response, but my sister waited patiently, bravely for me to give her one. "No," I finally said. "No, I don't."

She searched my eyes for any sign of prevarication and then nodded.

I wasn't sure if she believed me, but I couldn't give her any petty explanations for Philip's behavior. That would feel like a betrayal, a dismissal of the gravity of the situation. The only person who could give her those answers was her husband, and it was long past time for it.

My fury at my brother-in-law flared to life. Here his wife lay, doing all she could to preserve her life and that of their unborn child, battling her fear and uncertainty, and he was largely absent. He should be by her side, comforting her, helping her through this, not worrying about matters of Parliament or business or his estates.

This needed to end. Now.

Unfortunately, Philip was nowhere in the house. Which left me with no outlet for my anger and frustration. So instead, I sat down to do what I could to advance the investigation while I waited for him to return. I took out my sketchbook and drew the faces of all the men who had been involved in some way with Lady Drummond's life and death—family, friends, lovers, servants—anyone I could think of. Perhaps they would prove useless, but at the very least they would help me to review and prioritize the information we knew so far. And if we could visit the Chemist again and he happened to recognize one of them, the drawing just might prove to be exactly what we needed to finally catch the killer.

I awoke the next morning in a sour mood. I'd fallen asleep over my sketches, and developed a painful crick in my neck, as well as smudged the last drawing. Philip had returned sometime while I was slumbering, but tempted as I was to wake him and vent my foul temper on him, I knew our conversation would go better if he was well rested and I was calmer. Much as I'd wanted to confront him the night before, I now recognized that I needed him to see reason and admit the folly of his current actions. Approaching him in a towering rage was probably not going to help my cause.

I stretched out on Alana's comfortable fainting couch in the drawing room and ordered a pot of strong, black coffee instead of my normal cup of chocolate. Then I settled in to wait for Gage or Philip to appear, whoever came first. In the meantime, I finished my sketches and tried not to glance at the clock every five minutes.

I knew Gage well enough to know that, if at all possible, he would have spoken to his father the night before. And if not then, he would have hunted him down this morning. Neither of us slept well when there were things to be confronted, especially if there were strong emotions involved.

So when the morning stretched on toward midday and he still had not arrived, my impatience and irritation began to get the better of me. He had promised to share what he uncovered as soon as he could, and unless his father had left to return to London—something I highly doubted since I was still engaged to his son—I had a difficult time believing their confrontation had not yet occurred.

I abandoned my sketches to pace before the hearth. Philip had also not yet emerged from the guest chamber, but short of pounding on the door, there was nothing I could do about it. I pressed my hands to my face, feeling the worry and resentment and helplessness that had been surging inside me for days rise up and threaten to pull me under. It was as if I was treading water as wave after wave crashed into me, each one bigger than the last. Whenever I allowed myself to think about any one of the things battering my life and that of my loved ones, it was as if they all came rushing in on me. Alana's and the baby's precarious health, the uncertain state of her marriage to Philip, Gage's continued refusal to confide in me, his father's disapproval, the enormous wedding my sister was planning, Lady Drummond's murder. It was all too much.

I forced myself to breathe deeply, trying to clear them all from my mind, but they would not go away. I couldn't stay here. I needed to get out, to go somewhere, anywhere. Lifting my mink brown skirts, I charged for the door to collect my cloak. I refused the carriage, instead setting out on foot. I needed to move, to breathe the fresh air, not stew in another enclosed space.

I was several blocks away before I remembered why it might not be a good idea to set off on my own. I glanced around me, suddenly conscious of every person, every movement in my vicinity. Pulling my cloak tighter, I hurried in the direction of my nearest acquaintance's home. I suspected that might have been the destination I was truly headed anyway.

But instead of Lady Stratford, it was Lady Bearsden who received me in her parlor.

"Come in, dear. I'm afraid you've just missed Charlotte. She stepped out on a rather secretive mission." The older woman's eyes gleamed with excitement as she leaned forward to confess. "I suspect she's not strictly following the rules of mourning, but we shan't say anything." Her lips pressed together in a sly smile.

I was surprised to hear such a thing. Lady Stratford had always been eminently proper, even mourning a husband who had tried to kill her. But I didn't let her great-aunt know that. She seemed to be taking entirely too much pleasure in her niece's rebellion as it was. "Oh. Well. I hope I'm not interrupting anything," I replied, even though it was clear I was not.

"Of course not, dear." She reached out to pat my hand. "I'm happy for the company." She wagged her finger at me. "You still haven't brought your charming fiancé and his father by for a visit."

"Yes. I'm sorry. You're right. We've just been so busy with our latest inquiry."

She nodded sagely. "Lady Drummond." She sighed. "I can't believe she was murdered. And in her own home. What is the world coming to?"

I nodded in commiseration.

She tilted her head. "Well, how goes it? Do you have any suspects? Anyone I know?"

I could barely keep up with all of her questions. "We're at a bit of a standstill, I'm afraid. And a bit flummoxed as to which way to turn next." I wasn't sure why I was being so honest with her. Perhaps it was the weight of all my worries, or my troubled sleep the night before. All I knew was that I was tired and unhappy, and I couldn't be bothered to hide it all anymore.

Lady Bearsden seemed to sense this, because her demeanor changed. She suddenly became less animated, and far more maternal. "Tell me. Maybe I can help," she offered sincerely.

So I did. I ignored the fact that she was a gossip, or at least that she associated with a number of them, and laid out the entire inquiry for her from beginning to end. By the time I'd finished, an hour had passed and we'd taken tea, but Lady Bearsden confessed she was as baffled as I was. I did, however, recall a few things that I'd overlooked or forgotten I'd known, and my head didn't feel as muddled as it had before.

"I've never met this Mrs. Dubois," Lady Bearsden said, rehashing any thoughts I supposed she felt might be helpful to me. "And I suspect I never shall."

I hid a smile at her disappointment.

"But I know Lord Henry." She smiled. "Such a lovely man. I can't believe he would ever do such a thing. And I'm acquainted with Lady Rachel and her sister, though I knew their mother better." She tsked and shook her head. "Such a sad tale."

I'd begun to nod without really listening when she suddenly leaned toward me.

"Lord Corbin was not a very nice man, you know. There were even rumors for a time that he killed his wife. Nothing could be proven, of course. But that didn't stop everyone from speculating."

"Wait. Who?" I asked, trying to figure out what I'd missed. I felt a surge of anticipation run along my veins, sensing this was important.

"Lord Corbin," she repeated and, then seeing my blank stare, elaborated. "Lady Rachel's father."

I indicated my understanding.

She settled back into her seat, shaking her head again. "He was a hard man. It was probably a blessing for those two girls when he died of an apoplexy."

I sat straighter. "He died of an apoplexy?"

Lady Bearsden nodded, oblivious to the change in my mood.

"She told me her husband also died of an apoplexy."

"Poor dear," she murmured. "And now her friend."

This did not seem to strike her as odd, and perhaps it wasn't. Heaven knew, an apoplexy seemed to be a physician's explanation for anything they couldn't easily diagnose. But I couldn't help but note the coincidence. Though what Lady Drummond had in common with Lady Rachel's cruel father and her abusive husband, I didn't know.

Regardless, I began to reassess everything Lady Rachel had done and said since the moment she visited me after Lady Drummond's death. She had seemed so distraught, and perhaps she had been, but for a different reason.

I thanked Lady Bearsden for listening to me and reminded her how much trust I'd placed in her by telling her all I had.

"Don't worry," she told me with a shrewd look. "I may be friends with a bunch of busybodies, but that doesn't mean I don't know how to keep my own counsel." She flashed me a coy smile. "It's just more fun to be well informed of everyone's foibles. Especially at my age."

CHAPTER 28

I puzzled over Lady Rachel during my walk home. Could she have poisoned her friend? But why? It simply didn't make any sense.

And it all was no clearer to me when I returned to Charlotte Square than it had been when I set out. But I felt certain Lady Rachel had some part to play in the riddle. I just didn't know what. Yet.

Gage was waiting for me in the drawing room. I paused in the doorway to study him, trying to assess how well his conversation with his father had gone. The sun from the front window shone down on his golden curls where he sat bent over my sketchbook as he flipped through the pages. His boots were splattered with mud, indicating he'd gone for a long ride. Perhaps that was the reason for his tardiness.

"These are extremely well done," he commented without looking up.

"But I'm missing one," I replied obliquely, crossing the room toward him.

He looked up in question, but I refused to elaborate.

"You first," I told him, settling into the corner of the fainting couch next to his chair.

He tipped his head in assent. "I suppose that's only fair." But then he fell silent.

I waited as he leaned forward to set the sketchbook on the table and then straightened his waistcoat. I narrowed my eyes. He was gathering his thoughts, deciding exactly what to reveal. I'd watched him do it often enough, just usually not with me. "What did your father say?" I prompted, telling myself not to get angry.

He inhaled deeply before finally replying. "He admitted he had courted Lady Drummond the year after my mother died."

"That must have been difficult to hear."

He nodded, still staring at the rug, and lapsed back into silence.

I tucked my legs up underneath me, trying to be patient. But my annoyance got the better of me. "Did he say why? Or explain why he elected not to tell us?"

"He thought it would be good for him to take another wife, to have a hostess for his dinner parties, and someone to come home to since the war was over. Lady Drummond seemed the ideal choice." Gage exhaled heavily. "But . . . she wasn't my mother. And in the end, he decided they wouldn't suit."

I could understand now why Gage was having so much difficulty relaying this information to me. It must have come as a shock to know his father had considered taking a second wife. And then to hear why his father had decided against it, stated just as succinctly as Gage had put it, I was sure. Well, that made Lord Gage seem altogether quite human, and far more sympathetic than I was comfortable with, given the way he had treated me. It sounded like he had truly loved his wife, and as pleased as that made me for Gage, it irritated me to think the man was not entirely unfeeling.

"That sounds reasonable," I said in a gentler voice. "So why did he keep such an association secret?"

Gage glanced up at me, and I could tell from the shuttered look in his eyes that he was about to close me out. "He told me. I had to force it out of him. But he asked for my discretion."

"Even from me?" I asked, keeping a carefully neutral tone.

"Specifically from you, and . . . I promised I would keep his secret, so long as it wasn't relevant to the inquiry."

My jaw tightened. That was the same wording he'd used with me, when he promised to share what he learned. "And I suppose you've deemed it as such?"

"Yes."

I glared at him, letting him know with the snap of my eyes how displeased I was. "And how do you know it's not relevant? Perhaps I know something you do not that will make it so."

"Because I know. You'll just have to trust me on this."

I lowered my gaze to brush at the folds of my skirt, trying very hard not to raise my voice. "I see. And does Lord Drummond know about his friend's courtship of his wife?" I couldn't help asking.

He sat back, resting his ankle across his other knee. "Yes. Actually, my father introduced them."

"How happy for Lady Drummond," I drawled sarcastically.

"Quite," Gage admitted in a clipped voice.

I brushed at my skirts once more and then clasped my hands together in front of me. "So is this the type of behavior I'm to anticipate in the future? Where you and your father share confidences and push me out of investigations?"

He frowned. "Now you're just being unreasonable. You can't expect me to reveal my father's secrets just because you want me to. The same way my father can't expect me to reveal yours."

I clenched my fingers, hating his scolding tone of voice. The fact that he was correct only made me madder.

"Either you trust my judgment or you don't," he added, dropping his leg and resting his hand on the arm of the fainting couch next to me. His voice softened. "You will be my wife, and I will always share with you what I can. But there will be some confidences I cannot tell you, some secrets I cannot share."

"Does that include your own?"

He stilled, and I knew he hadn't anticipated such a question. The light in his eyes dimmed. "That's not fair."

"You're right. It's not," I agreed. "You've told me over and over that you'll tell me everything when the time is right. But that time never comes. And when I ask you about it, I end up being the one to apologize for pushing you." I gestured broadly with my hands. "So tell me, once and for all, are you ever going to confide in me? About your past? About your family? About *Greece*? As you said, I'm going to be your wife. Do I not deserve to know you as well as you know me?" I sat back, staring at him intently. "Or do *you* not trust *me*?"

His face turned red. "Why does it matter so much to you? Will it change how you feel about me?"

"I suppose it depends on what secrets you're keeping," I snapped back.

The color drained from his face, and I had to wonder what exactly he was hiding from me that would make him react so. "I don't know what to say, Kiera. It's not easy for me to talk about my past."

I threw up my hands. I was so tired of being sympathetic on that point. "And you think it was easy for me?" I demanded. "I had to share the most terrible, wounding experience of my life with you just to prove I was innocent of a crime I didn't commit."

"I know."

"We didn't even like each other at that point. At least you'll be sharing your secrets with your future wife."

"I know," he bit out, silencing me.

I gazed into his flushed countenance as he breathed heavily. The anger drained out of me, leaving only hurt and confusion. "Then why won't you tell me?"

His eyes were a well of secrets I couldn't begin to swim to the bottom of. And when he turned away, I began to believe for the first time that he would never give me the chance.

"I can't answer that, Kiera. Not now," he told me.

"You can't? Or you won't?" I murmured hoarsely.

He did not reply, but simply rose to his feet and left. I wrapped my arms around myself to hold myself together as his body moved farther and farther away from me and then disappeared from sight. I wanted to look away, but I couldn't, even though the separation growing between us physically hurt. Somehow I breathed through the pain, digging my fingers into my upper arms to hold back the tears welling in my eyes.

I refused to cry. I couldn't. Alana and the children needed me to be strong. Lady Drummond needed me to stay focused. Whatever became of Gage and I would happen regardless of whether I fell apart or not.

When finally I felt composed enough to lift my head, it was to see Philip standing in the doorway leading from the back parlor. From the look on his face, I could tell he had heard at least a portion of my and Gage's conversation. I just didn't know how much.

At first he said nothing, just stood there looking at me. I thought for a moment he would turn around without speaking and leave, but then he pushed away from the door frame.

"That was not very well done of you," he murmured, shaking his head in gentle reproach. "You expect too much."

My brows snapped together. "Do I?"

"Yes," he replied, stopping to lean against the back of one of the green brocade wingback chairs positioned near the hearth. "I know you're scared, Kiera. But fighting with him is not going to help."

I stiffened at this pronouncement, refusing to acknowledge the hollow feeling in the pit of my gut that said he might be right. I was not going to listen to this. Not from him.

"I see. *You* propose to lecture *me* on my relationship?"

Philip's shoulders lifted, clearly sensing he was treading on hazardous ground.

I stood, clasping my hands in front of me. "Then I shall return the favor."

He lifted his hands and started to turn away.

"No!" I snapped, startling him. "I have waited days to have this conversation with you, and it is happening. Now."

He stared at me as I crossed the room toward him in just a few angry strides.

"You want to talk about being scared? *You* are the one responding out of fear. And in the stupidest way possible."

His head reared back. "Stupid?"

"Yes, *stupid*." I had planned to approach this with more subtlety, but it was too late now. My anger over his interference had gotten the better of me.

His nose wrinkled in disdain. "I hardly think attending to my estates and parliamentary . . ."

"You're avoiding your wife because you're afraid she'll die," I stated baldly.

He stilled like a rabbit sensing danger.

"These matters of business and politics you've been so busy with. They're not so urgent. You're simply looking for excuses. Maybe you've even begun to believe them yourself. But the truth is, you're scared."

His eyes dropped to the floor and I moved closer, pleading with him across the chair between us.

"Well, I'm scared, too, Philip. But if the worst should happen . . ."

His hands clenched into fists where they rested on the back of the chair and he turned his head to the side as if to deny it.

"If Alana should die, at least I'll have the comfort of knowing I spent as much time as I could with her during her last few weeks. Will you be able to say that? Or will you hate yourself for making these paltry excuses not to talk to her, to lie in bed beside her, to hold her?"

Philip closed his eyes, as if flinching from that reality.

"She needs you."

At the desperate tone of my voice, he finally opened his eyes to look at me.

"She needs *you*, Philip. She needs your comfort, your strength. Your love." I shook my head despondently. "I don't know if she can make it through this without it."

His face was pale. "I've never stopped loving her."

"Yes, but have you told her that lately? Have you shown her?"

He didn't say anything. He didn't need to. I could see the shame and sorrow in his eyes.

"It's not too late," I told him quietly. "So for all of our sakes, *please* do something about it while you can."

I didn't wait for a reply, just turned and left, giving him the space to think about what I'd said. As I would think about what he'd said about Gage.

I wasn't sorry for confronting Gage with his continued refusal to confide in me. What I said was true. I was the one who kept apologizing for pressuring him, but the time for patience was at an end. The date of our wedding was inching closer; my sister nearly had it all planned. If we were going to pledge to love and honor each other for the rest of our lives, then he needed to trust me enough to share his life with me. All of it. Past, present, and future.

But no matter the truth behind the sentiment, I should not have reacted in anger, especially when he told me he couldn't share his father's secret. I had lashed out at him instead of attempting to discuss things in a calm, rational manner. I was treading on unfamiliar ground with our relationship, and I hated how disoriented and nervous that made me feel, and perhaps a little oversensitive.

I sighed, weary of arguing with Gage. We had bickered more in the last two weeks than we had in twice as many months. I needed to find a better way of debating with him, or else risk becoming one of those quarrelsome couples no one was happy to be around. Or worse, no couple at all.

Philipa called down to me through the railing from the floor above my bedchamber in a voice that I knew she thought was a whisper, but really wasn't a whisper at all, asking me to come play with them. Since she'd risked punishment sneaking out of the nursery just to ask me, I felt I couldn't say no. Though I supposed that meant I was rewarding bad behavior. I shook that worry aside. The children were as frightened as all of us. They deserved some leniency.

That was where Figgins found me sometime later, knee deep in blocks as I helped Malcolm build a fort and Philipa an enchanted castle, while Greer tottered around attempting to knock them down. Earl Grey was stretched out on the rug nearby, his new favorite spot to take a nap.

"My lady, Lady Stratford is here to see you," he said.

I sat up straighter, nearly toppling the guard tower I was constructing. For her to come calling on me was a breach in mourning etiquette, and as lighthearted as Lady Bearsden was about it, I knew her niece was not.

I apologized to my nieces and nephew and joined the butler in the hall. "Did you place her in the drawing room?" I asked, moving toward the stairs.

"Yes, my lady."

"Good. Send for some tea, please."

Lady Stratford sat on the edge of a chair, gazing out the window. When she heard my footsteps, she rose gracefully to her feet with a sheepish smile. "I hope I haven't come at a bad time."

"No," I hastened to reply. "Is everything all right? Your aunt?"

"Is fine. I know I'm breaking protocol by coming here," she added hesitantly.

I brushed her words aside, settling into the chair next to hers. "As if I care. I told you I didn't think your late husband deserved any observance of mourning. I'm just surprised to see you, because I know the rules do matter to you."

"Well, this mattered more."

I glanced at her quizzically, wondering what she meant.

She pressed her hands together in her lap. "My great-aunt told me you called this morning."

"Yes. She was very kind, and actually quite helpful."

"She said as much." Her lips curled in a crooked grin. "Well, crowed as much."

I smiled back. "So long as she only crows to you."

"Oh, she can be trusted." She inhaled deeply, as if working herself up to reveal something she didn't wish to. "But the reason I wasn't there was because I was confirming a suspicion I had. The rumors that have been circulating about you, the old gossip that someone stirred up again . . ." She shook her head. "Lord Gage didn't start it."

I nodded slowly, having already half suspected as much. "Do you know who did?"

She grimaced. "Lady Rachel Radcliffe."

My eyes widened in surprise. "You're sure?"

"Yes. Everyone my aunt and I were able to speak to could trace the rumors back to one source. Lady Rachel."

I rose to my feet and paced toward the hearth, where I stopped and turned back. "I'm stunned, but I feel like I shouldn't be," I admitted. "It makes perfect sense now that I think about it. She discovered very early on that I was suspicious of Lady Drummond's death, and that Gage and I were investigating. I told her to keep it quiet, but clearly she did not listen. And then to rekindle those old stories about me . . ." I pressed my hand to my mouth, thinking. Knowing everything I did now, it all seemed so obvious.

I grunted in exasperation. "I feel so foolish. I should have guessed from the beginning."

But I had been blinded by sympathy, empathizing with the misuse Lady Rachel had received at the hands of her late husband. I had related to her too much, and she had exploited that.

"I think you're too hard on yourself," Lady Stratford said. "You had no reason to think she had a motive for doing such a thing, while Lord Gage plainly demonstrated he did."

"I didn't," I admitted. "But after speaking to Lady Bearsden, I've begun to see a disturbing pattern."

"Well, no one else saw it. So don't castigate yourself."

I crossed back toward Lady Stratford. "Thank you for telling me."

"Of course." She spoke as if it were the simplest thing in the world, but I knew it wasn't.

"You called at homes all over Edinburgh to trace the source of the rumors, didn't you? You disregarded mourning etiquette just to help me."

She offered me a small smile. "Well, it was the least I could do. You saved my life, after all. I couldn't very well sit on my hands when I knew I could help. And don't forget Lady Drummond was my friend, too. I want her murder solved just as much as you do."

I reached for her hand and squeezed it. "Well, whatever the motives, I appreciate your disobedience of protocol." I tilted my head. "You know what they're going to say?"

"What's that?"

"That I'm a very bad influence on you."

Her soft gray eyes twinkled. "Let them."

After Lady Stratford left, I sat down to write two letters. The first was to Gage, explaining everything I had uncovered that day. No matter the current strife between us, we still had an inquiry to solve, and I needed his help.

It was a measure of his distraction earlier that he'd forgotten to ask what I'd alluded to at the beginning of our discussion, but I laid it out for him in ink. And I asked him to arrange an appointment with Dr. Abercrombie for early the next day. Now that I knew the right questions to ask, he might prove far more informative.

The second note was to Bonnie Brock. Being sure now that he could read and write, I jotted off a quick request for another meeting with the Chemist. I knew this meant we would have to wait for nightfall and I was anxious to finish the inquiry sooner, but there was nothing to be done about it. I gave the letter to Rosy, who seemed displeased to be utilized as a messenger yet again, and settled in to wait.

CHAPTER 29

Early the following afternoon, Gage and I were shown into the parlor with the porcelain birds again. We waited quietly, as we had during the carriage ride, speaking only to discuss the inquiry. Uncomfortable as it was, I preferred it that way. I was ashamed of my poor temper the day before, but I wasn't yet ready to apologize. Not without Gage stating something of his intentions to either trust me or not.

Dr. Abercrombie admitted he was surprised to see us. "I thought I'd told you everything I knew the other day when you called," he said, sinking into a well-loved chintz-covered sofa across from us.

I glanced at Gage, who nodded for me to take the lead. "I'm afraid we didn't know the right questions to ask you, but now we do."

The physician opened his hands face up, telling me to begin.

"Were you the physician of either the third Earl of Corbin or a Mr. Josiah Radcliffe?"

He sat back deeper against the cushions, and I knew I had hit upon something. "I'm not acquainted with Lord Corbin, but yes, I was Mr. Radcliffe's physician."

Gage and I shared another look, and I could see the same anticipation in his eyes that I felt.

"We know his death was said to have been caused by apoplexy.
Were you the physician to decide that?"

His mouth flattened into a grim line. "I was. And I know what
you're going to ask next. I've heard about Lady Drummond's poisoning." He sighed. "Yes, I found Mr. Radcliffe's death somewhat . . .
abnormal, but at the time I had no reason to believe it was murder."

I leaned forward eagerly. "How was it abnormal?"

"Mr. Radcliffe had been in what I would have called peak health, and
while it's not impossible that he could have had an apoplexy, it was certainly unusual. He also vomited profusely prior to his collapse, and was
able to gasp that his insides were burning. These two things did not sound
like the symptoms of an apoplexy to me, but the rest did." He rubbed his
temples. "Perhaps I should have insisted on further examination, but his
wife was already weeping almost hysterically, and when I suggested an
autopsy, she fainted. I had to administer a sedative to calm her."

I frowned. I could only imagine.

"I could see no evidence of foul play, so I attributed his death to an
apoplexy."

I nodded, knowing there was no use criticizing the man for his decision. He had done what he thought was best, and since no one else had
raised doubts, there had been no one to dispute it. However, I suspected
he would think twice before ignoring such abnormalities again.

"But what does this have to do with Lady Drummond's letter?" Dr.
Abercrombie asked.

"We think she was coming to ask you about Mr. Radcliffe's death,"
Gage explained.

The physician's eyes widened. "Why? Was she related?"

I pushed to my feet. "No. We think she suspected he had been
poisoned to death. And that she knew by whom."

·   ·   ·

"It looks like your misgivings were correct," Gage said once we had returned to his carriage. "Now what do you propose to do? Confront Lady Rachel?"

I shook my head. "We have no proof. Just a string of events that appear to be coincidences."

He tapped his fingers against his knee. "We need some way of linking Lady Rachel to the Chemist and the cream he poisoned with monkshood."

I leaned forward to peer out the window. "Which is why we're paying another visit to him tonight."

Gage fell silent, so I turned to look at him. His eyes were watchful, revealing little of what he thought.

"I wrote Bonnie Brock and asked for him to arrange another meeting. It seemed the only way we could obtain the answers we need." When he still did not speak, I clenched my fingers in my skirt, resisting the urge to snap at him. Instead, I added calmly, "Perhaps I should have consulted with you first, but it seemed the only solution to our problem."

"No. You were right," I was relieved to hear him say. He frowned at the floor. "There is no other choice." His eyes lifted to mine. "But what did you have to promise Kincaid in return?"

"Nothing."

His eyebrows arched. "So we'll be in his debt."

I suddenly became very interested in the passing scenery. "Maybe."

Gage fell silent again, and I had just allowed myself to believe he'd let the matter drop when he casually remarked, "Did you know that Lord and Lady Kirkcowan were robbed last night?"

"Were they?" I asked, hoping I'd displayed just the right amount of astonishment.

"Yes. Those jewels that Lady Kirkcowan stumbled upon in her

dresser. Well, they were stolen from her husband's safe. Along with a few other items."

"How terrible. Then I suppose she would have been better off keeping them in her dresser after all."

Gage's shrewd gaze told me he was not in the least bit fooled, but I wasn't about to admit anything to him. I stared back at him, blinking my eyes innocently.

When it became clear I was not going to talk, he turned away, the corners of his lips curling upward in a smile. "Much better," he said with approval.

"Much better what?" I asked.

"Acting, my dear. Acting."

This time Bonnie Brock directed us to meet him at the entrance to Robertson's Close, across from the Royal Infirmary, I supposed to make it more difficult for us to memorize any part of the route to the Chemist's shop. He also instructed us to dress in the plainest clothes we owned. After the incident in Grassmarket, I didn't need the reminder. I wished to blend in as much as possible. Being recognized once was enough for me.

We arrived promptly at sundown, leaving Gage's carriage closer to High School Yards and walking the remainder of the way to our rendezvous point. I thought my drab slate gray gown and old forest green cloak hid my status quite well, particularly in the dark gloom of an Edinburgh night. Gage was dressed in an old pair of trousers, a frayed greatcoat, and a low-brimmed hat. The strong smell of sawdust coming from his clothes made me suspect he was wearing the garments he wore while woodworking.

My lips curled at the thought that our scents might also mask our social standing, for I was sure the stench of linseed oil and gesso clung to my gown since I often painted while wearing it.

"Do ye find something amusin'?" Bonnie Brock's familiar brogue asked me.

I turned in surprise, clutching my sketchbook to my chest, though I should have known he would choose to sneak up on us.

He arched a brow in curiosity.

I glanced to Gage. "Only that you could probably smell us coming before you saw us."

Bonnie Brock sniffed. "Aye. But ye still smell sweeter than most of the city." His head turned aside and his jaw tightened. "Ye havena the stench of filth and desperation."

I didn't know how to reply to that, so I didn't try.

"Let's get this o'er wi'," he grumbled, and then nodded his head to the left. "Come."

We fell in line much like before and set off down the close. Our track seemed to twist and turn all over the city until I had no idea which direction we were walking in. He seemed to be trying even harder than before to confuse us. I wondered if he realized that only served to make me think the Chemist's shop was closer to the infirmary than he wanted us to know.

When finally we entered the courtyard where the Chemist was located, Bonnie Brock held out his hand, halting as if he sensed something Gage and I could not. He made us wait in the shadows while his men fanned out, inching along the perimeter of the square.

Bonnie Brock watched them through narrowed eyes with his arms crossed over his chest. His greatcoat was unbuttoned once again, as I'd begun to expect, though I now understood it was to give him easy access to the weapons held inside rather than because he did not feel the cold. Though I assumed he was more impervious than I was. I'd never seen him shiver.

"Did you speak to the porter?" Gage asked without preamble from where he stood on my other side.

"Aye," Bonnie Brock replied without looking at him. "He was

useless. Didna have any idea who the man was that gave him the letter, and he could only describe him in the vaguest o' terms."

"Which may be a clue in and of itself," I asserted. Now knowing what I did, I wasn't surprised.

Both men turned to look at me.

"You'll see," I replied.

One of Bonnie Brock's men reappeared to signal to him in a way that I assumed meant the area was safe, for he struck off across the courtyard. I hurried to keep up.

Nothing in the Chemist's shop appeared to have changed. It was still sparse and filthy, and the stifling scent of dust and decaying vegetation hung over the space like a miasma. However, the Chemist seemed more tired than the last time we had visited. His shoulders sagged and his garments hung on his frame like laundry on a line. Though I supposed it could be that he simply was no longer intoxicated with whatever drug he had taken before. His pupils were normal sized and his movements shaky.

He nodded to Bonnie Brock before turning to us. "You again," he said wearily.

"Yes. We just have a few more questions."

He sighed as if this was a great inconvenience, but he couldn't be bothered to argue about it. "Aye?"

"You told us about a man who asked you to mix monkshood—devil's cap . . ." I corrected, remembering that's what he'd called it ". . . into a jar of cream."

"Aye."

"You said you couldn't describe him because he was wearing a hood and hid his face. But I hoped you might try. I brought a few sketches I made, and I wondered if you could identify him from those."

He stared blankly at me.

"It could prove a tremendous help," I wheedled.

He sighed again and nodded.

I moved forward to lay my sketchbook on the counter, opening it to the pages I most wanted him to look at. "And by chance, do you recall whether you mixed devil's cap into anything else? Such as a bottle of rosewater or a vial of lavender oil, for instance?"

His eyes took on a faraway look. "Oh, aye. I forgot aboot the lavender oil. Same lad," he declared, lifting a finger. "He wanted teh be able teh sprinkle the devil's cap o'er some sort o' fruit, but I told him the taste'd be too bitter."

I looked to Gage, whose mouth was flattened in annoyance, clearly thinking the same things I was. Why hadn't he recalled this the last time we visited him?

The Chemist bowed his head to examine my drawings, and no more than a few seconds passed before he pointed to one of the pictures. "That's him."

I stared at him in surprise. I hadn't even shown him the sketch I had made of the man in a hooded cloak. "I thought you said his face was hidden."

"Aye. It was. That first time. But no' when he visited me today."

My eyes widened. "Today?" I lifted the picture he'd pointed to. "This man visited you again today?"

"Aye."

A sick feeling of dread flooded through me, turning my stomach. "What did he want?"

"Another jar o' cream laced wi' devil's cap," he answered matter-of-factly.

"The same type of jar?"

He tipped his head. "Slightly different."

I didn't ask for further clarification. I didn't need it. I snatched up my sketchbook and charged toward to door. "We have to go. We have to go *now*!"

I reached the top of the stairs and began to charge across the courtyard before Gage caught up with me and grabbed my arm.

"Kiera, slow down. What's going on?"

"The cream," I gasped, barely able to speak through my panic.

He clutched my shoulders. "Take a deep breath, Kiera. What about the cream?"

"It was meant for me, but I . . ." I pressed a hand to my forehead. "I gave it to Alana."

Gage's brow furrowed in confusion.

"Ye gave your sister poison?" Bonnie Brock asked, looming over us to the left.

Gage scowled at him. "Back up, Kiera. You're not making sense."

My muscles were screaming at me to move, but I inhaled deeply and tried to gather my thoughts. "The day before she died, Lady Drummond ordered some creams and ointments from Hinkley's for my sister, because of the dry skin caused by her confinement."

Gage nodded in understanding.

"They were delivered the morning of Lady Drummond's death, and . . . I suppose Lady Rachel saw them when she came to visit me," I elaborated, thinking aloud. "I gave them to Alana as Lady Drummond wished. But if Monahan just collected another jar of cream today, as the Chemist confirmed by pointing to his picture, then I can only assume it was meant for me since their other attempts to get rid of me failed." My chest tightened in fear. "But I gave my jar to Alana, so . . ."

"Yes, yes. I understand," Gage replied hastily, turning to Bonnie Brock. "We need to go back."

He nodded grimly, before barking instructions to his men.

Our return trek through Edinburgh was far shorter than our initial trip, and I could only assume Bonnie Brock had taken pity on me. However, each minute we traveled still felt too long as I prayed desperately I was wrong. That the cream had not been meant for me. That it had not been delivered to Charlotte Square.

But I knew with chilling certainty I had been right. The poison was intended for me. And if Alana used the tainted cream on her skin in her weakened condition, it could prove terrifyingly and agonizingly fatal.

CHAPTER 30

Gage hustled me into his carriage and shouted orders to his coach-man. Then while the coach raced through the streets of Edin-burgh, he sat clutching my hand as I perched on the edge of the seat, staring out the window. All I could do was keep praying over and over that my sister would be safe, even as my body strained forward, trying to will the coach to move faster.

I slid to the right as the carriage rushed headlong around a corner and a lump pressed against my leg. Reaching down, I wrapped my hand around something tucked into the pocket of my skirt beneath my cloak. I stuck my hand inside to extract a cloth bag tied with a draw-string. Feeling the smooth surfaces of each individual gem through the bag, I realized what it was, and glanced at Gage to see if he'd noticed.

His gaze was sharp with reproach. I opened my mouth to explain, but he closed his eyes and turned away. "I didn't see anything. I don't want to know."

I pressed my lips together and tucked the bag filled with Lady Kirk-cowan's jewels back inside my pocket, pausing only long enough to wonder how Bonnie Brock had placed them there without my noticing.

At Charlotte Square, I nearly jumped from the carriage without waiting for the footman to lower the step. Only the realization that a broken ankle or neck would not help me get to my sister faster made me pause. However, the second footman, who sat by the door on some nights when we were out, was not at his post, and I was forced to pound on the door. I wanted to shriek in frustration.

When finally the lock clicked open, I pushed my way through the door, waving my hands to halt the footman's stammered excuses. "Was a package delivered today? A jar from Hinkley's?"

The footman stared at me as if I'd grown two heads.

"Was a package delivered today?" I demanded angrily.

When he still didn't answer, I rushed past him and lifted my skirts to race up the two flights of stairs to my sister's bedchamber.

"Ah, yes," the footman finally spluttered, calling after me. "The man said there was somethin' wrong wi' the jar the shop delivered a fortnight ago. He apologized and said he was replacin' it . . ." His words trailed away, but he'd already told me what I needed to know. That man had likely been Monahan, pretending to be an employee of Hinkley's.

My heart leapt into my throat and I hiked my skirts even higher to take the stairs two at a time.

"Kiera," I heard Philip shout in confusion from below as he stepped out of his study, but I didn't stop to explain.

I didn't stop to knock either, but simply charged straight into Alana's chamber. Jenny startled, nearly dropping the jar in her hands.

"Kiera," my sister said, pushing herself up on her elbows so that she could see me over the mound of her bare abdomen.

I raced around the bed to yank the jar of Hinkley's cream from Jenny's grasp. "Have you rubbed any of this onto Alana? Has she touched the cream or the jar in any way?"

"No, my lady," Jenny stuttered, blinking at me in bewilderment. "Not this jar."

I exhaled and nearly collapsed in relief.

"What is going on?" Philip asked in alarm from the doorway. Gage stood beside him, with his eyes politely averted out of courtesy to Alana, whose nightdress was still ruched up, revealing her stomach.

"It's poisoned. The new jar of cream they delivered today," I clarified. "Lady Rachel thought I was the one using it."

Jenny stared down at the cream still smeared on her hands in horror.

"You need to wash that off. Now."

She turned to hurry from the room, but Alana stopped her.

"Use mine," she told her, lowering her nightgown to cover her exposed skin.

Jenny hesitated but a second and then plunged her hands in the bowl of water on Alana's washstand.

I pulled the cord next to Alana's bed to summon more servants.

Philip staggered across the room with his hand clutching his forehead. "Devil damn. If you'd been just a few seconds later . . ." He sank down on the bed next to his wife and reached out to clutch her hand between his. He stared into her eyes intently for a moment and then turned to me. "Why would Lady Rachel poison your skin cream?"

"It's how she killed Lady Drummond," I replied succinctly. The rest of the details could wait. I crossed the room to hand Gage the jar of contaminated cream. He lifted a hand to touch my cheek gently, letting me know he understood how shaken I was even if I was hiding it from the others. I wanted nothing more than to sink my head down on his shoulder, but there was Jenny to see to, and a murderess and her majordomo to catch.

Figgins appeared beyond Gage's shoulder, his attire in perfect order. No one would have ever thought he'd just been summoned from his bed. "My lady?"

I stripped off my gloves and cloak and handed them to him. "Jenny has been poisoned. She is not in great danger, but she does need to lie down. Send for Dr. Robert Graham to look at her. He will know what to do."

The unflappable Figgins nodded. "Yes, my lady."

I turned to Jenny, beckoning her toward the door now that she had finished scrubbing her hands. "Have a maid replace the water in Lady Cromarty's chamber, and send Bree up to me."

"I'm here, m'lady," Bree said, emerging from behind the butler.

"I need you to look after Lady Cromarty," I told her, placing a hand on Jenny's back to guide her through the door past Gage. "Jenny may begin to feel ill, if she doesn't feel it already."

"But my lady," Jenny tried to argue.

"You need to lie down," I told her firmly. "We'll take care of Alana."

"Yes, my lady, but . . ." She lowered her voice. "I think she's gone into labor. She insists not, but I've been with her through three births." Her eyes were very serious. "I know when it's time."

I glanced back at my sister where she lay on the bed with Philip leaning over talking to her softly. There were lines between her brows, telling me she wasn't as free of pain as she wished us to believe.

I turned to Figgins. "Send for Dr. Fenwick as well."

He nodded and gestured for Jenny to come with him.

"Thank you, my lady," she said, before allowing herself to be led away.

"I'll fetch fresh water and a bowl," Bree offered, following them.

I leaned against the door frame, watching as my sister absently rubbed her belly in circles, soothing either herself or her baby, perhaps both. She looked so small, so frail, lying in that bed. I was used to her being robust and lively, bossing me around as she'd done since before I could even remember, not timid and frightened, uncertain she would see the morning. Even when she struggled to give birth to Greer, and the physician couldn't stop her bleeding, she'd stayed strong and determined, refusing to give in. That was the Alana I wanted to see now, not this weak, cowering woman.

There were just too many things that could go wrong. Her strength could fail. Infection could set in. She could bleed out. I bit my lip, refusing to allow myself to list all the others. I had no way of knowing what would come, but I was going to do everything in my power to make sure my sister and her child lived.

My nerves tightened in fear and anticipation, like a corset string ready to snap. I made myself breathe deeply, settling myself for the battle to come.

I felt the warm press of Gage's hand against my back and turned to look up at him. The tenderness and assurance shining in his eyes at once comforted and heartened me. I rested my head briefly on his shoulder, absorbing his strength, and then forced myself to step back.

"Is your father still in Edinburgh?"

He tilted his head quizzically. "Yes."

"Take him and Sergeant Maclean, if you can find him fast enough, to detain Lady Rachel and her majordomo." I looked him determinedly in the eyes, not wanting him to disregard my wishes. "I don't want you going alone. They've proven they're reckless and ruthless, and possibly desperate. I'm already terrified for my sister. I don't need to be worrying about you, too."

He lifted his hand to caress the back of my neck. "I will. Send word to my quarters when your sister is safely delivered."

His confident words bolstered me. "I hope to be cradling a new niece or nephew in my arms before daybreak."

"I would like to see that."

The gentle tone of his voice caught at something inside me. "Would you?"

He leaned toward me. "Very much."

We stood staring at each other for a long moment, and then I smiled. "Perhaps tomorrow."

"Yes."

I breathed through the catch in my chest. "Stay safe."

"You, too."

I expected him to release me then, but instead he pulled me close and kissed me soundly for all to see. I didn't fight him or worry about the impropriety, but simply sank into the feel of his mouth on mine, his body supporting me. Until he'd pressed his lips to mine, I hadn't realized how much I'd needed this. To know that no matter how much the world around us crumbled and faltered, together we were still strong.

I clung to that truth and clutched it close to my chest through the rest of the night, comforting and restoring myself from it, and finding the courage to face whatever must come.

At first Alana tried to argue when we told her Dr. Fenwick had been sent for, but she was swiftly silenced when her face contorted from a labor pain. Fortunately they were still short. I'd barely had time to round the bed to the opposite side when the pain began to subside.

She breathed for a moment before lifting her head to renew her protests. "But it's too soon. The baby isn't due for a couple more weeks."

"He should be fine," I assured her, perching on the side of the bed to hold her hand.

"Greer was three weeks early," Philip reminded her. "And she turned out well. Small, but perfectly healthy. This baby will be, too."

Alana gripped his hand, seeming to soak up comfort from his touch and the sound of his voice as much as his words.

"Besides, I'm afraid you don't have a choice. If this baby is ready to come, then he's going to make his appearance, whether you wish it or not." I reached up to brush a strand of hair back from her forehead. "He's taking after you already."

She smiled weakly.

Bree returned with the water, and I stood to help ready the room for the baby's arrival. The housekeeper had been woken and was standing by to assist, as was a kitchen maid, who was warming large quantities of water on the stove. We gathered linens and cleared the space around the bed and on the tables nearby. The hearth was tended and a pot was lined with blankets to cradle the infant close to the fire should it become necessary.

And all the while, Philip sat calmly by Alana's side, talking to her in a soothing voice and helping her to breathe through the pain. I expected him to excuse himself at any moment, for most men did not attend the delivery of their children. It was believed not to be their place. He had followed such a custom with his other three children, but this time he continued to stay. Even when I sat down on the edge of the chair by Alana's bedside, he remained steadfastly by her side.

Watching him with her warmed something inside me that had gone cold these past few weeks, and I felt a tremendous release to know that their marriage wasn't broken. It had only faced a trial. One they would overcome. Proof, perhaps, that a happy, well-suited marriage was possible, just not a perfect one.

Alana's labor pains grew steadily more intense and closer together, as expected, but the blood spotting her linens concerned me. It was not a large amount, but enough to make me anxious for the physician's arrival. I was about to call for Figgins and ask if he knew what was taking so long, when Dr. Fenwick strolled into the room with his bag.

"So the wee bairn has decided he wants to be born in March after all," he declared, removing his coat and unbuttoning his cuffs to roll up his sleeves.

Alana laughed feebly. "It appears so. Unless he plans to make me labor for more than twenty-four hours."

"Well, let's see, shall we?"

I stood to the side as he examined Alana. He was well trained and steady under pressure, so I could not tell whether the blood he saw had alarmed him or not, but he took a bit longer than expected to lower the sheet again, even waiting through one of her labor pains.

"Oh, I dinna think we have long to wait noo," he stood up to tell Alana and Philip. "A March baby he'll definitely be. How is the discomfort?"

My sister inhaled shakily. "Manageable."

He looked at her closely. "Well, you tell me if it isna."

He crossed to the table, where he set his bag and began to remove some of the instruments from inside, but all the while his eyes were surveying the room. I noticed his gaze stayed longest on the precautions we had taken with the warming pan and extra coal. This chilled me, though I tried not to let it show.

I moved to stand next to Dr. Fenwick, ostensibly to help him set up his instruments. "Are there any other preparations we should make?" I asked in a low voice so that the others could not hear us. My eyes darted toward the hearth, letting him know exactly what I meant.

"Nay, you seem to have arranged things well." He glanced over his shoulder at Alana. "I heard that Lady Cromarty's maid was poisoned."

"Yes. Another physician should be examining her now, but I anticipate she will not suffer much ill effect. We seem to have caught it in time."

"That's good to ken. And Lady Cromarty was not harmed?"

"No." I exhaled. "Thank goodness."

Dr. Fenwick offered me a tight smile.

Alana groaned as another labor pain began and we both moved to help her. I took hold of her other hand while Dr. Fenwick watched the clock on the mantel. When the worst had subsided and my sister relaxed back into the bedding, Bree moved forward to bathe her brow with a cool cloth.

"All right, Lord Cromarty," the physician said as he pulled an apron over his clothes. "Noo is the time when I usually suggest the husbands leave."

Philip met my gaze across Alana's body. Her chest rose and fell steadily as she rested between pains. But although her eyes were closed, I could see she was still gripping her husband's hand.

His eyes hardened with resolve. "I'm staying," he replied decisively.

Dr. Fenwick did not seem surprised by this. "Then I will simply remind you that all our attention must be on your wife and child. Should you feel faint or ill, please remove yourself from the room." His words were prosaic, almost as if spoken by rote.

And Philip responded in kind. "I will."

He looked up at me again and I saw the man I had to come to rely on and admire staring back at me from behind his eyes. A little bit of the fear clutching at my heart began to unravel. If I could have said something, I would have, but words failed me, and the moment passed as Alana audibly inhaled. We turned as one to coax her through her pain, encouraging her to breathe as evenly as she could.

Onward the hours stretched as we supported and comforted her as best we could while Bree stood quietly in the background doing whatever else was necessary. Dr. Fenwick oversaw the proceedings, but there was really little he could do until the time was right or, heaven forbid, something unfortunate happened. He alternately examined Alana, timed her labor pains, and sat in the chair near the hearth, waiting for her body to ready itself to give birth.

When the time finally came, I could tell that my sister was exhausted. Between labor pains she lapsed into a dazed stupor, almost falling asleep. But with urging from Dr. Fenwick and help from me and Philip, she rallied herself to push. Bree assisted the physician, and I could tell from the tight pucker of her lips that something was not quite right, but I didn't dare leave Alana's side to find out what it was.

Then just as the first wash of morning light began to filter through the curtains, Dr. Fenwick ordered her to give one more push, and a mewling cry met our ears. Alana fell back against the bedding propping her up and peeled open her eyes, trying to see.

The physician didn't immediately speak, working with the infant as he was. The babe's sounds had subsided to a whine and I could see that his skin appeared blue. Dr. Fenwick stuck his finger inside his mouth to extract something, but all the while his eyes kept darting up from what he was doing to look at Alana.

"Lady Darby, your assistance please." His voice was calm, but urgent.

I moved toward him quickly as he directed Bree to give me the towel she was holding.

"Clean him off as best as you can and place him in the warmin' pan." He glanced up at Philip, adding almost absently, "The bairn is a boy."

I gathered him into my chest. His tiny whimpers tore at my heart. I could see now what had compelled the physician to hand the baby to me. Alana had lost a significant amount of blood, soaking the linens around her.

I turned away, telling myself to focus on the child so that Dr. Fenwick and Bree could attend to Alana. With the utmost care, I wiped the baby's skin clean and swaddled him in another towel before placing him in the cloth-lined pot we had prepared and kept warm. Then I knelt down beside him to watch his tiny chest rise and fall with each rattling breath.

Though I was frightened of what I might see, I forced myself to look back at the bed. Alana lay still and pale against the covers as Dr. Fenwick frantically searched for the source of the bleeding. A pile of bloody linens covered the floor at the base of the bed. But it was Philip's face that was most wrenching. His hands rubbed up and down her arms as he spoke to her in a voice gone hoarse from hours of talking, somehow keeping it composed and level. However, his gaze was agonized, begging her to open her eyes, to stay with him.

I turned away, pressing my hand gently to the tiny baby's chest, and prayed.

CHAPTER 31

Hours later I collapsed into the chair before my dressing table and laid my head in my hands. My muscles ached from the night of exertion and the strain of the tension that had coursed through me. My head swam with fatigue, but I could not sleep. Not yet.

"Lie doon, m'lady. Or you'll collapse," Bree urged me with her hands planted on her hips.

I looked up at her reflection in the mirror. "But Alana . . ."

"Is restin' safely. I'll keep an eye on her. As will Lord Cromarty."

"And the baby . . ."

"Wee Jamie is tucked up in the nursery wi' two nannies watchin' o'er him, no' to mention a trio o' excited older brother and sisters. So there's naught for you to do but sleep."

I sighed. "I will."

Bree continued to stand there with her gimlet eye fixed on me.

"I will," I responded more firmly in exasperation.

She narrowed her eyes in skepticism, but left the room.

She was right, but it was still difficult to allow myself to seek the oblivion of sleep. I was worried I would wake to find that everything had gone horribly wrong while I was slumbering.

Dr. Fenwick had been able to stop the bleeding, and with rest, Alana's body had begun to recover. Her pulse was now strong, her temperature normal, and she had eaten half a bowl of beef broth to sustain her. The baby had also improved, flushing a healthy shade of pink and nursing hungrily from his mother. They had decided to name him James Kieran, after my and Alana's father, and the woman who was sure to be his favorite aunt, they jested. I was touched by the gesture, and charmed by my newest nephew, who, as I'd predicted, had already become dear to me.

I pressed a hand to my aching head and stared at myself in the mirror. As expected, I looked terrible, with half my hair falling from its pins and dark circles under my eyes. But the gut-wrenching fear that had almost immobilized me earlier was gone, replaced by vigilance and caution.

I'd still not heard from Gage, and I hoped that for once his silence meant something good. Perhaps he was waiting to hear from me first. I reached for a piece of foolscap to jot off a quick letter telling him of Alana's safe delivery, knocking the cloth bag Bonnie Brock had slipped into my pocket the night before from the table. The contents spilled partially out on the floor. Sometime in the middle of the night I'd left it in my room and then forgotten about it.

I bent over to retrieve the bag and the gems, and then emptied the sack on the dressing table to give it all a cursory examination. Everything I had not promised to Bonnie Brock and his men seemed to be there, including the real version of the diamond and sapphire necklace Lady Kirkcowan had worn to Inverleith House. But there was also a slip of paper. I unfolded it to read.

A pleasure doing business with you. My compliments to Lady K.

You still owe me a favor.

I scowled at Bonnie Brock's writing. Apparently our business trans-action had not counted, and now I was in his debt. Which was not a place I wished to be.

I managed to fall asleep for a short time before Bree woke me, as instructed, to tell me that Gage had called.

His eyes scolded me as I entered the drawing room hastily dressed and still bleary-eyed. "Have you even slept?"

"A few hours," I replied, forbearing, quite admirably, I thought, from telling him he was not supposed to indicate to his fiancée at any time that she looked anything but lovely.

He shook his head and held out his hand to me, pulling me toward a settee in the corner. "How is your sister and the babe?"

"Recovering well." I didn't try to hide my relief. Even though Bree had assured me both were thriving, I had insisted on peeking in on Alana and the baby before coming down to see Gage, just to see for myself that they were healthy.

He ran a hand comfortingly down my back. "I'm glad to hear it."

I exhaled, trying to banish the fear I'd felt the past sixteen hours and shake some of the cobwebs from my mind. "Were you able to apprehend Lady Rachel and Monahan?"

He nodded grimly. "Yes. On the road to Glasgow."

"Glasgow?" I repeated in surprise.

"At some point yesterday it appears they began to fear they had revealed themselves."

I glowered. "Before or after they delivered a jar of poisoned cream to my sister?"

Gage shared my anger. "Presumably after. So they decided to flee to Glasgow, where they hoped to book passage to Belfast. Monahan admitted he has family there."

"So they confessed?"

His mouth flattened into a thin line. "Not exactly."

"What does that mean?"

Whatever he was about to say clearly displeased him. "Lady Rachel refuses to speak to anyone but you."

At first I was surprised, but the longer I considered her request, the more sense it made. If Lady Rachel had been misused by both her father and her husband, she must have a real mistrust of men. Or most men. Monahan seemed to be the exception. I could understand her not wishing to discuss such a delicate subject with a man if there was a woman she could deliver her confession to instead.

But I also suspected she hoped to engage my sympathy, to sway me to her side as she had so successfully done throughout this inquiry. Well, she was in for a surprise if she thought I would not be scrupulously fair and logical in my reviewing of her testimony. I was not a fiddle to be played for her benefit.

"Where is she being held?"

"Due to her status, she's currently under guard at her town house. But Monahan is being held at the police house."

I rose to my feet. "Then take me to her."

He was slower to stand. "Are you sure? You've had a long and difficult night. This can wait until you're better rested."

I rubbed my fingers in a circle over my temple. "The sooner this is over, the better for everyone."

This time when I was shown up to Lady Rachel's upstairs parlor, it was not by her choice. Out of necessity, she had been confined to the rooms attached to her bedchamber, where she could more easily be guarded until other arrangements could be made. As such, I found her pacing before her hearth in agitation, though she made an admirable attempt to hide it when I entered the room.

She was dressed all in black, though whether she was supposed to be in mourning for Lady Drummond or herself, I didn't know. Whatever the reason, the stark color paired with her dark hair and eyes and creamy skin made for a striking picture. One I was certain the guards had noticed. At my request, Gage had not accompanied me into the room. I wanted to speak to Lady Rachel alone without any distractions, and without the presence of a man to unsettle her, whether in truth or feigned for our benefit.

We stood staring across the room at each other. I was unprepared for the fury that swept through me at the sight of her. I knew I was angry with her for nearly poisoning my sister and her unborn child, but I thought that was under control. However, the white-hot rage that made me want to fly across the room and do her bodily harm said otherwise.

She seemed to sense this, and did her best to defuse my anger. "I'm sorry. I truly didn't know you'd given the cream to your sister."

I tilted my head, studying her. "But you intended it for me." It wasn't a question, but a bald statement of fact. She'd intended to kill me.

She nodded hesitantly. "Yes."

"You saw the package from Hinkley's that day you visited me," I said, wanting confirmation. "After you discovered your plan had succeeded. You'd killed Lady Drummond."

Her knuckles were nearly white where she clasped her fingers together over her abdomen. She turned to the side, and I wondered if she was considering denying it, but then she spoke in a choked voice. "Yes."

I crossed the room toward her, keeping the settee between us, for her safety, not mine. "Why?" I demanded. "I thought Lady Drummond was your friend. I thought you empathized with her. Why would you murder her the same way you murdered your father and husband?"

"You don't understand. My father and husband deserved to die. They were cruel, heartless monsters. And they deserved to rot in hell for what they'd done."

"Because they misused you?"

Her eyes hardened. "Perhaps you had a happy childhood, but I did not. My father regularly beat my mother whenever it pleased him. And when my sister and I crossed his path, he beat us, too. But it was more than that." She reached out a hand to pluck at the flowers in a vase on the side table. Her expression turned cold and emotionless, as if this was the only way she could speak of it. "My mother tried to leave him once, and he punished her by branding her with his signet ring."

I gasped in horror, but she didn't even seem to notice.

"So she would understand she belonged to him, and that no matter where she ran, she could never escape him. He made my sister and I watch, so we would learn that lesson as well. That's when I realized we would never be free of him unless he was dead."

"So you poisoned him?" I guessed.

She shook her head. "Not then. I was too weak. If I'd been stronger, my mother would still be alive and my sister . . ." Her hand tightened, crushing a fragile bloom. "Well, Father wouldn't have turned his attentions to her if I'd done what I needed to do sooner."

I swallowed, imagining what it must have been like for her to grow up with such a father. What would I have done? Would I have had the strength to poison him to protect myself, my sister, and my mother? I knew Alana would have. She was like a tigress when it came to defending me or our brother, Trevor, or any of her children.

I frowned, realizing Lady Rachel was doing exactly what I'd known she would, and I was doing what I'd sworn not to—empathizing with her. "Then how did you end up married to Mr. Radcliffe?"

She looked up at me for the first time since she'd begun to talk about her father. "Blind infatuation. Skilled acting." Her mouth twisted bitterly. "I didn't realize until a week after our wedding what a horrible mistake I'd made. The kind, solicitous man I thought I'd married was really a harsh, controlling bastard. The signs had been there. I'd just been too imprudent to see them."

"So you decided you needed to poison him, too?" I tried to keep the skepticism out of my voice, but it must have seeped through, for she scowled.

"I thought you of all people would understand. After what you went through with Sir Anthony. Didn't you ever wish him dead?"

Her words left a sour taste in my mouth. "Yes," I admitted. "But I never considered murdering him." Whether that made me more moral or just feebler, I didn't know.

She lifted her chin. "Well, perhaps your husband's mistreatment was not as bad as mine. But when I killed my father, I swore I would never allow another man to ever hit me again, and Mr. Radcliffe did much more than that." She crossed her arms over her chest and turned to glare at the portrait above her fireplace of a younger version of herself. "Spare the rod, spoil the wife," she bit out before whirling back toward me, flinging her accusatory words at me. "Monahan knew. *He* understood."

"Which is why he helped you kill Mr. Radcliffe. And later Lady Drummond."

Lady Rachel continued to glare at me, but then her eyes dropped as if she'd lost her nerve.

I rounded the settee, trailing my fingers over the cushions. "Even if I could understand your reasons for killing your father and your husband, even if I could appreciate your suffering, what about Lady Drummond? Why did you murder her? Did *she* deserve to die as well?"

"No," she replied in a small voice.

"Then explain to me *why* you poisoned her," I ordered in clipped tones. When she didn't immediately reply, I ruthlessly continued, "Was she too beautiful? Did you envy her all her friends? Or perhaps her new lover?"

"No," she protested. "None of that. She . . . she was wonderful. Perhaps too wonderful," she added dejectedly.

"What does that mean?" I snapped in annoyance.

"One day after Lord Drummond had been particularly brutal to her, I suggested that perhaps something could be done. And then I let slip that I was not inexperienced with ridding oneself of cruel men." The lines around her eyes tightened in betrayal. "I thought she would be sympathetic, that she would be grateful for the offer, but instead I could tell she was shocked and then disturbed by my suggestion. I tried to laugh it off, but I realized I'd exposed my secrets, and I had no guarantee she would keep them."

I crossed my arms over my chest. "So you decided, then and there, that your closest friend must die."

"No," she replied, sounding ironically affronted. "I watched and waited, hoping she would forget about it. I hoped our friendship and common suffering would be enough to convince her to overlook what I'd said. But then I discovered she'd sent letters to people near my childhood home, asking questions about my father's death, and I began to suspect they weren't the only inquiries she'd made into the matter. I . . . I was afraid she would find proof of what I'd done, and that she would have charges brought against me. And I knew I had to stop her."

She spread her hands open wide, imploring me. "Why would she do that? I didn't understand. I still don't. She was my friend. I didn't want to harm her. But why couldn't she leave it alone?"

"Perhaps you should have asked her that instead of poisoning her," I suggested mercilessly.

Her hands dropped to her sides, and I could see in her eyes for the first time that she was beginning to understand I was not going to be swayed by her account.

"Why did you choose to poison her with the skin cream and lavender oil?"

"I knew she used them regularly," she replied in a subdued voice. "I gave her the cream as a gift a few years ago, and she's used it ever since."

"I suppose it was easy enough to swap them out with the poisoned versions one day when you called on her. Then you just had to wait for them to work their magic."

Her brow furrowed. She clearly didn't like my cynical tone. "There was nothing easy about it."

"And when did you decide I must die also?"

She at least had the grace to flush. "When I heard you had been there when Clare died, and then I saw you with the cream. I . . ."

"You panicked?"

"Yes. Of all the rotten luck. And I couldn't figure out how you'd gotten on to the cream as the method of poisoning so quickly."

"I hadn't," I told her, wishing I'd only been so prophetic. It would have saved us all a great deal of trouble.

"Oh." She frowned and collapsed into a chair. "Well, I thought you had. And I decided the best way to prevent you from uncovering the truth was to start the rumors again to deter your efforts."

"And when it didn't, you tried to have me hit by a carriage. And when *that* didn't work, you sent me a forged note supposedly from Bonnie Brock Kincaid."

"Yes. Monahan noticed you talking to him that day after you visited me. He sent the note and paid some men to denounce you when you arrived at the White Hart Inn." She looked up at me with a speculative gleam. "You have some very interesting friends."

I ignored her implied question. "I'm afraid your majordomo has made a very powerful enemy because of it. Bonnie Brock doesn't take kindly to being impersonated."

Lady Rachel waved it aside. "Monahan's in the police house. They can't hurt him there."

I arched my eyebrows at her display of naïveté. "I wouldn't count on that."

She sat straighter. "What do you mean?"

"Bonnie Brock and his men can get to a person anywhere. The fact that Monahan's in the police house only makes him easier to find." I moved toward the door. "If I were him, I would be more afraid of what Bonnie Brock is going to do to him than the outcome of his trial." Perhaps it was cruel of me to say, but after everything she'd done, I thought she deserved to fret and worry for once.

"But you can stop him."

I paused and glanced over my shoulder.

"You can tell him to leave Monahan alone. That he's harmless now. Please," she pleaded.

On the one hand, it was good to see she actually cared about someone other than herself; on the other, her appeal only vexed me. She had murdered her friend to keep her secrets, and tried several times to murder me, nearly killing my sister and new nephew in the process. That she thought I would take any pity on her or her majordomo for what would happen to them next was preposterous.

"Bonnie Brock doesn't listen to anyone," I told her. "Especially me." In this case I knew it to be true. Besides, I wasn't about to waste another favor on her behalf. Not now. Not ever.

CHAPTER 32

Lady Kirkcowan called at Charlotte Square early the next morning, just as my note had directed. At half past eight, much of society was still in bed, and those people who were out and about would be too busy to pay attention to the comings and goings of one lady. She looked even paler than I remembered, which was saying something. Though it was to be expected, given the recent burglary at her home.

"I must say, I was surprised to receive your letter," she murmured after offering her congratulations on the birth of my nephew. We sat in a pair of beige linen chairs positioned between the two front windows.

"I'm sure. But when you know the reason why I asked you to call on me, you'll understand why I couldn't come to your town house instead." I removed the cloth bag from the pocket sewn into the lilac apron of my white jaconet morning dress and held it out to her.

She looked at me in confusion before accepting it.

"Open it," I prodded.

She slowly pulled the string and then tipped part of the bag's contents gently into her hand. Her wide eyes flew up to meet mine. "What . . . How . . ."

"There's no need for you to know the details, though I'm sorry to say that some of the pieces had to be sacrificed to the cause. I hope you don't mind."

"Mind?" Her voice wobbled. "Of course not. I thought . . ." She inhaled, pressing a hand to her mouth. "I thought they were gone forever."

I smiled in commiseration. "Store them somewhere safe. And given recent events, I would suggest that place be outside your home."

Her lips pressed together and tears gathered in her eyes. "Thank you. I don't know how I can ever repay you for your kindness, but . . ."

"There's no need," I assured her. "Just put them to good use."

She sniffed. "I will."

"And if anyone happens to ask you why you visited here today, tell them it was to congratulate my sister on her new baby. No one will question that."

A smile blossomed behind her eyes and brought some much-needed color into her cheeks. "A boy, isn't it?"

"Yes." And I proceeded to tell her all about wee Jamie.

Later that morning, I sat by the window in the nursery, rocking Jamie while I watched the other children play in the square below. He listened for a time as I explained the antics of his brother and sisters, and then he fell asleep swaddled in his soft blankets. At which point, I should have laid him in his crib, but I wanted to hold him close a little while longer. One of the nursemaids would be along soon enough to take him down to Alana so that he could nurse, but for the meantime he was mine to snuggle.

Which was how Gage found me, rocking and staring down at Jamie's sweet pink cheeks. I glanced up as Gage's shadow fell over us.

"Is this the little bruiser?" he asked, kneeling to get a closer look.

I tilted Jamie so that he could see.

"A fine fellow," he proclaimed. "Though he's quite bald."

I smiled at him indulgently. "Many babies are."

"Truly?"

I nodded.

"Well, the only babe I've ever seen belonged to my cousin, and she had a head full of dark curls." He sank back on his heels. "Although come to think of it, my aunt did make some slighting remark about the child inheriting her father's Celtic ancestry."

This was the first time Gage had ever mentioned any members of his family to me other than his mother and father. "Which aunt would this be?" I asked casually, trying not to alert him to the significance of his disclosure, lest he stop talking.

"My aunt Matilda. My mother's sister," he clarified.

"Do they live in London?"

"Some of the year." He lifted his gaze to look me in the eyes, letting me know he was sharing this information consciously. "The rest of it they spend in Devon near where I grew up."

I stood slowly and crossed the room to Jamie's cradle, tucked into the warmest and quietest corner of the nursery. He turned his head and gave a tiny baby sigh as I placed him inside and adjusted his blankets. My heart melted at the sight of him so cozy and content. Then I returned to the window, where Gage stood staring out into the sunshine.

He wrapped his arm around my waist and pulled me in close to his chest. We stood that way for a moment, watching the children run around the square and the carriages pass by in the street below. It was a peaceful respite, but I knew Gage had not come here simply to hold me close. There was too much between us that needed to be said, and I could tell from the subtle tension in his back that he was aware of that fact.

He inhaled as if rousing himself to the task. "Sergeant Maclean has been apprised of Lady Rachel's confession. He said there will be a trial. I'll have to give testimony, but that could be weeks from now. Until then it's up to the magistrate's court to decide what to do with her and Monahan."

"So we'll be staying in Edinburgh?"

"At least until May, perhaps June. Such is the life of the inquiry agent at times." He looked down at me. "I hope you don't mind."

I shook my head. "Not at all. I'm not sure I'm ready to leave my sister yet." I glanced over my shoulder. "Or Jamie."

"Once the trial is over, I'd like to go away for a time, just the two of us." His eyes narrowed in thought. "I hear the Lake District is lovely. Perhaps Lord Keswick could recommend a place for us to let."

"That would be nice."

As much as we needed to discuss all of this, I knew he was merely working himself around to the real matter at hand. I remained patient, as anxious as he was about the conversation to come.

And finally he came to it. "There are some things I need to tell you. Things I need to say. And I would prefer if we weren't interrupted." He turned to look at the cradle. "Is there someone who can watch the baby?"

I took hold of his hand. "Come with me." I pulled him across the room and rapped softly on the door closest to Jamie's cradle. It opened almost immediately. "Jamie's asleep in his cradle," I told the nursemaid.

"Aye, m'lady," she replied with a smile.

I guided Gage out of the room and down the hall to my art studio, where I unlocked the door with the key in my pocket. Once I'd closed it behind us, I turned to face him. "There. No one should disturb us here."

He nodded solemnly and began to pace around my easels and tables, rubbing his hands over and over the thighs of his trousers. I had never seen him so nervous, even when facing down a murderer. I perched on the edge of a stool and watched as he wore holes in his shoes and his trousers.

He cleared his throat. "As you know, I have difficulty trusting people, and there's a reason for that. I just don't like to talk about it. And as I'm sure you've guessed, it has to do with Greece."

He paused before one of my tables and began to fiddle with my brushes laid out in their case, rolling them round and round. "I was twenty-four and visiting Italy when I heard about the Greeks' struggle for independence from the Ottoman Empire. I was young, and idealistic, and searching for adventure, and I got caught up in the romantic idea of revolution, of freeing the country of Socrates and Plato from the barbarian horde. So I set sail for Morea to join the revolutionaries."

"That sounds noble enough," I offered, unclear where his story was headed.

"In theory perhaps, but in practice . . ." he shook his head ". . . it ended up being the least noble thing I've ever done."

I wanted to go to him, to hold his hand and touch his arm, but I realized he needed the distance to tell his story, so I waited as he gathered his thoughts again.

"I became fast friends with a pair of brothers who were the sons of a local chief. And . . . I fell in love with their sister, Rika."

I felt a sharp pang in my heart hearing him say those words about another woman. I knew that had been long ago and far away, and I could not have expected him to live to the age of thirty-three without having cared for at least one other woman before me, but it was still difficult to hear. Fortunately, he spared me the details of her beauty and courage and sparkling wit, or so I imagined her.

"We were nearly inseparable. She was also part of the revolution, riding with us on campaign. I wanted to marry her, but she insisted we wait to discuss such a thing until after Greece's independence was won." His mouth twisted bitterly. "It wasn't long before I learned why."

He lifted his gaze to look at me. "Do . . . do you know much about the Greeks' war?"

"No," I admitted. "I'm sorry."

He held up his hand. "Don't apologize. The fact that you don't might make this easier." He grimaced. "I took part in the siege of a city called Tripolitsa. It dragged on for months, and then finally in late September we were able to break through at a weak spot in the city walls and overrun the town in a matter of hours. A great victory, but . . . it's what happened next that will haunt me for the rest of my life."

He stared blindly at the wall over my head, pain etched into the lines of his face, and I was reminded suddenly of my friend William Dalmay, who had suffered from severe battle fatigue. The sight sent a chill of foreboding down my spine.

"The Greeks weren't happy with simply conquering the town; they wanted to punish them. They began to massacre the Turks—slaughtering men, women, and children. I . . ." He closed his eyes and swallowed. "I pleaded with them to stop, but they were like savages, intent on violence and torment. And my friends, they were some of the worst. I later heard them bragging that they'd each murdered upwards of ninety people during the three days the butchery took place."

I pressed my hands over my mouth, shocked by the picture he painted. "Why did they do it?" I whispered.

He shook his head. "They claimed it was in retaliation for the massacres the Turks had perpetuated before, and perhaps it started out as such, but this . . ." He shook his head as if to deny the images his mind conjured. "This was more than that. So much more."

His eyes searched the floor, as if there would be an answer written there among the paint splatters. But then I recalled he hadn't told me all.

"And Rika?" I asked tentatively, holding my breath.

"She called me a weakling and a coward for not taking part."

My mouth dropped open.

"And when I told her I was leaving Greece and begged her to come away with me, she laughed and told me she had never loved me. She was only doing as her father and brothers had asked, keeping me interested so that I would continue to fund their revolution with my English money. She'd never intended to marry me. She'd never cared for me at all." His voice was flat and emotionless, but I knew he was speaking that way to hide a great hurt, one that had wounded him deeply, and shaped him into the man he was today.

I rose to my feet and crossed to where he stood dejectedly in the middle of the floor.

"I was such a *fool*," he berated himself.

"No," I corrected him gently. "She was. You were merely young and idealistic, like you said."

He scowled in frustration. "I should have seen what was happening. There were signs, but I ignored them."

"Perhaps. I can't say. I wasn't there. But I do know that you have to stop blaming yourself for what others did." I grabbed hold of his elbows and made him look at me.

He rested his hands on my waist. "I blame myself for not trying harder to stop them."

I wished there was something I could say to lift that burden from him, but I knew better. Who of us was not plagued by the memory of a time when we suspected we could have tried harder or done more? So instead I turned my attention to the subject I could address.

"I understand now why you have a difficult time trusting people. First your mother's maid, and then Rika. It's a wonder you let me know you at all."

"Well, once I'd established you weren't a murderess, and you weren't interested in my money, it was a bit easier." His teasing words sounded hollow, but it showed he was trying to let go of the painful memories.

"How did you know I wasn't interested in your money?" I challenged playfully, trying to help him.

The corners of his lips curled upward in the beginnings of a smile. "First of all, because you didn't think I had any." He arched his eyebrows in gentle rebuke.

I wrinkled my nose. "It's not that. I knew you weren't a pauper. I just never really gave it a great deal of thought."

He smiled a bit brighter. "Secondly, you are perhaps the least avaricious person I know. You married a minor baronet when you could have aimed much higher. You own little jewelry, and your sister is constantly pestering you to be fitted for new clothes. The only thing you seem eager to spend money on is pigments and canvas."

I flushed under this recitation of my spending habits. "Well, it's good to know what's most important."

He leaned down so that our heads almost touched. "And lastly, you admitted to me that you never planned to remarry. That one unhappy marriage had been enough."

I had forgotten that.

"So for you to change your mind and accept me I knew was not an easy thing for you." His pale blue eyes softened with affection. "Am I wrong?"

"No," I said in a small voice.

"But all those things were simply proof of what I'd already come to know, even if I too often allow myself to doubt that truth. That I could trust you. With my life, with my past, and perhaps most importantly, with my heart." His voice sharpened with sincerity. "I do trust you, Kiera. More than anyone in the world, even if it doesn't always seem like it. I told you that you might have to prod me at times. I've become used to concealing my past, and it's not an easy habit to break. But you're right. If we are to wed, then I need to be able to share everything with you, not just my wealth and my bed."

I moved my hands around to press them to his chest. "I understand it's hard."

"I know you do."

"I just need you to try. Not fob me off at every opportunity."

He nodded. "I will. I promise."

And this time I could tell he truly meant it. Something behind his eyes had changed, and I had to wonder at it.

I ran my fingers under the lapels of his frock coat. "What brought you to this conclusion? Did something happen?"

"My father," he admitted.

I tilted my head in curiosity.

"He has always kept secrets from me, but I realized the other day that he also kept them from my mother." His gaze strayed over my shoulder, as if thinking back. "I remembered an argument I overheard them have one time, and how unhappy my mother was when he refused to talk about his time away from us. As a child I hadn't understood, but I recognize now that they were almost strangers. They wed for love, but then they drifted so far apart. Perhaps it would have been different if my father hadn't been away so much of the time, at sea and manning the naval blockade against France, but somehow I think it might actually have been worse. With the war and the Royal Navy keeping them apart, at least they could blame something other than themselves."

His eyes locked with mine. "I don't want that to be us. I don't want to live separate lives in the same bed."

My throat constricted at the earnestness of his voice. I gripped his lapels harder. "I don't want that either."

"Then we'll have to consciously curb our inclinations toward secrecy to keep it from becoming so." He squeezed my waist in emphasis. "And hopefully, in time, maybe we won't have to try. It will simply become natural."

"I feel like I've already made great strides in that direction," I admitted, and then smiled. "And a year ago I'm not sure I would have ever thought I would be able to say such a thing."

"A year ago I'm not sure I would have either."

I smirked, looking up at him coyly through my eyelashes. "Not even with Lady Felicity?" I teased, naming the girl his father had been intent on him marrying.

He grimaced. "Especially not with Lady Felicity." His eyes narrowed in mock reproach as he leaned closer. "But you know that."

"I do?"

"You should," he growled, and I smiled.

But there was still one more thing bothering me, and he could tell. He pressed a gentle kiss to my brow. "What is it?"

"It's only . . . Do you think your father will ever accept our marriage?"

"In time," he replied, sounding less concerned than I had expected. "When he realizes there's nothing he can do to change it. He's not accustomed to being challenged, and you certainly do that, my dear." He grinned. "It's good for him."

Then a tender light entered his eyes. "But what you're really asking is whether I'm willing to endure his disapproval, and the answer is yes. Unequivocally, yes." His voice dipped lower as he leaned in so that his lips were just inches from mine. "Is that what you needed to hear?"

"Yes," I replied, becoming distracted by his proximity.

"Good."

We didn't speak then for a good long while, our mouths being otherwise occupied. I gained a new appreciation for the breadth and strength of Gage's shoulders, and the privacy my studio afforded.

When reluctantly we parted, he did so with a groan, pressing his forehead to mine. "Do we truly have to wait until August to wed?"

"If we want to be married in St. George's as Alana has planned."

"And do you? Do you *truly* want that?"

I gazed into his eyes, which demanded my honesty, and at last admitted the truth aloud. "No."

His shoulders dropped. "Then why are we?"

"Because I didn't want to disappoint my sister. And I knew she needed something to distract her during her confinement, especially these last few weeks."

"But now that's over. So don't you think you should tell her how you really feel?"

I dropped my gaze. I knew he was right. But I still hated to upset Alana. She'd done so much for me. I hated to ruin her excitement.

He squeezed my shoulders. "Kiera, I realize you know your sister better than I do, but in this instance I'm quite sure she will just be glad to see you happily wed. It will not matter to her how it's done."

"Do you really think so?"

"Yes," he stated with certainty.

I nodded in acceptance, feeling as if a great weight had fallen from my shoulders.

"So how would you like our wedding to be?" he prodded.

"Something simple and private. Family and a few close friends. I don't need a grand affair or people who are barely acquaintances discussing my gown. A small wedding breakfast. And preferably sooner than August." I paused in my recitation to study his face. "But perhaps you would like a larger wedding . . ."

He shook his head. "I only want to marry you. I don't care how it's done."

My chest filled with warmth.

"Though I will say I definitely approve of your request that it be sooner." He pulled me close. "Much, much sooner."

So we wed two weeks later, with our family and a handful of our dearest friends by our side. And although the day was not without its hitches—including a missing necklace, a muddled cat, and a frightful tempest—the most important part was perfect. The part that made me Gage's wife.

It is sufficient to say we were happy. Though we should have known our peace could not last, for soon enough we found ourselves embroiled in another inquiry, this one at the request of the Iron Duke, the Duke of Wellington himself. That it should take place in Ireland was intriguing enough, but that it involved the death of a nun was both shocking and unsettling. And as we swiftly found out, also treacherous.